HOODLUM

ALSO BY K'WAN

Street Dreams

Gangsta

Road Dawgz

HOODLUM

K'WAN

 ST. MARTIN'S GRIFFIN ❧ NEW YORK

www.stmartins.com

ISBN 0-312-33308-0
EAN 978-0-312-33308-9

First Edition: August 2005

10 9 8 7 6 5 4 3 2 1

ACKNOWLEDGMENTS

Gone but not forgotten: Donald Goines and Iceberg Slim. Had it not been for these two gentlemen, some of us would still be working nine to fives.

It seems like every time I think I'm tapped out, another story pops into my head. God has truly blessed me and I'm thankful for it.

You know, every time I see my name printed somewhere or people enjoying my stories, I find myself wishing that my mother was here to see it. Then I realize that she is here. Maybe not in the physical, but definitely in spirit. I have an unconditional love for this woman for several reasons: It's hard for a young woman to raise a knucklehead on her own, but I was an entire fist. My mother loved me enough to comfort me when it was necessary, yet let me learn through trial and error. When she left here, she passed her gift on to me, and thus I share it with you.

FOR THE HOOD:

This is for all the people who held me down or offered words of encouragement. I'd like to send a very special shout out to Sonny Black. One day somebody took me under the wing, and I was fortunate enough to be successful. I only hope I can do the same for you. The game is wide open. Black Dawn, Inc. (home team for the New Year), Tony 'TM' Council (Hold ya head, cuzo. Playing fair didn't work, so they chose lies as their weapons of choice. This is the strategy of cowards.), Ty, Cousin Shae aka Enough, Mark, Party Tyme, Coo-Coo Killz, Party's Angles (summer nights on 114th help me create some interesting characters), my nigga Shannon Holmes (you opened the door, fam. All I did was step through it. Thank you.), my extended family in Bed-Stuy, Hard Body Records, Nakeya and Dawn (my home girls from Philly, I have yet to be fed), Richard from B-more, Thomas Long, Anthony Whyte, Eric Gray, Mark Anthony, Darren Coleman, Al Sadiq Banks (I see you, soldier. Get money.), Jamise L. Dames, Brandon Massey, Yasmin Shiraz (the tour was enlightening), Brandon Mc Calla (Pay attention to what you're doing and leave them broads alone!), Tracy Brown, Kashamba Williams, T.N. Baker, Nikki Turner, and the whole T.C.P. roster. Whether we're still signed to the label or not, we know where it started. All the talented authors who came behind me and added their voices to this genre, keep doing what you do, putting it down for the hood. Coast 2 Coast, Arc, Passion 4 Reading, Raw Sistaz, and the rest of the book clubs that held me down. Mad love goes to all the bookstores and vendors who continue to support me and push my books. If I missed you, I'm sorry. You'd think after four books I'd have thanked everybody.

A very special thanks to all the readers. You guys have been in my corner since day one. I thank you from the bottom of my heart for your continuing faith in my talent.

I would also like to acknowledge the people who talk breezy about me when they think I'm not listening. I thought about saying something witty, but I'll keep it simple. WATCH YOUR MOUTHS!!!!

Enjoy the story.

PRINCIPLE

"*PASS THAT BLUNT,* nigga," Legs said, switching the dial on the beat-up Chrysler's radio. Legs was light-skinned with nappy hair that he either wore in braids or an unkempt 'fro. He was known throughout the hood as a nigga that was always down to ride. He was a young cat trying to make a name for himself and that's part of the reason Tommy had selected him for this particular errand. Murder without motive.

"Fuck you, bitch-nigga." This was Amine. He was a short, dark-skinned kid who wore his hair in a short twist. He was an easygoing cat, who enjoyed a good laugh, but a wise man wouldn't judge him by face value. Amine was always down to put in work just to say that he did.

These were the two that Tommy had chosen to collect a debt owed to his family by a dude named Heath who ran numbers out of a grocery store on 131st and Lenox. Heath had a decent thing going, but he was a degenerate gambler and notorious fuckup. Tommy had loaned Heath some money a few months back so he could get back on his feet. Heath had been quick in taking the money but hesitant about paying it back.

The amount of money that Heath owed wasn't really worth making a stink over, but there was a method to Tommy's madness. Heath was one of the few people operating an illegal business in Harlem that didn't grease Tommy's or Poppa's palm. Heath was fortunate enough to be running one of the few number holes that was still pulling in respectable bread. Tommy wanted in, but Heath shut him down. He was an old head and was connected to the guineas. Strong-arming him might've caused a stink in relations between the Clarks and the Cissarros. But if Heath was wrong Tommy could have him killed and no one could really raise a stink about it.

Legs and Amine were both street-smart as hell, but between all the weed and sherm they dabbled in, they didn't have a lot of common sense between them. Tommy had given them instructions to try and get the money without getting rough. Tommy had watched the both of them grow up so he of all people knew better. Even if Heath paid the debt they were still likely to shoot him, if not break a bone or two.

"Fuck, we've been waiting on this nigga for almost an hour," complained Amine. "What's good with this nigga, Legs?"

"Easy, youngster," cooed Legs. "Don't be so quick to go get it. Nine times outta ten chaos will come if you wait long enough. That's just the way of the world."

As soon as Legs had finished his sentence Heath came strolling around the corner of 132nd and Lenox. He was strolling like he didn't have a care in the world. The silly mutha fucka even had the nerve to be wearing a lime green sports coat. He looked like a walking target.

Legs tapped Amine and slid out of the car. His partner got out and came around the back to join him. When Heath caught sight of the two, he slowed his pace a bit. He couldn't place the two kids who were grilling him, but the menacing looks they were giving him screamed trouble. Heath started to backtrack but the venom in Legs's voice gave him pause.

"Don't even do it like that," Legs said, easing up on Heath. "If I gotta chase you, I'm just gonna gun you down right here."

"What's this all about?" asked Heath.

"Come on, son," Amine cut in. "You already know what it is. Where the fuck is Tommy's money?"

"Oh," he said trying to muster a grin. "I was gonna call him about that, but I lost his number. I would've just rolled through the hood to holla at him but I ain't had a free moment. You know how it is?"

"Nah," Legs said, pulling his .45. "I don't know how it is. What I do know is that you better drop what you owe so I don't have to shoot yo' old ass."

Activator from Heath's salt-and-pepper curl began to drip down the side of his face as he pleaded, "Come on, fellas. What's all the gun business about? I'm sure we can talk about this."

"Man," Legs sighed. "I'm not really trying to go through the motions with you right now. Do you have Tommy's money or not?"

"Hey, no need to get bossy. You know I've been running the streets since before you and Tommy were born. Can I get a little respect?"

"I see you wanna do this the hard way. Amine," Legs said, looking at his partner, "do you mind?"

"Sure thing," Amine said, pulling a small .22 from his back pocket. Before Heath could cop a plea Amine shot him once in the foot. The gun sounded like a small firecracker, but Heath's roar of pain overshadowed that as he hopped around and eventually collapsed. The few people who were on the street took off in any direction other than the one Heath and the two gunmen were in.

"Now," Legs said, kneeling beside Heath, "let me ask you this shit again. Do you have Tommy's money?"

"Jesus," Heath cried. "You shot me in the fucking foot . . . my fucking foot."

"Oh, so you don't hear me, huh?" asked Legs, leveling the .45 with Heath's eye.

"Hold on, hold on," pleaded Heath. "Don't kill me!"

"Do you have the money?" asked Legs.

"I can give you half, but I need a day or so to—"

"Hold up," Legs said, cutting him off. "You mean to say that with all the money you're pulling in over here and you can't pay my man a measly twenty grand?"

"Sorry mutha fucka!" Amine said, kicking Heath in the ribs.

"Man," Heath picked up. "I ain't got that kinda bread laying around. It's gonna take me at least a couple of hours."

"Get up, Heath," Legs said, extending his hand. When he saw that Heath was hesitant to take the assistance he softened his tone. "Come on, Heath. We ain't gonna do nothing to you." Reluctantly Heath allowed Legs to help him up. "Its a'ight, man," Legs said, placing his arm around Heath's shoulder. "You know what, Heath? You're about a sorry mutha fucka. Tommy's been good to you, why would you wanna stiff him on some short bread?"

"I wasn't gonna stiff him," Heath lied. "On my dead mama, I was gonna pay him his cake. I got about ten on me and I can get the rest later on tonight."

"You know, Heath, if it were up to me then that would be fine, but I ain't the one who makes the laws on these streets. That would be Tommy. See, a nigga like me just enforces them. Just like in situations like this, when a shit bag like you tries to cross a good dude like Tommy. I'm sorry, Heath, but we just can't have that."

Before Heath could utter another word, a .45 slug tore through his torso and exploded out his back. Legs stepped over him and put another slug in his cheek. A young Hispanic man who had been off-loading a truck in front of a store spared a second too long to look at Legs. "Fuck is you looking at," barked Legs. "You got an eye problem?" The young man shook his head and ran off.

Legs and Amine went to work tearing Heath's pockets off. The lying son of a bitch only had about eight thousand on him. It would do though. Tommy had told the youngsters that they could keep whatever they snatched off the man. It wasn't really the money that Tommy had Heath killed over. It was the principle.

BABY BROTHER

THE YUKON THUNDERED along the BQE dipping in and out of traffic. "All Eyes on Me" was playing at full volume as the vehicle seemed to sway to the beat. The truck jumped from the left lane to the right without bothering to signal. Some of the other motorists beeped their horns and gave the driver the finger, but he didn't give a shit. His boss was in a rush and they were holding up progress.

"How much longer?" asked the dark-skinned man sitting in the backseat.

"Not much, Tommy," the driver said. "The exit's just up ahead."

"Cool," Tommy said, going back to his *Daily News*. "Let me know when we get there." After reading about the fifth article on someone that got a raw deal that week, Tommy closed the paper. The news was always so damn bad. "Fucking depressing," he whispered.

"What ya say, Tommy?" the driver asked.

"Nothing, Herc. Just thinking out loud, man." Tommy looked

at the back of Herc's massive bald head and grinned. Herc might've been one of the biggest and ugliest sons of bitches in the world, but a friend like him was priceless. He was loyal and didn't talk much, but the love was true between him and Tommy.

The truck finally pulled up near the terminals. "Be right back," Tommy said as he hopped out.

Tommy walked over to the gate where he was supposed to meet his charge and checked the arrival time. The young lady at the gate informed him that all of the passengers had exited the plane already. Tommy scratched his head and looked around. He was sure that he hadn't missed him coming in so where could he be? Tommy heard a giggle to his rear and turned to see what the cause of it was.

Two flight attendants were taking their time getting off the plane. One was a dark-skinned sister, sporting fish-bone braids. The other was a Puerto Rican girl with a wrap. In between them was the person that Tommy came to meet: his baby brother, Shai.

Tommy just stood there and watched as the flight attendants hung on Shai's every word. He couldn't hear what they were being told, but they were going for it. Shai just smiled and soaked it all up.

The brothers were very similar in appearance. They both had their mother's dark skin and their father's Trinidadian features. The only difference was that Tommy was broad with a low caesar, while Shai was thin with waves. Other than that they were almost identical.

Shai noticed Tommy waiting for him, but that didn't make him move any faster. He took his time as he relieved the flight attendants of his bags and kissed them both on the cheek. He put on his coolest walk and headed in Tommy's direction.

"What up, Slim?" Tommy said, spreading his arms.

"Nappy black," Shai capped. "What da deal, Buckwheat?" They had been calling each other names for years, but they were tight as hell. "Damn," Shai said, rubbing Tommy's stomach. "You got fat, kid."

"Good living," Tommy said, patting his stomach. "Good living. So, what up with you?"

"Same shit, man," Shai said, looking at his shoes.

"That's all you got to say?" Tommy asked.

"What do you want me to say?"

"You can start by telling me how you managed to get kicked out of school. Shai, what the fuck were you thinking?"

"It wasn't my fault, Tommy," Shai protested.

"It never is," Tommy said, shaking his head. "Shai, you gotta learn to take responsibility for your actions. Ever since we were kids, you were always blaming others for your mistakes. You can complain about how it wasn't your fault until the cows come home, but didn't nobody make you bet on that damn game. Now look what the fuck you've done."

Shai wanted to argue with Tommy, but he knew that he couldn't. His older brother was totally right. Until recently, Shai had been the star point guard at NC State. He was awarded a full athletic scholarship out of high school and was supposed to be the next big thing. Unfortunately for Shai, he was lured by the idea of fast money. Against his better judgment and common sense, Shai started betting on the games. It was a good little hustle until a sore loser reported him and Shai was suspended from school. Now he was home to face the music.

"Guess it doesn't make sense to argue about it now." Tommy shrugged. "You're grown and this is your life. I just hope Poppa doesn't kill you."

Shai cringed at the thought of going home to face their father. Poppa had verbally lashed him over the phone at least three times already. Shai had disappointed him and tarnished their family name at the school. Poppa took great pride in the name he had made for them. Their family had their hands firmly planted in the underworld, but their father was a respected businessman and pillar of the community. Having his son suspended for something like gambling didn't look good on them and there was no doubt in Shai's mind that he would suffer for it.

After grabbing Shai's last bag from the belt, they maneuvered their way to the waiting car. Shai looked at the truck and nodded his head in approval. Tommy always did have refined taste in cars. The forest green Yukon on 23s was a testament to that.

Shai found himself grabbed from behind in a vise-like bear hug. "Break yo'self, fool," Herc said, lifting Shai off his feet. "What's my name, huh?"

"Aw damn," gasped Shai. "Put me down, man."

"Say my name."

"A'ight. Wilmont."

"You trying to be funny?" Herc asked, tightening his grip.

"A'ight, a'ight. Herc."

"What?"

"My bad, man. Big Herc."

"That's better," Herc said, releasing him. "I see you still a lil' punk?"

"Fuck you, fat boy."

Herc jerked back but he didn't squeeze Shai anymore. He was just as happy to see him as Tommy was. They weren't related, but Shai was like his little brother too. They all grew up together. The three men piled into the truck and sped off. Shai looked out of his window like a tourist.

He had only been away for a few months, but it felt like a life-time. The city had that effect on its natives. No matter where you went or how long you stayed away, no place else ever really feels like home except the Apple. Shai took in a chestful of the toxic air and smiled. He was home.

CHAPTER 1

FAT MIKE TESSIO HAULED his three hundred and some-odd pounds up the tiny steps in front Bellini's House of Pasta. He ran a chubby hand across his gelled hair as he looked in the door's reflection. After fixing the lapel of his polyester suit, he proceeded into the restaurant. His second set of eyes, Nicky Tulips, brought up the rear as usual. Mike and Nicky greeted some of the staff and proceeded to the back booth where Ginerro "Gee-Gee" Giovanni, underboss of the Cissarro family, sat.

Ginerro sat at his usual booth sipping a glass of fruit juice. At his side was his bodyguard, Louie Bonanno. Ginerro looked at the fat man coming in his direction and kept on sipping. Even when Fat Mike was standing directly in front of him, he still didn't budge. After an uncomfortable pause Ginerro cast his cold gray eyes on Mike.

Mike could feel the chill run down his spine as the bastard just stared. Gee-Gee was an old-school mobster. He was first introduced into the secret society back in 1951. For more than three decades, Ginerro killed and ordered dozens of men murdered, all at the behest of the Cissarros. Over the last twenty some-odd years, he had served as underboss to three different Mafia chiefs, always seeming to miss his turn at the big time. A lot of the soldiers joked that it was the reason the old man was still around. He refused to die until he had his shot at the throne.

"How ya doing?" Ginerro asked, looking up at Fat Mike.

"I'm good, Mr. G," Mike said sheepishly, kissing him on both cheeks.

"Got something for me?" the old man asked.

"Yeah, here you go." Mike carefully handed a brown paper bag to Louie. "It's all there, boss."

"Good. So, how's business?"

"Right as rain, Mr. G. Couldn't be better."

"You still having them nigger troubles uptown?"

"Nah, we took care of that. All of them guys down there is scared of Poppa and they know Poppa is wit' us. They've been paying up."

"What about Poppa?"

"Well . . ." Mike stuttered. "He's pretty much got his own thing going. He don't give us no trouble." Mike chose his words carefully so as not to tip Ginerro off; Gee-Gee had no idea that Tommy and Poppa had been making side deals for the heroin that the Wongs were hitting him with. In the Mob the rule against drugs was very simple: Deal and you die.

"Fuck him," Ginerro said, slamming a bony fist into the table. "He's gotta give up a taste like everyone else. Poppa's got a lot of friends, but he ain't a part of our thing. Don't you come around here telling me what some spade uptown has got going on. If he's got action on any of our turf, then he pays too. Who the fuck is Poppa? You scared of this guy, Mike?"

"Nah, Mr. G. Fuck I got to fear from some nigger living in a big house? Let's just say that he pays homage to our thing."

"Damn well better be. Poppa keeps the niggers in line like the good little shepherd. That's all he'll ever be to us. The day you start acting like some fucking boot is bigger than our thing, is the day you ain't fit to be a part of it."

"Yeah, Mr. G. You don't have to worry about me fearing anybody except you."

"You better say it until you learn it, Michael. Now, you and this sneaky motherfucker"—he motioned toward Nicky—"get outta here."

Mike and Nicky left without saying a word. He was an underboss and Mike was just a crew chief, it was really a no-win situation. At least for the moment. That old fuck was going to step down whether he wanted to or not, Mike would see to that.

Shai's people lived on a modest estate right outside of Elizabeth, New Jersey. It was a Colonial house that sat alone in the middle of an open field. It was made of a brick-like texture that was painted a gray hue. From a distance it looked like a castle that had lost its place in time. The yellow brick drive snaked the distance of a city block from the house to the black iron gate in the front. The lawn was decorated with trees and stone gargoyles that watched the main road for intruders. Shai and Tommy had nicknamed them "the watchers."

At the rear of the house was a replica of an enchanted forest with all kinds of trees and vegetation. What made the whole thing really look crazy was the artificial pond that replaced their swimming pool. There was a green light built into the bottom of the pool that gave off a mystic effect.

Herc pulled the truck through the gates and up the circular driveway. Two men walking pit bulls on chains nodded at the big man as he passed them. The truck pulled to a stop in front of the house and unloaded its passengers. Shai looked up at the house as if it were his first time seeing it. Shai hadn't always lived out this way; he actually grew up in the projects. His father moved them all out here during his junior year of high school.

Shai and Tommy had gotten halfway up the front steps when the oak double doors swung open. A local Mob figure named Jimmy Malone came tripping down the steps, followed by one of his button men. The gray suit jacket he wore didn't do much to hide the bulge under his arm. He flashed a broad grin as the trio approached.

"Lil' T," he said, extending his hand. "What say, huh?"

"The name is Tommy," Poppa's eldest said, wearing a false smile. "And I say, don't forget it."

"I can dig it," Jimmy said, brushing off Tommy's comment. "Heir to the throne and shit."

"And you know this, *paisan.*"

"This kid," Jimmy said, tapping his bodyguard, "such a fucking ballbreaker. We'll probably starve once this guy is running the show."

"The faithful shall prosper," Tommy said, brushing past Jimmy and walking toward the house.

"I still love ya, T," Jimmy said over his shoulder. "Later, fellas." He nodded to Herc and Shai. Herc just stared, while Shai nodded back.

"Who was that?" Shai whispered to Herc.

"Trash," the big man grumbled. Shai left the situation alone and followed Herc into the house.

The trio crossed the foyer and beheld the marvel that was Poppa's domain. The interior was almost as spectacular as the exterior. The front doors led them to a circular room that served as the foyer. The room was lined with a plush red carpet that sunk in when you stepped onto it.

This living room of the house was where Poppa would sometimes entertain visitors. It was a wide-open space, decorated in antique furniture with a large crystal chandelier hanging from the gold-colored ceiling. In the center of the receiving area was a long carpeted staircase leading to the upper rooms. On either side of the stairs were doors leading to other sections of the house.

Poppa stepped out from one of these doors, wearing a blue smoking jacket and puffing on a thick cigar. Their father was a huge man. Not as big as Herc, but he wasn't a lightweight. He stood about six three and sported a trimmed beard. His auburn dreadlocks swung freely as he came down the steps to greet his boys.

Shai looked at his father's face, but didn't know what to make of it. Poppa was skilled at making his face unreadable. Shai didn't know if he was going to hug him, or snuff him. He knew Poppa was pissed, but didn't know to what degree. "What's up, Pop?" Shai asked, grinning. "You look good."

"Thanks. I been trying to exercise here and there, when I can. Getting old, you know?"

"Nah, what are you, about twenty-one?"

"Flattery will get you everywhere, boy. So what's up?"

"Nothing," Shai said, shrugging as if he didn't know what Poppa was talking about.

"Herc," Poppa said. "Why don't you take the bags upstairs? I wanna kick it with these two for a minute."

"Sure thing, Poppa." Herc scooped all of Shai's bags in one arm and lumbered up the stairs.

"Shai," Poppa said, stepping a bit closer. "Do I strike you as a fool?"

"No, sir," Shai whispered.

"Then don't play me like one. You know what I'm talking about. What the hell is your problem?"

"Poppa, I'm sorry—"

"I don't wanna hear that, Shai." Poppa cut him off. "You were fortunate enough to get a free ride to school and you turn around and fuck it up? I didn't raise no idiot, did I?"

"No, sir."

"I didn't think so. I'm disappointed in you, Shai. Very disappointed."

"I know," Shai said, lowering his head. "What I did was stupid, I know this. At the time, I wasn't thinking about it. I needed some extra bread and instead of asking for it, I tried to hustle it up on my own. Pop, all I wanted to do was show you that I could earn a buck. I didn't think it would get this bad."

"That's just it." Poppa shook his head. "You don't think, son. I've busted my ass for over thirty years in these streets so my kids could get a proper upbringing. This stunt you pulled was stupid."

Shai understood where Poppa was coming from, but he sure as hell didn't agree with his philosophy. In Shai's mind, money made the world go round, and he craved it in his life. Poppa always made sure he had what he needed, but what about what he wanted? Shai was the type of dude that liked "having thangs." He had expensive taste and loved to floss.

Poppa gave him enough to live very comfortably, but Tommy's little brother liked to splurge. Shai needed to have the finest of everything: women, cars, gear. What he didn't get from Poppa or Tommy he hustled up on his own. Gambling wasn't the only racket Shai had going on down South. He sold weed to the blacks, Ecstasy pills to the whites, and liquor to the browns. The shit was all profit to him.

"I know"—Shai nodded—"I'm sorry."

Poppa looked at his youngest son and sighed. He was pissed off with Shai for getting himself kicked out of school, but he couldn't be too mad at him. Shai had grown up around dirt all his life. Poppa tried to keep his two youngest shielded from it, but it was bound to rub off. Shai was talented and smart, so there was still a chance for him to make it right. Gambling on games was a serious matter and Shai had drawn a lot of media attention because of it. He could probably play for another Division One school, but it would take time and money.

"Come in here and let me talk to y'all," Poppa said, heading down the hall. He took his boys through the door to the right, which led down a corridor to Poppa's office. Poppa approached the office door and removed an odd-shaped key from his pocket. He placed the key against a panel on the wall and stepped back. There was a brief hissing and then the door swung inward. Poppa stepped to the side and welcomed his children into his sanctuary.

Shai looked around the room in astonishment at the redecorating that Poppa had done. The last time that Shai had come into this particular room it had resembled a large, yet modest, office. Now it looked like a miniature apartment. There was a steel desk set in front of a big window. Mounted on the wall above the window was a large battle-ax. A console about the size of a filing cabinet sat off to the right. Inside the console were a dozen or so small monitors. With these monitors Poppa could see almost the entire house, as well as the surrounding lands.

The walls were decorated with pictures of the children when they were young, as well as photos of Poppa with various city and state officials. Poppa had sure come a long way from the corner hustler he was twenty years prior.

"You like?" Poppa asked, smiling at Shai.

"Yeah," Shai said, scrunching up his nose. "It's a'ight."

"Shai, you're so full of shit. You know you're feeling it."

"Yeah, Pop. I can't even lie to you, this is the jump-off. Of course"—he tapped his chin—"I would've done it a little different. Maybe a bed in the corner . . . some candles."

"That's my brother," Tommy cut in, "forever the player. Slim, your problem is that you think with the wrong head. That shit is gonna get you into trouble one day."

"No more than your itchy trigger finger," Shai said with a smug grin.

"Why don't y'all cut that out?" Poppa asked, sitting behind his desk. "I brought y'all in here to talk. Sit down, fellas." The brothers did as they were told, taking the leather chairs opposite Poppa's desk. "Shai, that was some dumb shit you did, but you can't let that stop your flow. You gotta get right back in the fight and know not to fuck up a good thing. What you got planned for the summer?"

"I got a few things lined up," Shai answered, still looking around the office.

"I hope so. You know that we don't sit around on our asses in this house. I got a friend that plays for the USBDL. He's running a basketball camp in New Rochelle this summer. Thought maybe you'd like to check it out. Supposed to be other Division One play-ers there too."

"I dunno, Pop."

"Well, what do you know? I thought you loved to hoop."

"Oh, I do. But I thought I'd just kick back this summer. Maybe hang out in the City?"

"Oh, hang out in the City, huh?"

"Yeah, kick it around Harlem."

"Shai, you just got your silly ass kicked out of a school that I've been spending thousands of dollars to send you to. Boy, you ain't hardly in no position to be negotiating. No matter how 'old school' you might think I am, I'm always street first. I know what's on your mind before you think it." Poppa grinned at his son.

"Come on with that, Pop." Shai flashed an identical grin. "I'm just trying to chill and get my head together. I've always liked the City more than I liked it out here. I don't know anybody. At least I know the City. Besides, some of my teammates from school will be in the City for the summer."

Poppa looked at Tommy with a "he can't be serious" look. Tommy just shook his head as his father took the floor. "What kind of jackass do you take me for? You don't hang with them squares when you're away, so I'm supposed to believe that you're gonna hang with them in the City? The only reason your ass is itching to get back to the City, is to hang with Swan and them old thug-ass niggaz."

"But, Pop—"

"'But Pop' my ass." Poppa cut him off. "I know you, Shai. You came from me, so I know how you think. Let me put you up on something and you better pay attention. Swan, he's a good kid, but he's doing dirt. Him and all them niggaz you hang with is on the grind. Why the hell would you wanna go and stand around on a hot-ass block and ain't getting no money?"

"Pop, you know that's my click."

"Yeah, Shai. I know that's ya click, but hear me out. The City ain't no playground. These lil' niggaz is out there killing and dying, all in the name of a dollar. If we ain't losing soldiers to the grave, we're losing 'em to the system. Either way, it ain't for you."

"But, Pop, you never had a problem with me hanging in the City before."

"Yeah, that's when Tommy was out there. Your brother's upper management now. He ain't in the field no more. There won't be anybody out there to watch over you, Shai."

"I'm hip, Pop. I don't need no babysitter," Shai said coolly.

"Shai, it ain't about needing no babysitter," Tommy cut in. "Them streets ain't no joke."

"Tommy, I ain't no sucker. I can hold my own. Who knows, maybe I can help you out with the business this summer?"

"You must've fell and bumped yo' damn head," Poppa snapped. "It bad enough I gotta worry about Tommy, but you won't have no part of that."

"Pop, you know I ain't built for no job," Shai pleaded. "I'm not trying to play no corners or nothing like that. I can just kick it with Tommy when he makes his rounds."

"Shai, this isn't even up for discussion. You will not be running around the City like that. Especially with all the drama that's been popping off. No Shai, you can't roll with Tommy."

"Damn, Pop. You act like I'm a punk or something. I grew up learning the same things that you taught Tommy. What makes me so different?"

"The difference is, the family has a different plan for you. Tommy has made his choice. I can't say that I agree with it, but that's his choice. If he's gonna be out there getting money, then I'm gonna make sure he's doing it the right way. You, on the other hand, you're a schoolboy. You had an opportunity that none of us did. You slipped, but you'll bounce back. Get that education, Slim. Lord willing, you might even make it to the League. I'd much rather have you playing in the League instead of a prison yard."

"I can take care of myself, Pop."

"Shai." Poppa sighed. "You so damn hardheaded. Just like your mother."

At the mention of his mother Shai got quiet. She was somewhat of a touchy subject in their household. Their mother had left them when Shai was about six. She got tired of playing housewife and sought to recapture her youth in the streets. As it turned out, the streets ended up capturing her. Their mother had given up on them to chase rock. For a while she would pop up from time to time, mostly when she needed something. She would stay around for as long as it took to squeeze some money out of Poppa and then she'd be gone again. Poppa tried his hardest to help her, but you can't help someone that isn't ready to help themselves. So Poppa did what he thought was right: he banned her from seeing her children.

Tommy had always been in the streets so he understood what had happened to her, but Shai couldn't deal with it. In his eyes, she was nothing more than a coward who was afraid of responsibility. He tried to understand and still love his mother to some degree, but his heart wouldn't let him. In his eyes she was as dead as an autumn leaf.

"Look," Poppa said, speaking again, "the summer is damn near on us and it's too late for us to get you back into school this semester. I'm gonna give you a play this weekend, but I'll be expecting you to come to me with a plan by Monday."

"Thanks, Pop," Shai said sarcastically.

"Thanks my ass, Shai. Have your fun, but stay out of high-traffic areas. Do you understand?"

"Yes, sir."

"Good, now get outta here before I come to my senses. I wanna talk to Tommy."

Shai hopped up and headed out of the office. The old man was being a mother hen, but he'd come around sooner or later. The important thing was that Shai had gotten his way. It was summertime in Harlem and nothing could've been sweeter.

Tommy remained silent until his little brother had left the office. He knew exactly what Shai was thinking. Shai was far from stupid, but he was young and impressionable. He'd just have to make sure his brother stayed out of harm's way.

"You sure that was the right thing?" Tommy asked. "Letting Shai run loose in the streets unattended?"

"He'll be all right," Poppa said, relighting his cigar. "Gotta let go sometime. Besides, Shai is a good kid. Street-smart too. I raised all my boys in the real world, not that sheltered, fantasy shit."

"I can dig it, Pop, but you know it's getting crazy out there?"

"Everybody knows that Shai is a square peg. Ain't got nothing to do with the streets. Besides, who's gonna be crazy enough to fuck with one of y'all?" Poppa asked confidently.

"Right as usual, Pop. You know I'll lay something down for my lil' one."

"There you go, Tommy. You can dress a nigga up in a suit and give him all of the education in the world, but you can't take the hood outta him. When you gonna wise up, boy?"

"Come on, Pop, you know how I get down."

"Yeah and that's why I pulled you off the streets. It was getting too damn expensive cleaning up after you."

"Pop, you know I ain't never blast on nobody that ain't have it coming."

"Whatever, Tommy. Let's just get down to business. You speak to them Wong boys?"

"Yeah, Pop. Got it all set up. Me and Herc is supposed to meet up with 'em tomorrow night. After the party."

"Okay, that's good. You sure this is what you wanna do?"

"Yep," Tommy said confidently. "Mike and them niggaz been half stepping for too long. It's time to find a new supplier."

"Who's to say that they won't pull the same flake shit?" Poppa asked.

"I don't think so, Pop. Word on the street is these dudes do square business. They don't deal with too many people, but I hear that their shit is off da chain. The meeting should go well."

"Let's hope so, Tommy. This is your call, so it's up to you. If the

Asians set out a better deal, then do what you gotta. Remember though, be careful when you fuck with them Triads. Dangerous folks, Tommy. Dangerous."

"Shit, Pop. Ain't a nigga alive as dangerous as me and Herc."

"Don't let that pompous-ass attitude get you caught up in some shit. I don't plan on outliving none of my kids."

"Don't worry," Tommy said, standing to leave. "I hear you."

"I know you hear me, but make sure you're listening."

"Man, I ain't scared to go at it with nobody, Poppa. Every nigga bleeds."

"Boy, ya head is like a rock." Poppa sighed. "Discretion is the better part of valor."

"Yeah, and war is in the nature of man," Tommy capped.

"Don't get cute, lil' nigga. I don't care how many bodies you've dropped, don't forget who taught you the game. We understand each other?"

"Yes, sir."

"Good. You young boys ain't got shit on the old-time gangsters. You better wise up, Tommy. By splitting with the Italians, the deck is about to be stacked against you. This situation is a lot touchier than you might realize. It ain't like we're just dealing with Fat Mike and his dope, but we've also got relations with the Cissarros as a whole. We've always operated independently of the Italians, but they play a role in our power structure. When they cut us in on some of their people, we made quite a few dollars."

"Fuck them," Tommy spat. "What about our rackets that we cut them in on? We kick them back a taste on quite a few of our endeavors. They say it's a partnership, but it's more like we keep the niggers in line and keep our bullshit from spilling over into their backyards. If you ask me, we ain't nothing but some well-trained watchdogs."

"Well, I don't recall asking you, Tommy. When you take over, you're free to do as you please. For the moment, I'm master of this house. You just continue to be my strength in the streets and we'll be straight. Okay?"

Tommy didn't bother to answer his father, he just kept walking. Old age didn't seem to be making Poppa soft, but he was damn cautious. He seemed to be taking the idea of retirement more and more seriously. It was okay, though. Poppa had put in enough work over the years. If he wanted to play the background, then it was all good. Tommy liked being in the mix. He didn't have a problem parleying with the Asians. If they decided to get crazy then he would teach them the universal language: iron.

"Damn," Detective Brown said, "somebody did poor Heath dirty."

"You ain't lied, brother," his partner, Detective Alvarez, agreed. "I guess it's a pretty sure bet that his mama will opt for a closed casket."

"That's some cold shit, partner. Ain't you got no respect for the dead?"

"Fuck 'em," Alvarez said, lighting a Newport. "You do dirt, you rest in it. We all know the rules."

"True enough, partner. True enough."

Detectives Brown and Alvarez continued to examine the crime scene, while drawing strange glares from some of the plainclothes officers who didn't really know them. "Minority Report," as they were playfully referred to, didn't look like your average cops. As opposed to the off-the-rack suits that most of their fellow detectives wore, they draped themselves in the style of the streets they protected.

Tony Brown was a short, light-skinned man. He had a round face that had forgotten how to smile. He had seen some things on the streets that made him bitter toward everything, even the system he served. Brown was the more serious of the two.

Jesus Alvarez was the prankster. He was a very tall Puerto Rican guy. In addition to being an overall sarcastic bastard and pain in the ass, he considered himself to be a ladies' man.

"So what've we got so far?" Brown asked, flipping through his notepad.

"Numbers man takes a bullet, film at eleven," Alvarez said

sarcastically. "Far as we can tell, it was a robbery that went sour as hell."

"Doesn't make sense, J," Brown protested. "Everyone around here knows that Heath was a connected guy. Even if it was someone that knew him, why rob him in the street instead of just hitting his numbers spot? Heath is the top dawg so he's not gonna be carrying money. What's this all add up to?"

"Come on, bro. If you know something let me in."

"This was an execution."

"In broad daylight? Come on, man."

"The writing is on the wall," Brown insisted. "Whoever killed Heath was close up on him. He had powder burns all over his clothes. Trust me on this one, partner."

"Detective," a uniformed officer said, approaching them, "we've got somebody over here that you might want to talk to."

The detectives followed the officer to a squad car on the corner. There was a man sitting in the backseat that looked like he was going to shit all over himself. Something or someone had him rattled.

"What's his story?" Alvarez asked.

"Seems he was out here when it went down," the detective said, nodding toward the man in the car. "The thing is, he's not talking. Guy's scared to death."

"Let me talk to him," Alvarez said, opening the back door. The detective slid onto the seat next to the man. "What's good, *papi*?"

"I just want to go home," the man said, sounding frightened. "I don't want trouble."

"Trouble, who's giving you trouble?" Alvarez asked, faking concern. "All we want to do is find out what went down here."

"I dunno," the man lied. "I know nothing." He shrugged.

"Listen," Alvarez said, leaning closer, "nobody's gonna do anything to you, bro. We look out for our own. You understand?"

The man looked into Alvarez's eyes and saw the signs of camaraderie. He felt much more comfortable talking to a fellow Latino than the white officers who had originally been questioning him. "Two boys," the man blurted out. "They come and talk to the dead guy. They talk about something, but they no argue. Then the fat one shoot him in the foot, but the other help him up. Then, *bang-bang.* The one who help him up, shoot him. He ask what the fuck I looking at and I run 'cause I scared. Then I call you."

Brown's theory was right: Heath had indeed been executed. "So what else happened?"

Poppa sat in his recliner, rubbing his temples. It seemed that the warmer the seasons got, the more he had on his plate. Over the last few years, he had built a sizable empire. He had played God and executioner to his followers, for more time than some of them had been alive. Poppa would forever be remembered as a player in the game, but his tenure was coming to an end.

His bitch of a wife had left him with the responsibility of raising three kids on his own, with the headache of running businesses that danced on both sides of the law. Poppa had done a good job balancing the scales, but retirement would allow him to do better. The small box on his desk buzzed, snapping him out of it.

"Yeah!" he barked, holding down the TALK button.

"Poppa," a metallic voice squawked. "Hope is waiting for you in the Navigator."

"What the hell for?"

"Ah . . . you're supposed to take her to basketball tryouts."

"Shit!" Poppa cursed. He had totally forgotten about taking Hope to tryouts. The day was wearing on, and Poppa still had things to do. "Have Duce take her and I'll be there in a while. Tell her I have a meeting, but I'll be there."

Somewhere in Florida

Artie checked his watch and noticed that it was still early. He had an asshole full of drug money and the rest of the afternoon to fuck off. At least until his man Steve came down with the rest of the packages he was bagging up. Artie figured that he'd go to the mall to kill a few hours.

Artie climbed into his Acura and began his journey across town. He took a deep pull off his Newport and let the smoke roll from his mouth. He was feeling good. So good in fact that he never noticed the blue Chevy following him.

Artie parked his car at the rear of the mall. He could run in, get what he had come for, and run out. Artie's plan was foolproof, or so he thought. When he stepped out of the car and found himself staring down the barrel of a Desert Eagle, he realized that even the best laid plans had flaws.

"Aye, nigga. You know what it is," Malik said in a Southern drawl. "Come up off that shit, like now." Malik was a big man, but he moved as silently as the grave while he and his partner crept up on Artie.

"Ain't this a bitch," Artie cursed. "Y'all niggaz know who you're robbing?"

"We know just who you is, fuck nigga," Gator hissed. "Now do like the man say and come up off yo' shit, fo' I have to peel ya mutha fuck'n potato."

Artie looked from Malik to Gator and cursed himself for not having a pistol. Many thoughts ran through Artie's head at that moment. He looked down at the cross hanging from his neck and remembered how long he had saved up to get it. He thought about the birthday present for his son, which he had come to the mall to get. Artie decided at that moment he wasn't going out like that.

"Nah, man," Artie mumbled.

"Fuck did you just say?" Malik asked.

"I said I ain't giving y'all niggaz shit."

"Boy," Gator cut in, "is you retarded or some shit? That shit swinging 'round yo' neck ain't worth dying over."

"I can't let y'all jack me," Artie said, trying to fight back the tears.

"Oh, hell no," Malik said, reaching for Artie's chain. "You gonna unass that shit."

When Malik moved, so did Artie. He caught Malik off guard with an overhand right. The blow didn't drop Malik, but it stunned him long enough for Artie to grab for his gun. Artie put up a fight that neither of the robbers had expected.

Gator looked on in amusement as the little fella gave Malik one hell of a fight. When he thought that he had seen enough, Gator took his .357 and clubbed Artie in the back of the head. The smaller man collapsed to the ground, clutching at the gash on the back of his head.

"Enough of this silly shit," Gator said in an icy tone. "Now come up off yo' shit, before I put lead to yo' lil' ass, nigga."

Gator expected the fight to be over, but he was mistaken. Artie looked at the man with desperation in his eyes and lunged for the gun. Unlike Malik, Gator wasn't for the bullshit. As soon as Artie got within spitting distance, Gator pulled the trigger. The blast hit Artie in the face and tore part of his skull to shreds. Malik jumped, but Gator didn't flinch.

"Look what the fuck you made me do," Gator said as he bent down and went through Artie's pockets. "Done made me pop this ol' fuck-nigga."

"That little mutha fucka snuck me," Malik said.

"Puss-ass nigga. Go through the mutha fuck'n car and see what he was holding. Stupid mutha fucka."

Malik knew better than to argue with Gator. There was no telling how he would react. Malik took two steps and froze as he heard trouble arrive.

"Mall security. Don't move!"

Malik looked at the white man dressed in the tan-and-brown uniform. Had it been a few years ago, they would've just run or beat the hell out of the rent-a-cop, but it was a new millennium and the rent-a-cop was armed.

"Put the guns down and get on the floor!" the security officer barked. He was scared to death, but the sounds of sirens approaching in the distance gave him some courage.

Malik made to comply with the officer, but Gator stopped him short. "What the hell are you doing?"

"I'm doing like he say," Malik explained.

"Fool, you can't be serious," Gator said in disbelief. "That nigga ain't 'bout to shoot nobody."

"I said, on the ground!" the officer repeated. By now there was another security unit on the scene, so the first officer's confidence shot up another notch. "This is your last warning, boy. Get your ass on the ground."

"If it ain't one thing, it's a fucking 'nother," Gator said. He fired from the hip, hitting the officer in the stomach. Malik panicked and tried to run. Before he made it anywhere the other unit opened fire. They laid Malik out right on the spot.

"If you want something done right," Gator mumbled as he hit the ground and crawled for Malik's gun. With both pistols in hand Gator popped up from behind a car and laid his thang down. The windows on the security cruiser shattered as Gator hit it with multiple slugs. The ensuing screams told him that at least one of the cruiser's occupants was no longer with them. Gator continued to fire off shots as he backed out of the parking lot.

A police cruiser arrived on the scene, killing any ideas Gator might've had about getting back to the Chevy. He was now a caged rat searching for another means of escape. Gator ran around to the side of the mall hoping that he could snatch a car to make his getaway. To his dismay, there was neither time nor opportunity. He would have to find another way or hold court with the Dayton PD.

As luck would have it, a young man was pulling out of the lot on his motorcycle. When Gator made his move the man never knew what hit him. Gator clothes-lined the man so hard that he almost took his head off. He really didn't give a shit though. His driving force was that they still had the death penalty in Florida.

Gator tossed his spent .357 and opted to go with the Desert. Another security officer came running around the bend as Gator picked up momentum. The dumb-ass officer jumped right out in front of him. Gator jerked the bike, causing the front wheel to become airborne. Before the security officer could react, Gator tore into his face and chest with the bike tire. The guard didn't even live long enough to see Gator hop the tiny divider leading to the street.

A police car tried to cut Gator off, but he leaned his weight to the left, causing the bike to fishtail. When one of the officers attempted to get out, Gator opened fire, shattering the window and making the officer rethink his play. Gator revved the bike and sped in the other direction.

To his surprise, one of the remaining security officers was standing in the street with his gun drawn. He fired a shot, grazing Gator's arm. Gator lost control of the bike and skidded along the ground. The security officer, trying to be a hero, approached the fallen gunman. He figured that if he apprehended the man before the police did, he would be a hero in Dayton County. He never figured that Gator had plenty more tricks up his sleeve. Gator hopped up off the ground and landed a hard right to the security officer's gut. When the officer doubled over, Gator followed with an uppercut. The security officer went to pass out, but Gator held him upright. He yoked him from behind, using him as a shield as the police drew their weapons. In the blink of an eye, a robbery had turned into multiple homicide and kidnapping. Neither of which Gator planned to stand trial for. It was either get away or die in the streets.

The officers advanced on Gator but didn't dare to fire a shot for fear of hitting the security guard. Gator had no such reservations as he opened fire on the police. The first officer took one in the chest, taking him out of the firefight. The second one dropped to the floor and crawled for safety.

Gator, still holding the security guard, backed down the street, desperately seeking another escape. People cursed and blared their car horns at the black man standing in the middle of the street. Gator looked to a beat-up brown station wagon and saw an opportunity.

An elderly dark-skinned man was sitting behind the wheel of the car trying to figure out what the traffic jam was about. He had no idea that he was about to be Gator's ticket to freedom. Still gripping the security guard, Gator made his way to the wagon. The man looked on in shock as Gator snatched the driver's-side door open.

"Don't shoot," the man pleaded.

"Don't fret, old-timer," Gator sneered. "These hot ones ain't for you. But I will be needing ya bucket. Get the fuck out!"

The old man raised his arms and exited the wagon without protest. Gator tossed the security guard into the driver's seat, while he climbed into the back. He placed the pistol to the back of the security guard's head and said, "Drive, mutha fucka!"

CHAPTER 2

SHAI GOT OFF THE HIGHWAY on 155th Street and took 8th Avenue downtown. It had been quite some time since he really got to hang out in the hood. Shai rode slow and watched the honeys go back and forth. There were some thick lil' mamas at NC State, but they weren't built like the females in the City. Their whole gutter-ass attitudes were a turn-on for Shai. He was a sucker for a hood rat.

Shai cruised 8th until he got to 114th Street. Before he made the left, he threw in his 50 Cent CD and got low in the ride. "Wanksta" blared from the speakers as Shai got his low ride on across 114th Street. Due to him slouching and the tinted windows, people really couldn't see who was in the ride. He just peeked over his shoulder and laughed as the haters watched his 20s spin.

Shai pulled up in front of a building where some dudes were standing around clicking. Shai recognized his peoples so he decided to have a little fun. "Hey!" he shouted, still hiding his face behind the tint. "Any of y'all niggaz know Swan?"

Most of the other dudes backed away from the car, except for a skinny, light-skinned kid wearing a white T-shirt. "Who that?" asked the kid.

"You Swan?" Shai asked, trying to hold in his laughter.

"I said who that?" Swan said, backing away.

"I got something for you, son," Shai said, rolling the window down slowly. Before he could get it down all the way, a .38 appeared in Swan's hand.

"How you want it?" Swan asked, raising the gun.

Seeing that his joke was about to go too far, Shai rolled the window all the way down. "Easy," Shai said, showing his hands. "You gonna pop ya dawg?"

"Shai?" Swan asked, smiling. "Is that my nigga? The mutha fuck'n prince of the underworld? When you blow into town, cat?"

Shai stepped out of the ride and accepted his friend's greeting. "A lil' while ago. I see you still out here on one?"

"You know how it is, Shai. We can't all inherit a big house. Some of us gotta work for it."

"I can dig it. So, what's up with the gang?"

"Up and down, kid. You know how it goes down 'round here. My little brother Joe just caught a bid."

"That lil' nigga out here doing dirt?" Shai asked in disbelief.

"Please believe it," Swan confirmed. "I tried to tell the lil' nigga this here ain't no joke. These young cats got hard-ass heads."

"How much time they give him?"

"Gave that boy sixty-six years," Swan said sadly.

"Damn, lil' ass Joe-Joe. Fuck he do, kill somebody?"

"Nah, him and his man was riding down to VA wit' like four birds in the trunk. Police tried to pull them over for a busted taillight and the dumb mutha fucka that's driving dips off. They ran for about a good twenty minutes or so before they wrecked. Joe was already on probation, so that didn't help his cause any. Then the nigga he was wit' cold snitched."

"You're serious?"

"I bullshit you not, kid. Mutha fucka ain't even wait till the trial, he started talking in the sheriff's station. Ya pops paid for the lawyer out of his own pocket, 'cause it was his work. But the snitch killed it. The fucked-up part was that I was supposed to take the work down there. I ended up going to Atlantic City with this bitch, so I got lil' Sleep to do it for me. I didn't know he was gonna gas my brother to go with him."

"So what happened to Sleep?"

"Fuck you think?" Swan said venomously. "A mutha fuck'n shiv happened to that rat bastard. Had that boy cut from ear to ear, then they broke the blade off in his ass. That dribble mouth sack of shit took my lil' brother's life away, so I took his."

"Damn. Did Poppa flip out?"

"Did he? That's where I got this," Swan said, pointing to a scar under his eye. "Poppa beat me like I was a nigga in the street. Said that the only reason he didn't kill me is because he loved me like family. To make it worse, he cast me out, dawg. Got me out here with these stupid-ass niggaz," he said, motioning to the soldiers in front of the building. "How long I known ya family, Shai? I know I fucked up, but this shit is crazy."

"You know how Poppa is, Swan. But fuck that, what's up with you?"

"Same shit, different day, Shai. I'm just trying to live. Ya know?"

"Ain't we all, brother."

"I'm good now though," Swan said, throwing phantom jabs. "I got my road dawg back. The streets better look out now."

"I ain't on that shit, Swan." Shai waved him off. "Poppa's already pissed at me for getting kicked outta school. I ain't trying to hear his mouth."

"Damn, son. You got kicked out?"

"Yeah, man." Shai sucked his teeth. "Nigga snitched on me behind that gambling shit."

"Man, you ain't push his shit back?" Swan asked, making a gun with his fingers.

"Nah, kid. It ain't even that serious. I was in enough trouble, so I just bounced."

"That's some bullshit. Niggaz be on that faggot shit. Don't

sweat it though, it's money out here, son. Wit' us together, we can do some things. Just like old times." Swan folded his arms across his chest.

"We used to kill 'em out here." Shai smiled.

"Hell yeah." Swan gave him a punch. "You was the only nigga I knew that could take a pound of bullshit weed, and have niggaz thinking they had some fire."

"You know what I say," Shai said, smirking, "if it smells like watermelon, then it must be. Mutha fuckas spent all that money on some backyard boogie and a little watermelon puckers." A few summers ago, Shai ventured into selling weed. He wanted to get some high-powered shit, but niggaz was selling it too high for him not to have a spot. Shai found a way around the bullshit. He bought regular weed and doctored it up to be something else. If it smelled exotic, Shai could sell them on it being so.

"Those was the days," Shai continued. "We could've got our fucking heads handed to us behind that shit."

"But we didn't," Swan pointed out. "You always knew how to do your shit without it getting ugly. Just like a true gentleman."

Shai smiled.

"Yeah," Swan continued, "if we had you on the team, we could do some shit."

"Nah." Shai waved him off again. "I ain't really trying to go there, Swan. Poppa don't want me on the streets. This is Tommy's thing."

"Don't beat me in the head, Shai. You know damn well you got hustler in your blood. Shit, we was flipping them pounds of weed like hotcakes. Ain't nothing for us to set up shop again. I fuck wit' Tommy on the hard drugs. Coke, dope, shit like that. It shouldn't be a problem if we do us on the weed tip."

"Yeah, until Poppa finds out and whips both our assess," Shai joked. "But fuck that. How's the lil' one?"

"Mara, that's my heart," Swan said proudly. "I live and die for her, baby."

"'Bout how old is she now?"

"She about to be three, son. It's funny 'cause while you was at the prom, I was up in labor and delivery."

"Life is crazy like that, kid. But you doing right by her, ain't you?"

"That's a silly-ass question, Shai. You know me, man. Giselle is a stone-cold bitch, but that ain't got shit to do with Mara."

"Fo' sho'."

"Hey, Shai," two passing girls said in unison. Shai waved at the girls and gave them his winning smile. The girls giggled and kept going. Swan shook his head.

"You ain't even been on the block five minutes," he teased.

"Don't hate, nigga. I'm the prettiest nigga in Harlem," Shai joked as he licked his fingers and ran them along his eyebrows.

"Front'n-ass nigga. Yo, let's spin the hood, kid."

"You ain't said nothing but a word," Shai replied as he got into the driver's seat. Swan got in on the other side. Shai cranked on the CD player and pulled the car into traffic.

"Star, quit playing and get your coat!" Tish shouted, trying to find her house keys. She had been having a rough day, and her niece Star wasn't helping. This was the usual routine when her sister didn't come home: Tish would be left to tend to Star. At times, she got pissed, but she tried to understand her sister. It was hard raising a child by oneself. That's the reason Tish didn't have any.

Honey had always been the rebel around the house. She pretty much did what she wanted to, even when they were kids. When she came home one day and told her mother that she was pregnant, it didn't really come as a surprise. Instead of her mother trying to understand, she called Honey every name under the sun and gave her a clear ultimatum: "Give your baby up for adoption, or get out." Honey chose the latter.

In the beginning, it was really hard for her. She was a teenage mother with no job and no skills. Honey was always too proud to accept help, so welfare wasn't an option. Besides, since she wasn't eighteen, she'd need her mother to handle the paperwork. There was no way in hell she was going to do that. She'd just have to find another way.

So she just coasted. Honey looked for work, but she was either too young or underqualified. In the meantime, in between time, Honey had men throwing themselves at her left and right. Having a baby accented her already shapely body. It was around this time that Honey realized just how much of an asset a woman's body could be. She decided that instead of trying to work for peanuts, she'd just use her natural assets to get what she wanted.

Guys constantly showered her and Star with gifts. It was cool, but it wasn't hers. When a man gives you something, he usually wants something in return. Honey wasn't above fucking for a buck, but it wasn't really her style. She needed to find a way to generate her own income. It was around that time she was introduced to stripping. A girl she knew coaxed her to try it once, and like most girls, Honey was addicted to that fast cash. She hadn't looked back since.

Tish tried not to be judgmental of her sister. She didn't agree with Honey's career choice, but she understood survival. She had often tried to coax Honey to explore going back to school, but she only half listened. Honey was caught up in the glitz and glam of the streets. She sold herself on the idea that she'd find the balla to snatch her off her feet and take her to paradise. Not likely.

"Star, let's go!"

"So where we at?" Shai asked, coasting up Broadway.

"I don't know, nigga," Swan replied. "You act like you ain't from New York. Oh, I forgot. Youz a Jersey nigga, right?"

"Fuck you, Swan. You know where I'm rep'n. Man, that weed gave me the munchies. How 'bout we go find somewhere to grub?"

"A'ight," Swan agreed. "I know this little spot uptown where we can get some seafood at a reasonable price."

"Sounds good to me," Shai said.

"In a minute. I got a run to make," Swan told him.

"Swan, you know I ain't riding wit' no work in the car," Shai warned.

"Shut up, fool," Swan joked. "I ain't gotta pick up no work, I gotta go snatch some bread from this cat on Amsterdam."

"What, you playing messenger?" Shai asked.

"Hardly." Swan smiled. "Insurance money."

"You mean extortion money," Shai pointed out.

"What the fuck ever. All I know is that I'm supposed to pick the bread up from homeboy. Whatever arrangements he's made wit' ya brother is none of my concern. I sell crack, nigga. I don't know nothing about that other shit."

"Just hurry yo' ass up," Shai said, sucking his teeth.

Swan directed Shai to a bodega on 102nd and Amsterdam Avenue. He pulled the Camry in front of the joint and double-parked. There were some dudes standing in front of the store, trying to look hard. They strained their eyes to see who the occupants of the car were. When they saw Swan hop from the car, they all turned their eyes and went back to what they were doing.

"What up, ahk?" Swan asked, stepping into the bodega.

"Swan, what's good?" said a young-looking Arab boy wearing a fitted Raiders cap. "My pops is stocking the shelves. Dad!" the boy yelled down the aisle.

A man, who looked like the boy twenty years older, popped his head up from behind some cereal boxes. He looked around the front of the store and stopped his gaze on Swan. He dabbed his tan face with a handkerchief and gave Swan a yellow-toothed grin.

"What up, shorty?" Kareem asked.

"Told you about that shorty shit," Swan said playfully. "You got that for me?"

"Yeah," Kareem said, pulling a healthy-looking envelope from the pocket of his smock. "It's all there, but it's almost a shame to give it to you."

"Quit talking crazy," Swan said, taking the envelope and thumbing through the bills. "We've got a beautiful thing going over here. Y'all move our product and pay taxes, while we provide you with the goods you sell at a generous discount. What's better than that?"

"Yeah, that part is cool, but you guys are slipping," Kareem admitted. "We pay you for protection, but those kids from the projects have robbed us twice this month. I had to go into the rent money to pay you guys."

"Robbed?" Swan asked in surprise. "I didn't know anything about that. Kareem, you know you my nigga. Why didn't you come to me?"

"Since you got into that trouble with Poppa, you don't get over this way much. I tried to tell that other guy, but he didn't follow up on it," Kareem explained.

Swan suddenly became furious. Kareem and his family were good people. They paid on time and they never came up short. Their store, just like several others in Harlem, were under the protection of the Clark family.

"Don't worry, Kareem," Swan said. "I'm gonna take care of this shit, right now. Would you know these kids if you seen 'em again?"

"Why not?" Kareem asked. "It's not like they wore masks."

"A'ight. So we'll take a walk over to the projects and handle this shit," Swan said, leading the way out of the bodega.

Swan walked past the car, not saying a word to Shai. Shai noticed him and wondered what the deal was. Not wanting to be left out of the loop, Shai climbed out of the ride and followed Swan and the Arab man.

"What the deal?" Shai asked, finally catching up.

"Wait for me in the car," Swan said over his shoulder.

"What up, we got beef or something over here?" Shai asked, ready to hold his partner down.

"We ain't got shit," Swan said, checking his gun. "I gotta go fix a problem for my man Kareem."

"So, I'm with you," Shai said.

Swan looked at Shai and sucked his teeth. He knew Shai wasn't a punk, but he also knew that Tommy would murder him if anything happened to Shai. They were already right there, so Shai was in it.

Swan just hoped that he would be able to hold him and his man down with one gun.

"There they go." Kareem pointed to a group of young men standing in front of the building. "The fat one," Kareem said, indicating a dark-skinned kid who was smoking a cigarette. "That's the main one. The other dudes are just flunkies."

"A'ight," Swan said, shoving the barrel of his gun into his pants pocket and covering the butt with his shirt. "Shai, you stay here with Kareem until I call for you."

"What you gonna do?" Shai asked.

"Man, stop asking so many fucking questions," Swan snapped. "Just be easy and watch a nigga work."

Shai looked on in confusion as Swan hunched over and walked toward the boys. He couldn't think for the life of him what Swan was up to. Regardless of what it was, he was gonna hold Swan down. He didn't want to get hurt in the process, but if it happened, he was ready.

"Say, man," Swan said, swaggering toward the boys. "Who's working?"

"What?" a short, light-skinned kid asked. "Fuck you talking about?"

"You got coke?" Swan asked, scratching his arm.

"Nah, man," the light-skinned kid said. "We don't know nothing about that shit."

"Come on," Swan pleaded. "I ain't no cop. I'm just trying to get a quick buzz."

"Why don't you buzz yo' ass from 'round here," the fat kid cut in.

"It ain't even gotta be like that," Swan said, reaching out and touching the fat kid's shoulder.

The fat kid grabbed Swan's arm, which was just what he expected him to do. When he tried to move Swan's right arm, Swan came up holding the gun with his left. He jammed the pistol into the fat kid's gut and smiled wickedly as his whole team froze in place.

"Chill, man," the fat kid pleaded.

"Fuck that chill shit, big boy," Swan said, jamming the gun farther into his stomach. "Talk that fly shit now."

"Chill," the fat kid repeated. "We selling weed over here. Take it all and the money."

"Thanks," Swan said, digging into the fat kid's pocket. He removed a small bankroll and shoved it into his pants pocket. "But this ain't about no paper. Yo!" Swan called to Shai and Kareem.

Shai looked at the Arab man and shrugged his shoulders. He walked over to his friend, followed by a frightened Kareem. Shai looked each one of the boys in their eyes as he took his place next to Swan. He was nervous as hell, but he held his face.

"You know this man?" Swan asked, nodding toward Kareem.

"Yeah," the fat kid said sheepishly.

"This is my people," Swan said, moving the gun from the fat kid's gut to his temple. "And being that he's my people, he falls under the protection of my family. The Clark family." Swan noticed the fat kid began to sweat at the mention of the Clarks. "You've wronged this man, but you're gonna make it right. Isn't that so?"

The kid nodded.

"Good," Swan said. "Now I want you to say something with me: *When I come home, I'm gonna pay back every dollar I stole.* Say it, mutha fucka!"

"I'm gonna pay back every dollar I stole," the fat kid repeated.

"Nigga, say it right," Swan barked, cocking the gun.

"When I come home, I'm gonna pay back every dollar I stole."

"Good," Swan said, backing up. "That wasn't hard at all. You niggaz make this shit right. Any questions?"

"Yeah," the fat kid whispered. "Where am I going?"

"Oh, shit." Swan laughed and leaned against Shai. "I damn near forgot to tell you." Swan shot the fat kid, once in each leg. "The hospital, pussy. Don't fuck with my people!" Swan swept the kid's crew with the pistol. No one dared move. He smiled, knowing that his point had been made.

. . .

Shai drove the car with both hands, casting a glare at Swan from time to time. He had gone to bat with Swan at his side more than once, but that was back in high school. With age came a coldness to Swan that Shai wasn't quite used to. You had to be cold to play the game. If what Swan did was everyday life in the game, Shai was happy to be a square.

The two men talked back and forth and continued to spin through Harlem. Swan took Shai to Land & Sea, where they stuffed themselves with seafood and sipped mixed drinks. It felt good to kick it with his man again after so long. Even though Shai made it home for just about every break, they rarely got to see each other during the school year. While Shai was away at school, Swan would be in the City. Then when Shai was in the City, Swan would be OT. That's why the summertime was so important to them; it was the only time of year that the two of them could really kick it.

"Damn," Shai said, stuffing another shrimp in his mouth. "This shit is good."

"You never been here?" Swan asked.

"Nah. I heard of this place before, but I really was fucking with One Fish Two Fish. But this here is the jump-off. Plus the food ain't as high."

"Shai, cut that shit out. You know you ain't hardly pressed for no cake."

"Swan, I'm just as broke as every other college nigga."

"Please. Yo' daddy is caked up, man."

"That's his paper, son. I don't count that, 'cause I ain't make that."

"You serious?"

"Yeah, man. I work at this fancy-ass hotel down there. Shit, them folks tip good too. I clear quite a few dollars in tips on the weekend."

"Damn, I need to come down there with you, Shai."

"Wish it was that simple." Shai sighed. "Niggaz gave me the boot, kid."

"Shai, you let them backwards-ass crackers catch you slipping? I'm disappointed in you," Swan said.

"It wasn't even like that. A mutha fucka told on me. Nigga lost some paper and got upset. It ain't my fault he lost, but the bitch-ass nigga told on me. They started to bring me up on charges but Scotty dead'd that shit. Kicked my black ass smooth out though."

"What you gonna do, Shai?"

"I dunno." He shrugged. "Guess I'll ride out the summer and see what comes up."

Shai's attention was temporarily diverted when he heard the restaurant door open to his rear. He watched as three gorgeous young ladies came into the establishment. They were three shades of brown and Shai wanted to taste them all. Before Swan could say anything, Shai was on his feet and headed in the direction of the ladies.

"Excuse me," Shai said, half bowing, "my name is Shai, and I will be your host for the evening. May I escort you to my table?"

The girls looked at Shai and laughed. Shai had them grinning so he knew that all he had to do was choose. Blonde, redhead, or brunette? So many choices. The blond girl stepped forward and addressed Shai's comment.

"I dunno," she said, eyeballing him. "You don't look like no waiter to me, shorty." She stood there looking like something straight out of *Black Tail*. Shorty had a butterscotch complexion, with caramel eyes. Her hair was dyed blond and cut into a style that the girls weren't wearing up that way just yet. Her black low-rise jeans exposed her round ass and washboard stomach.

"Baby," Shai said, taking her hand. "Service is in my blood. What's your pleasure? What you need?"

"You hear this nigga?" the blonde asked, looking to her crew. "Look shorty, you're cute as hell, and witty on top of it, but this ain't a good time."

"What, you up here wit' somebody, ma?"

"Something like that, shorty."

"My name ain't shorty. It's Shai."

"And my name ain't ma. It's Honey."

"Honey," Shai said out loud. It made sense. This lady was definitely sweet paradise. Shai looked at her round breasts and made up his mind. He needed to have her. "So," Shai picked up. "Now that we know each other, can we exchange numbers?"

"Are you serious?" Honey asked. "I told you I was in here with somebody."

"It's all good, Honey. I respect everything you saying right now, that's why I ain't just snatch you up and bounce. Homey can have his fifteen minutes of fame, I just want my chance to find out what makes you shine the way you do. Is it wrong for a man to be curious about why the Lord creates such miracles?"

Honey tried to hold it, but a smile burst onto her face. This cat knew all the right things to say to a chick and he was handsome as hell. When she looked at the way he wore his sweatpants, only exposing a touch of his colorful boxers, she was open. There was something about this kid's style that made her wet. She didn't know if it was his confidence or the James Dean–like sneer that he wore, but something about the young man made her wanna take a chance. Only not at that moment.

"Like I said," Honey continued, "I'm here with somebody, so I can't even holla at you like that. Thank you for the kind words though." Honey allowed the *real* waiter to lead her and her team to their table, while all Shai could do was watch her switch away.

Shai's fantasy was broken up when someone bumped him from behind. Shai stumbled forward a few paces, but managed to keep his cool. He turned around and found himself confronted by a dark-skinned kid. He was a skinny dude, who walked with a bop. He wore a leather jacket when the weather was pretty nice outside. Shai knew what that was about. The kid glared at Shai with his veined, red eyes and searched for a reason. Shai was about to get crazy, when Swan tapped his arm.

" 'Sup, Bone?" Swan said to the dark-skinned cat.

"Young Swan," Bone said, still not smiling. "What you doing this far north?"

"Came to get something to eat with my peoples."

"Oh, you know this nigga?" Bone nodded toward Shai.

"Yeah, this Shai. You don't remember him?"

"Nah. Fuck is he?"

"This is Poppa's son."

"What Poppa?"

"Only one Poppa, dawg."

"I thought Tommy was his only son?"

"Nah. Shai is the youngest. He went to junior high with us."

"I don't know this cat, but he looking at me all crazy and shit. I thought he had a problem or something."

"Nah, Bone. Shai is a civilian."

"Well, you better teach him to be careful where he's standing." Without another word Bone and his peoples went to join Honey and her girls at their table. Shai just stood there staring at Bone's back.

" 'Sup wit' that dude?" Shai asked. "He acting like I did something to him."

"Nah," Swan said. "Ain't you, it's Tommy he's salty with."

"Fuck he do?"

"Bone used to work with Poppa. Tommy caught him stealing and slapped him around. Banned him from the block. Only place Bone can get money now is way up here. Got his own little team up here. Ain't many of them, but they're some mean sons of bitches. Steer clear of them cats, Shai."

Shai shot one more glance in Bone's direction, before returning to the table with Swan. Now Shai understood why Honey didn't want to holla; she was rolling with that fake-ass gangsta Bone. He didn't look so tough, but if Swan was leery of him, then there must've been something to him. Swan didn't scare easily.

Honey strolled back to where her friends were piling into one of the booths. She had gotten a kick out of exchanging words with Shai.

He was cocky as all hell, but there was something about him that turned Honey on. Also, there was something very familiar about his name.

She had seen the youngest Clark boy around, but had no idea who he was or what he was about. Unlike Tommy, Shai didn't make his name on the streets. Honey thought the kid was cute, but her mind really wasn't on socializing at that moment. She was thinking about her life.

It seemed like she was running in place. Between her "job" and the men she had taking care of her, she lived pretty comfortably. Her rent was paid, and she stayed fly, but there was a serious lack of stability. Men came and went like clockwork, but none of them could be taken seriously. All they wanted was a piece of ass or a pretty face on their arm. Sometimes she felt like the whore her mother always said she would turn out to be. More often than not, Honey wanted to give up, but she had to be strong for Star.

"Damn, girl," Honey's friend Paula said. "Don't you hear me talking to you?"

"Huh?" Honey asked, snapping out of her daydream.

"I was asking you if you were working tonight?"

"Sorry, Paula. My mind was somewhere else."

"Um-hm," Stacy butt in. "Probably thinking about shorty over there."

"Please." Honey blushed. "Ain't nobody thinking about that lil' boy."

"Speak for yourself," Paula spoke up. "The kid is fine."

"He a'ight," Honey said nonchalantly.

"Bitch, stop fronting," Paula remarked. "Anyway, I was asking if you were working the club tonight. I could've picked you up and we could've split the cab."

"I don't know, Paula. I get tired of shaking my ass for these crab-ass niggaz. Always talking that Willie shit, but you gotta damn near beg a nigga for a tip. That shit is wack."

"Better get in where you fit in," Stacy said.

"Easy for you to say." Honey snaked her neck. "I don't see yo' ass getting thigh burns on no fucking poles. That shit is a headache."

"You know work ain't Stacy's style." Paula nudged her. "She's one of those flat-back hoes!" They all had a good laugh, then Paula went back to the original topic. "So, you gonna push up on shorty or not?"

"You still wit' that shit?" Honey sucked her teeth.

"You better act like you know," Paula said. "That nigga is connected to paper. Money and handsome . . . that's a winning combo, bitch."

"Whatever." Honey waved her off, wondering what the hell her friend was so excited about. "Anyway, what am I supposed to do with that nigga Bone up in here? Y'all know how he do."

"Don't remind us," Paula said. "That boy don't hardly know how to act. I don't even know why you mess with that nigga."

"Me either," Stacy added. "That boy's got a face that only a mother could love."

"Fuck you, bitch," Honey said, laughing. "Bone's got money and his dick is a'ight."

"Fuck Bone," Paula said, looking around to make sure that Bone wasn't within earshot. "I'm giving Shai your number."

"No the hell you aren't," Honey protested.

"Baby girl, stop acting like that. Bone ain't your man or nothing, so why not?"

"He isn't my man, but I'm here with him. Besides, he's on his way over here. How do you plan on getting Shai the number without Bone peeping it?"

"Honey," Paula said, scribbling on a napkin, "watch your girl work."

Frost sat on the leather couch he had just purchased for his mother, rolling a blunt. The latest videos were playing on the fifty-three-inch television that took up nearly one entire wall. The deep white carpet that lined the living room floor felt good to his bare feet. Frost smiled with pride.

Frost was a small-time hustler who Tommy had fired for being incompetent. He was one of those cats that thought they knew the game inside and out, but really didn't have a clue.

When Tommy fired him, Frost scrounged up a few dollars and bought some grams. He eventually flipped those to an ounce and so on. He hadn't reached bird status, but he was determined to get there. There were quite a few crews in the hood that wanted to get at Frost or get with him. He didn't care either way because he figured that he was the smartest nigga in the hood.

Swan had caught him hustling on the block and whipped his ass for it. Tommy had decreed that Frost had to be cast out, much like Bone. But instead of doing what Bone did and relocate to another hood, Frost did it the lazy way: He took his show on the road.

Frost would post up on different blocks and sling his work. Then he would get up off the block before anyone noticed what he was doing. Being that he had a few workers under him to hold him down, he was able to be everywhere at once. He figured that if he kept doing it like this, he wouldn't get caught.

The two men ate the rest of their meal and called for the check. When the little Mexican waiter brought the bill, there was a folded piece of paper with it. Shai unfolded the paper and eyed the phone number on it. When he looked up, Honey was staring at him. She shot a quick wink and went back to her conversation with Bone. Shai smiled to himself as he put the number into his pocket. Bone might've talked a good game, but Shai was the true player.

After gorging on seafood, Shai convinced Swan to go with him to the gym. Swan protested, 'cause sports weren't his thing, but Shai insisted. Even though Shai wasn't in school, he still had to take care of himself. Just because he had gotten expelled didn't mean that he was going to give up on his dream. Shai was determined to make it to the League.

At first Shai and Swan were just shooting around, but soon people started coming in. The guys decided to run a full, but Swan opted to sit it out. Instead he just watched Shai do his thing. Swan was thoroughly impressed by his friend's skills. Shai was hitting the cats on the court with all kinds of moves. Shai hit his opponents with everything from crossovers to jump shots. To add insult to injury, he dunked on a loudmouthed kid, who thought he was nice. Swan always knew that Shai had skills, but watching him was something out of this world. It was like poetry in motion.

CHAPTER 3

AFTER DROPPING HONEY AND her peoples off, Bone hit the hood to handle his business. He sat on a wooden chair in his apartment, sifting through a pile of cocaine with a playing card. Everything that needed to be put on the streets was bagged and ready to go. The overs were for Bone to do with how he saw fit. A good portion would go into his nose and the rest would be used for entertainment.

Bone scooped a pinky nail full of the powder and inhaled it. There was a tingling in the back of his nose that quickly spread to his skull. Soon his face and nose were numb. Bone smiled, knowing that the coke would be moved quickly on the streets. He pushed back from the small table and walked to the window.

From the view of his apartment on 204th and Broadway, there wasn't much to see. Traffic, commotion, and the grit of the city. There was no beauty, only shades of gray. It wasn't much to look at, but it was Bone's domain: the section of the city that Tommy had banished him to.

The slight by his onetime friend still stung when he thought about it. He was younger than Tommy, but his ambition and hustle easily matched that of his elder. Tommy was Poppa's heir, so by right of birth the City would come to him. Bone was to be one of his lieutenants. That was, until their falling out.

Bone knew he was wrong for skimming, but he had to eat. He was getting money under Tommy, but he would never be truly allowed to know his worth. He would always be second to Poppa's boy. Bone's greed got the best of him and he lost his position. He should've been thankful that he was allowed to live, but Bone didn't see it that way.

Tommy thought he was being slick by letting Bone live and banishing him as an embarrassment. He wanted to show that he could play God with people's lives. He was always an overconfident mutha fucka and that would be his downfall.

Money was slow going for Bone and his followers at first. Every dope man in the City knew that Bone had been cast from the promised land and would be desperate. They either wouldn't deal with him, or would double the price. Bone had no choice but to suffer the losses if he wanted to continue to eat. When Fat Mike had agreed to hit him off, things had started to look up. The only problem was, Mike would only give Bone the runoff from Tommy's shipments. It was either too weak, or not enough to really get right. It allowed Bone and his team to keep their heads above water, but something had to give.

Time was ticking on the streets of New York. The reigning king was getting on in years and there were quite a few crews who were uncomfortable with Tommy taking over. If Bone played it right, he could come across as the lesser of two evils and gain support. In order to do this, he would have to prove his worth to Mike. With the Italians behind him, it would be a whole lot simpler to step up.

Bone took one last look out over the City and returned to his little wooden chair and his pile of cocaine. The wheels in Bone's mind began to spin as he thought on what he had to do next. He continued to shovel coke into his nose, letting his wicked thoughts roam.

. . .

Gator paused and ducked into a doorway as the police car sped by. He knew he was in a bad way and had to get the hell out of Florida. When the coast was clear, he resumed his walk.

The night air whipped against his bare arms, causing chill bumps to run up and down his limbs. He cursed himself again for having to throw away his baseball jacket, but there was no way he could've kept it. In addition to being filthy with soot, it was stained with the security guard's blood. He could've let the young white guy go, but why risk it? Gator put two in the guard and set him and the station wagon ablaze. By killing him, Gator had time to think about his next move.

He had a few dollars on him, but hardly enough to make an inconspicuous exit from the state of Florida. If he stayed, his days would be numbered. He needed to get gone, but had no way to do so on his own. With nowhere else to turn, Gator stopped at a pay phone outside of a McDonald's and placed a collect call to New York.

Poppa sat in his office going over some last-minute details for his retirement/launch party. This party was going to be the event of the year. Poppa had invited any and every heavy hitter he knew to come out and celebrate with him. Not only was he getting out of the game, but he had an investment on the ball that was sure to make him richer than he already was. This was cause to celebrate indeed.

A soft knock on the door brought Poppa's attention to his study door. "Come on in," he yelled out.

Butch stuck his head into the office. Butch was Poppa's bodyguard. He was about six feet and weighed maybe two hundred pounds, but contrary to how he might've looked the man was very dangerous. Butch served in Desert Storm as a member of an elite group called the Bone Collectors. They would seek out sacked villages and military structures and finish off any- and everyone who might've survived the initial attack.

When Butch came home and Uncle Sam kicked him in the ass and told him to try and live off $567 a month, Poppa scooped him up. Butch had been putting people to sleep for the drug lord ever since.

"Poppa, you busy?" Butch asked.

"Nah, what's up, Butch?"

"Mo Black is here to see you."

"Oh, you can send him in."

Butch nodded and dipped back into the hallway. A few seconds later Mo Black came strutting into Poppa's office. Mo was a very plain-looking character. He had an even brown complexion with a light mustache and a close fade. He was wearing a pair of JCPenney slacks and plain black leather jacket. To look at him, you'd never know that he made Poppa hundreds of thousands of dollars a year selling Ecstasy and angel dust.

Poppa had Mo living in a quiet town in upstate New York. To his neighbors, he was just a guy who owned a small moving and storage company, and lived quietly with his wife and kids. But it was all a lie.

The woman was Mo's girlfriend, Vivian. She was just as scandalous as he was. The kids were her sister's foster children. The sister was so high off crack most of the time that she never bothered to question why Vivian had offered to take the kids in. She didn't really care. All she knew was that she got to keep the foster care check that Vivian received for them once a month.

Mo used the moving company, which Poppa had financed, to ship large quantities of product inside the furniture. They would take people's furniture apart, pack it with the work, then they'd put it back together again. They paid off local troopers along the route just to minimize the hassle. By the time the furniture reached its destination, the truck had already been intercepted along the way and the drugs off-loaded. They were so efficient that people never even knew that they were paying to ship narcotics all over the eastern United States.

"Mo Black," Poppa said, smiling. "What it is, brother?"

"Poppa Clark," Mo said, embracing his elder. "Good to see you."

"So what goes on in hick's ville?"

"You know how it is, Poppa. Why you had to stick me in that mud hole, is beyond me."

"Because that's the last place the police would think to look for a damn dust plant, young'n. So what you got for me?"

"As always I come correct, Poppa. I've got one and a half in the trunk and I got another one and a half for you on the come around."

"I knew you'd say that." Poppa smiled. "Your money is always on time, son."

"Of course it is. I just don't see why the hell I'm stuck in Klan Land to prove it."

"Mo, how can you not see the beauty in it? With you being way up in west bumblefuck you don't have to deal with these knuckle-headed-ass kids. Besides that, you still get to maintain a fairly low profile. Silence is golden."

"Something that I've been exercising since I came to work for you six years ago. I've watched and learned from the greatest. Poppa, if I live to be a thousand your jewels will still be embedded in my brain."

"I know, Mo. That's why you're one of my closest lieutenants."

"True. So what's going down on the streets, Poppa?"

"Mo' money, mo' problems."

"This is the game we play," Mo said, grinning. "We all know the stakes before we roll the dice."

"Ain't this some shit," Poppa said, chuckling. "I brought you into the game and you're dropping jewels on me?"

"Hey, we all learn something new every day."

"So how we looking on that new town? I heard it's sweet up there."

"Oh, that's coming along nicely, but there are a few setbacks. I'm having a little trouble out of some Jersey cats that already had something going out that way."

"What they slinging?"

"Mostly rock. A lil' powder here and there."

"So why don't they just fall back? You only sell dust, Mo. I don't see how that's gonna step on their toes any."

"I tried to explain it to the kids like that, but you know how niggaz is. Always wanna see who can poke their chest out the furthest."

"I can dig it," Poppa said, lighting a cigar. "I know you and your peoples ain't really the killing kind, so you want me to send somebody up there?"

"That might not be such a bad idea."

"Okay. I'll get in touch with Priest."

"Hold on. No offense Poppa, but I don't want Priest around my business. That cat spooks me."

"Okay. So maybe I'll put one of the other soldiers on it. Swan might be good for this one. Or the new kid, Legs."

"Whoever. Just keep Priest down here with you."

"Scary ass. So when you want this problem addressed, Mo?"

"Shit, we can leave whenever. The only reason I'm staying in town for more than a day is because of the meeting, but we can handle it right after that," Mo said, standing.

He shook Poppa's hand and left the office. Poppa liked Mo and didn't really care for the idea that some out-of-town cats had tried him. Poppa would be sure that they answered for it though. His influence and power stretched a long way and they were going to find out that you don't fuck with Poppa Clark's family.

Shortly after his conversation with Mo, Poppa's cell rang. The caller ID flashed a Florida number. Poppa still dealt with quite a few people down that way, but only a select few had his cell number. He hit the TALK button and listened as the caller spoke frantically. "Uncle T, I need your help."

After the game, Shai dropped Swan off and went back to the house. He was glad to get a chance to get out and stretch his legs. It had been a while since he had been on the court. The whole time he was balling, he kept imagining that he was still in school playing ball. The roar of the crowd, the thrill of taking that last-minute shot. Shai missed that more than anything.

Basketball had always been his one true love. He had caught the bug when he was about four years old. Poppa and some of his buddies were watching the Lakers game on television and Shai had slipped in with them. From the moment he saw Magic Johnson handle the rock, he was hooked. Shai sat there and watched the whole game without uttering a word. He wanted to be just like Magic.

Shai had been careless with his dream. At the time, it seemed like a good idea to bet on the games. It kept extra bread in his pocket and made him popular with some of the more unsavory characters on campus. What he didn't think of was getting caught. For an extra few hundred dollars a day, Shai nearly destroyed his dream.

Between what Poppa gave him and his other hustles, Shai was good. His problem was that he had gotten greedy. He saw what kind of money the white boys were making and wanted in. He had a lot, but he needed to have it all. Greed was the downfall of many a man, and in that capacity, Shai was no different.

Now he was dangling in limbo. There was no doubt in his mind that he would be able to get into another school, but the question was, how long would it take? Shai shrugged, 'cause there was nothing else he could do at the moment. The summer was fast approaching, so his little dilemma would have to wait until fall. He was back home until further notice, so he decided to just ride it out.

The house was quiet, so he figured his siblings were out. Shai glanced around at the expensively furnished mansion and dreamed of the day when he would have one of his own. Unlike Tommy, Shai was determined to make his own mark on the world. He climbed the carpeted steps and headed to his domain. When he got to his bedroom, Poppa was standing near the bookshelf, looking at some of his old trophies.

" 'Sup, old man?" Shai said coolly. In his mind, he was preparing himself for another speech. This was something that he really didn't need at the moment. He had to get dressed and meet back up with Swan, so they could hit the streets.

"Hey, Slim," Poppa said, removing one of the trophies from the shelf. "Hope you don't mind. I was just in here reminiscing. You always were the athletic one." Poppa held up the trophy.

"You know how I do," Shai responded, jump shooting a pair of socks into the laundry hamper.

"Sure ya right." Poppa smirked.

"So, you ready for retirement?"

"I really can't say, Shai."

"What's the matter, Poppa? I thought this was what you wanted?"

"It is, Slim," Poppa assured him, sitting on the edge of the bed. "I've been in them streets a lot of years. Some people don't get a chance to step off."

"You did."

"Yeah, I guess I did. I can't lie though, I'm gonna miss them streets. They've been good to an old man. They fed me and in return, I treated them fair. While I was running the show, shit was smooth as silk."

"You're saying that like it's gonna change when Tommy takes over," Shai said, with a raised eyebrow.

"I dunno, son." Poppa shrugged. "See, I lasted as long as I did in the streets 'cause I kept a low profile and I was humble with it. I treated everyone according to how they conducted themselves and kept the beef to a minimum. Tommy is a different case. Your brother is a stone gorilla. Always in the mix and shooting his gun off."

"Yeah, Tommy is 'bout his business," Shai said, smiling.

"Lil' nigga, please." Poppa waved him off. "Let me drop a jewel on you, son. Just because you drop a nigga or two, don't make you 'bout nothing. You gotta know when to talk and when to fight, son. Tommy is gonna make himself hotter than a firecracker in them streets. I keep trying to tell him to let the soldiers handle certain shit, but your brother and that damn temper of his." Poppa shook his head.

"So why don't you pick someone else?" Shai asked.

"Because Tommy is my blood. By right, this is his. He's earned it."

"And what about me?" Shai questioned. "What have I earned?"

"You've earned the chance to be something in life," Poppa said seriously.

"Wow," Shai said sarcastically.

"Don't be funny, Shai. I'm serious. You might think that this life is all about spending money and driving big cars, but there's two sides to every coin. Remember, I told you that."

"Yes, sir."

"Shai, life has a greater purpose for you. Tommy is my heir, but you will be the glue that holds this family together. I want Hope to look at you and see that good does live in this house. Teach her, as I've tried to teach you. I love Tommy, Shai. Just like I love all of my kids. He has a bright future ahead of him, I just want him to live long enough to spend it. I've tried to teach him about being poised, but it is what it is. You know, I never said this out loud, but I've always wished Tommy was more like you."

"Like me?" Shai asked, amazed. "What the hell do I know?"

"Shai, it ain't what you know, it's how you carry yourself. You're a born thinker and a gentleman."

"Thanks . . . I think."

"Just telling you what I know, son." Poppa shrugged. "Oh, well. Tommy's a hothead, but he ain't no damn fool. Eventually, he'll grow out of it. At least, I hope he does. I don't plan on outliving any of my kids." Poppa dropped a few more jewels on Shai and went to his office.

Shai knew his pops was a wise old dude. You didn't come as far as Poppa Clark had without having some sense. He'd been laying his gangsta down for thirty-something years and Shai was glad that he was getting out of the game. But in a sense, he envied Tommy. His big brother was about to inherit one of the largest criminal empires in the eastern United States. He was about to have the money and the power. Damn, he had it made.

Honey put the finishing touches on her makeup and was ready for the world. It was the weekend and she and her girls were hitting the club. As if it had to be a weekend for them to party. Before Bone had dropped them off, she made sure to hit him for some bread to get her hair and nails done. She had her own money, but it felt better to spend his. The nigga had to make himself useful some kind of way.

As she looked at her freshly did hair, she chuckled to herself. The way Paula had slipped Shai her number was smooth. Her girl always had a plan. Honey was hesitant about giving him the number, but she was curious as to what he was about. Had they been alone, she might've let him treat her to something to eat while she picked his brain. But this wasn't the day for that; Honey was with that fool-ass Bone. Wasn't no telling what he would've pulled if he'd seen her talking to Shai.

Bone was always up in Honey's mix. "Where you going, who you going with?" That was his MO. She always had a believable enough story for him and most of the time he went for it. He would give her a song and dance about it, but Honey would break him off with some pussy or a short shot of head and all would be well again. After her little bout with Tommy, Bone had been a comfort to her. Now he was just a pain in the ass. Honey needed a way to get rid of him, but for the moment she was gonna bleed his pockets.

Shai moved through the crowded club wearing his million-dollar smile. Everyone was greeting Shai and telling him how happy they were that he was back. It felt good to be among his true peoples. The whole scene was a stage and Shai was the star performer.

Clubbing wasn't in the original plan, but Shai was on his thirsty shit. Swan didn't really do the club scene, but his friend wanted to party, so he allowed himself to be dragged along. They found a decent little spot on the West Side and decided to pop in.

Shai finally managed to make his way to the bar to order his drinks. He copped a Long Island iced tea for himself and a shot of yak for Swan. As Shai turned to make his way back through the crowd, he bumped into a familiar face. She stood there looking like a grade-A winner, rocking a pair of white linen pants and a black shirt that she wore tied in the front. Her hair was done up differently, but her angelic face remained the same.

"Small world," Shai said, smiling.

"Small indeed," Honey agreed, returning the gesture. "So, you a regular in here?"

"Nah," Shai said, sipping his drink. "First time. How about you?"

"I come here every so often."

"Right. So, what you drinking, ma?"

"Oh, you treating?"

"Wouldn't have asked if I wasn't."

"Okay. In that case, you can get me a cosmopolitan." Shai ordered Honey's drink and it came in less than two minutes. "Damn," she said, accepting the drink. "These people ain't never come with my drink this quick. You must be a VIP."

"Nah, I just know how to get what I want. I'm used to having my way."

"Is that right?"

"Yep."

"So, you one of those confident cats, huh?"

"As confident as they come. My daddy always taught me and Tommy that nothing's out of our reach."

"Hold up," Honey said mid-sip. "What Tommy?"

"Tommy. That's my older brother."

"Brother? What's your name again?"

"Shai. Shai Clark."

Honey almost dropped her drink as two and two amounted to four. She could've slapped herself for not making the connection. The slick-talking brother from the seafood spot was one of the notorious Clarks. Honey knew that Tommy had a little brother, but she had never met Shai before that day. Her mind told her to leave it alone, but her greed and curiosity wouldn't let her.

"So, you're Shai Clark?" Honey asked, moving closer.

"The one and only," he said, smiling. "You've heard of me?"

"Yeah, I heard about you."

"So, you know my reputation for being every woman's dream?"

"More like every woman's whore. I've heard of you, Shai. They say that you ain't no good."

"People say a lot of things, Honey. Some of them are true, some of them aren't. You know how mutha fuckas like to talk."

"So is what they tell me about you true?"

"Hardly," he lied. "I've made some poor choices over the years, but I'm far from a whore."

"Yeah, right. Why don't I believe you?"

"Honey, what you chose to believe is up to you. I could sit here and shoot you some bullshit story in an attempt to sway you, but that ain't my style. I let my deeds speak for me."

"Deeds, huh? So Mr. Shai, what would you do to prove to me that you're not a whore?"

"All I can do is show you the person that I am, as opposed to the person that people make me out to be. I don't break my neck to accommodate nobody, but I hate to have filthy rumors circulating about me."

"You talk a good one, Shai."

"I do everything good, Honey."

Honey stood there trying to read Shai, but it was useless. He wore a hell of a game face. Shai could talk that sweet shit until his lips fell off, but Honey was far from stupid. Shai didn't hustle but he was connected to money, which was almost as good. Honey knew just what was going on inside the youngster's head. She had something he wanted and he had something she wanted: fair exchange.

"Okay," she continued. "We'll see, Shai." Honey thanked him for the drink and turned to walk away. Shai grabbed her arm before she could move away.

"So you just gonna take the drink and skate?" he asked.

"I said thank you, didn't I?" she shot back.

"Come on, shorty. You gotta come better than that," he said, giving her a wicked smile.

"So you trying to say I owe you something for this drink?" she asked with an attitude. Honey began to fish around in her purse for her money.

"Easy, love," he said, stopping her from pulling the dough out. "I don't want ya paper. All I wanna do is dance wit' you."

"Dance?" she asked, crinkling up her nose. "I thought gangstas didn't dance."

"I wouldn't know," he said, grabbing her hand and leading her onto the dance floor, "I ain't no gangsta."

To Honey's surprise, young Shai was quite the dancer. The DJ spun the new G-Unit and Joe single and the party got live. Shai grabbed Honey by the waist and began to sway to the beat. At first she acted stiff, but as the song played on, she got more into it. They just grooved with each other, not trying to get too crazy, but the mood shifted when "Nasty Girl" came on. Honey backed up against Shai and started to grind on him. He kept pace, but was having trouble focusing on his movements and not her body. Honey's scent drifted into Shai's nose, causing him to get aroused. She rubbed her hand against his face as she continued her little performance.

Honey turned to face Shai and ran her leg up his. When Shai tried to touch her thigh, she moved his hand away. Honey licked at Shai's neck seductively, but never touched him. The whole time they danced, she teased him. She would make sure that he was good and excited, then backed up off him. This continued until the mood shifted again and gangsta rap was the theme. Honey took that as her cue to exit. She gave Shai a friendly kiss on the cheek and turned to leave again.

"Listen," he said, stopping her. "I hate to be pushy, but I'm feeling you, ma. I'd like to get to know you a lil' better. Say, why don't you snatch up one of your girls and the four of us can go to breakfast when the club lets out?"

"We'll see, Shai," she teased him. Honey knew Shai was used to getting what he wanted, so she had to bait him.

"Don't disappoint me, Honey." Shai watched Honey saunter back through the crowd. Of all the females in the club, Honey had to be one of the baddest. She could play hard to get all she wanted, but Shai was confident that he would beat that. He was a player, how could he lose?

The night dragged on with more drinking and more partying. Shai must've danced with just about every chick in the joint. When it was all said and done, he had a good buzz and a pocket full of numbers. After a bit of searching, he linked up with Swan and was ready to go. As they made their way to the exit a scuffle broke out by the bar. At first there was just a lot of shouting and pushing. Then came the gunshots.

Shai was stuck at first. He tried to run for the exit with everyone else, but Swan pulled him to the ground behind an overturned table. After a small stampede, security managed to get the situation under control. Shai got up from the floor and looked at his ruined Versace slacks.

"Damn," Shai said, out of breath, "fuck was that shit all about? Niggaz up in here shooting."

Swan looked at Shai and laughed. "Welcome home, Shai. Welcome home."

Honey sat in the back of the cab, looking out the window. The Temptations sang about sunshine on a cloudy day and Honey hummed along. That was the second time she had bumped heads with Shai and the second time he had left an impression.

"Look at this ho," Sharon teased. "I know you ain't over there swooning over no dick?"

"Please." Honey played it off. "I'm just high."

"Bullshit," Stacy said from the passenger seat. "I seen how you was all up on the young boy."

"That wasn't just any young boy," Paula cut in, "that was Shai Clark."

"Tommy's little brother?" Pam asked in shock. "Bitch, you dead wrong."

"I ain't trying to hear that shit, Pam," Honey protested. "That shit wit' Tommy was ages ago. Besides, Shai is cute."

"Bet he got a few dollars put up too," Sharon said, giving Paula a high five.

"All y'all think about is money," Honey said.

"Like you don't," Paula cut in. "Miss me with that shit, Honey. We know you, like you know us."

The girls continued to laugh and talk for the remainder of the ride. In front of her girls, Honey acted as if she was only half interested in Shai. She was actually very interested in him. She wanted to see what he was all about. She hoped that her luck would hold out and he wouldn't be as much of an asshole as Tommy. Shai was a very intriguing character, and the fact that he had a few dollars didn't hurt.

Shai stood on the line inside of White Castle waiting to order his food. The inside was like a small after-party, loaded with drunk club-goers. Shai was accompanied by Swan as usual and another cat from the block named Snoop. Snoop was a tall, pole-thin cat, who sported a nappy Afro. They called him Snoop because he could find out dirt on anybody. Names, addresses, birth dates. Snoop was a wiz on the Internet.

"That shit at the club was crazy," Shai said.

"Please," Swan cut in, "that ain't nothing unusual. Niggaz get to drinking and don't know how to act. That's why I don't go to clubs no more. Only reason I went tonight was because you wanted to step out. Other than that, I would've been on the block."

"That shit blew mine, Swan. The worst part about it was that I had some ass lined up for us."

"You serious?"

"Yeah, shorty and them from the restaurant. The blond chick."

"Blond," Snoop cut in. "You talking about Honey?"

"Yeah," Shai continued. "You know her?"

"Yeah, me and every other mutha fucka in the hood. Shorty used to dance at Heat when it was open. Heard she does private parties now."

"Snoop, you mean that fine bitch is a ho?" Shai asked in shock.

"Don't put words in my mouth, Shai. I know she's damn sure a stripper, but the ho part is just what people say."

As hard to believe as it might've been, Snoop was hardly wrong. If he said that Honey shook her ass for cash then she probably did. He would've never guessed that the object of his affection was getting down like that. He wasn't too bothered by it though. As it stood, Honey was just another chick that he was trying to fuck.

After a good twenty-minute wait, the gentlemen had successfully placed their orders and received their food. They decided to post up and try and holla at some of the ladies. The night was still young and none of them had any place to be just yet. Shai was getting the number from a brown-skinned young lady when Tommy's Yukon pulled up to the curb.

Tommy had traded in his suit for a pair of jeans and some Timbs. His forty-inch cable swung from side to side as he approached his little brother. When Tommy hopped out of the truck, Shai noticed that some of the crowd began to disperse.

"What up, Slim?" Tommy asked.

"Ain't nothing," Shai said, hugging his brother.

"You was over at the club a lil' while ago when they started shooting?"

"Yeah, me and Swan was on our way out when it happened."

"All ya people straight?"

"Yeah, we ain't have no part in that shit."

"I'm glad that you're safe, Shai, but I told you about them clubs. Why don't you take your lil' ass to a lounge or a club where they don't allow boots and jeans from time to time?"

"You know how we do, Tommy. That's just our style."

"Please, y'all out here looking like three little ragamuffins and you talking about style. You can't be serious?"

"That's a'ight, Tommy. We couldn't all grow up in the eighties. Nigga, you just stopped buying tight jeans. Ya *Thriller* jacket wearing mutha fucka."

The brothers traded insults for a few minutes before Tommy got serious again.

"Yo," he said tapping Shai's arm. "Walk wit' me to the truck. I need to holla at you." Shai followed Tommy to the truck to see what the word was. "Listen," Tommy continued, "you know how Poppa is about you being out in the streets, right?"

"Yeah, I know Tommy."

"So why the fuck do you insist upon putting yourself in harm's way?"

"What you talking about, Tommy? All we did was go to the club."

"Yeah, but look what kinda club you went to. Them hole-in-the-wall spots ain't no good, man. Things are different around here now. Poppa's made a lot of money over the last few years. With money, comes animosity. With animosity, comes enemies. We got plenty of those, Shai. There's gonna be a whole lot of shit going down real soon. Tensions between us and other crews are already high. We killing 'em in the street. Niggaz is sick right now."

"I feel you, Tommy. But you know I ain't into this kinda shit. Why you giving me the lecture?"

"Ain't no lecture, lil' brother. More like a reality check. You think that because you play ball at some fancy school that niggaz won't come for you? You better wake the fuck up, yo. Your last name is Clark, same as mine. That means that you're bound to this thing we do by blood. You may not live in our world, Shai, but its rules still apply to you. Take heed to what I'm telling you."

"A'ight, Tommy."

"Don't just say 'a'ight,' Shai. You better pay attention. Look, I know you'll think about what I'm saying, but you gonna do what

you please anyhow. So hold this down," Tommy said, passing Shai a
.32. "That ain't to be running around looking for trouble, or flashing it for ya peoples. That's a last resort. Always try to bow out
gracefully. If that don't work, go out with lead. If Poppa finds that,
you didn't get it from me." Tommy hugged his brother and hopped
back in the truck.

Shai stood on the curb soaking up his brother's wisdom. Tommy
was crazy as all hell, but the boy had plenty of sense. Poppa
wouldn't have it any other way. Shai looked down at the tiny hand-
gun and felt the coolness of the metal. A rush of power shot through
him that was almost dizzying. Shai would hold many guns over the
years, but he was nineteen when he got his first one.

It had been a long day for Shai. He had been on the receiving end of
several lectures, nearly shot, and met the woman of his dreams. Not
bad for his first day back. If he was lucky, he might live long enough
to get kicked out of another school. Shai silently giggled at his own
twisted logic.

"Fuck you laughing at?" Swan questioned, as he exhaled smoke
from his nose.

"Inside joke," Shai responded.

"Yo, Shai." Bump spoke up from the stoop he was sitting on.
"Now that you home, what you gonna do? You gonna be working
with Tommy?"

"Nah," Shai said. "Poppa ain't trying to hear that shit."

"News flash," Snoop cut in. "Poppa ain't running the show anymore. Tommy is the H. N. I. C."

"God help us," Dave mumbled.

"Tommy is handling the day-to-day business, but it's still
Poppa's show," Shai informed him.

"Did you see that shit?" Bump asked, staring at a figure huddled
in the shadows a few yards away.

"Who, son with the hoodie?" Swan asked.

"Yeah," Bump said, getting off the stoop. "That mutha fucka just made a sale."

"You know him?" Swan asked, staring at the kid, who was nervously looking up and down the block.

"Nope."

"Oh, hell no," Dave said. "Don't nobody hustle on Poppa's streets but us."

"Let's go handle this shit," Swan said, retrieving his pistol from behind a trash can.

Swan started across the street, with his crew in tow. Shai continued to lean against the railing, puffing the half-gone blunt. All he needed was more drama. He had intended to mind his business, but Swan had been drinking and he was armed. He was wild enough sober, so there was no telling what he would do drunk. He cursed and followed his team, blunt in hand.

"Yo," Swan called to the kid. "Fuck is you doing?" The kid started to walk away, but Swan trained his gun on him. "Don't fucking move."

"Chill, yo," the kid pleaded.

"Nigga"—Bump poked his finger in the kid's chest—"you must've lost ya fucking mind. You know whose block you're hustling on?" The kid shook his head. "Poppa's, mutha fucka."

Shai saw that the kid was visibly shaken. He didn't appear to be more than thirteen or fourteen. He was too young to be hustling on anybody's block, but the drug lords didn't discriminate when it came to age. If you were down to bubble, then you could get a spot. That's just the way it went.

The crew began to take turns slapping the kid up, while Swan looked on and laughed. The kid was crying uncontrollably and looking around for help that would never arrive. He was on a drug-infested block in the middle of the night. If he was lucky, he would just get the shit beat out of him. Shai had finally had enough.

"Okay, fellas," Shai said. The crew didn't seem to hear him, 'cause they continued slapping the kid around and kicking him in his ass. "ENOUGH!" Shai bellowed. Everyone froze in place. Shai stepped through the mini–lynch mob and helped the kid to his feet. "How old are you?" Shai asked, looking at the kid's bruised face.

"Fourteen," the kid whispered through bloody lips.

"Look at me," Shai said, holding the kid's face so they were eye to eye. "This isn't for you. You're young, so I spare you this one time. Don't look for it to happen again. Get the fuck outta here."

The kid looked at Shai, not sure whether it was a joke or not. He looked around at the shocked crew and Swan still holding the pistol, and decided to make his exit. He ran down the block as fast as his young legs could carry him. When he disappeared around the corner, Shai turned to face his crew.

"Was that necessary?" Shai asked.

"That nigga violated," Bump snarled. "If Tommy were here, he would've let us stomp the nigga out."

"Well, Tommy ain't here," Shai said icily. "You're supposed to be a fucking hustler so act like you got some sense. He was a child. If something had happened to him, do you know how hot this block would've been? If y'all niggaz took the time to think once in a while, you might make it off the corners one day. I'm out."

Shai headed up the block to where his car was parked. Bump sucked his teeth, while Dave and Snoop just looked on in shock. Swan smiled.

CHAPTER 4

SHAI WAS AWAKENED THE next morning by a loud thumping
on his bedroom door. The digital clock on his nightstand read ten
thirty. Way too early for him to be up on a Saturday morning. He
tried to drown out the thumping with a pillow, but it only got
louder. "Come in!" shouted a sleepy Shai.

The door creaked open and Poppa stepped through it. He was
dressed in a dark-green linen suit, with his dreads tied off in the
back. Poppa looked at his wreck of a son and shook his head.

"Rough night?" Poppa asked, sitting at the foot of the bed.

"Kinda," Shai said, sitting up. "Me and Swan went out last
night."

"Kicked it around the City?"

"Yep, you know us."

"Heard there was a shoot-out in one of them hip-hop clubs y'all
like to go to."

"Yeah, Pop. I heard something like that, but we wasn't there,"
Shai lied.

"Um-hm. I'll take your word for it, Shai. Now, get up and get dressed."

"Dressed? Pop, it's Saturday."

"I told you about it over the phone, before you left to go to the airport yesterday. Little get-together for a friend of ours. You remember Bill O'Connor, don't you?"

"I think so. He's a cop or something, right?" Shai knew exactly who he was, but he'd never let on to Poppa.

"Used to be. Became a high-profile lawyer a while back. My man is about to get his name on the ballot for assistant district attorney. He's the guest of honor at this lil' thang."

"Dang, I gotta get dressed up for some stuffed shirts from downtown?" Shai whined.

"Do this favor for your old man," Poppa said, resting a hand on Shai's shoulder. "You'll get to take some flicks with some bigwigs. Good publicity for a promising athlete such as yourself. Plus a few of the girls from a few of the pro cheerleading squads are coming out."

At the sound of that, Shai rubbed his hands together in anticipation. "Okay, Pop. I'll get dressed and be down in a few."

"Okay. Thanks, son." Poppa walked out of the room leaving Shai to get himself together.

Shai was still a little hungover, but the thought of partying with industry chicks motivated him. He slunk over to his walk-in closet and began the task of finding the proper outfit. As he looked over the extensive wardrobe, a particular 'fit caught his eye. He fingered the suit and recalled its origins. It had been a gift from one of his father's business associates, an Italian designer whose name escaped him at the moment. It would do nicely.

Shai went into the bathroom and looked at himself in the mirror. His eyes were bloodshot and his lips looked like powdered donuts. He turned on the hot water in the shower while he twisted a joint. When he lit it, he leaned out of the bathroom window so the smell wouldn't carry.

After finishing the joint, Shai stepped into the hot water. The heat felt good coursing through his body. He hadn't really stopped to take a breath since his return home.

Shai reluctantly pulled himself out of the shower. It was now a quarter to twelve so Shai had to put some pep in his step. He stepped into his boxers and slid into a pair of silk socks. By the time he got his pants on, his bedroom door flew open again. Shai was about to catch an attitude until he saw who it was. A teenage girl came barging into the room. Shai smiled as his little sister flopped onto his bed. He knew it wouldn't be long before Hope made a grand appearance.

"What up, chicken head?" Hope joked.

"What's good, two-piece?" Shai replied. He was about four years her senior, but they were still close.

Unlike the brothers, Hope favored their mother. She was a smooth chocolate color, with medium-length hair. Her high cheekbones and cat-like eyes made her look like one of those pretty African models. She had large firm breasts that stood up under her white Donna Karan blouse. Her chunky bottom almost burst the seams on her cream-colored skirt. Hope was one of those girls that had developed way before her time.

"Why you ain't come say hi when you got in?" Hope asked.

"I had to handle something," Shai said. "Business, ya know?"

"Yeah, I know *your* kinda business, Shai."

"Get outta here, girl. You don't know what you talking about."

"Yeah, I do. Shai, you ain't nothing but a whore."

"Hey," he said, faking anger. "Where'd you get that dirty word from?"

"Please, look it up. But I know about you, Shai. The girls talk."

"Yeah, what they say?"

"They say how you be doing 'em. Shai, Shai, Shai," she sang. "Like you God's gift. You remember when you came up for Christmas break last year?"

"Yeah."

"Well, you told Poppa that you was going out with Swan, but

you really went off to see Minister Brown's daughter. After Poppa told you to leave her alone, you still went off and slid with her."

"Your story got a point, Hope?"

"Sure does. The way I got it is y'all went back to the minister's house. You knew he was hosting bingo at the church. Yeah, Shai, I heard. She did all kinda nasty stuff for you. Put it in her mouth and all," she said, giggling.

"What?" Shai asked, surprised. "Where you getting your information from, girl?"

"You forgot that she go to my school? She told all the girls at Saint Mary's how Shai Clark does it."

"You don't go listening to everything you hear, Hope. Females talk for the sake of hearing themselves talk. I can't help it if I'm young and pretty," Shai said, slipping on his shirt. "You need to be glad we got the same genes."

"Forget you, Shai. I can't help being a diva," she joked.

Hope was a miracle baby. She, like the rest of them, had the same mother and father. It was Poppa's last attempt at reforming their mother. This was back when she had first got caught up. She was doing her thing with whoever was holding weight, all in the name of her monkey. Poppa had reached out to her in a last attempt at salvation. He managed to get her straight and bring her back to the dime that she used to be. Their mother stayed clean long enough to get pregnant for the third time.

Poppa thought that he would be able to save June before her addiction took complete control. Over time the call of the streets became too strong for her. Poppa was so caught up in his business that he didn't know June was getting high again.

June went into labor prematurely in the fall of 1988. Hope Elise Clark came sliding out of their mother's ass at 6:15 A.M. She weighed a whole pound and a few ounces. The doctors said that she wouldn't live through the week. Poppa was beside himself with grief. He felt that it was his responsibility to keep June clean. If not for herself, then for the little girl that she carried. The first month was the hardest, but after about seven weeks Hope was ready to go home. That's how she got the name Hope. Poppa's baby girl beat the odds.

Poppa was overjoyed to have his baby girl home, but he had come to the end of his rope with June. Poppa laid his hands on June for the first time. It was Hope's second day home from the hospital. One of Poppa's men had spotted June copping from a local dealer. Poppa had the dealer put to death, but for June there was only one penalty: exile.

After giving June a verbal and physical lashing, Poppa stripped June of all her valuables. Credit cards, jewels. All of it gone. He cast June from the mountain and down with the sodomites. Poppa decreed that if June was content to live as the savages did, then it was only fitting that she live among them.

June tried to fight him in court, but she didn't have any type of leverage. Poppa was a modest businessman with connections, while June was an uneducated drug addict. She wasn't allowed to see her children or interact with them unsupervised. June stayed high so much that after a while, the supervised visits stopped. Poppa played the role of both parents for all three children.

"Why aren't you dressed yet?" Hope asked.

"I'm trying," he said. "It takes time to look good, shorty. Now get yo' ass up outta here." Shai popped Hope on the butt with his belt as she scooted out the door. He'd have to keep an eye on her. There were too many thirsty niggaz in the world to let her run wild. He knew because he was one of them.

Honey was awakened by her phone ringing. She sucked her teeth and put the pillow over her head. To her disappointment, it didn't help. She tried to ignore it, but the phone kept ringing. After about the sixth ring, Honey snatched the cordless off the charger.

"Hello!" she barked, not bothering to hide her irritation.

"Hello, Melissa," a proper voice said.

"Who is this?"

"This is Mrs. Johnson, from the library. Did I wake you?"

"Yes."

"Good," the woman said smugly. "What's up with you? I had you scheduled to take your GED practice test today, but you never showed up."

"Oh, I had to take care of something," Honey lied.

"Melissa, this is the second time you've missed it. Is everything all right?"

"Listen, I got a lot going on in my life right now," Honey said with an attitude.

"Well, apparently education isn't one of them," Mrs. Johnson said. "Listen, Melissa. I'm gonna be frank with you. You need to figure out what you want to do with your life. You're a young and intelligent girl. Don't throw your life away. Set an example for your daughter."

"Hold on, you don't even know me," Honey snapped.

"But I know plenty of girls like you though. Baby girl, the clock is ticking. You might be pretty and dress real nice, but what good is that gonna do you when you're forty and have nothing to show for it? The odds are against us already, just being black women, but being an uneducated black woman makes those odds damn near insurmountable. You need to think about what I'm saying to you."

"Look," Honey said, feeling the sting of the truth, "I don't have time for this right now. I'll come down during the week and schedule myself for another test. Good-bye." Honey hit the OFF switch and put her head back under the pillow.

Legs sat in front of the big-screen television tapping away at the Xbox joystick. The five or six homies assembled in the basement apartment were laughing their assess off as Legs used an aging Emmitt Smith to run for an eighty-yard touchdown. He was whipping Amine's ass in a game of Madden football. The win would be sweet, but the hundred dollars that Amine would be coughing up was sweeter.

"That nigga is serving you," joked a tall kid named Harry.

"Fuck you," Amine shot back. "Why don't you just suck Legs off and get it over with? Can't stand a dick-riding mutha fucka."

Amine reached for the bottle of Cristal that was sitting next to him. He looked at the bottle and frowned at the corner that was left. "Damn, son. Niggaz ain't got no more drink?"

"Nah," said Harry. "That's the last of it there. I think we got some beers in the fridge."

"Beers?" Amine asked with a frown. "Nah, son." Amine fished around in his pocket and took out a wad of bills. Everyone eyed the money as Amine peeled off three one hundred dollar bills. "Go get some more Cristal and a bottle of Henney."

"You rolling like that, huh?" Harry asked.

"Straight cheese," Amine replied. "Tommy takes care of his own, duke."

"Fuck outta here," Marshall said, speaking for the first time. "I work for Tommy too, but my pockets ain't looking like that. What the deal, son?"

"What can I say, dawg? I'm eating."

"So why we ain't eating like that?" Harry asked.

"'Cause," Amine responded, sounding like he was talking to a group of children, "you niggaz is just corner boys. Me and my man Legs is putting in major work. Now take ya ass to the store and quit asking questions, fool."

Harry made eye contact with the other soldiers in the room before taking the money. Legs caught the look that was going around and didn't like it. He was cool with all the soldiers on hand, but there was no telling the lengths that jealousy could make a person go to.

"I'm trying to tell y'all, niggaz," Amine continued, "you gotta step ya game up if you ever plan on seeing cheese. Salad-ass niggaz is running around waiting on a handout, that ain't what's up. You gotta prove yo'self, dick. I don't give a fuck what I gotta do to move up. Tommy gives the order to kill, then it's on. I'm trying to get my stripes. Yo Legs, remember that nigga Heath? Yo, that shit was—"

Legs, who had become disgusted with his friend's antics, cut him off in midsentence. "Yo, dawg," Legs said, tapping Amine's leg. "Let me holla at you for a minute." Legs didn't even wait for a response.

He just walked out the front door and hoped his friend would have the good sense to follow. Amine threw out a few more choice insults to the soldiers before joining his partner outside.

When Legs spoke, he did so in a hushed tone. "Fuck is wrong with you?"

"What you talking about, kid?" Amine asked.

"All that stunting shit. Nigga, is you crazy?"

"Come on, dawg. I'm just having a lil' fun. Why don't you chill?"

"Because, dumb ass," Legs said heatedly, "your fucking mouth is either gonna get us knocked or robbed."

"Nah, Legs. You got it all fucked up, dick. Those is our peoples in there, kid."

"Amine, you don't know what the fuck you're talking about. Niggaz talk, same as bitches. Then you in there styling on peeps like you better than them or something."

"I was just playing with them, b. My niggaz know it's love."

"Ya niggaz? Amine, you don't know them niggaz like that. You just met 'em when Tommy put you on. You don't know what the fuck is going on inside their skulls. How does that look, we're all working for the same cat, yet me and you are the only ones sitting on some change? That shit is looking real suspect."

"Whatever, Legs. You supposed to be a killer, nigga. Act like it. You acting like you shook or something."

"Hold on," Legs said, putting on his most serious face. "Nigga, I put you down with this, son. Never forget that. Fear don't live nowhere in this heart." He beat on his chest for emphasis. "It ain't about being scared. It's about being smart. All you gonna do is bring the heat on us. If the police don't catch wind of your wild-ass stories then Tommy might."

"I ain't wetting that shit, man." Amine waved him off. "I'm keeping it funky."

"I guess there just ain't no talking to you," Legs said, shaking his head. "You're grown, partner, I can't speak for you, but I'm gonna take the money and do just what the fuck Tommy told me to do: get low."

"You do what the fuck you want, but I ain't hardly going underground for killing a piece of shit like Heath. I'm gonna have some fun with this bread."

Legs watched his partner turn and walk back into the basement apartment. If Amine wanted to put himself on front street, then so be it. Legs, on the other hand, wasn't talking any chances. He didn't like the idea of ending up in prison or on anyone's hit list. Legs flagged down a cab and headed for Penn Station.

Tommy sat in the back room of Shakers going over paperwork. Shakers was one of the businesses that Poppa owned. It was a gentlemen's club where you could come have drinks and watch the stage show. Shakers also had a back room where regulars could come and gamble. It was one of the first spots that he opened when he began legitimizing his assets. Poppa had since moved onto bigger and more lucrative investments, but he held on to Shakers for sentimental reasons.

Tommy's thoughts were broken up by a knock on the office door. "Come in," Tommy said, without looking up. Herc stuck his huge head inside the office door. "What is it, Herc?"

"This clown is here to see you, Tommy," Herc said, annoyed.

"Who?"

"That skinny wop. What's his name? Freddy Delupa or something?"

"Oh, you mean Freddy Deluca? You can send him back here." Herc went off to get Tommy's guest while Tommy got ready to receive him. He made sure that all of the paperwork was put away and the .32 that he kept inside the desk drawer was within arm's reach.

Freddy Deluca was a messenger boy for Fat Mike. Tommy hadn't gotten around to telling them that they would no longer be lying down with the Cissarros. They would hear about it sooner or later if they hadn't already. They could either accept it or not. Tommy was ready to give it to them however they wanted it.

Herc came back, followed by Freddy and a weasel-faced man he didn't know. Freddy was draped in a white suit and matching shoes. His curly locks sat up on his head in an Afro-like fashion. He greeted Tommy with a warm smile, but Poppa's eldest boy wasn't so easily duped. He had learned a long time ago to look deeper under the surface of what a person showed you.

"Tommy," Freddy said, smiling. "How ya doing, *paisan*?"

"I'm good, Freddy. So what brings you down to the gutter? You slumming?"

"Tommy, why do you say such hurtful things? Can't a guy come down to visit with his ace boon coo—"

"Watch ya fucking mouth." Tommy cut him off. "I don't play word games, mutha fucka. What do you want?"

"Sorry, Tommy. I didn't mean no disrespect. Got a little business I wanted to talk with you."

"So, talk."

"Okay, T. We got this stuff that's coming in about two weeks from now. High-powered shit, Tommy. Thing is, the shipment is hot. As in *burning*. We need to dump this shit, like fast. The hows and the whys ain't important. We just need to get rid of it."

"I don't know about this, Freddy," Tommy said, casually lighting a cigarette. "I'm still trying to move the last shit y'all hit me with. The potency was weak. I tried to put a three on it and it turned to shit."

"We know, Tommy. We got burned on a deal and it filtered down to youz guys. You know how it is?"

"Nah, Freddy. I can't understand that. I didn't give you no funny money, so why I gotta get funny product? I got a rep to protect, same as y'all, Freddy. How does that look on me?"

"Whatever, Tommy. Let the past be the past. I'm here to talk to you about the present. Can you do this thing for us?"

"I dunno, Freddy," Tommy said smugly. "Let me get back to you on it."

"Tommy, Mike says that he would consider this a personal favor."

"Like I said, I'll get back to you."

Freddy looked at his partner and shook his head. He said something to the man in Sicilian and the man nodded. Tommy didn't know what they were saying, but he didn't like it. His hand dipped to his lap and fingered the pistol he retrieved from the drawer. Using his foot, he tapped on a yellow switch that was hidden beneath the desk. This would activate yellow lights that were situated throughout the club, letting Herc or anyone on staff know that something was about to go down in the spot. Herc saw the light and took his position outside the office door with a shotgun at the ready. Had Tommy tapped the red light switch, Herc would've come in blasting.

"Fuck is that shit all about?" Tommy asked. "You mutha fuckas speak English around me."

"Don't worry about it," Freddy said, moving toward the door. "You've said your piece. We'll be in touch."

"What you mean by that, Freddy?" Tommy asked, getting hostile.

"You know, I thought we were friends, Tommy? Friends don't turn their backs on friends in a bind."

"Ain't turning my back on you, Freddy. I'm just telling you what I know. We moving major weight over here, baby. Can't get overstocked."

"*Major weight,*" Freddy muttered. "Some people forget their places in the scheme of things."

"And what's that supposed to mean?"

"You know what the fuck it means, Tommy. We put you and Poppa on the map."

"You must be crazy," Tommy snapped. "We do our own thing, chump. With or without the Italians, we eat. All y'all do is try to funnel that bunk-ass dope through us. Without the Clarks, y'all spaghetti-eating mutha fuckas wouldn't see a dime in the black hoods. Fuck, we don't really need you." Tommy folded his arms.

"Bullshit," Freddy shot back. "Ain't no way that them bigwigs downtown would've given you shines the time of day. We brought you in."

"What'd you call us?" Tommy asked, standing up.

"You heard," Freddy said, poking his chest out. "A shine. You know, *shoeshine*?"

Herc caught the ass end of the conversation and burst into the office. He moved to stop what he knew was coming, but he was too late. Tommy was already going. He cracked Freddy in the jaw with the butt of the pistol, sending him crashing into the wall. The weasel-faced man tried to draw his weapon, but Herc had him. He landed a gut shot that knocked the man's wind out.

"Fucking greaseball," Tommy said, slapping Freddy. "You come into my place disrespecting me?" Another slap. "Fuck you and your fat boss. We don't bend for nobody. You piece of shit you. Open ya fucking mouth." Tommy put the barrel to Freddy's lips. "You had a lot to say before. Open that big-ass trap now."

"Tommy," Herc cried. "Fuck is going on?"

"Just teaching this guinea mutha fucka a lesson."

"Tommy," Herc said, easing in his direction. "This ain't no good for us. Let him go, Tommy."

Freddy could see the rage burning in Tommy's eyes. Fat Mike had sent him down here to ask Tommy a favor. Freddy was just a soldier, he wasn't even a made guy. But that hadn't stopped him from coming down and playing big shot. A front that was about to cost him his life.

"Tommy," Herc said, putting a hand on his shoulder. "Don't fuck up what we got going over a messenger boy. Let him up."

Tommy gave Freddy one last shove and let him up. "Pussy," Tommy said. "You come in here talking that shit like dagos got a say in Harlem. Fuck you and Fat Mike. This is nigger heaven up here. Fuck outta here!"

Freddy gathered himself up off the floor and tucked his tail between his legs. He had brought his nephew Carlo to the meeting in an attempt to impress him with his sway over the blacks. All Freddy ended up doing was embarrassing himself. He was stupid to come down and try to muscle Tommy Clark. Tommy came up under the old codes. All Freddy could do was suck it up and think of a good story to feed his capo.

Herc watched the Mafia men leave and rubbed his head in frustration. Slapping Freddy Deluca around was a bad move; there was bound to be a backlash. "Dumb stunt," Herc mumbled.

"What?" Tommy asked, taking a pull of his cigarette.

"Slapping that dago around," Herc spoke up.

"Fuck him!" Tommy shouted. "Sons of bitches come into my place and wanna sling insults. Fuck them Mafia niggaz. I ain't scared."

"Ain't about being scared, Tommy. It's about being smart. You putting your hands on that dago could cause a lot of bullshit."

"Fuck 'em. Greaseball mutha fuckas." Tommy popped a lot of shit, but he knew he had fucked up. Nothing was etched in stone with the Wongs yet, so burning Fat Mike wasn't the wisest thing to do. The Italians could make things very uncomfortable for Tommy. Not impossible, just uncomfortable.

"So what've we got so far?" Brown asked, as he pulled the Buick into traffic.

"Well," Alvarez said, lighting his cigarette, "seems homeboy knew more than he let on yesterday. Apparently, Heath knew the kids that killed him. They walk up on him, exchange a few words, and *bang*. His ass is dead."

"Simple as that, huh?" Brown asked. "Well, Mr. Simple As That, do we have a description of these kids?"

"I'll do you one better," Alvarez said, tossing a folder onto Brown's lap. "Pictures, my man."

Brown took one hand off the wheel and used it to flip open the folder. Inside were mug shots of two young kids who looked familiar to Brown. He knew he had seen the faces before, but he couldn't place where.

"Fuck are these jokers?" Brown asked.

"I let our informant sift through some mug shots and these were the faces he pointed out. The chubby one is Amine Barrett. The other one is his partner Herman Johnson. Or Legs, as he's called in the streets."

"Legs," Brown said, scratching his head. "Why does that name sound familiar?"

"It should. You've had to see him coming in and out of the station. He's spent more time in there than we have. He's best known for robbery and petty extortion."

"Oh, I think I remember this kid. Didn't he come through homicide a while back?"

"Yep. Had him in for questioning in that kid's murder last summer. Never got anything to stick on him though."

"This doesn't make sense though, J. Other than that incident with Legs, those two aren't known for murder. Besides, they're barely old enough to pee straight."

"That don't mean shit, Tone. There's no required age to murder."

"Very true," Brown said, turning the Buick west. "So do we have any leads as to where we might find Mr. Johnson or Mr. Barrett?"

"Warm at best," Alvarez admitted. "The kid Legs is a nomad. No family, no permanent address, no ties."

"What about the other kid?"

"We got an address from about two years ago. I don't know if his people still live there or not."

"We can always check it out. If he doesn't live there, he probably still plays that hood. If he isn't out there, someone's got a lead on him. Where we headed, J?"

"A Hundred Forty-fourth and Lenox. Harlem world, baby."

Brown mashed the gas pedal causing the Buick to jerk. He ran through a red light and almost caused an accident as he merged with the northbound traffic on the West Side Highway.

By about twelve thirty the driveway started getting crowded. Cars, trucks, and limos were pulling up left and right. Poppa stood to the side of the house with Hope greeting the guests. He flashed his widest grin as he shook the hands and kissed the cheeks of various political officials and entertainment personalities. Poppa had turned out to be a respected businessman. Long way from the street thug that he was so many decades ago.

In the early days, when he came over from Trinidad, Poppa had made quite a name for himself. Back then, he was working part-time as an enforcer for a local Mob boss down in Miami. Poppa was known for his brutality and his way with a machete.

Poppa looked out at the guests sprinkled over his vast lawn. He had risen from a poor refugee to a kingpin. Shortly he would be on his way to becoming one of the most respected businessmen in the country. He had come a long way all right. A hell of a long way.

"Look at my fucking head," Freddy said, touching the purple knot Tommy had given him. "That spear-chucking son of a bitch has gotta go."

"Hold on," said Fat Mike, flicking the ash off his cigarette. "Slow the fuck down, Freddy. You don't come in here telling me who goes and who doesn't. I'm running things down here. Understand?"

"Sorry, Mike."

"That's more like it. Now tell me what happened."

"It's like I said. I went down to Shakers to see this prick, just like you asked. I lay the offer out to him and he starts talking reck-less. That spade called you all kinds of filthy names and said that you should go fuck yourself."

"Tommy Clark said this to you?"

"On my mother's eyes, Mike."

"I dunno," Mike said, rubbing his chin. "Tommy's a hothead, but he isn't stupid. He knows that saying or doing the wrong thing could catch him a dirt nap, regardless of whom his father is. It just sounds fishy."

"What's fishy?" Freddy asked, getting animated again. "Some nigger slaps around one of your soldiers and it's fishy? Mike, I don't wanna sound like I'm outta line or anything, but this shit ain't right. Had this happened to a soldier from another family, that eggplant would be stiff right now."

"Well," Mike said, flashing Freddy an evil glare, "this ain't another family. I'll tell you what else: had someone else heard you make that statement it wouldn't look good on you. Makes you sound like you're not happy with us. Is this so?"

"No, no," Freddy pleaded. "I love this family. All I'm saying is that I felt disrespected by this Tommy kid. If he can get away with slapping soldiers around, who's to say that he wouldn't try it with a made guy?"

The thought of Tommy's crazy ass running up on him didn't sit well with Mike. In all actuality, he really didn't care that Tommy had kicked Freddy's ass. Chances are Freddy probably said something to set him off. But right or wrong Mike couldn't let it slide. He had to do something to make it right so he could save face with the other soldiers.

"Tell you what," Mike said, getting up from his recliner. "I'll handle it."

"Thanks, Mike."

"Don't worry about it, Freddy," Mike said, throwing one of his flabby arms over Freddy's shoulder. "We'll get it all worked out, Freddy. I always take care of my own."

Angelo made his way through Newark Airport, followed by his second in command, Fritz. Angelo was a very tall and thin man. He had soft olive skin and hazel eyes. He also had curly black hair that he wore in a low cut. When Angelo walked, he seemed to be flowing instead of taking actual steps. He was as silent as a snake and twice as deadly. It was for this reason that Poppa had chosen him for the mission.

"Fuck is this nigga at?" Fritz asked, again looking at his watch.

"Patience," Angelo shushed him. "Our charge has to maintain a low profile. He can't very well be standing around out in the open. It was hard enough getting his hot ass on the plane without arousing suspicion."

"This is some bullshit," said Fritz, adjusting the crotch of his Pepes. "I ain't no fucking babysitter."

"We ain't babysitting, man. Poppa asked us to pick his nephew up from the airport and bring him back to the City. Simple as that."

"Still sounds like babysitting to me. Why the fuck doesn't this cat just hop in a cab?"

"Fritz," said Angelo, pinching the bridge of his nose. "We went over this in the car already. The boy is hot, with a capital 'H.' All I really know is that the kid is Poppa's nephew from Florida. He got into some kind of trouble and had to get low. So here we are."

"Florida, huh?" Fritz asked, stroking his thin mustache. "Probably another one of them front'n ass niggaz, talking all crazy."

"I don't know, man. I only met Gator once, but I heard the kid is a gangsta."

"Gator? Are you serious? Man, I can't wait to see what this fool looks like."

"There he is over there," Angelo said, motioning to a man slouched near the pay phones. Gator noticed Angelo at the same time and began slinking in his direction.

To Fritz's surprise, Gator was hardly what he had expected. Gator was a man of average height. He stood maybe six feet. He had a square jaw that seemed to be hinged by iron pikes. Though his waist was slim, almost to the point of looking feminine, his chest was broad. On his head, he wore a rasta-type cap, pulled low.

Gator's menacing brown eyes swept over the people that milled around the airport. He was scanning for any signs that someone might recognize him or that the law might be hip. Gator might not have the advantage of a pistol, but he worked best when his back was against the wall. Before his escorts had arrived, Gator had taken the liberty of loosening several of the iron rods that supported the rope dividers for the ticket lines. If need be, he could get to one of them and bash his way out of the airport.

Fritz inadvertently took a step back as Gator approached. The man didn't come at him sideways, but there was something about him that screamed "Get the fuck back!" His brown face bore battle scars, and his nose was somewhat crooked from being broken more than once. Gator looked from Fritz to Angelo and smiled, exposing two rows of crocodile-like gold teeth.

CHAPTER 5

SHAI STEPPED OUT onto the lawn looking as sharp as ever. He wore a black pinstriped suit, with a matching vest. He was going to wear a tie but decided not to at the last minute. Instead he let the red silk shirt hang open. The three-quarter suit jacket stopped exactly at the knee. All eyes were on him as he glided over to where his father was standing.

Poppa was standing near a six-foot swan made of ice, talking to two men. The first man Shai didn't recognize, but he knew the second man was Sol Lansky. Lansky was one of Poppa's business partners. He was a Holocaust survivor who had taken up roots in New York shortly after World War Two. He started out with just a little pawn shop on the East Side. It was through this shop that Sol fenced stolen goods for the Mob. He eventually opened up a liquor store a few years down the line. The one liquor store turned into three and so on, until eventually Sol had a chain of liquor stores. He might've looked like a humble shopkeeper but Sol Lansky had money and heavy underworld connections.

Poppa and Sol had heard of each other but neither had ever had a reason to do business. That was until about 1987 or so. Sol was having a problem with one of the local crews around his store. He reached out to his Mob connections, but they figured that settling beefs between niggers and Jews wasn't on their immediate things to do list. Poppa had always admired the old businessman, so he stepped in and made Sol's problem vanish. They had remained friends, trading favors over the years. When Poppa made his decision to go legit with the majority of his money, Sol took him on as a partner. The duo amassed millions over the years.

"Shai," Sol said, flashing a wide grin. "How you been, son?"

Shai walked over and shook the elderly man's hand. He made sure that his grip was firm but didn't apply much pressure. Sol's little gnarled-up digits felt as if they might snap off if he squeezed too hard. The charcoal-gray suit that he wore hung loosely on his slim frame. As withered and gray as Sol might've seemed, he was a tough old bird. Shai had heard rumors about the Jew in his prime.

"Good to see you, Sol," Shai said.

"Sorry about the little trouble you got in."

"Shit happens," Shai shrugged. "I'll get back on track."

"I know you will," the old man said, patting him on the shoulder.

"Besides, if I don't, I'm sure I can depend on you to give me a job. Maybe vice president of your company?" Shai joked.

"Yeah, you're a ballbreaker, just like your old man."

"Watch it, Sol," Poppa said. "I hear you got a mistress or two in the stash."

"Poppa, you'll forever be a putz."

"Damn right. Oh, Shai, I've got somebody I want you to meet. This is Bill O'Connor, the guest of honor." Shai smiled and shook the redheaded man's hand. He knew who Bill was, but tried not to let on. It was Bill who got Shai his Ecstasy connect; his son was Shai's supplier. He'd never tell Poppa this though. Bill said that the reason he looked out for Shai was because he liked the way he handled himself. They both agreed that it would be best if Tommy and

Poppa never discovered the extent of their relationship. City official or not, Poppa wouldn't have hesitated to have the man killed.

"Been some years since last I saw you, kid," O'Connor said with a wink. "I hear you're quite the scholar."

"I try," Shai said humbly.

"Well, at least you're going," O'Connor continued. "A lot of young people decide to skip college and pursue other things. You understand where I'm coming from?"

"Yes, I do. That life isn't for me. Poppa and Tommy have got bigger plans for me."

"Good. Speaking of Tommy, where is that crazy guy?"

"He'll be here," Poppa said. "Running a little late."

"And speaking of running," Bill said, "I hear Tommy's gonna be running your street operations?"

"Yeah." Poppa nodded. "I'm done, Bill. My time in the streets is over. I tried to convince Tommy to hand it up, but this is what he wants."

"I know it's what he wants, Poppa," Bill said, scratching his chin, "but do you think he's ready for it? I mean, don't get me wrong, Tommy's always been a good earner, but he's not the most subtle kid. Running this on his own might be a bit much for him. It's a big job, Poppa. Tommy's smooth as silk, but he isn't the most diplomatic kid. There's already a lot of tension on the streets with you stepping down. Maybe giving Tommy total control will make it worse before it gets better?"

"Look, Bill," Poppa said defensively, "I know just what kinda kid Tommy is. Hell, I made him. I know he's a little rough around the edges, but so were we back in the day. Tommy's still got some growing to do, but he'll be okay. Besides, who the hell else could I get to take care of things on the streets?"

"What about the kid?" Bill asked. He made it seem like an honest question, but he had an ulterior motive. He had made quite a bit of money with Shai through his son. He knew that if somehow Shai had a say-so in what went on with the Clark organization, he could profit from it. Bill liked Poppa, but deep down he just saw him as another avenue to get money.

"Shai knows the streets," Bill continued, "but he ain't poisoned by 'em. Maybe you should think about letting him play a part? I'm not saying to give him total control either, but maybe he and Tommy could balance each other out?"

"Doesn't sound like a bad idea," Shai cut in. As soon as the words left Shai's mouth, he wished he could take them back.

Poppa's burning gaze fell on Shai. "Nothing doing," Poppa said, shaking his head. "That ain't for you, Shai. Fuck that!"

"But, P—" Bill tried to reason.

"This conversation is done, Bill." One of the security guards came over and whispered something into Poppa's ear. Poppa nodded and sent him off. "If you'll excuse me, gents, I've got something to attend to in the house." Poppa walked off, leaving Shai to play host.

Shai sucked his teeth, but he made sure that Poppa was out of earshot before he did it. He and Bill looked at each other, but didn't say anything. They just went their separate ways. Sol cast a curious glance at the both of them, but let it go.

Poppa walked into the receiving area where his visitor was waiting. The man sitting on his sofa was light skinned with a curly Afro. When he noticed Poppa come into the room, his visitor pulled his six-nine frame from the love seat and moved to greet the lord of the manor.

Poppa had first met James a few years back out in Queens. He was a young college hoop star who was working as a coach for a team that Shai was playing for. The young man was a bit of a loud-mouth, but his game was serious. He and the young Shai spent a lot of time together. He kept him off the streets, so Poppa took a liking to him, even invited James out to the house a few times.

"James," Poppa said, shaking his hand. "How you been?"

"I've been good, Poppa. Just trying to perfect my game and raise my kids."

"Good man. So, how's the career going?"

"It's been up and down, Poppa. Even tried my hand overseas. My latest paycheck is coming from the DBL."

"Don't fret, James. I'm sure you'll get called up soon enough."

"Well, that's kinda what I wanted to talk to you about. I need a favor, Poppa."

"Here we go again." Poppa sighed. "It seems like that's the only time I see you, James."

"Poppa, it ain't like that."

"Don't bullshit me, James. You remember the last time you came to me for a favor?"

"Yes, Poppa." Sometime prior James had gotten into trouble at the university. A girl on campus had accused James and some of his friends of sexual assault. James had come to Poppa in tears talking about how he was being framed. Poppa felt sorry for the young man so he pulled some strings for him and made the problem go away. Turns out that James was fucking the girl. The real slap in the face was nine months later when the girl had James's baby.

"James," Poppa said. "I ain't doing shit for you."

"Poppa, I know I fucked up at school and all, but I've been try-ing to get my life together. I swear to you. I just need you to do me one last favor."

"What is it?"

"It's like this: I get a call to come and try out for the Knicks not so long ago. The coach and the rest of the front office loves me, but the GM wants to be a hard-ass about it. It's like the fucking guy hates me."

"What did you do to make him hate you, James?" Poppa asked, knowing there was more to it.

"Okay, Poppa. While I'm up here for the tryouts, I meet this girl at a hotel. Fine lil' white chick. Ya know? Anyhow, we're at the bar drinking and she wants to take the party back to her room. So I say fuck it. To make a long story short, I bang this broad and find out after the fact that she's the GM's niece."

"You still ain't learned, huh?"

"Poppa, you got me all wrong. Once I found out who this chick was I backed off. The only thing is, she got offended. Told her uncle that I took advantage of her. This might be my last shot, Poppa," James pleaded.

Poppa had intended to tell James to go and fuck hisself, but as he listened to the story he started to feel sorry for James. He wasn't a bad kid; James just didn't make good choices. Couldn't fault the boy for being stupid. Poppa gave a last look at James and his big heart got the best of him.

"Okay," Poppa said, lighting a cigar, "I'm probably the biggest asshole to ever step off of a boat, but I'm gonna give you a play. I'll see if I can have someone speak with this man. This GM."

"Thank you, Poppa," James said, reaching to hug him.

"Save your thanks," Poppa said, holding him at arm's length. "I haven't promised you anything. I only said that I would try. I want you to understand something though. If I do what you've asked of me, then you will return the favor?"

"Of course, Poppa."

"Okay, James. Go on out back and join the party." James made to leave, but Poppa stopped him short. "One more thing, James. If you cross me, I'm going to have you killed. Do you understand?"

"Yes, Poppa," said James timidly. He smiled at Poppa and made his way to the backyard. As he crossed the vast receiving area, he felt his legs trying to give out. There was no doubt in his mind that Poppa would make good on his threat.

Tommy came into the room just as James was leaving. Poppa waved him over to where he was standing. Tommy had hoped to avoid Poppa for as long as he could. He hadn't gotten around to telling Poppa what happened with Freddy. He knew Poppa was going to flip about how he handled it, so he wanted to wait until after the party.

"You just getting back from the City?" Poppa asked.

"Yes, sir," Tommy said.

"So what took you so long?"

"Had a little situation, sir."

"Situation?" Poppa asked. "Everything cool?"

"Yeah, I got this," Tommy lied.

Poppa could tell by the look on his firstborn's face that he was holding something back. "Give it to me straight," Poppa demanded.

"I had some trouble at the club earlier. I kinda pistol-whipped Freddy Deluca."

"You did what?" Poppa said, grabbing Tommy by the collar. "Tell me you weren't stupid enough to give them white folks a reason to kill you."

"Wasn't my fault," Tommy pleaded. "Freddy came into our spot disrespecting me."

"You kids kill me," Poppa said. "Always using respect or lack of it as a reason to resort to violence."

"Pop, it ain't like this cat is a made guy. He works for Fat Mike."

"Made or not he's still connected. Tommy, if you're gonna run this thing, you gotta learn to use your fucking head. You wanna go back to them Spanish niggaz uptown, wit' ya tail between ya legs to buy theirs? You still haven't secured a definite heroin connection and you're pissing on the one you have. If his boss takes what you did as a slight, then this could really jam us up." Poppa let Tommy go, but he was still glaring viciously at him.

"I'm sorry Poppa," Tommy said, easing out of arm's reach. "I fucked up."

"Damn right you did. Tommy, you could've gotten yourself killed behind this dumb shit. Then where does that leave me? I'll tell you. Doing life in somebody's prison. 'Cause God knows if them Italians lay hands on my family, I'm gonna personally kill them mutha fuckas."

"Fuck it, Poppa. If the dagos want a war, then they can get one. We'll blow those bastards back to the boot."

"Tommy, do me a favor and shut up for a minute. You need to use your head sometimes. A war with the Italians is the last thing we want right now. We got guns and soldiers, but we don't need the heat. In addition to the thing that you're working on with the Wongs we got something else on the ball. This is big, Tommy. Regardless of what happens, I'm out of the game soon. If you choose to keep this thing here going, you're more than welcome to the headache."

"So, what you guys got cooking up, Pop?"

"Don't worry about it, Tommy. You just worry about this little obstacle in front of you. You could either make this right with Mike or try and seal the deal with the Wongs. Now go get dressed. We got people waiting on us."

Poppa headed back to the party leaving Tommy to his own thoughts. Tommy was fucked with no Vaseline. After what had gone down at Shakers there was no way he was crawling back to the Italians. His best bet was to make the deal with the Wongs. If Mike had a problem, then so be it. All Tommy could do was to be ready if it came.

"Why the hell did you do that?" Sol asked, taking a slow sip of his cognac.

"Do what?" Bill responded.

"You know what the hell I'm talking about, Bill. You know how Poppa feels about Shai, so why even put that out there?"

"Hey," Bill said, pointing a finger at Sol, "I'm trying to protect my investments here. Poppa and me been doing business for a while now. Not as long as you guys, but long enough. I make a lot of money through Poppa, and I like it that way. I love Tommy like family, but I don't wanna depend on him to eat. He's good at what he does, I can't take that from him, but the kid is too damn wild."

"Bill, this is Poppa's choice," Sol said. "I'm not comfortable with it just yet, but I don't have a choice. This is Tom's thing and he's gonna run it the way he sees fit."

"I'd still bet my money on Shai," Bill said, in a matter-of-fact tone. "He's a good kid, and the soldiers respect him."

"Bill, you must not be hearing me," Sol said, setting his drink down. "Poppa Clark would never go for it. He's the captain of the ship and we ain't gonna rock the boat. Get me?"

"Yeah, Sol. I get you." Bill nodded his head in agreement, but he had his own agenda. He didn't have anything against Tommy, but he wasn't exactly comfortable with him taking over the streets. Poppa kept all the crews in line with diplomacy; Tommy would do it with pistols. It was only a matter of time before the feds or one of the other crews took Tommy down. Poppa had worked too hard to build his empire to have it squandered away by his hotheaded son. It would break Bill's heart if something happened to Tommy and it would break his pocket if he couldn't get his tribute from their drug profits.

Harry came out of the liquor store sipping on the bottle Amine had purchased. The youngster was throwing money away and running his mouth to anyone that would listen. Harry was sure to find a way to use it to his benefit sooner or later. He cracked his bottle open and took a swig. No sooner than he took a gulp, a shit-brown Buick screeched to a halt in front of him. At first Harry thought it was the police, but he wasn't so sure when he saw the black man and the Puerto Rican coming in his direction. He breathed a sigh of relief when the Puerto Rican pulled out his badge.

"Fuck y'all want?" Harry asked, trying to sound tough. "Pressing me behind some drink. That ain't nothing but a ticket."

"Ticket," Alvarez said, taking a sip of the liquor. "Nah, you got it all fucked up. We ain't here to write no tickets, son."

"Fuck kinda cops are you?" Harry asked in shock.

"The worst kind," Brown said, grabbing Harry by the neck. "I'll personally put two in ya slimy ass and say that you resisted arrest."

"What y'all want?" Harry asked.

"Info, player," Alvarez said evenly.

"I don't know anything!" Harry pleaded.

"Oh, you're a wiseass?" Brown asked. Before Harry could respond, Brown tossed him headfirst into the rear door of the car. "Look," Brown said, scooping him up. "This is the deal, yo. You're gonna stop playing with us and start talking."

"All we wanna know is where to find Legs or Amine," Alvarez cut in.

"I don't know who you're talking about," Harry lied.

"See," Brown said as he unholstered his nine, "this is that bullshit. I'm gonna shoot this mutha fucka."

"Easy, partner," Alvarez said, knowing that what Brown said wasn't a threat. "Let's just take the lil' nigga for a ride. We'll see if we can get him talking down by the Hudson."

As Brown and Alvarez grabbed Harry and forced him into the backseat of the Buick, he didn't feel so tough anymore. Harry knew that the information he was withholding wasn't worth what they were going to do to him.

CHAPTER 6

TOMMY HAD ARRIVED at the party a while ago, but he was acting strange. The whole time he just sat by the pond chain-smoking and talking on his cell. This was very unlike him. Shai was about to inquire about Tommy's mood when Butch tapped him on the shoulder.

"Poppa wants to see you in the conference room," Butch whispered.

Shai gave Tommy one last glance before following Butch to the manor house. As he crossed the lawn, he noticed that certain people had disappeared. Sol, along with a few others, had made a discreet exit. There was something going on and Shai had a feeling that he was about to find out.

He walked into the circular room that served as Poppa's council chamber. There was a round table in the center of the room and a wide-screen television. Other than that, there was no real furniture to speak of. This room wasn't decked out like the rest of the house. The conference room was strictly for business.

As Shai walked in, he felt a little uneasy. Assembled around the table were some very big fish, on the criminal as well as legitimate levels. Poppa motioned for Shai to come and take the empty seat on his left. Tommy had come in and occupied the one to the right.

"Come on in, Shai," Poppa said. Shai nodded and took the seat next to his father. "Shai, I called you in here because some very big things are in the works. Things that will not only affect members of this family, but our communities as a whole. Let me introduce you to some people. You already know Sol and Scotty here," Poppa said, motioning to Lansky and a brown-skinned man wearing a dark blue suit. "That'd be a waste of my breath, so I'll move on."

Shai knew the man called Scotty all right. Martin Scott, known as Scotty to his friends, was a defense attorney from across the water. He and Poppa went back to the eighties, when Scotty was selling drugs to grind up enough money to pay for his education. Poppa let Scotty hang around and do odd jobs for him. Poppa saw that the youngster had too much potential to toss it away chasing a dollar. When it came time for Scotty to go off to school, Poppa fronted him the money. When Scotty finally finished law school and tried to pay Poppa back, he wouldn't accept the money. Poppa called it an investment. Scotty did legal work for Poppa off and on, but he was still allowed to open his own practice. Not bad for a little black kid from the projects.

"This gentleman to your right"—Poppa nodded toward a balding white man—"is Antonio Bratsi. Bratsi is our friend from out of Atlantic City."

"How ya doing, kid?" Bratsi nodded.

"Next to Bratsi," Poppa continued, "is Phil Greene. Phil is one of the men responsible for building our estate. He owns several contracting companies and is also the head of one of the few minority unions on the East Coast."

"What's going on, Shai?" the fifty-something black man asked.

"Shai," Poppa said, "what is said in this room is to stay in this room. Understand?" Shai nodded in agreement. "Good. Well, gentlemen, let's get to it. We all came in here today for the same reason.

Through our combined resources we have the opportunity to become billionaires."

"Sounds good, Tom," Phil said. "I got a general idea of what's going down from the proposal that Scotty submitted, but what're we really trying to do?"

"Well, as you all know, the gambling rackets bring in billions of dollars on a yearly basis. That's not even including the backdoor games that go on all over the world. In Nevada, the people who own those places are making a killing. Even over in AC people are catching the itch. The place Tony runs is one of the smaller ones and that still checks at least a few mil' in a good month."

"Poppa," Phil said, "that's all fine and good, but what's that got to do with us? Tony's the only one with ties to the casino rackets and he's not even an owner."

"My point exactly. If the Italians can profit the way that they are off of the casinos, then why can't we?"

"My friend is right," Sol cut in. "The old ways are dying out. We've all fought long and hard to get where we are, but we deserve more. Tony, you've been in the casino rackets since the old days. Do you think that it's fair to say that you deserve a piece for yourself?"

"Of course, Sol," Bratsi said. "I busted my hump for over thirty-something years dredging around in Vegas for those guys. Things get a little rocky, and the little guys get pushed out. Hey," he said, shrugging his shoulders, "I got no hard feelings. I just feel that my services were never totally appreciated. I would love to have my own, but I don't have the finances to make it happen."

"And that's where we come in," Poppa picked up. "If we pool our collective resources, we could make this thing work. Sol and I will front the majority of the cost, 'cause it's our baby, but you gents will have to play your parts. In return, you'll be given shares of the joint."

"What do you need from us, Tom?" Phil asked.

"That's the sixty-four-thousand-dollar question." Sol smiled. "Each one of us has a purpose in the grand scheme of things. For instance, our friend Tony has a connect that can get us a gaming license.

The man he's chosen is an average Joe, but the important thing is that he's clean. No record or anything. Tony will run the day-to-day operations, but the license will be in his connect's name. Besides that, Tony knows the casino layout and the area. Phil, we'll use your people for the construction. It'll open up more jobs for your guys, making you more popular than you already are. Not bad in an election year. Besides, we'd feel more comfortable keeping it in the family, so to speak. If all goes well, we'll be up and running in less than a year."

"Less than a year?" Phil asked in disbelief. "Building a casino is no easy task."

"But that's the beauty of it all," Sol continued. "There's a certain hotel out that way that's bumped into some unexpected financial problems. They have graciously offered to sell us the place at a discount. The first payment has already been submitted for Clark Lansky, to take over the property. The beauty of it all is that there's a few acres of vacant land with some warehouses sitting on 'em that are just collecting dust. Some of our dummy companies have already started buying up the surrounding turf."

"So," Phil said, "that brings us back to the initial question. What makes us so special that you wanna cut us in?"

"It's like this, Phil," Sol explained. "This is a big venture. Poppa and me can't just walk in there and drop that kinda bread on a spot. Even though we both have very successful businesses we still couldn't account for that kind of money. It would bring too much heat on us. Now if we were to take on some partners, we could pull it off."

"I can't speak for Tony, but I don't have that kind of money." Phil shrugged.

"Phil," Poppa said, getting frustrated, "I think you're missing the point. We're not asking you to put up no dough. You would be a co-owner, in name only. It would really belong to me and Sol. Minus your *small* percent for the trouble."

"That's all well and good," Phil said, "but what's the upside, besides a phony title?"

"First of all," Poppa said, sounding a little annoyed, "it's not like you're doing it for free, Phil. Of course we'll be paying your guys top dollar for the work. Not only that, but that will boost your clientele something fierce. Instead of throwing stones at the plan, embrace the beauty of it. We don't really need you to make it work, Phil. But I would love to have you aboard."

"Well," Phil said, not wanting to be left out, "in that case, when do we start?"

"As soon as possible. Scotty has already drawn up the paperwork. Each one of you will get a package containing the contracts, a mission statement, a rough floor plan, and a sizable cash bonus. All we need to do is cross the 'T's and dot the 'I's and we can get started."

"Sounds like a plan," Tony said.

"That's the kinda talk that I like to hear," Poppa said, softening his demeanor. "Let's drink on it."

The men picked up the glasses that were sitting in front of them. "To long life and big money." The partners toasted it and sealed the deal.

After the meeting let out the men returned to the party. All except for Shai. Poppa asked him to stay behind so they could speak privately. Shai was very impressed by what he heard at the gathering. The cats that Poppa dealt with had real money. These were the kind of men that you couldn't help but notice when they entered a room. Not because they were flashy or had big mouths; these men emanated power.

"So," Poppa began, "what did you think?"

"That hotel and casino thing is a boss idea, Pop."

"That's not what I meant, but thanks. I was talking about the meeting in general."

"I would say it went well." Shai scratched his chin, where signs of stubble were beginning to show. "A casino will bring in some long dough. And the way you railroaded those stooges was priceless."

"What do you mean?" Poppa asked, faking ignorance.

"Come on, Poppa. This is your baby boy you're talking to. You and Sol got some long paper, but you know if it looked like y'all was putting all the money up, it would only be a matter of time before the IRS came looking at you funny. So you call in the three stooges."

"Why do you keep referring to them as 'stooges'?" Poppa questioned.

"Because that's what they are. Poppa, you and Sol could've taken your proposition to anyone else, but you chose those guys for a reason. Antonio has been under the Mob's boot for years, but is still struggling to make ends meet. He sees you as a way to get on the map. His motivation is revenge. Your guy Phil, I read about him in the *Times* once or twice. Very few people know that it was the Italians who helped him make his climb through the unions. He sees siding with you as a way to establish himself as more than just a front man for the dagos. His motivation is insecurity."

"Are you done?" Poppa asked.

"No," Shai continued. "The glue that holds them together is greed. They actually think they'll have some say-so over this whole project. You, me, and Sol know different. They're nothing more than pawns in all this. Part of the reason you chose them is for their individual assets. The other reason is because they aren't the sharpest knives in the drawer. Those two guys are nothing more than scapegoats. The minute they get besides themselves or try to cross you, they'll disappear and no one will miss them. This will leave you and Sol as the sole owners of the casino, legally. It's a win-win for you."

"Spoken like a true Clark." Poppa smiled proudly. "You're learning."

"I had an excellent teacher."

"Indeed. I know you hear about my legal dealings, but I wanted you to see it firsthand. Do you see what kind of doors money can open up? Dirty money is cool, but this money here is the sweetest.

This money spends anywhere, you know why? 'Cause it's all accounted for. As long as the government gets their cut and you can prove where it's coming from, you're good."

"I know that's right, Pop. That's why when I make it to the League I'm gonna live just like you."

"Never like me, son. Things always improve with the newer models. Remember it."

"I will."

"But realistically speaking," Poppa said, sitting down, "what if you don't make the League? I'm not trying to jinx you or say that you're not good enough, but you know the odds just as well as I do."

"I know, Poppa. That just means that I just have to step my game up."

"I feel you, Shai, and I got your back. But nothing is promised to us. What I'm stressing is the importance of education. If you make it to the League and blow out your knee the first game, what're you gonna do? At least if you have your degree, it gives you a second option."

"I can dig it, Pop. Of course I'm gonna finish school, but I wanna be a ballplayer. If that falls through then I guess I'd have to find another hustle."

"True indeed, Shai. I know you boys don't think I'm gonna be around forever. Man, I'm about to give this all over to Tommy. I'm done with it, Shai. Once I get this casino up and running I'm out."

"I dunno," Shai said, scratching his head, "you've been on the grind so long, it's hard to believe you're stepping off."

"No bullshit, Slim. When I say I'm out I mean it. But I still need one of my own to look after things in the event something happens to me."

"Sure you do. That's what you're grooming Tommy for, right?"

"That was my original plan. Your brother is a good kid. He knows how to earn and he damn sure gets the job done, but he doesn't have a head for business. Don't get me wrong though. Tommy can take a kilo of dirt and bring you back some paper, but he's no negotiator. His first reaction to everything is violence. He's in his element when he's in the streets. You're a bit of a different case."

"If you say so, Pop."

"Listen, Slim, there's a lot going on right now and I need everybody to do their part, including you. In this game that I've chosen to play, tomorrow is a blessing."

"Me?" Shai asked. "What do I know about anything?"

"Shai, you don't give yourself enough credit. It's not that different than what you do on the court. You bring that ball across the half-court line and distribute it however you see fit. It's up to you who scores or not. Same thing in the boardroom. You call the shots."

"Guess I never really thought about it like that, but this is your business. I wanna stand on my own, not live off of a handout."

"Shai, I'm not planning on just handing you anything. Of course you're gonna earn your way in life, but you don't have to start at the bottom of the barrel to do so. I've busted my ass in the streets all of these years for my children. This," he said with a sweep of his hand, "is for y'all."

Shai just nodded.

"Never fear," Poppa said, placing his hand on Shai's shoulder. "It's not something you'll have to worry about anytime soon. You just focus on keeping your grades up and improving your game. When the time comes you'll be ready." Poppa smiled at Shai and left the room.

Poppa snatched the small hand radio from his desk and hit the TALK button. "Duce," Poppa barked. "Have our other guests arrived yet?"

"Yeah," Duce replied. "The last of the lieutenants arrived about ten minutes ago. I got them situated in the boathouse. Herc is keeping their asses in check, but you know they're gonna get antsy soon."

"Tough shit. They gotta wait. I'll send Tommy down there in a while, but we gotta wrap this party up first. Keep the drinks flowing, but don't have them fools getting drunk. I'll get wit' you in a minute." Poppa put the radio down and exhaled. Retirement was so close that he could almost taste it. His casino would be up and running in close to no time and he would be making an asshole full of money, even with Sol as a partner. Thinking of his friend made him recall their conversation from earlier.

Poppa had voiced his anxieties about leaving the hotheaded Tommy in charge of such a vast operation. He was a good leader, but his temper would be his undoing. And then Bill came up with a solution that both offended and puzzled Poppa.

When Bill had first suggested making Shai part of the operation, Poppa thought he was joking, but there was no humor in Bill's face. He seriously expected Poppa to bring Shai in. The suggestion was laughable. Poppa was not foolish enough to think that Shai didn't do a little dirt here and there, but he was hardly in Tommy's league. No, he would be the good son.

Poppa would continue to encourage Shai to pursue his studies and dreams, but he wanted to ensure that he had something of his own. Tommy had the streets, but what about Shai? What would become of him were Poppa not around? Shai too would need something to call his own.

Honey pranced through the dimly lit club, wearing nothing but a thong and a pair of clear stiletto heels. There were a few men inside the club drinking, but they weren't really spending any money. This was one of the main reasons that she hated working the day shift.

Honey had been stripping off and on for the past two years. When she first took up the trade, it was supposed to be temporary. She just wanted to hustle up enough money to take care of her daughter and put something away for college. It hadn't worked out as she expected. She had money put away, but it wasn't enough just yet. It seemed like something was always coming up to set her back. On more than one occasion she had considered getting a regular job, but quickly pushed that idea aside. She had gone to high school, but didn't have any real skills. The thought of working somewhere for a small paycheck didn't sit well with her. Honey liked the independence stripping allowed her, so she continued to do it until something better came along. That was two years ago and she was still shaking her ass.

She plopped down at the bar and ordered a mimosa. It was a little early to be drinking, but she doubted that anyone would raise much of a stink about it. She sorted through the wad of bills and sucked her teeth. She had been working for two hours and had barely made two hundred dollars. By the time she paid the tip out, it would've hardly been worth it. Something had to give.

Honey thought on her second encounter with Shai. It was weird the way she kept bumping into him. It was as if fate was trying to throw them together. She really dug Shai. He was cocky, handsome, and caked up. He seemed to be a good dude, but the reality of it was that Honey needed a come-up. She could see herself getting involved with Shai, but she had issues. Namely Bone.

Honey had been dealing with Bone for quite some time. He had been a factor in her life since her daughter was an infant. They weren't officially a couple though, at least not to her they weren't. Bone saw it differently when it was convenient. They both did their thing, but Bone tended to get crazy over her. One kid she had been seeing found himself the recipient of a pistol-whipping, courtesy of Bone. He was free to fuck whomever he wanted, but he tried to keep a leash on her.

Bone could be a sweetheart, but he was too damn possessive. He acted like just because he spent paper on her, he had ownership rights. If he wanted to act like her husband, he needed to put a ring on her finger. Until such time, Honey would do what she wanted. Fuck that, business was business. Honey was a chick that wanted to have the best of everything. Bone served a purpose, but Honey needed more. If she had it her way, Shai would be the avenue to get to it.

. . .

Shai walked back to the party trying to process the conversation that he and his father had had. It made him feel good to know that Poppa had a plan for him. He was never jealous of Tommy, but he sometimes felt that Poppa favored the elder. It wasn't until he got older that he realized Tommy was being groomed for a greater purpose.

Midway through the party Shai was about done. He had shaken more hands and kissed more cheeks in one afternoon then he had all through college. Poppa invited all of the bigwigs to the party. There were models, athletes, and politicians galore gathered in the backyard. This had to be the networking event of the year.

Poppa called for the crowd's attention.

"Friends and esteemed guests," Poppa began. "I would like to thank all of you for coming out and helping us to make this little gathering memorable. Most of you already know me, but for those of you who don't, my name is Thomas Clark. Co-CEO of Clark, Lansky & Co. Realty. But this day isn't about me. We've all gathered here today in honor of a stand-up guy. My friend and yours, Bill O'Connor. Come on up here, Bill."

"Thanks, Tom," he said, shaking Poppa's hand. "Thank you all," he continued over the applause. "You know Thomas and I go back a long way. I remember when he was just a skinny kid outta Miami trying to make his fortune in New York. Back then I was just a sergeant with the two-two. Both of us still too green to know a stock from a bond. Now look at us. I'm fortunate enough to have a shot at a city office and Tom is one of the most savvy businessmen that ever took a crap between a pair of shoes. Thomas Clark is living proof that hard work and dedication can carry you a long way. I just wanted to say thanks to you all for coming out. When the polls open, VOTE BILL O'CONNOR FOR ASSISTANT DISTRICT ATTORNEY!" The crowd applauded as Bill wrapped up his speech.

Shai looked at his father and nodded. One thing Poppa always knew how to do was pick a winner. From the looks of things O'Connor was a sure bet to win that ADA spot. With him in their pocket Poppa and Sol would be quite powerful.

. . .

Poppa had shaken hands and woven his way from the party to his private study. He had a few last-minute things to tie up before he attended the second gathering that was already taking place in the boathouse. The door slid open silently, causing Poppa to raise his head. Security didn't radio ahead to notify Poppa as they were instructed to do with the other guests. He was used to this particular person coming and going unseen. Technically, he didn't exist.

The visitor stood in the doorway and waited for Poppa to wave him in. His face sported new growth from lack of shaving for a few days. His head was clean and smooth except for the scar that ran from the center of his head over his patched left eye. He placed his hands inside the sleeves of the dusty black robe that he wore and stepped into Poppa's chamber. As he nodded slightly at his benefactor, the dingy white collar that lined his neck became visible. This was Priest, Poppa's friend and watchdog.

"Come on in and have a seat, Priest," Poppa said calmly.

"Thank you," Priest said. "Once again, thank you for inviting me into your home. I come to you a humble servant and avenging angel. Your will be done."

"Can I offer you a taste?" Poppa asked as he poured himself a drink.

"No," Priest responded in an almost sane voice. "Alcohol clouds one's judgment. If it's all the same to you I'd like to get right down to business."

"Okay," Poppa said, taking the chair opposite Priest. "Seems that we've got a little situation within our organization. This lil' clown from 'round the way has been getting light fingered. I don't know how Tommy didn't catch it. Probably all that damn weed he smokes. Good thing I count my own pennies, huh?"

"Indeed."

"These kids think that because I'm getting on in years that I'm slipping."

"Hardly, Poppa."

"At first I was gonna let it slide and just kick the shit outta the boy, but in light of the way things are going in the streets lately, I think a message is in order."

"You don't have to say any more," Priest said, standing. "I'll handle it."

"I know you will, Priest, but this is special. I want every one of these niggaz on the streets, whether they work for me or not, to know that the name Clark still means something."

CHAPTER 7

THE BROWN BUICK SKIDDED to a stop on 125th and Amsterdam. The back door swung open and a body came rolling out. Before the body hit the ground the Buick was off again. Harry lay on the ground suffering from a massive beating. His right eye was closed and his ribs felt like they were cracked. He had held out as long as he could, but the detectives used unique interrogation tactics.

"Are you sure?" Sol and Scotty asked simultaneously, looking at Poppa.

"Yeah, I'm sure," Poppa said. "I've given it some thought and I'm sure. Get it done."

"Poppa," Scotty spoke up. "That's a big responsibility to put on him."

"I know it, Scotty, but I gotta do it," Poppa explained. "This is the right thing."

"If you feel that way about it," Sol said. "I ain't got a problem with it. I think you're a cagey old bastard, but I'll support you on this one."

"Thanks, Sol. Make it happen, Scotty," Poppa ordered. "But remember what I told you. Shai is not to find out."

After conducting his business with Sol and Scotty, Poppa was ready to address the soldiers in the boathouse. The people that still lingered at the party didn't even notice Poppa slide off. He was followed closely by Butch, who kept his hands near his .45s.

When Poppa walked into the meeting room, everyone fell silent. He was a large man, but hardly the largest in the room. Poppa just had a presence about him that made him seem larger than life. Each of the lieutenants looked at Poppa with mixed emotions. Some looked at him in awe, others in admiration, and some were not impressed. Whatever their feelings, they all gave Poppa their undivided attention.

"At ease, boys," Poppa said in an easy tone. "I ain't gonna take up much of your time. I just wanted to say a few things to you, then I'm gonna let Tommy have the floor."

Poppa looked around at the assembled men before him, remembering each face and how they had risen to their positions. It had been a long and violent time for most of them, but they stood in those positions because they were willing to do what was needed to come up. They were ambitious and dangerous. This made them very efficient and very dangerous. For the most part, Poppa trusted his lieutenants, but there were a few among their number that would need watching.

"First off," Poppa continued, "I want to thank those of you who were able to attend this gathering. Those who aren't present, such as Angelo and a few others, are absent with my permission. Now, I'm sure you've all heard the rumors about me retiring from the game. Allow me to confirm the rumor. Tommy has been the boss of this family in everything but name, for quite some time. Soon it will be official, but not just yet," he said, glancing at his son. "Just because I'm not active on the streets, doesn't mean that I'm not kept informed. Y'all keep doing like you're doing and respect Tommy's words as if they were my own."

"That shouldn't be too hard," Mo Black cut in. "He's about a bossy son of a bitch as it is." The whole crowd erupted into laughter. Mo Black was always saying some off-the-wall shit and making people laugh. He was a good-natured soul like that. Always good for a laugh. The soldiers would need to keep their spirits up in the weeks to come.

"Fuck you, Mo," Tommy said jokingly.

"He ain't wrong," Poppa added. "You love to give orders. But seriously, there's something that ain't so funny that needs to be addressed. Tommy, you have the floor."

Poppa nodded to the crowd and took a seat in the corner, near Butch. Tommy stepped up to the front of the room and looked at his father. Poppa gave him the nod and he began speaking.

"Soldiers," Tommy barked unexpectedly, "we're approaching a dark time and a golden age, all at the same time. When my father steps down, we will be losing one of the greatest leaders that the streets have ever known. I know I have big shoes to fill and I can't say that I will ever be able to accomplish what he has, but I will try with all that I am to do so. I love each and every one of you as if we were blood. Under me, I will strive to make sure that there is never an empty belly in our camp or our families. I come to you in love and with a promise of great things. Follow me and be rewarded."

Tommy looked out at the lieutenants who were cheering and patting each other on the back. Tommy was pleased at their reaction, to say the least. In his heart of hearts, he believed in the things that he was preaching to his men. But Tommy was born of the beast, and war was in his blood. He would never be content to do things quietly, as Poppa did. He was rash and bullheaded and his actions would show it. In time, Tommy would probably grow out of it, but time was no friend to no one.

"Gentlemen," Tommy said, quieting the crowd. "There is still more for us to discuss before we rejoice. Things are gonna be different. We Clarks have become a force in this game. I plan to establish us as an independent force. No more will we bow to the Italians or anyone else. Poppa and his endeavors with the Cissarros is what it is, but it's about time we put Mike and his crew in their places."

"That could jam us," Lucius, who sold dope in the Marcy Projects said. "Mike be setting that weight out."

"Well, Mike ain't the only person holding weight," Tommy protested.

"So, you saying that we should go back to fucking with Poppy and them from Broadway?"

"I ain't saying that. Them niggaz is more crooked than the fucking Italians," Tommy said seriously. "Don't even worry about it, kid. I got this situation under control."

"So what are we gonna do?" Lucius asked, not sounding convinced.

"Do what you do. Get money, my nigga," Tommy insisted. "That fat mutha fucka is gonna bow down like everyone else. If this goes there, it's only gonna be two types of niggaz left in the world. Pussies and soldiers. Which are you?" he asked the crowd.

"SOLDIERS!" they shouted in unison.

Tommy looked over to Poppa, who nodded his head in approval. Tommy looked back to his crew and smiled. He knew some of them followed him out of love, while others did so out of fear. It was nice to be loved, but fear felt much, much better.

Swan was supercharged after the meeting. Tommy had the whole crew ready to ride out after his speech. To Swan, it was better than a Sunday in church. The real crowd-pleaser was the appearance of Poppa Clark. The old man hardly ever came out to fraternize with the soldiers, but this meeting called for his personal attention. What was even more surprising was that Poppa had requested to meet with Swan privately afterward.

After talking a little shit with some of the lieutenants, Swan was escorted by Herc to one of the back rooms. He had a lump in his throat the size of an apple. This meeting could be what he needed to put him back on the map. Ever since he had been stripped of rank, Swan hustled day and night trying to prove that he was still worthy.

Swan entered the room expecting to see just Poppa and Tommy, but he was surprised by the presence of Mo Black. He looked to each one of the men respectively and tried to figure out what was going on. Poppa was smiling, so at least he knew he hadn't done anything wrong.

"Come on in, Swan." Poppa waved to him.

"You wanted to see me?" Swan asked. His voice was soft, but he made sure to keep eye contact with Poppa.

"Yeah, kid," Poppa responded. "I got something that I need done and I need you to do it."

"Anything, Poppa. You know that."

"Glad to hear it. This is the deal, son. My man, Mo Black"—he motioned to Mo—"he's doing some stuff for me out of town. He's making us a lot of money and that's truly sweet indeed. But he's got a problem. Some knuckleheads are trying to stop my shine. This is not good and needs to be addressed. Dig?"

"Yeah, I dig, Poppa. You want me to fix Mo's problem. You got it."

"I knew I could count on you." Poppa smiled. "There'll be a few dollars in it for you when you get back."

"I'll get right on it, Poppa. Anything else?"

"Nah, that's all."

Swan turned to leave, but Tommy stopped him short. "Swan. You do this without fucking up and I'll promote you. You'll be given full lieutenant status and privileges. You have my word on that."

Swan just nodded and continued back the way he had come. He gritted his teeth and grinned at the opportunity he was being given. He had been waiting for a chance to get back into Poppa's good graces. He knew that he could probably go up there and squash whatever was going on without killing, but this was too sweet to fuck up. Blood would have to be spilled. When Swan stepped to them boys upstate, he was going to shoot first and ask questions never.

CHAPTER 8

HONEY SAT IN THE nail salon on 134th and Lenox Avenue while the little Asian man put the finishing touches on her airbrushed design. She tapped her foot impatiently, but this didn't put a rush on his work. Honey had a full day ahead of her and spending over an hour breathing the harsh nail fumes wasn't part of her plan.

After she left the club, she had stopped by Bone's to get some shopping money. She knew that Bone would be coming in from the streets around that time and he would be too tired to want sex. Sex with Bone wasn't one of her favorite things to do. He was hung like a ten-year-old, but acted like he was a champion lover.

The little Asian had finally finished doing Honey's nails. She tossed two twenty dollar bills at him and headed out into the streets. As she pulled her cell out to call a cab, it began vibrating. Honey started not to answer it, because the number was restricted, but what if it was important? After a brief debate Honey flipped the phone open and pressed TALK.

"Hello," a masculine voice said. "May I speak to Honey?"

"Who's calling?" she asked, trying to disguise her voice.

"Shai."

Honey didn't respond at first. She figured that he might call her sooner or later, but she had banked on later. She hadn't even had a chance to set up a game plan for him yet. Oh, well. As long as she had him on the phone she might as well go with the flow.

"Shai who?" she teased.

"Oh, it's like that?" he said, sounding a little offended. "I thought my name was pretty original, but I guess you know a few guys named Shai?"

"I'm just teasing you, Shai. What's good?"

"You."

"Is that right?"

"Please believe it," he said. "Tell me where you are and I'll come through and scoop you."

"Slow down, player," Honey warned him. "I didn't even say that I was free."

"I know, ma. But you are."

"How do you figure that?"

"Simple. You didn't say that you weren't when I first threw it at you."

"You've got a smart mouth, Shai."

"Baby," he said, trying to sound sexy, "my mouth has got an IQ of one hundred and twenty, along with three different speeds. You better ask somebody."

"Boy, you're crazy."

"Yeah, crazy about you, ma. So are you wit' it?"

"I guess so."

"What do you mean, 'I guess so'? Baby, don't cheat yourself out of a golden opportunity. I just wanna kick it, and see where your head is at. No harm in that, right?"

"If you say so, Shai. But check it, I can't get away right now. Can you come and get me later?"

"I guess so," he said, mimicking her. "I'll give you a ring when I come through the City and we can work out the details."

"A'ight, Shai. That'll work."

"Cool. So I'll get at you later, ma." Before she could respond he hung up.

Honey looked at the phone and shook her head. Shai was stuck on himself with a capital "S." He was rude and had a slick mouth, but that's what attracted her to him. She had a good mind to stand him up, but after thinking on it she decided not to. She would meet with Shai when he called. Then she would see if he could back up the things he was saying.

Teddy sat in the spot counting up the take for the night. There was about ten thousand in total. Well, eight and a half after he skimmed his cut. Even though Poppa had extended his courtesies to the young man, it wasn't enough. He felt like he deserved more.

Teddy gave the managers of the next shift their instructions and left the spot. He and his partner, Tic, walked down Old Broadway and set out for the liquor store. It was the weekend and they were gonna get pissy drunk with Poppa's money.

As he and Tic rounded the corner, they spotted a dusty old man standing on a milk crate shouting. He was wailing about the second coming of Christ and a whole bunch of bullshit that neither of the youngsters really wanted to hear. With nothing better to do they decided to harass the street-corner preacher.

"Why don't you get up outta here with that shit!" Tic shouted.

"Yeah," Teddy chimed in. "Don't nobody wanna hear that shit."

"Boy," Priest said, stepping off the crate. "Ain't you got no respect for your elders?"

"Hell no," Teddy said, giving Tic a pound. "You need to get your ass off my corner before I take out your other eye."

"These are the Lord's corners," Priest said, with a smile. "Would you stop me from spreading His word on *your* corner?"

"Damn right," Teddy sneered. "This is Teddy's corner, not the Lord's. He ain't got no work on this block."

"Oh," Priest said, moving closer to the pair. "So you're the infamous Teddy?"

"Ha-ha," Teddy laughed, giving Tic another pound. "Yeah, nigga. I know you've heard of me."

"Indeed I have."

With his right hand he wrapped his rosary beads around Teddy's neck and held him to his chest. When Tic moved to help, Priest pulled a silenced .22 from his priest's robe. He squeezed off two shots, hitting Tic in the head and heart. When the young man dropped Priest turned his attention back to Teddy.

"Ye who hath no faith," Priest said, applying pressure. "Come into my breast so that I might show you the will of God."

"Get off me," Teddy said, struggling. "Man, you don't know who you're fucking with. I work for Poppa Clark!"

"I am well aware of this, you wicked little boy. It was he who sent me to claim your thieving life. Now," Priest said, pulling his eye patch free. Teddy almost gagged as he looked into the empty hole where an eye should've been. "Look into the blind eye of justice and prepare to face judgment."

Priest jerked at the steel wire that held his beads in place and snapped Teddy's neck. Next he took out a stiletto and plucked out both of Teddy's eyes. Once that was done, he flipped over the crate that he had been standing on and retrieved the bleach container that held the battery acid and began splashing it on Teddy's already mutilated face. The icing on the cake was when he hacked off both of Teddy's hands. Once the other street hustlers got a glimpse of Teddy, they would think three times before stealing from Poppa.

"Come on, Swan. Tell a nigga something," Shai pleaded.

He had been on Swan the whole ride back to the City for details on the meeting. Swan couldn't believe his friend. Tommy had let Shai borrow his Lexus for the evening and all he could think about was what went on at the meeting. Swan wanted to get out and enjoy the night.

"Just be easy, dawg," Swan said as he stuffed some white T-shirts into a duffel bag. "I told you that I gotta do something for your father. I'll only be gone for a day or so."

"Damn, Poppa got you on a top secret mission?" Shai asked, lighting the blunt that dangled between his lips.

"Yeah, man. Keep your fingers crossed, Shai. If this goes down the right way, I'm getting a promotion. No more short paper."

"They gonna make you a lieutenant?" Shai asked excitedly.

"That's what Tommy said," Swan confirmed. "He says if I perform this service to the letter, I'll be given domain over west Harlem. From a Hundred and Tenth and Morningside, to a Hundred and Thirty-fifth and Lenox will belong to our crew."

"That's what's up." Shai exhaled a ring of smoke and passed the blunt. "My nigga is finally gonna get his stripes. You da man, dawg."

"Yeah," Swan said flatly. Ever since Poppa had assigned him the task, his stomach had been doing flip-flops. Swan had killed men before, but that was in the heat of battle. This was something different. Poppa had trusted him with carrying out an organized hit. His instructions were to go out there with Mo and inform his competition that he would be opening up on their turf with Poppa's blessing.

As simple as it sounded, Swan knew that it would hardly go down that way. You couldn't just walk up and tell a hungry nigga that you were gonna eat off his plate and expect it to be all good. Blood would have to be drawn. At least if the roles were reversed, that's how Swan would respond. Even though he was going on behalf of Poppa, he was still violating. He had no right to go into another man's yard and tell him to starve. But right or wrong, Poppa's will was law. If he had ordered Swan to murder the men and their families, it would have to be done. It was all in the name of progress.

"Look," Swan said as he passed the blunt, "I'll fill you in on all the gory details when I get back. While I'm gone, occupy yourself with something other than the block."

"Come on with that shit," Shai snapped. "You starting to sound like Tommy."

"Never that," Swan corrected him. "I'm just telling you what's best. You wasn't at that meeting Shai, so you don't know what's really hood. It's about to be some shit behind this thing with the Italians. Niggaz is about to turn it up in the streets. This shit is gonna pop off, Shai, and a bullet ain't got no name. If you don't listen to nobody else, listen to ya dawg."

Before Shai could respond, Giselle came in the front door. She was carrying two large shopping bags and an attitude. She sniffed the air then looked from Swan to Shai, who was now holding the blunt. Shai knew she was about to start up.

"Damn," she said, dropping her bags. "Y'all couldn't light an incense or nothing? You act like I wanna walk into a cloud of smoke when I come home. Pass that shit."

"Sorry, Giselle," Shai said, passing the blunt.

"Where you going?" she asked Swan.

"I got something to do," he said. "I won't be gone long."

"Every time I turn around, you've got something to do," she barked. "You need to start giving me straight answers instead of speaking in riddles."

"Don't ask me about my business," he warned her. "I said I won't be gone long. Leave it alone."

"I know you ain't trying to stunt for Shai," she said, looking him up and down. "Don't come at me like one of these bird bitches y'all be tossing up."

"I'm going to get something to eat," Shai said, knowing where the argument was leading. "Get up wit' me on the later side, fam'," he said, hugging Swan.

"My nigga." Swan returned the hug.

"You ain't gotta run off, Shai," Giselle told him. "We're all adults, let's talk about it."

"I love you too, Giselle," Shai cracked as he slipped out the door. As he headed down to the elevator, he could hear Giselle questioning Swan. He slapped his thigh and laughed at his friend and his girl. It was times like those that Shai was glad to be a player.

CHAPTER 9

POPPA SAT IN THE back of the Bentley smoking a cigar and going over some paperwork. Scotty had gone over the paperwork three times at Poppa's request, but he felt as if he had to do it again. The closer he got to retirement the more on edge he was. He wanted the switch of power to go smooth and without effort.

"Here they come," Butch said from the front seat. Poppa gave him the nod and he got out to open the door for his boss. Poppa stepped out of the car and leaned against it, near Butch. They both eyed the car that was approaching them.

Angelo stepped out of the car while the two passengers held their positions. Poppa wanted it this way. He wanted to feel Gator out through Angelo, before deciding how to deal with him. Poppa greeted Angelo with a warm smile.

"What's good, Angie?" Poppa asked. "Everything go okay?"

"Did you expect any less?" Angelo asked smugly. "You know me and Gator go back a taste, he was cool."

"How's he sounding?"

"Sounds cool. As you instructed, I didn't talk to him about too much in front of Fritz, but we did get to speak a bit."

"So, what's the deal?"

"Pretty much like he said." Angelo shrugged. "He did some real dumb shit, but he's pretty sure that no one can finger him."

"Knowing Gator, he probably killed anyone who got close enough to get a good look at him. Fuck it. Send him over. I'll holla at you and Fritz later on. I need y'all to handle something for me."

Angelo nodded and turned back the way he had come. He leaned into the car and exchanged a few words with the occupants. After a few seconds, Gator emerged from the car. He straightened his broad shoulders and moved to where his uncle was standing.

" 'Sup, Uncle T?" Gator asked nervously.

"Shit, you tell me," Poppa said coldly.

"Got into a lil' trouble back home."

" 'A lil' trouble,' " Poppa said, raising an eyebrow. "Fool, you shot a bunch of mutha fuckas and one of them was a cop. You know how much fucking heat you're bringing to my doorstep?"

"Sorry, Uncle T. I didn't mean to get you caught up in this shit. Gator handles his own. But I didn't know where to turn. I just needed to get up outta Florida to plot my next move. I won't stick around and bring heat down on you. I'll be gone in a few days," Gator said, defeated.

"No," Poppa said. "I won't turn you away. You're June's nephew, so you're my family too. You're gonna stay in New York until I figure out what to do with you."

"Hey, Uncle T." Gator smiled. "You know I got ya back. Whatever you need I got you."

"I'll probably just have you hang out with Shai. Maybe the two of you can keep each other out of trouble."

"Shit, I ain't seen cuz in a while. How's he doing?"

"Head just as hard as yours," Poppa sighed. "It seems like he can't keep his ass out of trouble."

"His name Clark, ain't it?" Gator joked.

"Don't play with me, Marquis," Poppa said, using Gator's birth name. "You just watch your step while you're in New York. You're under my supervision, so act like it."

"Yeah, fo' sho', Poppa. I'm gonna get low wit' cuz and take in the sights."

"The hell you will," Poppa informed him. "Just because you gotta lay low doesn't mean I ain't gonna put yo' stupid ass to work. We pull our weight around here, Gator."

"Yes, sir."

"Now get out of here. Angelo will take care of you until I handle my business."

Gator quickly spun away from Poppa, so he couldn't see the smile that he was sporting. He had expected Poppa to be way harder on him, but he knew that he wouldn't turn June's nephew away. Poppa was doing big things in New York and Gator figured he might as well get comfortable and get his too.

Darkness fell over the city and New York came to life. The working stiffs were tucked into their safe havens, leaving the streets to the hustlers and people of the night. Herc pulled the Yukon in front of a tiny restaurant in Chinatown. Tommy stepped from the rear of the truck decked out in a gray business suit. The black briefcase hung at his side as he strolled toward the spot, followed by Herc.

"I don't like this, Tommy," Herc complained.

"What's not to like?" Tommy asked. "If everything is on the level, then we stand to make a sweet deal."

"It's too good to be true, Tommy. All the years that we've been running around in Harlem these fucking slant eyes ain't never taken an interest in our thing. Why the generosity now?"

"Don't know, Herc. And truthfully I don't care. All I know is that I smell money."

"Still don't like it, Tommy. Shit stinks if you ask me."

"Well, I didn't ask you, Herc. Stop being so fucking paranoid and come on." Tommy walked toward the restaurant. Herc shrugged his massive shoulders and followed his friend inside the joint.

When they entered the restaurant, there were a few people inside enjoying their dinner and some dudes sitting at a table playing a game that neither one of them recognized. When Tommy and Herc walked in, the players all stood at attention. They conversed among themselves in Mandarin Chinese and fixed their attention on the two black men.

"You lost?" an Asian man wearing a tank top and leather jacket asked. His English was perfect except for a slight accent.

"Nah," Tommy said. "We ain't lost, son. Came to see Billy Wong."

"He know you?"

"Yeah, tell him Tommy's waiting on him."

Leather Jacket said something to one of the other players and a young boy went off into the back. After a few minutes the boy came back speaking in Mandarin. Leather Jacket motioned for Tommy and Herc to step forward. The other players got up from the table and formed a semicircle around the two men.

"Fuck is this?" Herc asked, reaching into his jacket. Before he could clear his weapon, there were four semiautomatic pistols aimed at them. Herc raised his hands and reluctantly allowed one of the Asians to remove his .45.

"Easy, big man," Leather Jacket said. "Just a precaution. Don't know how you guys do it uptown, but we don't talk with guns down here. Your pistol will be returned to you when our business is conducted. Now, can you raise your arms so we can search you, Tommy?"

Tommy didn't like it, but what could he do about it at that point? They had come too far to turn back now. Besides, if they tried to turn back, it might've been looked at as a sign of weakness. There was nothing weak about Tommy. Poppa had always taught him to fear no man. If ever the chips were against him, die with pride.

Tommy stepped forward and raised his arms. One Asian patted him down, while another searched the case. He admired Tommy's parcel and placed it back in the case. After assuring that they held no hidden dangers, the young men were allowed to pass.

Leather Jacket led them through the kitchen area to a thick wooden door near the fire exit. He knocked in a pattern and waited. After a few seconds the door opened exposing a dimly lit corridor. Leather Jacket nodded at the doorman with the Uzi under his arm and kept walking. The corridor stretched a few dozen feet and stopped at another door. The difference was that this door was steel and had a rubber seal around the frame. Leather Jacket knocked on this door and awaited entry. The iron door hissed open on hydraulic hinges and welcomed Tommy and Herc to a world alien to theirs.

When the room's seal was broken, a fog of marijuana slapped them in the face. Herc, who wasn't a smoker, found himself a bit dizzy. Tommy on the other hand took in a chestful. There was another smell in the air that Tommy didn't recognize. It was sweet with a touch of evil. Strange indeed.

The man who opened the door was a brute. He was almost Herc's height, but wider across the chest. "Shoes," he grumbled. Tommy and Herc nodded, removing their expensive shoes. He squinted at the trio and waved them in with his AR 15.

The room was decorated straight out of eighteenth-century China. The floor was laced with a red carpet. If you looked closely at the rug you could see the gold threads crisscrossing it. The walls were covered in expensive-looking tapestries and the doors were made from real bamboo. There was no furniture in the room to speak of, except a few small glass tables. The only things to sit on were some throw pillows. In the center, lounging on a red satin pillow, was Billy Wong.

Billy looked like the royal emperor himself. He had on a traditional silk robe that was the color of bluest oceans. Silver angels danced along the sleeves and bottom of the robe. Billy watched his visitors through half-closed eyes, as he took deep pulls off a bong.

Two young black girls rested their sleepy eyes on his lap, staring into nothingness. The master of the house greeted his guests with a lazy smile.

"Tommy," Billy said, extending his free hand, "good to see you, brother."

"Thanks for having me, Billy."

"Please, you and your friend have a seat. I hope you don't mind the pillows?"

"Nah," Tommy said, sitting cross-legged. "It's cool, Billy."

"Good. I see you've met Max?" Billy said, nodding at Leather Jacket.

"Yeah," Tommy said, looking over his shoulder. "We've met. Uh, is it cool to talk?" asked Tommy, nodding at the girls.

"Them," Billy said, taking a breast in each hand, "high off of opium. We could probably take turns ass-fucking them and they wouldn't be any the wiser. Care for a taste?"

"Nah, I'm good. Before we begin, Billy, I have a gift for you. May I?" Tommy asked, pointing at the case. Billy nodded in approval. Tommy popped open the case, revealing a strange mask and a jeweled dagger. "For you," Tommy said, bowing his head and presenting Billy with the items. "I believe they're from the Yao Era?"

Billy looked at the gifts and nodded in approval. Poppa had schooled Tommy well on dealing with foreigners. Always learn their customs and make them feel respected. Sure enough, it was working. The mask and dagger had cost Tommy a pretty penny, but he just looked at it as an investment in his future.

"Nice," Billy said, running his finger across the flat end of the blade. "Authentic?"

"Damn well better be," Tommy smiled. "As much as I paid for 'em."

"You know your stuff, Tommy. Are you familiar with Chinese history?"

"I like to know a little about everything. Keeps me open-minded. Ya know?"

"Indeed. And I have a gift for you." Billy reached under his pillow and produced a sugar bag packed to the brim with the prettiest green buds Tommy had ever laid eyes on. "We grow this stuff right in our yard back home. I also do my homework, Tommy. I'm familiar with your fixation with exotic plants."

"Good looking out," Tommy said, accepting the gift. "This smells proper. I wish I had something to roll with."

"Tommy," Billy said, pinching a bud from the top. "You can't smoke this kinda weed inside of a cigar. You've gotta hit this the right way." Billy stuffed the bud into the bowl of the bong. Using a glass lighter, he set the bud ablaze and inhaled. It smelled like the sweetest heaven to Tommy. "Here," Billy said, offering the bong. "Test it."

Tommy took the bong and looked at it for a minute. Tommy wasn't a bong man, but at the same time he didn't want to offend his host. Tommy put the still-smoking bong to his lips and inhaled. When the smoke entered his chest, it didn't even burn. It was when he tried to hold it that he had the trouble. The sweet smoke put a vise grip on his lungs and threatened to cut off his air. Tommy went into a fit of coughing and slobbering on himself. He handed the bong back to Billy feeling like a complete ass.

"Told you," Billy said, taking a pull. "This is some good shit. You gotta be careful with it. Now, let's talk a little business."

"Okay," Tommy said, wiping his mouth with a handkerchief. "I'm listening."

"We Wongs have been in this neighborhood for some time now. We have coexisted with the Italians, content to make what we could where we could. But you see, this is a new millennium. The old leaders have made way for new blood. A certain group of people, whom are loyal to my family, and our cause, has a way to get mass quantities of heroin into the United States. They only produce small amounts a few times a year and ship them to different ports—nothing too heavy. Their problem is that they don't have the means of manufacturing it in mass amounts, nor do they have the distribution. That is where we come in."

"How's that?"

"The Wong family has holdings in the legitimate world as well as the underworld. We have a processing plant in Jinan, right along the coast of the Yellow Sea. We use this particular plant to supply southern Korea, Shanghai, and parts of Vietnam. They in turn send it to other ports and it eventually makes it to the States. We see money off of it, but there are so many middlemen that the profits get chopped all to hell. We aren't particularly happy with it, but it keeps our product in circulation."

"Not to rush you, but what's that got to do with us?"

"I was coming to that, Tommy. As I said, we do our homework over here. We know that Poppa isn't happy with the current arrangement he has with the Italians. As it stands, Poppa is one of the biggest distributors of narcotics in the eastern United States."

"So, that ain't no big secret. Just about anybody with their hands deep enough in dirt knows or has at least heard about that. But if you did your homework, as you say, then you'd know Poppa is retiring."

"Indeed," Billy nodded. "That's why I wanted to meet with *you.*"

"Okay, Billy. You bring me down here to discuss a plan that's supposed to benefit both of us, but so far it sounds one-sided. We get to move all this shit and make an asshole full of money while you guys get the overs? Why ain't you just bring some of your people in to move it on the streets?"

"Good question, Tommy," Billy agreed. "They're several reasons but I'll give you the two most important. For one, there isn't much of a demand for heroin down here. The people of our culture are more spiritual in nature. I'm not saying that we aren't without our vices, but it'll pop better outside of our neighborhoods. The second is this, the elders amongst us are not so quick to stick their hands into narcotics. Much like the Italians, they're very leery of the heat that comes with that trade."

"Oh," Tommy cut in, "so as long as the niggers and spics are slinging it everything is everything?"

"Tommy," Billy said, resuming the negotiations, "don't look at it like that. Poppa is the undisputed lord of the underworld. This is the main reason that the Italians keep friendly relations with you blacks. United we can both sever our ties to a common pain in the ass."

Tommy sat stone-faced, kicking the idea around in his head. As he thought about it, he saw the beauty of Billy's plan and the offer. This would put them in a position to knock the other heroin pushers out of the box. Just as Tommy had anticipated, the deal was truly sweet. But there was more.

"Also," Billy picked up, "we are not without our own political connections. I'm sure we can get the elders of our family to extend some of their courtesies to the Clarks."

This bit of information caused Tommy to listen a little more closely.

"In a few years," Billy continued, "your family and ours can dominate the heroin trade in the United States. Blacks and yellows working together would make a powerful foe against mutual enemies."

All Tommy could do was grin. The deal that Billy Wong had set out was just what his family needed to smash the competition. The deal was sweet, but Tommy wanted more. For Billy to think he was just going to settle for dominance in the States was absurd. If he had connections abroad, Tommy wanted in.

"I will admit," Tommy began, "your offer is a sweet one. Like you, I wouldn't mind being young and rich, but I don't think you're factoring in all the details, such as your overseas heroin markets."

"What about them?" Billy asked suspiciously.

"Billy." Tommy grinned. "I've never considered myself a stupid man. If we distribute heroin for you, that puts us in a marriage of sorts. If a man messes with your spouse, then you gotta go to bat for 'em. You feel me?"

"Indeed," Billy said, hitting the weed again, "it would tip the scales slightly if we had you as an ally."

"Exactly my point, kid. See, we can lay down with this dope shit and all see some bread, but what about the perks? You get the protection of the Clark family, but what do we get?"

"I see your point," Billy said. "Tell me, Tommy. What do you want?"

"I want a piece of the overseas market. Nothing major, just a little slice to call my own, ya know? Set something up over there."

"I would have to talk to some of my elders about this, but I will consider it. Anything else?" Billy asked sarcastically.

"Since you asked," Tommy sneered, "yeah. Exclusive distribution rights."

"Tommy, that's asking a bit much."

"I don't think so, Billy. I know you've got other people moving that shit in the City, we ain't special. But ask yourself this, why haven't those other crews kept the Italians from getting in your ass? I think you need us a little more than you're letting on."

Billy wanted to take the dagger and slash Tommy's throat, but he kept himself in check. Tommy had proved to be slightly more cagey than he had given him credit for. If Billy gave Tommy exclusive distribution, he would make quite a few people unhappy. But with Poppa Clark as an ally, would it really matter?

"You are a tyrant as a negotiator, Tommy," Billy said, half joking. "We will take these things into consideration. Can you guarantee us that you will use your influence at the shipping yards to accommodate some of the Wong endeavors?"

"I'll get with Poppa, but I don't see why not. Give me some time to iron out the details and I'll get back with you."

"Sure, Tommy. I understand totally. Will forty-eight hours be sufficient?"

"That should do it," Tommy said, standing. "I'll get back to you as soon as possible." Tommy bowed first to Billy then Max. "I thank you for having us as your guests." Max escorted Tommy and Herc to the main entrance. Herc was given his gun back before Max bid them farewell. After seeing them off Max went to rejoin his brother.

"So," Max began. "What do you think?"

"Hmm," Billy said, rubbing his chin. "Tommy is quite the strategist, but he's not as good as me. He thinks he sees through us, but he's only half right. Tommy will go for whatever we tell him, because he's ambitious and we can help him get where he wants to be. Poppa is still officially the boss, but Tommy runs the organization. I think that he will influence Poppa to agree to our terms."

"You better hope so, Billy. If not, we're gonna be up shit's creek. I don't know why you put an order in for all that product and you haven't secured definite distribution. You know the Italians are shady."

"Because, my brother, I am a prophet. I see greatness down the road ahead. These fucking Italians have had us under their boot long enough. We've been giving them our product for less than what it's worth and they still try and cheat us. With the blacks behind us we will stand as a force to be reckoned with. In a few years time we'll push the Italians out of this part of the City for good. Besides, I'd rather do business with a nigger than a guinea anyhow."

"What's the difference, smart guy?" Max asked.

"The difference is, a nigger knows that he'll always be one step behind the white man and he's content with it. He takes what he's given and tries to either destroy it or make the best out of it. These Italians on the other hand, they think they're not niggers. These greaseball mutha fuckas think they equal to the real crackers. They run around living in a fantasy world where their dons are gods. Delusional mutha fuckas. If anybody can put the squeeze on these guys, Poppa can."

"That's some slick shit, Billy. Using Poppa's crew against the dagos."

"Nothing slick about it, bro. I'm just speeding up the inevitable. How long did you think that Poppa was gonna let them cheat him? Dudes like that don't go for the bullshit. All he was waiting on was a new supplier and I'm just filling a need."

CHAPTER 10

ALVAREZ AND BROWN HIKED up to the top floor in the run-down tenement. They had to step over a passed-out dope fiend to clear the last landing. When they got to the floor, they searched the tiny hallway until they found the apartment they were looking for. Brown reached out and tapped on the door lightly.

"Who the fuck is it!" shouted an angry woman from the other side.

"Ah . . . police," Brown responded.

The woman opened the door just enough to peek out. "Bull-shit," she said, looking them up and down. "Y'all ain't no damn cops."

"It's the truth, ma'am," Alvarez said, flashing his badge and winning smile.

The woman examined the badge thoroughly before opening the door all the way. As soon as she did, chaos spilled out into the hallway. A radio was blasting along with what must've been three different televisions. Kids were running back and forth through the house and a three-legged dog sat looking at the detectives from the doorway.

The woman who opened the door was much smaller than her big mouth would've led the detectives to believe. She was about five feet and held a baby under one arm. She was very young looking, probably somewhere in her early twenties. She had the face of a child, with the telltale signs of the harsh life she was living. Her eyes sported dark circles and her teeth were yellowing from smoking cigarettes. She could've been someone special in her day, but the streets had a thorough hold on her.

"It's about damn time," she said, snaking her neck. "I called you muthas an hour ago and you just getting here?"

Alvarez and his partner looked at each other, confused. Neither of them knew what the lady was talking about. "Excuse us?" Alvarez asked.

"Are you deaf? I said I called y'all an hour ago."

"Ma'am," Brown cut in. "We didn't get any call. We're here looking for—"

"Mutha fucka," she cut him off. "How you gonna tell me? I dialed nine-one-one then you two show up on my doorstep. I think that's the way it's supposed to go when you call the police?"

"Look, lady," Alvarez cut in, "we don't know nothing about that. We're here looking for Amine Barrett."

"I should've known," she said, shifting the baby to the other arm. "That mutha's in trouble again, ain't he?"

"Well, we don't know yet," Brown admitted. "That's what we're trying to find out. Who are you again?"

"Oh," she said, fishing a Newport from her pocket, "I'm his sister, Theresa. Though I'm a lil' ashamed to admit it. That boy has been rotten all of his life. Why y'all think our mother abandoned us? To get away from him and his rotten-ass daddy. The bitch did it slick though, 'cause she left his ass on me. I got four kids already and I gotta deal with his grown ass."

"Look, miss," Brown continued. "We aren't here to pass judgment on anyone. We just wanna ask Amine some questions."

"Yeah right," Theresa chuckled. "You mutha fuckas kill me. Put a suit on ya monkey assess and you think you're better than somebody. The funny thing is that when you clock out, you'll still be a nigga."

"Hold up, lady," Alvarez picked up. "How the hell did we get from asking your brother some questions to us thinking we're better than anyone? Did I miss something?"

"You might've, but I didn't," said Theresa, blowing smoke rings over the baby's head. "You come around here trying to play word games with me like I don't know what's going on. Y'all ain't come to ask no questions, y'all came to lock Amine up. Just keep it real?"

"Well, since you asked so nicely," Alvarez said sarcastically. "This is the deal. Ya dumb-ass brother has gone and gotten himself into some serious trouble. Seems that our young friend was either involved in or witnessed a murder. Now, we're trying to get to him and find out what really went down before he gets picked up for it and some redneck judge decides to stick a needle in his arm."

"Or one of the victim's peoples catches him and puts a bullet in his head," Brown added.

Theresa stood there with her mouth open. She had talked back to the police quite a few times, but these cops were different. They had a low tolerance for bullshit and they wore it on their sleeves.

Before Theresa could say anything else an older man, who was clearly drunk, came staggering to the door. "Fuck is these niggaz?" the drunk asked.

"Ray-Ray, get yo' drunk ass from around me," Theresa warned him. "These people are here for Amine."

"Well, that nigga ain't here," Ray-Ray slurred. "And he better not show his black ass 'round here no more. Lil' mutha fucka stole twenty dollars from me the other day. Thieving ass."

"As I'm sure you two have figured out, Amine ain't here," she said, addressing the aggravated detectives. "I ain't seen that boy in days and I can't say that I'm sorry."

"A'ight," Alvarez said, heading back down the stairs, followed by his partner. "If you see him, tell him that we're looking for him."

"Whatever," Theresa said. "Say, as long as y'all are here, can you help me get this drunk bastard out of my house?"

Brown and Alvarez looked at each other then at Ray-Ray and Theresa. Brown and Alvarez smiled at each other and shrugged. They enjoyed a hearty chuckle as they left Theresa and Ray-Ray to work it out amongst themselves. They hit the streets and continued to search for leads on the gunmen.

Honey and Paula sat at her kitchen table, smoking a blunt. Paula went on and on about the latest gossip. Honey nodded and smiled as her friend spoke, but she was only half listening. Her mind was on other things, namely Shai.

"Honey," Paula said, tapping her friend, "are you listening to me?"

"Huh?" Honey said, startled.

"Girl, what planet are you on? I've been sitting here running my mouth and you ain't even trying to hear me."

"I got a lot on my mind, P. Ain't nothing."

"Yeah, right," Paula said, twisting her lips. "Bitch, I know you. You've been in a zone all day. I know when something is on your mind, Honey. Which piece of dick is it now?"

"Why do you assume that my mind is on dick?" Honey asked defensively.

"Like I said, 'I know you.' Your mind is always on one of two things: money or dick. Now, I know it ain't money, 'cause you would've put ya girl on, so it's gotta be dick. Talk to me, Lissa."

Honey knew Paula knew her all too well. They had been friends and sometimes crime partners since grade school. They had gotten their periods around the same time and even lost their virginity together. If anyone knew Honey, it was Paula.

"It's nothing," Honey sighed. "Just thinking about life."

"Life?" Paula asked, scrunching her nose up. "What about it?

As far as I'm concerned, life is good. Bitch, you got your own crib, a beautiful daughter, and just about every nigga in Harlem sniffing around yo' trifling ass. What could be better?"

"I dunno," Honey said, twirling her fingers through her blond locks. "Shit is a'ight right now, but I just feel like . . . like it could be better. It's like, I got a lot and I'm thankful for it, but most of it is off the strength of somebody else."

"Girl, you feeling okay?" Paula asked, looking at Honey as if she were going crazy. "That's the best part. A nigga is supposed to take care of you. If you're sharing your pussy with them, they're supposed to share their finances with you. Fair exchange is never robbery. That's the first thing we learned. It's all about the come up."

"I know, Paula. But after a while, it all starts to seem routine." Honey shrugged. "We run game and niggaz trick dough. Same shit, different day. They play the game and we play it better, but what does it all amount to? Don't you ever want something that goes beyond that? Like a real relationship?"

"Hell no," Paula laughed. "Why the fuck would I want to wake up to the same mutha fucka every day? That shit is more drama than I need."

"I feel you, Paula. Most of these niggaz is headaches, but there's gotta be some good ones out there. You don't know how many times I wished I had a good nigga to take care of me and Star. A nigga to just be in my corner when I need him. I ain't no weak bitch, but sometimes I get lonely."

"Baby girl, then get a dog. Look, Honey, I understand where you're coming from, but that ain't life. Ain't no nigga gonna come in on a white horse and sweep you off your feet. That only happens in movies. These niggaz ain't shit, ma. You gotta get what you can, while you can."

"I know niggaz ain't shit," Honey agreed, "but there's gotta be a few good ones left."

"Like who? That young nigga Shai you've been swooning over?" Paula asked, looking into Honey's shocked face. "Don't look at me like that. I know you, Lissa. You've been stuck on him from the first time y'all met."

"Please," Honey said, waving her off. "It ain't that serious. He's a'ight, but I ain't in love with him or nothing."

"I should hope not. You know the golden rule. 'A nigga gotta pay to play.'"

"I know that's right," Honey said, giving Paula a high five, "and Shai ain't no different."

"Then you need to act like it," Paula said seriously. "You went through this shit before and look what it got you."

"But Shai ain't Tommy. That fool is a born street runner, while Shai is a square peg."

"He ain't that square. Shai has boned his fair share of hoes 'round here. That boy has got a slick tongue."

"Then it's up to me to show him what to do with it," Honey said, patting her vagina. "Ain't a nigga wit' a dick swinging that can run game better than me."

"That's the get-money bitch I know," Paula said proudly. "Fuck that, baby girl. It's all or nothing. Get that niggaz nose open and his pockets will follow."

CHAPTER 11

WHEN SWAN HIT THE BLOCK, there wasn't a soul in sight. This seemed unusual, because there were a group of fiends waiting to be served. He figured something had happened, because it was very unlike his soldiers to close up shop while they still had product to sell. After a bit of probing, Swan learned that his youngsters had been robbed earlier that day and hadn't been seen since.

Swan climbed the stairs to the second-floor apartment where they kept their drugs. He pressed his ear against the door and heard giggling coming from the other side. Slowly he inserted his key and released the lock. When Swan got inside of the apartment, he only got angrier. The soldiers who were supposed to be holding the block down were upstairs with several young ladies hanging out and drinking.

"What the fuck is this?" Swan snapped. "Y'all are supposed to be getting money and I find you partying?"

"Nah," said a soldier named Dave. "We was just getting low for a minute. Niggaz was creeping."

"So I heard. That's what I give you clown-ass niggaz hammers for."

"Wayne had the hammer," said another soldier by the name of Bump. "He had to go home and change his clothes. That's why we got low."

Swan exhaled deeply. "That has got to be the dumbest shit I ever heard. Okay, let's say for the sake of argument that it did go down like that. Why didn't y'all come up here and get the nine? Or why didn't you go knock on Sheila's door and get the three-eighty?"

"We was just about to do that," Dave lied.

"Nigga," snapped Swan, "I can't tell. Seems to me that y'all was more into these bitches than our paper."

"Who you calling a bitch?" one girl said, snaking her neck.

"Shut up," Bump warned. "We just took a lil' break. That's all, Swan."

"Oh, now I understand," Swan said, smiling. "Y'all just came up here to freak off right quick, is that it?"

"Yeah," Dave agreed.

Swan reached into his waistband and pulled out his pistol. "Fuck y'all think," Swan said angrily. "This ain't no mutha fucking temp agency. You want a coffee break then get a regular fucking job. Bump, you and this fucking clown-ass nigga Dave hit the block and see about my cheese. You bitches get the fuck up outta my spot."

Everyone in the apartment scrambled to gather up their things before Swan really flipped out. Bump knew that it was a bad idea when Dave had suggested it, but he still allowed his friend to talk him into it. Now he had to hear Swan's mouth. It was best to shut up and hit the block.

Swan watched his soldiers scramble to do his bidding. He had considered wilding out a little more but he didn't wanna overdo it. The soldiers had gotten the point. As Swan watched the last soldier leave the apartment, his phone went off.

"Hello!" he snapped into the receiver.

"Damn," Shai said on the other end, "fuck is wrong wit' you, kid?"

"What's popping, Shai? I ain't mean to sound like that, son. I'm just going through some shit right now. Where you at, fam'?"

"Right downstairs. Bring your punk ass on."

Shai sat in the Lexus GS playing with the various buttons. He was surprised that Tommy had let him hold the toy, but he wasn't mad at him. Shai rolled the seat back and hit SHUFFLE on the CD player. To his surprise a false panel came down from just below the glove box. Inside the little compartment was a chrome Glock.

Shai picked up the gun and looked at it curiously. His brother had guns stashed everywhere. In Tommy's line of work, you never could be too careful. Shai closed the compartment. Much like his father and brother, he believed in caution.

"So," Swan began, as he slid into the passenger seat, "what's good for tonight, player?"

"Trying to see now," Shai responded. "I'm supposed to meet up with a shorty later on, but I wanted to kick it wit' you before you head out."

"Damn you're thirsty. Who's the victim this time, Shai?"

"Honey."

"Stop lying."

"I kid you not, dawg. I got at her this morning."

"Let me find out you're trying to jam all the honeys out before the summer is over?"

"Nah, Swan. I'm just trying to see where shorty's head is at."

"Shai, don't give me that shit. You feeling this girl?"

"Please," Shai said, waving him off, "players ain't got no feelings."

"Yeah, right, Shai."

"Anyway," Shai said, changing the subject. "I hear y'all about to come under new management."

"Yeah," Swan said, in a disappointed tone. "Tommy Gunz is finally getting his wings."

"You don't sound overly thrilled."

"It ain't like that. You know I got mad love for Tommy. I just know shit is gonna be different. Fucking wit' Tommy, a lot of niggaz is gonna lose their lives."

"Let me find out the notorious Swan is going soft?" Shai joked.

"Never," Swan insisted. "I'm a warrior to the heart! I'd lay down my life for this family, son. It ain't about being scared, it's about being around to see my daughter grow up. I've been putting in work for Poppa since I was a lil' nigga. Poppa had people hit when they deserved to be. Under him, we had to check niggaz, but there was never the threat of war. With Tommy in charge, that's gonna change."

"Nah." Shai shook his head. "Tommy's gonna be okay. It'll be just like if Poppa were still in charge."

"No it ain't, Shai. Niggaz on the street is scared of Tommy. He's quick to bust his gun, plus he's got Poppa and the Italians behind him. Poppa is retiring and Tommy is breaking off from the Italians. Niggaz is gonna come, and we will have to go to war."

"Damn," Shai cursed. "What are you gonna do, Swan?"

"What can I do?" Swan shrugged. "I'm loyal to this family, no matter who is running it." Swan paused for a moment. He didn't want Shai to take offense at what he was going to say, but it needed to be said. "Shai, let me ask you a question. Have you ever thought of laying your claim to the seat?"

"Honestly, yes," Shai admitted. "I'm not saying that Tommy is doing a bad job, but I think things could be a little tighter."

"I know that's right," Swan agreed. "Tommy is a warlord. That's his strength, but we don't need that now. What we need is a leader. Someone who will help us raise the bar out here."

"And you think I could do it?" Shai asked suspiciously.

"I don't see why not. Shai, how many niggaz you had working for you down South?"

"About nine or ten," Shai said, searching his memory.

"And how many of them got knocked or shot up?"

"None."

"Exactly. Shai, you and Tommy are both great leaders, but your methods are different. Tommy moves on instinct, you make calculated decisions. Look at the way you handled that beef the other night. You could've let the fellas whip ol' boy out, but you didn't. You weighed your options and moved accordingly. The situation got handled with minimal violence. You're exactly the kind of nigga we need out here."

Shai laughed, but in his mind, he couldn't help but to think about it. There had been quite a few times when he would imagine that he wielded the kind of power that his father had. The fame, the flash, and a whole army at his disposal. Who wouldn't love the chance to be the man? But Shai knew there were harsh consequences to holding that seat.

"Where the fuck is we going?" Shai asked, trying to change the subject.

"Pull up on One-nineteen and Eighth," Swan directed. "They got this little spot over there and I wanna see what it's looking like."

Shai followed Swan's directions and found himself in front of an after-hours joint. Everyone that was at the place was from a ten-block radius. From the gate, Shai could tell that it was a neighborhood spot. Shai was never really one to do local spots, but he didn't have anything better to do at the time.

All eyes were on Shai as he joined his friend on the curb. Everyone from 119th Street knew who Swan was, but they didn't know Shai. He took the curious glances with a grain of salt and continued to the front of the lounge. As Shai stood outside kicking it with Swan, he heard a familiar voice.

"Shai," said the voice. "Is that you?"

For a minute Shai was afraid to turn around. He knew the voice, but until then he thought that he would never hear it again. Shai took a deep breath and turned around slowly. On that beautiful summer night on 119th Street, Shai was confronted by his estranged mother.

"Hey, baby," June said, flashing a yellow-toothed grin. "What you doing down this way?"

"'Sup, June?" he asked coldly.

"You know your mama. I'm just trying to hang in there. How you been?"

"Chilling."

"And school?"

"It's a'ight," Shai said, looking away.

"My boy," she exclaimed. "The college scholar. Peggy," June called to her partner, "come here, girl."

Peggy came staggering across the street to the front of the club. Peggy and June looked like a cracked-out Oreo cookie. While June was dark-skinned and still somewhat thick, Peggy was a skinny white girl. She raked her chipped fingernails down her track-ridden neck and winked at Shai. It got so bad that people were beginning to look. If Shai wasn't embarrassed before, he was now.

"Girl," June continued. "This is my baby boy, Shai. You know, the basketball player?"

"Oh yeah," Peggy slurred. "I know your son, June. I've bought shit off of him. Say, Tommy, you holding any of that bomb shit? I'll give you some head for it."

"Fuck outta here," Shai barked. "You got the wrong cat, white girl."

"Bitch!" June fired. "How you gonna say some shit like that to my kid? Shai don't sell no drugs and he damn sure don't want no cracker's lips on his dick."

"Geez," whined Peggy. "Sorry, June. It ain't my fault though. The kid looks just like his brother."

"I'm outta here," Shai said, brushing past the two ladies.

"Hold on, baby," June said, coming up behind him. "What, you don't wanna see your mama?"

"What do you want from me?" Shai asked, not bothering to face her.

"Want?" she asked. "I don't want nothing from you, Shai. Except to maybe see how you're doing. No harm in that, is it?"

"Look," he said, trying to remain calm. "I'm just out here trying to enjoy my summer. If you've never given me anything, can I please have that?"

"Okay, Shai," she said in a hurt voice. "I just wanted to see how you were. How's Hope?"

"Like you give a fuck," he said with a smirk.

"Shai," she snapped. "I might've slipped a lil', but I'm still your mother."

"'Slipped,'" he sneered. "I think that's a bit of an understatement."

"Don't get cute," she said, raising her voice. "You ain't too big for an ass whipping."

"Please, June."

"And what's wrong with you calling me mama every now and again?"

"You'd have to be one in order to qualify for the title. June, you ain't never been around for me or Hope. Anything your heart desired was yours, but I guess the larceny in your heart outweighed the love. You took everything Daddy gave you and made it wicked."

"Wicked?" June snaked her neck. "Let me tell you something, Shai Clark. Your father isn't an angel. He might keep y'all living in a big house, but look what he does to pay for it. So don't come at me with that spoiled bullshit he done crammed into you."

Shai's eyes flashed the hurt that his face would not divulge. "Same shit, different day," he mumbled, as he walked off.

"Yo, Shai," Swan called after him. "Hold up, kid." Swan jogged over to where his friend was standing. "You a'ight?"

"Yeah," Shai huffed. "I'm good."

"So you wanna come in or what?"

"Nah, Swan. I ain't really in the mood for that right now."

"So what're you gonna do, Shai?"

"Probably coast, kid. Gotta clear my head and shit, ya know?"

"You want me to roll with you?"

"Nah, I'm good. But thanks, Swan. I'll call you later and see what you're up to."

"So be it," Swan said, hugging his friend. "You hold your head on these streets. You hear me, Shai?"

"Fo' sho'." Shai broke Swan's embrace and headed for the GS. June was trying to get his attention, but he acted as if he didn't notice her. Shai revved the engine and eased the car from the curb. June was waving at him, but Shai couldn't see it. He blinded himself to any and all things associated with her. If you wasn't family, then you wasn't shit. That was Shai's motto. The woman who had ushered him into the world was dead to him.

Fat Mike sat inside of the tiny coffee shop going over the recent turn of events. Things in the streets were slowly but surely souring and he didn't like it. Tommy Clark was becoming more of a liability than an asset. He had made millions from the Clarks and their heroin ring. Poppa was a classy old dude, but his son was getting beside himself.

Mike knew he hadn't always played fair with the blacks, but the way he figured it, he was doing them a favor. They had the protection of the Cissarro family and a constant supply of heroin through him, but lately it didn't seem like enough. The blacks were finally discovering their worth. If they pulled out of their heroin agreement, Mike's pockets were gonna take an awful hit. If his income slowed, Mr. G would want answers. If those answers revealed his drug dealing, Mike would be up shit's creek. He had to get the problem resolved, immediately.

"Nicky!" Mike called out.

"Yeah, boss?" Nicky answered from the next table.

"Bring the car around."

CHAPTER 12

POPPA SAT IN HIS backyard smoking a Cuban cigar and looking at the stars. This was one of his favorite places to be when he wanted to think and that's just what he was doing: thinking. The winds of change were blowing and Poppa could feel it. His drug operations were growing, but so were the risks that came along with them. This was part of the reason why Poppa wanted to go legit.

In this new age of the hustle, what few rules that still existed were being drastically changed. No longer could disputes be settled through diplomacy. In the new millennium, lead was the law of the land. There was no longer a place for a wizened gentleman such as Poppa or those who came before him. The game was definitely going sour.

Poppa had much bigger plans for his future, as well as the futures of his children. He did what he did to come up so they wouldn't have to. Tommy was a different case though. From day one Poppa saw it in Tommy's eyes. The call of the streets sang loudest in his eldest son's ears. No matter how Poppa tried to steer him in another direction, Tommy kept his fascination with the streets.

Tommy had been getting into shit since he was a kid. There was a time when he had gotten kicked out of Catholic school for running a circle of dice games around the campus. Poppa always disciplined him for this kind of conduct, but he felt somewhat hypocritical in doing so. How could he tell Tommy not to hustle when that's how he was getting fed? When Tommy got too old to control, Poppa did the next best thing. He took him under his wing and showed him how to hustle the right way. Better to do it correctly than to do it ass backward and suffer.

Since becoming Poppa's protégé, Tommy had done his job efficiently. That is, up until recently. It seemed that Tommy's quick temper was hindering his growth. He had great leadership abilities and a good head for numbers, but Tommy didn't understand discretion. He would rather shoot you than sit down and talk about it. Poppa tried to teach him discretion, but it was pointless. The beast was just a part of who Tommy was.

"Poppa," Tommy said, coming into the backyard. "You busy?"

"Nah," Poppa said, sitting up. "Just thinking. Come on out, son."

"I met with the Wongs today," Tommy said, taking the opposite seat.

"How did that go?" Poppa asked.

"Seems that we have a new heroin supplier," Tommy said with a grin.

"And price?"

"It rounds out to about fifteen hundred or so cheaper per kilo than what Fat Mike was hitting us for—and dig the kicker, Poppa. On the first go around, they're giving us some birds for free as a show of good faith. Next go around, I figure we spend a few hundred thousand . . . maybe a cool mil' or so and make back a few million."

"A few hundred thousand," Poppa pondered. "That's a lot of bread, Tommy. Who's to say that I wanted to spend that much?"

"Poppa, you can't beat a deal like that. I even managed to get them to throw a taste of their overseas operations in."

"That's always a plus, depending on what it's gonna cost *us* in return."

"Poppa," Tommy said, standing. "We need this deal. I don't know if you've noticed it or not, but we're losing business trying to push the junk off that we're getting from the Cissarros. Poppa, we need to fuck with these Chinese folks."

"Gimme some time to think about it, Tommy."

"Poppa, the first shipment will be here in less than two days. I told Billy that we were moving forward with the deal."

"Oh, so you just took it upon yourself to speak for me? I'm the boss of this family, Tommy."

"Poppa, I didn't mean any disrespect, but what choice did I have? You said to fix things with Fat Mike or find another supplier. So I found somebody else."

"You got a lot of balls, boy."

"Poppa, you said that I'm going to be running the family, so let me do my job. Me and Billy can deal on that end. As far as whatever power moves you make with his peoples, that's up to you."

"Tommy," Poppa said, chuckling. "You're too much, you know that? I used to wipe your little black ass and now you're telling me what's what? Okay, Tommy, we'll do a lil' business with these Wongs. But before I speak to anyone, we gotta see if they can be trusted. Pick up whatever product they're setting out for you and see what you can do with it. If it's proper, then we play. But if these mutha fuckas try to put shit on us . . ."

"You ain't even gotta tell me, Poppa," Tommy said, patting his waist. "Let the games begin."

After speaking with Poppa Tommy had a lot on his mind. He needed to get some fresh air and clear his mind. Tommy and Herc cruised through Harlem, making their rounds. Tommy could've let someone else do it or trusted Herc to do it alone, but he needed to be in the streets. Being in the hood always helped him to think. It was his domain.

Poppa was handing the operation over to Tommy, but he still saw fit to tell him how to run it. He had a great deal of respect for Poppa and the things he had accomplished, but he didn't understand the way things worked anymore. Poppa had ruled the streets for several decades, but for the last few years he had been locked in an office playing corporate games, while Tommy lorded over the savages. It was a very new ball game.

Flashing lights in the rearview broke up Tommy's thinking session. You would've thought that with all the money they paid the police, they could avoid these routine traffic stops. Tommy wasn't worried about it though. He knew Herc had his pistols stashed, so they wouldn't have a problem. He had left his own gun in his car, but it suddenly dawned on him that he had let Shai hold the car. The color slowly drained out of his face. If Shai got stopped or something else happened because of his forgetfulness, Poppa was going to skin him. Literally.

"Hello?" yawned Honey into the cell phone.

"What's good?" Shai asked.

"Shai, is that you?"

"Yeah."

"Boy, it's two in the morning."

"Sorry, did I wake you?"

"Nah, I'm not even in the house. Where are you, Shai?"

"Just riding. No particular destination. Where're you at?"

"Down here with my girls at this wack-ass club."

"Word, how about I come scoop you?"

"What?" she said defensively. "You trying to put in a booty call or something?"

"Nah," he protested. "I just wanna see you. Maybe we can go get something to eat and talk? No funny business."

"A'ight. Well, I'm at NY's on Forty-eighth. You know where that is?"

"Yeah, I know the place. I'll call you when I get close."

"See you then, Shai." Honey hung up her cell and cracked a smile. She had originally thought that her night was going to be a bust, but Shai's late-night call changed things a bit.

The encounter with June had left Shai a bit rattled. It had been quite some time since he had seen his estranged mother. He usually avoided June when he saw her coming, but this time she had gotten the drop on him.

Shai couldn't understand why she still had that effect on him. He was old enough to put the madness behind him, but for some reason his heart wouldn't let him forgive June for abandoning him. He slapped his fist against the dashboard in frustration and the radio face flipped down. Inside the console was the shiny Glock.

Shai shook his head as he fingered the pistol. His brother was someone who liked to be prepared for just about anything. Shai stuck the pistol in his waist and felt the pressure of the butt against his abdomen. The pistol sent such a rush through Shai that he foolishly chose to hold on to it.

When Shai pulled up to NY's, the club was just letting out. There were people moving up and down the block trying to catch a ride or get their last-minute slide on. Shai sat low in the Lexus, laughing as people were trying to peek through the dark tints. Everyone was trying to figure out who was in the car. Shai knew to play his position and come out at just the right time.

Shai spotted Honey making her exit from the club. She and her friend were surrounded by a flock of vultures and hangers-on. Honey's golden locks were twisted in the front and she had Shirley Temple curls fanned out through the back. When she walked, her white riding pants looked like they were about to bust at the seams.

After a brief check in the mirror to make sure he was tight, Shai slunk from the car. His brown eyes swept over the crowd, taking in everyone's expressions. People were looking at Shai as if he were a movie star. Shai didn't have on a lot of jewelry or flash, but he carried himself like he was important.

Shai walked up to his soon-to-be-lady and gave her his Billy D smile. "Honey," he said, taking her hand. "Seems like a lifetime since last I saw you." Without warning he leaned in and kissed her on the lips. "Shall we go?"

Honey, as well as everyone else who had seen it, stood there in total shock. She didn't know whether to slap the shit out of Shai or return the gesture. She could tell right off that a night with him would be quite interesting.

"Ah," she stuttered. "Yeah, we can leave."

Shai directed Honey to the car and held the passenger's door open for her as she slid onto the leather seat. After making sure that she was secure he walked around to the driver's side and got in. All eyes were still on them as they pealed off into the night.

"I'm gonna ask yo' stupid ass one more time," Brown said, holding the kid by his face. "Where the fuck is Amine and Legs?"

"I don't know," the kid cried.

"Stop lying," Alvarez said, still picking under his fingernails with the cross they had snatched off the kid's neck. "You know something and you're gonna tell us, dipshit. If not, I'm gonna let my partner beat you bloody."

The kid suddenly felt very weak. If these were the same cats that beat up Harry, then he was in trouble. Besides that, if they happened to kill him, who better to cover up a murder than a cop?

The kid tried to remain tight-lipped, but when Brown knocked one of his teeth out with the butt of his pistol, the kid rethought his options. "Okay," the kid pleaded. "I'm not sure, but I think Amine went up to the Crystal Lounge."

"Was that so hard?" Alvarez said, patting the kid's bloody face. "All you had to do was tell us what we wanted to know and you could've spared yo'self an ass whipping. Oh well, my partner needed the workout anyway."

Brown dropped the kid on the floor and kicked him in his ribs one more time for good measure. "Clown-ass nigga," spat Brown.

"This shit is getting ridiculous. We've been searching for these punks all day and still nothing."

"Tone, you're one of those people that always sees the glass as half empty, when you should be looking at it as half full."

"How do you figure that and we still haven't found either of these fucks?"

"For one thing, we know now that we're only chasing one perp. The one thing that all these stories have in common is the fact that no one seems to have seen Legs in a minute. It's a good bet that he's dirty and got low. That puts him on the back burner for the moment."

"Okay, so what about this Amine character?" Brown asked.

"He'll be easy enough to track down."

"How's that when we haven't been able to find him all day?"

"Because the dumb shit is still here. Legs is the smarter of the two. He felt the heat coming and got out of Dodge. The stupid mutha fucka Amine is leaving a paper trail for us to follow. Amine was definitely in on the hit. Now it's just a matter of picking him up and getting a confession out of the bastard."

"You make it sound so easy, J."

"Actually it is, Tone. These punks ain't smarter than us. I remember when police work really meant *work*. These kids are getting themselves caught by being so damn disorganized. Lately, we don't have much to do. It's all a matter of being in the right place at the right time."

"Whatever, man. Let's just go pick this kid up so we can call it a night. One more killer off the streets. Hooray for us."

"It might run a little deeper than that."

"Here we go again," Brown said, slapping himself in the forehead. "What is it now, Sherlock?"

"I've been going over this in my head for a minute and it's still not adding up," Alvarez explained. "Heath was a well-connected guy. Ordering his execution took balls and money. These two dicks we're chasing don't strike me as the type to plan something like this on their own. Somebody else is tied up in all this and just using those dumb fucks as pawns."

"A conspiracy?" Brown asked.

"Isn't it always, partner?"

"Why did you do that?" Honey asked.

"Do what?" responded Shai.

"You know. Why did you kiss me back there?"

"Because I felt like it."

"So, do you always do what you feel, Shai?"

"Pretty much. I like to think that I'm in control of my own destiny."

"Well, I like to feel that I'm in control of my own body. Besides, what if your girl or someone she knew would've seen it?"

"Ain't got a girl."

"I find that hard to believe, Shai."

"I don't. But if I did, it wouldn't bother you that much."

"How do you figure that?"

"You're in the car with me, aren't you?"

"You think you've got all the answers, don't you, Shai?"

"Not all of 'em, just some of 'em. So where do you wanna go and eat?" he asked, changing the subject.

"You're the one with all of the answers," she said sarcastically.

"I know a spot. Hold tight, ma." Shai headed east toward the FDR and merged with the northbound traffic. Shai had been with plenty of women in his young life, but Honey was unique in her own little way. She wasn't the prettiest girl that he'd been with, but Honey had her own style.

While Shai was making a mental assessment of Honey, she was doing the same. She couldn't help but admire his style. He was thuggish, but classy with it. Shai was one of those dudes that would look just as good in a pair of whites and a T-shirt as he would in a business suit. She was very much attracted to the young man, but her motivation was what he could do for her. Shai was born to money and she had to have some of it, if not all. Honey was 'bout her paper.

"So," Shai said, breaking the silence. "You have a good time at the club?"

"It was a'ight," Honey said, pulling a cigarette from her white leather purse. "Too many thirsty niggaz."

"They be on ya, huh?"

"Stop acting like you don't know, Shai."

"Never that," he said, taking her cigarette. "The kid got too much class." Shai lit the cigarette and handed it to her.

"You're so full of yourself, Shai Clark."

"Why, because I'm confident? Honey, if I don't believe in me then who will?"

"Please, Shai. You know that even if you didn't play ball, you'd still be straight."

"I don't follow you."

"Shai, your father is a successful businessman. You've got a legacy and a half waiting for you."

"Honey," he said seriously. "It ain't even that kinda party. Some cats would be content with a handout, but not me. I'll make my own fortune, by my own means."

Honey was a little thrown off by the passion in Shai's words. Her friends had told her that he was a spoiled rich kid, but he didn't seem to be so at all. Shai was a pompous bastard, but he seemed to be very independent and focused.

"Damn," she said, patting his thigh. "You ain't have to get all sensitive about it."

"I'm too loose to be tight, ma," he said, placing his hand over hers. "I just wanted to let you know where my head was at. How about you? Tell me something about Honey."

"Me?" she asked, a bit startled. "What you wanna know about me?"

"I dunno." He shrugged. "Just tell me something that sums up who you are."

"Well . . . I'm twenty-one and originally from Queensbridge. I've been living in Manhattan for like . . . two or three years now. And I like strawberry ice cream." She giggled. "I guess that sums it up?"

"A lil' bit. Is the name Honey on your birth certificate?"

"Nope."

"So?"

"So what?"

"Are you gonna tell me what it is?"

"Not on the first date. I can't give you all of my goodies at once."

"I hear that," he said, getting off at the 96th Street exit. "So, you got any kids?"

This question must've caught Honey off guard because she hesitated before answering, "Yeah . . . a little girl."

"I see," Shai said.

"Is that a problem?" she asked defensively.

"Easy, ma." He grinned. "I didn't say anything of the sort. I'm actually pretty good with kids."

"Do you have any?"

"No, but I've got nineteen years of experience."

"You're silly." She giggled. "I think I can fuck with you."

Shai pulled the GS in front of a little diner on the East Side, not far from the movie theater. Honey eyed the diner nervously as Shai killed the engine. Of all the places to eat, he had to bring her to that one. Shai opened the door for Honey and she stepped out onto the curb.

"I like this lil' spot," he said, taking her by the hand. "They make a pretty good steak."

Shai led Honey into the small diner. As soon as they entered the place, the staff was greeting Shai with smiles and shakes. Honey had never received that kind of reception at the establishment with any of the other men she frequented the place with in the past.

Shai and Honey were escorted to an out-of-the-way booth in the back of the diner. She scanned the few faces that were gathered in the spot to see if there was anyone that could identify her. Luckily for her, the diner wasn't crowded.

CHAPTER 13

BONE HOPPED OUT OF the cab and almost fell against the hood, as he struggled for control of his equilibrium. The bottle of Hennessy that hung at his side was only half full. The other half was integrating with his liver. He and some of his friends had just come from the strip club downtown and broke luck.

The first girl was a real Amazon-type chick. She was about six feet tall with caramel skin and high cheekbones. She had legs like baseball bats and an ass shaped like a Valentine heart. The second girl was black as tar and thick as hell. She was short with a huge ass and big breasts. The yellow lipstick that coated her big lips made them look like a landing zone for penis.

The five of them staggered and laughed their way into the diner, with Bone bringing up the rear. The host looked at them warily and led them to a booth. Bone happened to look toward the back and saw the kid from the other day sitting with a girl that bore a striking resemblance to Honey.

. . .

"Geez, Mike," Nicky Tulips whined. "We've been riding around for hours and ain't seen one hair on that shine's ass."

"Just drive the fucking car," Mike barked from the passenger side. "The sooner we get this thing solved, the better. That package is as hot as a fucking Roman candle and we gotta get it moved before you-know-who starts getting wise."

"Okay, Mike. You say we gotta find him, so we'll find him. But what if he tries to give us the old fuck you, like he did Freddy?"

"Hey," Mike said, pointing a chubby finger. "I ain't Freddy. One of those fucks raises a hand to me and I'll shove it up his black ass. You gotta know how to deal with these people, Nicky. Tommy ain't like the rest of these humps. That kid is a gorilla to the heart. He's done a couple of jobs for us on the side and let me tell you, Tommy is a vicious son of a bitch. You gotta schmooze someone like that. Ya know? Make 'em think their opinion counts worth dick. Throw 'em some crumby perks and they're happy."

"Mike," Nicky said, stopping at a red light. "You already spoke to Poppa about it, so why we still looking for Tommy?"

"Because we still gotta move this package," Mike informed him. "Pull up across the light at that diner. I wanna get a sandwich."

Nicky was relieved to be stopping somewhere. Mike had been riding like a madman for the better part of four hours trying to hook up with Tommy, never once considering Nicky's bladder. He had to take a serious leak.

Nicky double-parked the car outside the diner and moved around to help Mike out. The big man waved Nicky off and hauled his bulky frame from the car. The two Mafia men cautiously moved the few paces to the diner entrance. When they got inside, they were given the same toothy greeting as Shai. The owner, who was a small balding man, came from whatever he was doing in the back to greet Mike.

After the exchange of a few pleasantries, Mike was offered a booth. He was about to decline and sit at the bar, but something in the back of the diner caught his attention. At first he had thought the young man sitting in the rear booth was Tommy, but as he looked closer he realized that it was the younger of the Clark boys. Shai was sitting in the back with a young lady and appeared to be having an exchange of words with a street punk Mike knew as Bone. A wicked plan began to form in the fat man's brain as he headed in their direction.

"You come here a lot?" Honey asked, as she slid into the booth.

"Only when I'm in town," Shai responded with a smile. "My pops put me onto this place a few years back. It's a nice atmosphere, but the food isn't outrageously priced."

"So, you dine based on price?" she asked.

"Not at all," he chuckled. "I think of food as I do women. You can't put a price on quality. I feel that the finer things in life are worth spending a few dollars on." Shai was about to go on when he saw a familiar face headed in his direction. It took a while to register but Shai put a name with the face sneering at him: It was the kid Bone. Shai knew from the look on Bone's face that he was out for trouble. He reached under the table and pulled out the Glock that he had "forgotten" to return to Tommy's car. Shai placed the gun on his lap and kept an eye on the approaching Bone.

Honey must've noticed the change in Shai's facial expression because she looked over her shoulder. When she saw Bone approaching them, she wanted to get up and run. But she couldn't play herself in front of Shai. Honey turned her attention back to the menu and tried to stay cool.

"What's really good?" slurred Bone. "You can't speak, Honey?"

"Oh," said Honey, faking surprise. "Hey, Bone. What're you doing here?"

"Shit," he snapped. "I should be asking you the same thing."

"Nothing much. Just came to get something to eat after the club."

"I'll bet," said Bone, staring at Shai. "So what, you sliding with this cat?"

"Knock it off, Bone," she said, with a wave of her hand. "Me and Shai are just chilling. Besides"—she glanced over at the two strippers—"you don't look lonely."

"Don't try to change the subject, Honey. You just trying to cover your own ass. Don't try and make this shit about me."

"Excuse me," Shai said, cutting in. "Do you two need a moment alone to talk?"

"Hell no," Honey snapped. "Bone is doing him. We ain't got nothing to talk about."

"Oh, I was just making sure that I wasn't causing a problem between you?"

"Nah, you're good, Shai. And Bone," she said, addressing him, "you need to stop trying to act like you're my man or something. If I want to have dinner with a friend, that's my business."

"Bitch," Bone snapped. "It's damn near daylight. This shit is more like breakfast."

"Hold on, player," Shai interjected. "There's no need for name-calling. I'm sure this can be resolved in an adult fashion."

"Oh, so you trying to be funny?" Bone asked, shooting Shai a cold stare.

"Not at all. I just ain't wit' all the conflict. If you wanna talk to Honey, be my guest. But keep the names to yourself. At least while she's with me."

"Ain't this some shit," said Bone, waving his friends over. "This nigga wanna play Captain Save-a-Ho."

"You must got me twisted with some other nigga," Shai said, fingering the gun under the table. "My name is Clark. Shai Clark." He looked Bone dead in the eye. Shai's voice was calm but his nerves were tingling. He kept wondering if Bone was gonna flex.

"Fuck you," said Bone, slapping their water glasses from the table. "You think 'cause ya last name is Clark you're some kinda don? Nigga, I'll twist yo' shit." Bone took a step toward Shai but stopped short when Shai placed the Glock on the table.

"Look fam'," Shai said very calmly. "I'm trying to be the bigger man about all of this. But if you wanna keep with all this gangsta shit, I'm wit' that too. What's good?" At the sight of the young man's gun, other diners began to exit the spot. No one wanted to be the recipient of a stray bullet. Shai's face showed no emotion but his heart was beating out of his chest. Word on the streets was that Bone was crazy and down to bust his gun. Shai wasn't a killer or anything of the sort, but fear had forced his hand. If Bone made a move, Shai would air him out.

Suddenly Bone was very sober. He had been feeling himself for a minute but seeing that Shai was strapped changed all that. Bone didn't really know Shai, but he knew Tommy. If the two brothers were anything alike, Shai would surely kill him.

"So it's like that?" Bone asked, still trying to sound tough.

"It ain't like nothing," Shai said, never taking his eyes off Bone's hands. "I told you I don't want trouble, but you don't seem to hear me. I've tried asking you, so now I'm telling you. Leave us the fuck alone."

"You lil' punk-ass nigga," Bone began. "I'm gonna—"

"Hey, hey," Mike said from behind them. "Fuck is going on back here?"

At the sight of the made man Bone calmed down a little bit. He knew that this was a Mob-owned joint, but he didn't realize that there was any Cosa Nostra about. If he had, then he probably wouldn't have gotten so rowdy. Unlike Shai, Bone knew just who Mike was, and what kind of power he held.

"Nothing, Mike," Bone said humbly. "Just a lil' misunderstanding between me and my girl."

"I ain't ya girl," Honey barked.

"Bitch, stop fronting," said Bone.

"I ain't gonna be too many bitches," Honey shot back.

"Listen, listen," Mike said, waving everyone silent. "You guys know better than to bring this kinda shit into my spot. If you wanna bicker then go outside. This is a diner, not a fucking wrestling ring."

"Let's go, Honey," demanded Bone.

"Please." She waved him off. "I ain't going nowhere with you. Burn it."

"Fuck you think you're talking to?" Bone reached out to grab Honey's arm, but Shai was a little quicker. He grabbed Bone's arm with his free hand and placed the gun to his head with the other.

"Fuck," Shai began. "You got a learning disability? She doesn't wanna go with you, kid."

"Are you crazy?" asked Mike, getting in between them. "I told the both of youz to cool it."

"Check this out," Shai said, addressing Mike. "I don't know who you are, and I ain't got no quarrel with you. But if this is a friend of yours then you might wanna take him for a walk."

"Okay, kid," Mike said, trying to contain his smile. "Just put the pistol away. Bone, why don't you take the ladies and go?"

"Mike," Bone asked, still at Shai's mercy. "You gonna side with this cat over me?"

"It ain't about siding, Bone. I just don't want this kinda heat in my joint. Do me a favor and take a walk."

"A'ight," said Bone, jerking loose. "I'm gonna bounce, but this shit ain't over, Shai. Not by a long shot."

"Take a walk, Bone," Mike reiterated, only this time his tone was much harsher.

Bone caught the look in Mike's eye and decided to let it go. He gathered up his team and headed for the door. He spared one last glance at Shai and bit down on his lip. Swan said that Shai was a civilian, but the youngster had put himself out there on some gangsta shit. If that's how he wanted it, then Bone would be more than happy to give it to him.

"You're Tommy's kid brother, right?" Mike asked, inviting himself to a seat.

"Yeah," Shai said, with a bit of an attitude. "Why, you got a beef with me too 'cause my last name is Clark?"

"Hardly," Mike said, putting his hands up in a submissive gesture. "You probably don't remember me. Mike, Mike Tessio?"

"Oh, yeah," Shai said, relaxing. "I've seen you at the house a time or two. You're in business with my brother Tommy, right?"

"Something like that, kid. Me and your brother do a little something from time to time. So, you're home from school, huh?" asked Mike, changing the subject.

"Yeah," replied Shai.

"I've seen a few of your games. You've got a jump shot like a white boy."

"Thanks, I think."

"Sure, kid. You know you put braces on my little girl?"

"How do you figure?"

"That game against Duke. Nobody expected NC State to have a snowball's chance in hell at winning that game, but old Shai Clark came through in a pinch."

"Dropped about thirty in that game, didn't he, Mike?" asked Nicky, speaking up for the first time.

"Thirty-one," Mike corrected him. "I had quite a few dollars riding on that game. Paid off big-time."

"Glad I could help out," Shai said, motioning for the waiter to bring the check. When the waiter came to their table with the bill, Mike intercepted it.

"Your money's no good here, kid," Mike said, crumbling up the bill. "It's on the house."

"Mr. Tessio—" Shai began.

"Call me Mike," he interrupted.

"Okay, Mike. I appreciate the kind gesture, but my daddy didn't raise no fools. Nothing in life is without its price. What do you want from me?"

"Come on, Shai, how you gonna insult me like that? You're my pal Tommy's little brother. Can't a guy just want to do something nice for a buddy?" Shai just stared at Mike blankly. Apparently Mike had underestimated Shai; he was more streetwise than he gave him credit for.

"Okay," continued Mike, "you got me. See, me and Tommy have been having . . . a difference of opinion. I got something on the ball that could make us some money, but I need Tommy to go along with it. But you know how your brother is."

"Yeah, I know just how my brother is," Shai agreed. "But what's that got to do with me? If you know my family as well as you claim to, then you already know that I don't get involved with my brother's dealings. I have my own life."

"Oh, I know this, Shai. I would never put you in harm's way, 'cause I know that ain't your thing. I also know that you and your brother are very close. All I'm asking is that you talk to him, Shai. Tommy had a fight with one of my guys, so things are pretty touchy right now. I just want him to know that I ain't salty. Freddy's a prick and that's just a given. But I don't want what went on between him and some goomba in my crew to spoil a beautiful working relationship. Ya know what I mean?"

"Yeah," Shai said, standing. "Like I said, I'm not a soldier in my father's army. I can speak to Tommy, for all the good it will do, but don't look for any miracles." Shai helped Honey to her feet and led her in the direction of the exit.

"Hey, Shai," Mike called out. "Hold on a sec." Mike pulled out a wad of bills, peeled five off, and handed them to Shai. "Just a little something for your time."

Shai looked at the money as if it had been dipped in shit. "Thanks, but no thanks," he said, looking Mike dead in the eye. "Poppa takes care of his own." Shai held the door for Honey and followed her into the night air.

Bone sat in the passenger seat of the cab, fuming. The encounter with Shai had him so mad that he didn't even wanna freak off anymore. After dropping the strippers home, Bone and his crew hit the bootlegger and headed back to the hood.

"Yo," Rah said from the backseat. "You a'ight, son?" Rah was a high-yellow cat with a chipped tooth. He was the youngest of the crew, so he asked dumb-ass questions from time to time.

"Fuck do you think?" Bone snapped.

"I'm just saying," Rah continued. "You sitting up there all quiet and shit, know what I mean? You actin' like them Clark niggaz got you rattled. I know that ain't the case 'cause you like the illest nigga in America."

"Ahmad," said Bone, turning to face the backseat. "You better tell this lil' nigga to shut up before I pop his ass."

Ahmad was Rah's older brother. He was a butterscotch color with hazel eyes. Ahmad was the quieter of the two and the easier to deal with. Ahmad considered himself something of a ladies' man, but he was a hustler to the heart. He could take a few grams of some bullshit and bring it back lovely. That's why he was Bone's right-hand man.

"Why don't you be easy, Rah?" Ahmad said, lighting a cigarette. "You don't know what to say outta ya mouth, that's why niggaz is always leaving you on the block."

"Whatever," Rah said, not bothering to take heed to the look his brother was giving him. "All I'm saying is that shit in the diner was wack. This lil' faggot-ass nigga flexing and shit. We notorious up-town, son. We should've mashed that nigga out."

"Rah, please," Bone cut in. "When Shai backed out that hammer, you was ready to run. And don't try to lie, nigga. I seen it all in ya face."

"Fuck outta here," Rah said, drawing a small .22 from his boot. "If it had jumped off, I was ready to bang, kid."

Bone and Ahmad looked at Rah's tiny pistol and both burst out laughing.

"Little brother," asked Ahmad, between giggles. "What were you gonna do with that?"

"What you think?" Rah shot back.

"Get yo'self killed," Bone picked up. "Niggaz like you always do some bird shit. That's why you spend the majority of ya career on the corner and the rest back and forth to the Island. You got so much to prove, but no fucking idea how to go about it."

"I would've started blasting. That's a start."

"Fucking idiot," Bone mumbled. "Even if you had gotten up the courage to pull out on Shai—matter fact, let's just say for the sake of argument you shot him. Poppa would've killed you and ya whole fucking family tree. You, I don't really fuck with, but I got a lot of love for ya brother and ya sister, so I wouldn't jeopardize them like that. You though, someone is gonna put a bullet in ya head sooner or later if you keep acting like these streets is a fucking game. What ya ass needs to do is go get a fucking job and leave this to the grown folks. Straight up."

"I can do me just fine." Rah pouted.

"You need to cheek ya little brother, Ahmad. If you love him, put him up on game, son."

Ahmad looked at Rah and sucked his teeth. He had told the youngster time and again to think before he spoke. Rah was just content to do and say whatever he wanted and think that being Ahmad's little brother would save him. Ahmad was a feared man on the streets as well as up north. He had done his first state bid when he was sixteen and proved himself from the jump. The first inmate to try Ahmad ended up shitting in a bag. It was pretty much the same on the streets.

"So what're we gonna do about this Shai situation?" asked Ahmad.

"Fuck that nigga," said Bone. "The only reason I didn't get at him right then and there is because he's connected. We ain't got the soldiers or the firepower to go at it with Poppa and Tommy. But best believe we're gonna make something happen. Shai's gonna learn his lesson, but we gotta go about it the right way. All we need is an angle."

Honey allowed Shai to lead her out to the car without a whole lot of effort. She was feeling both afraid and excited about the evening's turn of events. You only see that kind of stuff in the movies. Shai claimed that he didn't fuck with the streets, but Honey could tell from the way he moved that he had it in him.

And what about that Mike character who popped up? Honey had seen Mike in the newspaper once or twice, so she knew that he was somebody important. Mike was supposed to be some kind of mobster connected to the Cissarro crime family. The way he jumped on Shai's dick, Honey had assumed that she had made the right choice in pursuing Shai.

"It's getting late," Shai said, as he opened the passenger door for Honey. "Maybe I should get you home?"

Shai must've been out of his mind. With all that had gone on that night there was no way that Honey was just going to let Shai drop her off without letting her in a little deeper. If it took giving Shai some on the first date, then Honey was totally willing to do so. Shai was a prime catch and Honey wanted to get her claws in as deep as possible.

"What's the rush?" she asked, sliding into the Lexus.

"None really," Shai said, leaning down to her window. "Just thought with all the craziness that you might've wanted to call it a night."

"Nah, I'm good. Let's go somewhere and talk."

Shai shrugged his shoulders and went around to the driver's side. He slid behind the wheel and brought the machine to life. Before Shai pulled off, he looked at his cell phone. He had left it in the car before he and Honey went into the diner. The screen showed five missed calls. He figured they were jump-off calls so he didn't bother to check them. He wanted to give Honey his undivided attention.

Amine came staggering out of the Crystal Lounge, drunk as a skunk. He had been dancing with girls and popping bottles all night long. All courtesy of the money Tommy had given him and Legs for the hit on Heath.

He invited Legs to join him, but Legs declined. He insisted that they go low until the heat died down, just as Tommy had instructed them to. Amine teased his partner about being a bitch and insisted on going out anyway. Legs wished him well, and hopped the Long Island Railroad to his girl's house.

Amine couldn't figure why his partner was acting so scared, but he figured that the killer would come around. The way Amine figured it was, working for Tommy Clark made you damn near untouchable. This was true to an extent; if you were a member of Poppa's inner circle, then you got certain privileges. But a grunt like Amine was expendable.

Amine eyed the big-butt girl that came out of the club with him and smiled. Before he started working for Tommy, he could've never gotten with a girl like that on his own. Once Amine had put the word out that he was one of the drug cartel's *top killers,* everyone wanted to be nice to him.

Amine cupped the girl by her large ass and led her to the curb, where they would hail a taxi. There was a tall Puerto Rican cat sitting on a parked Buick eyeballing him. Amine had enough liquor in him to feel like he could take on the world. The nine tucked in his waistband cosigned it.

"What the fuck you looking at!" barked Amine. The man just smiled and kept his hands in his pockets. "You think I'm a joke?" asked Amine, getting more animated. "I'm funny to you?"

"Nah, *papi,*" Alvarez said. "You just look like this kid I know from Harlem. But he's a real gangsta mutha fucka."

"They don't come no more gangsta, son," Amine boasted. "You keep screwing me like that and you gonna find out."

"You ain't fucking wit' me, kid," Alvarez said, waving him off. "I'm connected."

"Connected? Who you wit', cracker?"

"First of all," Alvarez said, getting off the car, "I'm Puerto Rican. Second, I'm fucking wit' Tommy Clark."

The lie had its desired affect when Amine boasted, "Fuck you saying? I been on payroll for TC. You better ask about Amine, nigga. And I'm putting in work. What!"

Alvarez smiled as he removed the badge he had been concealing in his coat pocket. Amine looked wide-eyed as sobriety came back to him. He reached for his pistol, but realized he was too late when Brown placed his Glock to the base of Amine's skull. The jig was up.

"What up, gangsta?" asked Brown.

"Fuck you want from me, pig?"

"Well," Alvarez said, "we had originally come to ask you some questions. But in light of the situation"—he removed the pistol from Amine's belt—"looks like you're going for a lil' ride, son."

"Man, ain't this shit illegal or something?" Amine pleaded.

"Not really, my man," Brown spoke up. "You've just confessed to being a part of Tommy Clark's cartel to two police officers. Then we find you with this pistol that I'm pretty sure will come up dirty if we run it through ballistics. I'd say you're fucked, shorty."

"Looks that way," added Alvarez. "But then again, maybe you're not. All depends on if you can make letting you go worth our while?"

"I doubt it," Brown said, shaking his head. "This nigga is a fucking nobody. Probably ain't got but a few hundred in his pocket. Hardly enough for us to waste the effort. I say we book this cocksucker and see what we can get to stick on him."

"I don't know, Tony," Alvarez protested. "He still might be of some use to us."

"Fuck this lil' nigga, J. He's probably never even met Tommy Clark."

"But he claims he's connected."

"He's a fucking liar. I say we bust him, or give him a good ass whipping."

Amine looked back and forth between the two arguing detectives and saw his chances of getting away become slimmer and slimmer. If he'd only listened to his partner.

CHAPTER 14

BY THE TIME Shai made it back to his father's Jersey estate, the sun was just beginning to rise. It had been quite a full night for the young athlete: first the situation with Bone, then Mike pops up acting like he and Shai went way back. Shai had only been home a short time and already having his father's name had gotten him into some shit. Being a Clark was both a gift and a curse.

After they had left the restaurant, Honey had directed him to a secluded spot off Harlem River Drive, where they parked and got caught up in a deep conversation. Honey gave Shai a brief overview of her life. She told him about everything from when her father left her, to a boyfriend that used to kick the shit outta her. Honey also confessed to Shai that she stripped. There was no shame in her game. She had a child to raise and rent to pay. Stripping did it a whole lot quicker than flipping burgers. Honey was raw like that.

Shai told her about his life at school and his absentee mother. He also touched base on his basketball career and the pressures of being a young superstar. Shai talked about a lot of things that night, but never once did he mention his father's illegal holdings. Since he was a child, it was just an unspoken rule. *What goes on in the family, stays in the family.*

They kissed and explored each other during their little chat. Shai's touch was like silk to her. He made every nerve in Honey's body tingle. He cracked for the ass, but she backed him off. It's not that she didn't want to fuck him, 'cause the bulge she felt in his pants confirmed that he was holding, but she couldn't let him think she was a jump-off. Honey's plan was to make Shai fall in love with her. She would give it to him, but not before the time was right.

After spending a beautiful evening with his new friend, Shai dropped Honey off at her apartment building. He gently kissed her on the forehead and waited till she got in the building before pulling off into the night. After spending one evening with Honey, Shai's nose was wide open. It was unlike Shai to develop emotional attachments for any female other than Hope. His shrink had told him that the reason he treated women the way he did was because of his mother. Shai didn't wanna hear that shit. He was just a love-'em-and-leave-'em type of guy.

As Shai headed up the stone driveway, he noticed a figure sitting on the porch. It was dark, so he couldn't tell who it was. All he could see was a profile in the light of a cigarette. He moved closer to the figure as he made his way up the front steps. Shai peered through the darkness and made out his brother Tommy.

"What up, Slim?" Tommy asked, exhaling the smoke.

"Damn, what you doing out here at the crack of dawn?" Shai questioned.

"Waiting on you. I've been trying to call you all night. Fuck we pay ya high-ass phone bill for if you ain't gonna pick it up?"

"I was caught up, man. You know how it is, T."

"Man, pass my strap." Shai handed his brother the pistol and listened as he continued to speak. "Sometimes you do some dumb shit, player. Why didn't you bring the gun to me when you found it?"

"Man," Shai complained. "Ain't no telling where you was at when I realized I had the damn thing in the car. I didn't wanna have to come all the way to west hell to meet you then come back. That shit would've cut into my night. I was good with it."

"Dummy boy," Tommy teased. "What if one-time had pulled you over? Then what?"

"Pulled over for what? Your tags are up to date and I wasn't drinking. They ain't have no reason to pull me over," Shai said defiantly.

"Shai, you're one of them lil' niggaz that think they know every damn thing. The police don't really need an excuse to pull you over. Being black is enough. You're a young African-American male, riding around in a sixty-thousand-dollar auto. They're gonna figure either you stole it or you're doing dirt. Period. Man, you know how often I get pulled over just going from point A to point B? Shai, you got a lot to learn if you wanna run these streets. Stay in ya lane."

"I'm good," Shai said, storming past Tommy.

"Hold on," Tommy said, grabbing Shai by the arm. "Fuck is all the attitude about?"

"Look, Tommy," Shai said, facing his brother. "I don't know if you and Poppa have noticed or not, but I ain't a kid no more. I know what time it is out here, man. I ain't hardly ignorant to what you and Daddy are out here laying down. I've been around this shit all my life, yo. Same as you. Yet I get treated like a kid. That shit is wack. I'm a Clark too."

"Shai, it ain't all that it seems. This rep comes at a price."

"Trust me, big brother, I know what's good. Like I said, I ain't a kid."

"You just don't learn, do you Shai?"

"I'm hardheaded like my brother."

"Don't be funny, nigga. I'm trying talk some sense into ya lil' ass."

"Whatever. Oh," Shai said, remembering his talk with Mike, "I seen ya peoples."

"What peoples?" Tommy asked.

"The white boy. Fat Mike."

"Mike? Fuck was you doing with him?"

"I wasn't with him. Homie rolled up on me when I was out to dinner with Honey."

"Did he come at you sideways, Shai? I swear to God, I'll body that nigga today."

"Nah, he was cool. He actually squashed a beef I had with that nigga Bone."

"Bone? Shai, how the hell did you manage to get that nigga started?"

"I ain't do nothing to that nigga. He was mad 'cause I was wit' his bitch. I tried to be cool about it, but that dude is ignorant as hell."

"That's what life on the streets can do to you. The strong will prosper, while weak-minded niggaz like Bone perish. Shai, you better keep yo' ass off them streets before one of these niggaz decide that they don't give a fuck what ya last name is."

"I ain't stunting that shit, T. I can hold mine wherever."

"So you think you know what time it is, huh?"

"Pretty much."

"A'ight, Shai. You're grown, I can dig it. You think you're ready to see just how deep it can get?"

"I ain't no punk," Shai snarled. "I'm a man, just like you, Tommy. I can take care of myself."

"Okay, Mr. Man," Tommy said, flashing a sinister grin. "You say you can handle it, cool. You got it, Shai. Get ya z's on, baby bro. We gonna hang out tomorrow, ya heard?"

"Whatever, Tommy. I'll be ready." Shai walked into the house like he was cooler than an iceberg. He tried to sound confident but his heart was really racing. He knew he should've just listened to his older brother, but he had to show him that he could hold his on the streets. Now he had probably bitten off more than he could chew. Only God knew what kinda stunt Tommy had up his sleeve, but it was too late to cry about it. The die had been cast and Shai would just have to wait and see what the numbers read.

Honey felt like she was swooning when she walked into her apartment. The evening with Shai had been quite memorable. At first she had just planned on hollering at him to try and see what she could get out of the deal. Somewhere along the line the rules changed. Honey found herself actually digging the young man. Her friends had told her stories about Shai, but the man she had spent her evening with seemed so different than what people said. He was an intelligent and attentive young man. Quite a far stretch from the womanizer that the girls made him out to be.

Honey looked at her sister Tish, who was on the couch knocked out. She hadn't intended on staying out all night, but she didn't expect two men to draw iron over her either. When her sister woke up, she would explain what had happened. She would understand. If she didn't, oh well.

Honey walked into her daughter's room and found her sleeping peacefully. She stared down at the little girl and almost got teary-eyed. All she wanted for Star was a better life than the one she had been subjected to. There was no limit to the things that she would do and had done to provide for her daughter. She knelt down and kissed the little girl on the forehead. She loved Star with all of her being. Honey did some underhanded shit on the streets, but that was where it stayed. When she came home, she was Melissa.

With this in mind, Honey picked up her cell and dialed Shai's number. The voice mail picked up right away so she figured he must have it turned off. She listened to Shai's recording and found herself becoming aroused at the sound of his voice. After the beep Honey said, "Melissa." It probably wouldn't register to Shai right away, but once he thought about it, he'd figure it out.

Honey climbed out of her club outfit and slipped into a pair of plaid boxer shorts and a white T-shirt. She lay on her bed, looking at the ceiling and thinking. Falling for Shai was definitely not in the cards. She had no idea what had happened in the few short hours that they had spent together, but it was a feeling that she was unfamiliar with. Something about Shai seemed so right to her. When she looked into his eyes, she felt at peace. Falling for Shai wasn't supposed to happen, but it did. Now, the question was what to do about it?

CHAPTER 15

SWAN SAT IN HIS motel room, cleaning his guns and watching the news. He had been in the small town for a short while, but it seemed like weeks. There was nothing to see and nowhere to go. Not that he would've gone partying in the town anyway. Pleasure could wait until he got back to the City; he was there to handle business.

He and Mo Black had coasted through the town, trying to locate their adversaries. The crew was in the hood where they were supposed to be, but their leader hadn't shown his face yet. Mo wanted Swan to drive back to his place with him and try again, but Swan suggested that he get a room in the town and lay on the cat. Mo posted a man on the kid's block and instructed him to call Swan's room when the target popped up. So Swan sat and waited for his phone call.

His mind went to his friend Shai and what he was doing. Swan knew that Shai could take care of himself, but he was still worried about him. Shai was from a family of hustlers, but he didn't understand the world that they lived in. Swan faulted Poppa for that. He thought that by shielding Shai from it, it would make him immune to it. He was wrong. All that did was dull Shai's street sense. That's why Swan schooled his friend out every chance he got. Shai wasn't a square, but he wasn't a soldier either.

The phone rang, bringing Swan back to the situation at hand. Only two people knew where Swan was staying and Mo Black had his cell number. It must've been Mo's watcher. Swan picked up the phone, but said nothing. He listened as the watcher simply said, "It's time." Swan hung up the phone and prepared for his first professional hit.

Swan popped open his case and began to remove the items that he would need. He slid into a bulletproof vest and pulled a hoodie over that. He removed three handguns from the bag and began to hide them on his person. The two .40-calibers went into customized shoulder holsters and the .38 was strapped to his ankle. On his way out the door, he grabbed the sawed-off shotgun. It was time to earn his keep.

Shai was awakened by the covers being snatched off him. He looked around, sleepy-eyed, trying to figure who would be crazy enough to wake him after he had been out all night. To his surprise Tommy was standing over him dressed in jeans and a hoodie.

"Raise up, sleepyhead," Tommy barked.

"Come on, man," Shai said, pulling the blanket back over his head. "Too early for this shit, Tommy."

"Nigga, please," Tommy said, yanking the blanket again. "Get yo' ass up. This morning you claimed that you wanted to spin out with me, so I'm holding you to it."

"Damn, T. You was serious?"

"As a heart attack. Now come on, unless you've decided to stay in a child's place?"

The challenge had been made.

"A'ight," Shai said, rolling out of bed. "Let me hop in the shower and—"

"Nah," Tommy cut him off. "We ain't got time for that. Throw some sweats or some jeans on and let's roll. Where I'm taking you, there's nobody to be pretty for. I'll be waiting for you out front. You got five minutes, Slim."

Shai stood on shaky legs as his brother made his exit. His mouth felt like sandpaper and his stomach was doing flip-flops. His body told him to call it off, but his pride told him that it needed to be done. He had to show Tommy that he wasn't a kid. Just because Shai didn't sell drugs, this didn't make him any less of a hustler. He grew up in a crime family, how could he not have the streets in him somewhere?

Tommy called himself trying to teach Shai a lesson, but Shai was prepared for his brother's lil' outing. He would ride with Tommy all day and never flinch, no matter what he saw. He figured that the worst Tommy would do is make him play the block or sit up in a dope house. That was nothing to Shai. He did it with Swan all the time. What would be so different about this trip?

Four minutes and thirty seconds later, Shai came strolling out the front door. He was dressed in a pair of green fatigue pants and the matching jacket. His construction Timbs were loose on his feet, while his fatigue hat was pulled tight, partially covering his blood-shot eyes.

Herc looked at Shai and shook his head. He was hoping that the youngster had gotten cold feet at the last minute, but here he was in the flesh. He had told Tommy that it was a bad idea to bring Shai along. With the rising tensions in the streets, it was hardly a proper time to be teaching the kid a lesson. But Tommy was hardheaded, just like every other male in the Clark family.

"Looks like you had a rough night," Herc joked, trying to lighten the mood.

"Hell yeah," Shai confirmed. "I just got in a few hours ago."

"So why don't you stay home and get some rest?" asked Herc, hoping Shai would agree.

"He's good," Tommy cut in. "It's a light day. Shai will be a'ight."

Herc looked at Tommy and saw the look that he was giving him. He had tried to spare Shai, but Tommy had something to prove. He would've argued with Tommy, but it wasn't his place to do so. It was between the brothers. Herc just shrugged and went around to the driver's side, while Tommy got in the passenger seat and Shai climbed into the rear. There was no turning back now.

Amine was slumped against the overpass on 125th Street, clutching his ribs with his free hand. His other was chained to the structure. One eye was shut and his bottom lip was split down the middle. Every time he breathed, he could feel the pain from his broken ribs.

The two detectives had been working him over, trying to get information. Amine had tried to hold out, but he was getting weak. It came to the point where the detectives had given him a choice: a name or his life. After the beating that they had given him, Amine was sure that they would kill him, so he chose the easy way.

"Tommy," he rasped. "Tommy Clark."

Legs sat in the window of his girlfriend's apartment smoking a blunt. When he had first set out to lay low at her spot, he figured that he'd lose his mind being so far from the midst of action. To his surprise, it was a pleasant experience. Legs had gotten some well-deserved rest and was thinking a lot more clearly.

He hadn't had any contact with his crew, except when Tommy had called to make sure he arrived at his destination safely. He was surprised that he hadn't heard from Amine. It was unlike his partner to go without speaking to him for extended lengths of time. Especially with the way things had been going. Legs had a funny feeling in the pit of his stomach, but shook it off as jitters.

Legs put the blunt out and walked barefooted to the bedroom. His girl, Vanessa, was stretched across the bed, watching videos. Legs laid beside her and kissed her lightly on the cheek. Her yellow skin turned red as she blushed under her man's touch. He moved his hand from her wrapped brown hair, to her slightly protruding belly.

The fact that his girlfriend was pregnant was something that Legs kept from most people. Even his friend Amine. It wasn't because he was unhappy about it. That was hardly true. In fact, most of the money that he made on the streets he wired to her at her little hideaway. Legs didn't tell many people about his blessing, because he was careful. He knew that by coming to work for Tommy and Poppa, their enemies would become his. Poppa and Tommy had some very powerful enemies.

This didn't bother Legs too much, though. He had no fear of anything on two feet. Besides, with the way Tommy looked out for him he wasn't hurting financially. God forbid if something happened to him today or tomorrow, he knew that between what he had put away and the agreement he and Tommy had made, his unborn seed wouldn't have to go without. Unlike Amine, Legs was a planner.

When he found out about his girl being pregnant, he confided in Tommy. He explained his need for extra income and his willingness to earn it. Tommy had honored his request and agreed to keep his secret. In addition to working with his partner, Amine, Tommy also gave Legs other tasks to perform. It usually wasn't anything that another one of the soldiers couldn't handle, but Tommy would pass the jobs on to Legs. Legs didn't know it, but Tommy gave him these odd jobs so it wouldn't be like he was giving the money away. He wanted Legs to feel like he was earning.

Legs was enjoying his little vacation, but the call of the streets was ever present in the back of his mind. He had a few dollars, but by not being on the streets, he couldn't add onto that. He needed to be grinding, but Tommy's instructions were very specific: "Stay put till I call for you." So, stay put he did. Tommy was the boss and as long as he kept Legs fed, his word was law. Legs would be back in the trenches soon enough.

"Soon," he whispered. "Soon."

.   .   .

So far, it had been an easy day. Shai had ridden in the car while Tommy and Herc conducted business. The first stop was the Strand Diner on 96th Street. They had a light breakfast and discussed the business for the day. Next, they jetted through Brooklyn to check on a few spots they had out there. Everything was easygoing, until they arrived in Queens.

A young worker named Josh was waiting for them at the appointed spot. As they got up on him, Shai noticed he was sporting a black eye. Not a good sign. Josh had explained to them that some of the cats from the projects where he hustled had opened up shop. When Josh told them that they couldn't work there, they told him that they lived in the projects and the Clarks couldn't dictate where they worked. Now it was up to Tommy to make the situation right.

Josh hopped in the truck and the four of them drove the few short blocks to Queensbridge. It didn't take long for them to find the kids. They were posted up in front, selling stones like they had a license to do so. Tommy and Herc checked their weapons and prepared to approach the kids.

"What are you gonna do?" Shai asked from the backseat.

"What the fuck you think we're gonna do?" Tommy asked, annoyed. "We're gonna show them lil' chumps who the fuck is running shit."

"Tommy, you can't just hop out flashing your pistol in broad daylight. That could make the situation worse."

"Shai, don't try and tell me how to handle mine. You just play the back, like a good little observer."

Tommy's comment irritated the hell out of Shai, but he let it slide. "Let me talk to them," he said, getting out of the truck.

"Fuck do you think you're doing, Slim?" Herc asked, getting out to cut him off.

"Look," Shai said, leaning into the passenger side window. "Just let me holla at the kids, before y'all start shooting shit up. I'll take Josh with me, but y'all be on point, just in case." Shai started walking without waiting for Tommy's approval. Josh just shrugged and followed him.

There were about four of them in total. They were all young, ranging in ages from about fifteen to eighteen. They were dressed similarly in sweatpants or army fatigues. Shai noticed that one of them was wearing an oversized jersey, so it was a good guess that he was armed. What he also noticed was that their clothes were dingy and their footwear had seen better days. Shai knew just how he would come at them, he just hoped he didn't get shot trying to prove a point.

"'Sup, fellas?" Shai asked, with a pleasant smile.

"What you need, dunn?" a kid with fuzzy braids asked.

"I need to holla at you."

"Fuck you need to holla at us about?" the kid with the jersey asked.

"I need to discuss how you cats are moving. My name is Shai Clark, and y'all are hustling on turf that's already been claimed. We can't have that."

"This nigga must be crazy," Fuzzy spoke up. "This is the 'Bridge, son, and you ain't even from around here. How you gonna tell us we can't eat?"

"He must wanna go out like his man," Jersey added.

"I'm afraid you've misunderstood me," Shai said, keeping his voice even and his hands at his sides. "I'm not telling you that you can't eat. Every man has a right to eat. I'm just telling you that you can't continue to move whoever's rock you're moving, in my father's territory."

"How you figure we're working for someone else?" Fuzzy asked.

"Simple. If you were working for yourselves, you wouldn't be out here going hand to hand. The bottom line is, this has to stop. But I do offer compensation."

"Compen . . . what?" Jersey asked.

Shai shook his head in frustration. "Listen, how much do you make off a pack?"

"We get a hundred dollars off every G pack," Fuzzy said proudly.

"Well, now you get a hundred and fifty, plus the protection of my family."

"You got some nerve," Jersey said, exposing the butt of the nine that was tucked under his shirt. "What's to stop us from just popping yo' ass?"

"Because"—Shai nodded over his shoulder—"the large gentleman in the truck would cut you down with the machine gun he's holding before you could get away." The four men looked over Shai's shoulder and spotted Herc glaring at them from behind the wheel. They backed up a bit. "It's settled then," Shai continued. "Finish whatever work you have, then see Josh for the re-up. If anyone lays hands on him again, your mothers will be shopping for black dresses. Are we clear?"

The four boys nodded in unison.

"Jesus H. Christ. What the hell happened to him?" Lt. Andrew Jackson asked, scratching his balding head.

"Resisted arrest," Alvarez lied.

"I'll bet," said Jackson, seeing through the lie, but not really giving a damn. "So what did ya get from the prick?"

"Well," Brown cut in, "we've placed him at the scene of the murder, but he's not the triggerman."

"Is he saying who is?" asked Jackson, casting another glance at the battered Amine.

"He's done us one better, sir. He's named the man who gave the order." Alvarez smiled.

"Well, don't keep an asshole in suspense," Jackson said sarcastically.

"You're familiar with a Tommy Clark."

"Who isn't? He and Sol Lansky are two of the most powerful and crooked businessmen in the City. We haven't been able to pin a charge on either of 'em in years."

"Not that Tommy Clark, sir. We mean his son."

"That fucking wack job? I'm not surprised. But do we have any proof?"

"So far," Brown picked up, "all we have is his word."

"Good, but not good enough. Who was on the trigger?"

"Bright boy isn't saying, but we figure it was his partner, Legs."

"Where the fuck is this Legs character now?"

"We don't know, sir. But we've got some blue-and-whites on the street looking for him now."

"Not good enough. Use whatever means that you need to in order to crack this case. I don't care what you do, as long as it gets results. I want you and Alvarez on the streets day and night. You better not close your fucking eyes until you bring that murdering son of a bitch back to me in chains. When you're finished with that, bring me Tommy Clark. In chains or a box. Doesn't really matter."

The two detectives glanced at each other devilishly. Jackson had just released two rabid dogs into the streets and he knew it. He knew that even though they had orders to bring him back in cuffs or a box, they would most likely do the latter. The two detectives rushed off so quickly that they almost knocked over a file clerk who was standing by the water cooler.

"You wanted to see me, Uncle T?" Gator asked, strolling into Poppa's office.

"Yeah, sit down." Poppa put away the documents he was reading and addressed his nephew. "I got something I want you to handle for me."

"Anything, Poppa," Gator said excitedly.

"Angelo's gonna pick you up and take you into the City. A little mutha fucka 'round there has gotten beside himself and I want y'all to put him in his place."

"I'll fix him up real nice for you," Gator said, clamping his gold teeth down, sounding like two knives clashing together.

"I'm sure you will." Poppa smiled. "But that's a minor part of what I need you to do. Gator, I want you to spend some time with your cousin Shai. Things are getting restless on the streets, and I want to make sure he doesn't get caught up."

"You mean like a babysitter?"

"Yes and no. You and Shai are close enough in age where it shouldn't be an awkward situation. Swan is a good kid, but he's hot on the streets. Everybody knows he's running with Tommy's crew. You, on the other hand, are a fresh face. Nobody knows you, so you shouldn't be singled out. The important thing is that Shai doesn't think that I have you watching over him. He'd never go for it."

"I got you, Uncle T." Gator winked.

"Gator, y'all be careful out there. I'm trusting you with Shai's safety. If anything should happen to him . . ."

"You ain't even gotta say it." Gator flashed the Glock that Angelo had given him. "Me and cuz gonna be straight."

CHAPTER 16

HONEY HAD MANAGED TO successfully clean her house, knock out half her laundry, and prepare lunch for Star and her sister. Not bad after the night she had. But even after accomplishing all this, she still hadn't heard from Shai. It wasn't like she was sweating him, but she thought that she would've heard from him by then. She wasn't about to go out like a groupie and call him again. She was going to use this time to relax. That was when the phone rang. Honey rushed to the phone, knowing that Shai had finally come to his senses. She was thoroughly disappointed when she answered.

Shai sat in the back of the truck, listening to Herc rip Tommy. It seemed that Tommy thought he would have to swoop in and save his little brother, but this wasn't the case. Shai had handled the situation, without using violence, at the same time showing Tommy that he knew a thing or two about street etiquette.

Tommy's little outing was intended to deter Shai from getting caught up in the streets, but it backfired. All it had succeeded in doing so far was cause Shai to consider Swan's theory. Could Shai be an asset to the family?

Shai pulled his cell from his pocket and realized that he hadn't turned it on since the night before. When he hit the ON switch, the screen read six new messages. He called the voice service and listened to them. Two were hang-ups, two were from Jane, one was from Swan, wondering about his whereabouts. None of the messages really stirred anything in Shai except the last one.

The message was very short. In fact, whoever it was didn't really leave a message at all. It was just a name: Melissa. At first it confused Shai, because he couldn't catch the voice, but as he listened to it again, he caught it. It was Honey.

"Melissa," he said under his breath.

"What was that, Slim?" Tommy asked from the front seat.

"Nothing," Shai dismissed him.

He listened to the message twice more with a wide grin on his lips. When he caught himself smiling, he quickly straightened his face before Tommy or Herc caught him. He was beginning to earn their favor and didn't need to do anything stupid to change that. Shai dialed the number that Honey had called him from and waited.

Honey had a secret. A secret that very few people knew. After about an hour or two of half-ass sex and snorting girl, Honey was zoned out. She couldn't understand what it was about Bone that would always make her go against her principles. It was as if he had some kind of hold over her or something. She flexed her still numb fingers, trying to find a warmth that didn't seem to come. Cocaine always made her numb.

Bone was like a badass habit that she just couldn't shake. Whenever she was around him, she had no control over herself. Coke wasn't really her thing, but he could always seem to gas her to do it.

For her, it was just something that she did from time to time. For him, it was something that he did to get through to the next day. Honey might've bumped a little, but she knew that it couldn't become a habit. Coke could make you look old and haggard, and Honey got paid off her looks. She had to check it before it got out of hand.

Speaking of work, Honey looked over at the digital clock and saw it was almost time for her to do her thing. Back to the plantation. Night in and night out, shake your ass, get some tips. It was all routine to Honey. A routine that she was getting tired of. She had to find a better way.

Honey pulled herself away from Bone and stood over his sleeping form. There were times when she hated him with a passion and there were times when she felt for him. The coke that was racing through her brain told her to take his pistol and shoot him. With Bone dead, no one would have a hold on her. But that would be stupid. If she went to jail, who would take care of Star? Instead, Honey took some money from his pocket, slid on her clothes, and left.

Fat Mike sat in the passenger seat of the Caddy, chewing a cigar. He should've been pleased that he had finally got ahold of Tommy and got the street prince to meet with him. But this couldn't dull the ache of Gee-Gee's words. They stung him to the quick and put the Cissarro capo in a dark mood.

"So, you finally got ahold of that fucking boot, Tommy, huh?" Nicky asked.

"Yeah. Prick calls me this morning, talking about he's returning my phone call."

"So the kid brother got you in?"

"I dunno. Either that or he mentioned the fact that I approached him and Tommy got nervous. Either way, we'll finally get a chance to sit down."

"Hmm, what are ya gonna do, Mike?"

"I dunno. I'll see how Tommy acts when we meet. I'll move based on that."

"Fucking niggers," Nicky chuckled. "Mr. G let Poppa get too big, man. That spade has got too much power. Too much."

"You're right about that, Nick. Poppa has a lot of weight in this city. Even without the connections we sent his way, Tom Clark would be a heavy hitter in the game. The white faces on his coattail only double that power."

"Maybe we should talk to Mr. G about getting rid of Poppa?"

"That'll be our last resort," Mike told him. "Poppa is damn near a made guy. If it wasn't for his black skin, he might have already been sponsored into our thing."

"Thank God for small miracles." Nicky chuckled. "So, you think he's gonna move the dope?"

"If he knows what's good for him, he will."

"I hear Poppa's retiring soon. Gonna leave everything to Tommy officially."

"Jesus, Mary, and Joseph," Mike said, slapping his forehead. "Things will really go to shit then. The only thing keeping that fucking baboon Tommy in check is Poppa. If the kid gets free rein of the streets it'll be like the fucking thirties."

"So what does Mr. G think about all this, ah?" Nicky asked curiously.

"He ain't no fan of Tommy, but he doesn't give a shit which Clark is running the show. As long as the niggers are kept in check and he gets his tribute once a month, he's cool."

Nicky let a few ideas roll around in his head, before asking the next line of questions. "Okay, so we can't kill Poppa. What if we clip Tommy?"

"Hmm." Mike thought deeply on it. "That's always a possibility. But that'd be risky too. Poppa's still as vicious as ever. If we kill his boy, he's gonna come at us hard."

"Fuck him," Nicky said slyly. "We got the whole fucking Cissarro family behind us. We'd blow those fucking spear chuckers clean back to Africa."

"Don't underestimate those guys," Mike warned. "Poppa's got his shit together. He's got an army behind him and some friends in very high places. You don't get to be a boss without knowing how to play this game. Even if it is a crew of niggers. Besides that, what do you think Mr. G is gonna do to us when he finds out what our little war is about? You know the rules, Nicky," he said seriously. "Deal and you die."

"Mike, all I'm saying is somebody's gonna have to go. This girlie bullshit between us and them is gonna crumble sooner or later."

"I hate to admit it, but I know, pal. Poppa's crew is getting too strong and personalities are bound to clash. But when it happens, I plan to be ready. I got a few people that I've been looking at for the last few months. I have a number of candidates lined up if this thing with the Clarks goes sour."

"I knew you'd have a plan, Mike," Nicky said admiringly. "Anybody I might know?"

"A few people," Mike said, thinking on it. "One prime candidate though. Bone from Two Hundred and Fourth."

"I heard of Bone," Nicky said. "Mean son of a bitch."

"Mean indeed," Mike agreed. "But the question is, can he be controlled? Niggers like Bone ain't got shit to live for but the hustle. They'd sooner sell their mother's shit than do an honest day's work. Put a nigger like him in power and he might get crazy with it."

"At least he'd be easier to control than Tommy."

"That's what I'm hoping. Besides that, there's already bad blood between Bone and the Clarks. I'm sure he's just looking for a reason."

Nicky bit his bottom lip and eyed his boss wearily. He had a question on his lips, but was hesitant about asking it. Figuring it was something that needed to be addressed, Nicky just came out with it. "What if we could kill two birds with one stone?"

"How do you mean, Nick?" Mike asked.

"What if we could get rid of Poppa and Tommy in one shot?"

"How do you figure we do that?"

"Well," Nicky continued, "it's like you said before: We can't whack Tommy without having to worry about Poppa making a move, but what if we whacked Poppa instead?"

"Nicky, are you high?" Mike asked, seriously. "If we were to whack Poppa, Tommy would come after us with everything he had. Not to mention that we'd have to come up with one hell of a lie to tell Mr. G."

"Mike, you and I both know that Heath was connected. He ran numbers for Mr. G and Tommy had him wacked. If we could convince Mr. G that Poppa gave the order, that would give us a little leverage."

"True," Mike agreed, "but what about Tommy? He'd go ape shit. That could cause a lot of bloodshed."

"Yeah," Nicky smiled devilishly. "That's why we get someone else to do the dirt for us."

"Nicky, Poppa's like the fucking president. Who the hell are we gonna get to whack him out?"

"Bone," Nicky said seriously. "You said yourself, he's looking for a reason. Why don't we give him one? We tell Bone that if he whacks Poppa, he can have the City with our blessing. With our own pawn in the seat, you can still move your H, Mike."

"So far so good, Nicky. But there's still the Tommy factor. He'd come at Bone with everything he's got. Bone and his crew are strong, but no match for the Clarks."

"Yeah, Tommy's strong, but he's the one that gave the order to hit Heath. The police already got a hard-on for Tommy. If they can somehow be pushed in the right direction . . ."

"They'd put Tommy away," Mike said, catching on.

"Now you see where I'm going with it. Either way, we're rid of Tommy."

"Nicky," Mike said smiling broadly, "I'm glad you're on our side. We'll try talking to the Clarks first, but if they still don't go along with us, we'll put our plan into motion."

CHAPTER 17

SWAN SAT IN THE beat-up dodge, smoking a cigarette and waiting. He looked at the picture Mo's watcher had provided him with and shook his head. The kid he had been sent to speak with was tall and lanky, with a mouth full of gold. He sported one of those jail caesars with the half-moon and had a silly expression on his face. The kid didn't look very intimidating at all. But looks could be deceiving. It didn't really make a difference. He had no intentions of speaking with the young man. He was going to kill him.

Swan sat up when he saw the target bop out of the building, giving his crew dap. He was with a young white girl, acting like he was Poppa Clark himself. A few seconds later, he was joined by a huge man, whom Swan assumed was his bodyguard. Mo's watcher had never mentioned the target having a bodyguard. This was just another obstacle that he would have to get over.

Swan removed his .40s and placed one in each pocket of his leather jacket. He gave one more cautious sweep of the block and got out of the car. He walked at a normal pace, keeping his head down.

Blending with the crackheads that were coming and going, Swan got right up on the target before anyone even noticed he was there.

"What up?" Swan addressed the group.

"What you need?" a skinny hustler asked.

"I need to holla at y'all cats," Swan responded, keeping his hands tucked inside his jacket pockets.

"Fuck you wanna talk to us about?" the target asked, trying to look mean.

"This shit y'all got going on"—Swan motioned to the flow of people—"I need y'all to shut it down."

"Shut it down?" the target asked, looking at his crew. "Are you fucking crazy?"

"Not crazy, fam'," Swan said, looking him dead in the eye. "A messenger. Y'all probably heard of my boss, Poppa Clark?"

"From out of New York," the target said. "I heard of him. And?"

"And he's sent me here to talk to you. This thing y'all got is fucking up our business. I need you to shut it down or get on with us."

The target looked at Swan for a minute, then burst out laughing. His crew joined in and they had a laugh at Swan's expense. Swan wanted to wild out, but he had to play it cool. He was out-manned and probably out-gunned, but this had never stopped him before. Swan liked those kind of odds.

"Miss me wit' that bullshit," the target told him. "This ain't the City, fam'. Poppa don't run this. This is my shit. I say when we open and close."

"Dawg"—Swan tightened his jaw—"you ain't hearing me, are you?"

"Nigga, I heard you," the target shot back, "but that don't mean I'm listening. Why don't you get the fuck out of here before something happens to you, shorty."

It had become obvious that these fake-ass hustlers weren't going to listen to reason, but Swan had planned for this. He fired two shots from his left pocket. The first one caught the target in the gut and the second one severed an artery in his neck. The target dropped to the ground, choking on his own blood.

The bodyguard moved for his gun, but Swan was ready for him too. He removed the other .40 from his right pocket and popped him in the head. He too slumped to the ground. The white girl began to scream, while the target's crew stood there, frozen in place.

"Let's try this again," Swan said, waving the two smoking guns. "This shit is shut down! Ain't nothing popping. If I hear that you niggaz is still up here trying to sling, I'm dumping on the whole block. Women and children included. You silly mutha fuckas understand me?" The crew nodded their heads in unison. "Good."

Swan backed away from the crew and headed back to the car. As he walked back to the auto, he tried to contain his laughter. Mo had acted like these kids had a tight operation, but Swan was able to murder their leader with little effort. He couldn't wait until he got back to the block to tell Tommy about it.

Swan had just opened the car door when something slammed into his left shoulder. He fell against the car and tried to turn himself, when he was hit in the back. Swan slid down the side of the car and collapsed, partially inside. He looked over his shoulder and saw the skinny hustler coming toward him, holding a pistol.

Swan fought to stay focused. The pain from the gunshots almost caused him to black out, but he held it together. The slugs hit his vest, so he was good, but they still knocked the wind out of him. It seemed that the hustlers had a little more heart than Swan had given them credit for. The skinny hustler moved in for the kill, but Swan was waiting for him.

"Sucka-ass nigga," the skinny hustler said, advancing on Swan. "Trying to come up here with that shit. Who's shut down now?"

Swan had an answer for him when he popped up from behind the car door, holding the shotgun. He pulled the slide, then squeezed the trigger. The shotgun roared and spit fire into the skinny hustler's face. Before he could hit the ground, Swan hit him in the chest, sending the skinny hustler skidding into the street.

Without taking the time to admire his handiwork, Swan stepped over the body and began to fire at the crew. He caught one of them in the back, but the rest scattered. "Punk-ass niggaz," Swan spat. He limped back to the ride and flopped behind the wheel. The engine came to life and Swan got up out of there. He would make a brief stop at the motel to gather his things, then he was on the next thing smoking back to New York.

Tommy and his team walked into the restaurant on 93rd Street looking around suspiciously. He had finally decided to meet with Mike and get it out of the way. The fat man wasn't going to like what Tommy said, but he had to respect it. In case he didn't, he made sure he and Herc were strapped.

Tommy looked over at his little brother and tried to read his facial expression. He couldn't see a thing. Shai wore a mask of complete calm. He was neither excited nor scared. Tommy also noticed how his brother was making a mental note of his surroundings and the people. He had trained him well.

"Tommy," Mike shouted, raising a meaty palm. "Over here."

Tommy led the way to the table, with Herc in tow and Shai bringing up the rear. Mike was seated at the table with Nicky at his side. Tommy exchanged handshakes with the men, while Herc folded his arms aggressively. Shai just nodded.

"Sit down, fellas." Mike smiled. "Youz guys hungry?"

"Nah," Tommy said, sitting in the seat opposite Mike. "We're good. You said you wanted to talk, here I am. What's good?"

"Geez, Tommy," Nicky cut in. "Now is that any way to greet two pals?"

"Don't play wit' me, kid," Tommy said coldly. "We ain't never been friends, so save that slimy shit for the next bird, ya heard? Now as I was saying"—he turned back to Mike—"you wanted to talk to me?"

"Direct and to the point as ever," Mike said with a shake of his head. "Yeah, Tommy. I got a few things I need to talk to you about. The first being my man Freddy. What's up with that?"

"You should be more careful who you send to parley with me," Tommy said with ice in his voice. "That little mutha fucka came into my place talking out his ass. If a man comes into my domain and doesn't show the proper respect, then he gets dealt with accordingly. This goes for anyone."

Mike didn't miss the light threat. He let it go for the time being. "I can understand that, Tommy. But Freddy is a friend of mine and you beat him pretty bad."

"He got what his hand called for," Tommy responded dryly.

"Still," Mike said sternly, "he was one of my soldiers. Meaning he was under my protection. How does that look on me if I don't do anything?"

"Mike," Tommy said, matching his tone, "I ain't got nothing to do with what's going on in ya camp, or how it looks if one of yours gets stomped out. He disrespected me and I beat his ass. Period. Now however you wanna deal with that, is on you." Tommy made sure he was looking Mike square in the eye when he said this.

Herc had noticed his boss's tone and let his hands slide to where his twin .375s were tucked. Nicky had caught his motion and slid his hand to the Glock in his belt. Both men knew that their bosses could be hotheaded, so neither one knew what would come of the stare down. Either way they were both ready to do their jobs efficiently.

"Come on, T," Mike said, trying to defuse the situation. "You know I ain't one to raise a stink. I understand why you did what you did, but understand my position: Freddy is one of my soldiers. That means he's supposed to be untouchable to any and all outside of our order. I gotta have some type of restitution."

"Restitution?" Tommy asked, as if he had never heard the word before. "Fuck is you talking about? You want me to pay this nigga? Hell nah, son. I ain't wit' all that."

"Nah, not money. Maybe you could settle up some other kinda way? Maybe if you apologized to Freddy in front of our crew—"

"Fuck outta here," Tommy cut him off. "I ain't apologizing to that rat fuck. Fuck Freddy. Mike, I know you didn't call me down here for this shit. I thought you wanted to talk about that other thing."

Mike was beginning to get frustrated and Tommy knew it. It had been his plan since he returned Mike's phone call. He intended to get the Italian mad enough to do or say something stupid, then he would have a legit reason to cut him off. Freddy's ass whipping had been the result of poor judgment, but Tommy was going to turn that to his advantage.

"Okay," Mike said, gritting his teeth. "What's this I hear about you won't take my dope?"

"And? It's just like I told Freddy's bitch ass, we're getting shorted on that bunk you gave us. We gotta recoup."

"Tommy, did I miss something here? You boys sell dope for us, right?"

"No," Tommy said flatly. "My men sling heroin for my father and me. We buy it from you. We don't work for y'all, son. Please don't get it fucked up."

"Tommy." Mike raised his voice. "What the fuck is wrong with you? You forget your place?"

"Hell nah." Tommy smiled. "Actually, I'm just starting to learn it. And it ain't at the foot of your table, homie. We're an independent, just like y'all, baby. Treat us with some respect."

"Tommy, this shit you're talking is fucking the game up."

"No, you're fucking the game up!" Tommy shouted at the big man. "We, soldiers and captains, deal amongst each other, not civilians. Who the fuck gave you the right to approach my brother?"

"What?" Mike asked, startled. "I didn't—"

"Don't lie." Tommy cut him off. "Shai"—he spun to his brother—"did this nigga approach you the other night?"

Shai was caught totally off guard by the question. When he had told Tommy about his meeting with Mike he didn't expect him to put it out there like that. Everyone was looking at Shai, waiting for his response. The air was so thick that he felt light-headed. He looked from his brother to Mike and nodded.

"What's up with that shit, Mike?" Tommy asked angrily.

"You got it wrong, T," Mike assured him. "I just asked Shai to see if he could get you to talk to me. Nothing more. And if I were you, I'd watch my tone."

"Well, you ain't me, Mike. And I'll talk at whatever fucking octave I choose. I ain't one of ya goombas, so don't try to play me."

"Tommy, I think you need to slow down and think about the way you're sounding right now."

"Oh." Tommy smirked. "I know just how I sound. Like a nigga that's fed up. Honestly, y'all been shitting on us for a while and disguising it as friendship and fucking handouts. We know our worth now, Mike. Things are gonna have to change or we can't do business anymore."

Mike's face turned beet red with anger. He couldn't believe that the same kid he had seen running around playing corners was talking to him like a fucking nobody. It was obvious to Mike what was going on: the little prick had found another dope connect and was trying to cut him out of his taste. Before he could respond, Nicky was on his feet.

"You ungrateful nigger," Nicky shouted. "We put you on the fucking map. You fucking—"

"Go ahead," Herc said, raising his .357s. "Say it again."

Shai looked at the exchange in pure shock. The incident with Bone was intense, but it was nothing compared to this. Shai would've shot Bone if he had to, but he wasn't a killer. On the other hand, each of the four men locked in the current conflict were. If something didn't happen to stop it, there was gonna be some shit in the seafood restaurant.

"Gentlemen," Shai spoke up, startling everyone. "I don't mean to get in your business, 'cause I ain't got nothing to do with this street shit, but I think we should put the weapons away and talk about this. It wouldn't do either side any good if the police come up in here and find them hammers."

"Mind ya business, Shai," Tommy warned.

"No," Mike cut in. "The kid's got a point." Mike tried to sound like he was in control, but he was actually relieved that Shai had interjected. He really didn't want to bang out with Tommy, especially on even ground.

Everyone looked at Shai. The youngster was totally out of pocket for putting his mouth in their business, but he was right. They were about to get themselves caught up in some shit that they really didn't need. Mike and Tommy gave each other a final stare before waving their men down.

"Tommy," Mike said in a low tone, "when has it ever been a problem with you taking dope from me?"

"Since y'all started trying to clown us," Tommy responded defiantly. "That shit y'all been dumping on us for the last few months ain't been worth nothing. It had so much cut on it already, we couldn't even break even. With all due respect, why should our children go hungry, 'cause some guinea mutha fucka got a lil' greedy? That shit just don't add up to me, Mike."

"Listen." Mike smiled. "You take this weight as a favor to me and we'll settle up down the line, eh?"

Shai and Herc tensed. They knew by the undertone of Mike's voice that he was trying to give Tommy an ultimatum and they both knew that Tommy would respond by laying down the gauntlet.

"Fuck I look like to you?" Tommy snarled.

The glove had been thrown.

"You must not have heard shit I just said, Mike. We ain't fo' that shit, man. The Clarks can't afford to take too many losses. It's bad for business. You understand, don't you?" Tommy smiled coldly at Mike.

"You're making a mistake, Tommy," Mike hissed. "Don't do it like this."

"Y'all niggaz need to learn some respect," Tommy said slyly as he lit his cigarette. "We've been your watchdogs for too long, Mike. You mutha fuckas can't show us a little respect, then fuck it. Our business is concluded."

Tommy was the only one smiling. Shai glanced away while Herc kept looking from the Italian to his friend. People in the streets always said Tommy might be a lil' crazy, but Herc was sure that he was full crazy. He had just possibly started a war with the Cissarro family. A war that would record many casualties. This was bad.

Mike watched in shock as Tommy got up and turned for the door. He couldn't believe the balls on this nigger, but it was playing out just as Nicky had said. The Clarks were getting too big and something would have to be done about it.

"Okay, T," Mike said behind him. "We'll see about this shit."

Tommy never turned around to respond. He just kept walking for the door. Herc backed out, with his .357s at his sides, but still ready. Shai looked from Mike to Tommy and back again, trying to figure out what the hell went down.

CHAPTER 18

AS SOON AS SWAN returned to New York, he was brought to see Poppa. He was tired and his nerves were shot, but one didn't refuse a summons from Poppa Clark. When he came into Poppa's study, it was only Poppa, Butch, and Angelo. Swan's palms sweated rivers as anticipation swept over him.

"Come on in here." Poppa waved him in. Swan timidly stepped forward. "You did good, son. Real good."

"Thanks, Poppa," Swan said in a low tone.

"I know you done some stupid shit in the past, but it's all a part of a process. We make mistakes and we learn from them. Have you learned from yours?"

"Yes, sir."

"Swan, this is a great responsibility I'm about to lay on you. You will be the boss of the hoods assigned to you, answering directly to Tommy. You will be responsible for your soldiers, your turf, and Tommy's money. Do you understand and accept this responsibility of your own free will? Will you swear on the life of your child to put none before this family?"

"Yes," Swan said confidently. "I will lay down my life for this family, Poppa. All I want is a chance to prove myself."

"Come here," Poppa said, spreading his arms. Swan stepped forward and accepted Poppa's embrace. "You're in now," Poppa whispered in his ear. "Remain loyal and strong and you will prosper. Waiver and you will die."

Swan buried his face in Poppa's chest so he couldn't see the tears in his eyes. He wasn't crying because he was scared, he was crying because he was happy. Poppa had always treated Swan like a son. He showed him more love than his real father. Now Swan would be able to return the favor. He would murder or die for the love of his new family.

"I think that was a bad move, Tommy," Herc voiced.

"Here you go with that shit," Tommy said, irritated. "Fuck that greaseball mutha fucka. What he gonna do? That nigga got some frog in him, then let's do it. Fuck you mean you think it's a bad move?"

"Herc's right," Shai added. "I don't think Poppa would've approved of the way you handled that."

"What is this, a fucking mutiny?" Tommy looked from Herc to Shai. "The last I heard, I was running things in the streets, while Poppa is building castles in the sky. I say how things get handled on the streets. I might've been a lil' brass about it, but fuck it. Them Italians don't respect us, kid. Why should we keep fucking with them?"

"You could've at least waited until things were secure with the Wongs," Shai suggested. "They say they'll make good on it, but who the fuck are they?"

"Get a load of this shit," Tommy said, icing Shai. "You spend one day in the streets and you're giving me advice? Let me hip you to something, little brother. You might know the game, but remember who schooled you."

"You schooled him," Herc picked up. "But he's making more sense than you right now. Poppa's gonna flip if this shit blows up."

"So fucking what!" Tommy barked. "This is my show. Let the old man focus on retirement, I can handle this shit myself. I need some time to think on it. For right now, everybody just be cool and keep ya traps closed. I'll call a meeting of the street lieutenants tomorrow night. Before the meeting, I'll speak to Poppa. For right now, nobody says anything."

"The nerve of those fucking jigs," Nicky vented. "Tommy has got to go, Mike."

"Why don't you relax and let me think, Nicky!" Mike barked. He leaned back in the booth and massaged his temples. He cursed himself silently for not seeing this coming. That little prick Tommy had gotten another dope connect right under his nose. Mike had other outlets for his dope, but nobody was moving weight like Tommy. Now that outlet was gone. Mike had a serious problem.

"Fucking prick," Mike said out loud. "This fucking boot has gone too far."

"He's gotta go, Mike."

"Yeah." Mike rubbed his chin. "I think it's time to set the wheels in motion. I just wanna avoid an all-out war."

"So, what are we gonna do, let this spade spit in out faces?" Nicky asked heatedly.

"Hell no," Mike said, flipping his cell phone open. "Obviously there's no reasoning with Tommy. I plan to approach Poppa about it, but in the meantime, I'm gonna make sure my ass is covered."

"Who you calling?" Nicky asked.

"My insurance policy." Mike smiled.

"We always getting the bullshit jobs," Fritz complained.

"Why you always complaining about some shit?" Angelo said, annoyed. "Every time I turn around, you're complaining."

"I'm saying, yo, we always putting in work and never reap the rewards. Shit, I didn't even get invited to the meeting at Poppa's house."

"The meeting was for lieutenants. You ain't a lieutenant."

"I don't see why not. We put in more work than anybody Poppa has rolling with him. You got bumped up, why the fuck didn't I?"

"Maybe 'cause you complain so fucking much," Gator said from the backseat. "Ever since I got here you ain't did nothing but complain. You niggaz is living like kings under my cousin and you're beefing. You need to bring yo' ass down to Florida. We'll show you sweet-ass niggaz how to grind."

"Ain't nothing sweet about me, kid," Fritz assured him. "You better hold that shit down."

"Why don't both of y'all be cool," Angelo cut in. "We came here to do a job, so let's do it and get the fuck gone."

The tension between Gator and Fritz was obvious. For some reason Gator was distrustful of Fritz and vice versa. Neither man really wanted to be around the other, but they had been put together for this job. They would settle their differences down the line, but for right now Angelo was in charge and no one wanted to argue with him.

"Shane," Angelo addressed the fourth occupant of the car. "You see this nigga come out?"

"No," Shane said. "When I saw him go in, I called. While I waited for you guys I had a crackhead watching the door. He hasn't come out yet."

"And you're sure about what you told Poppa?" Fritz added, wanting to feel like he was saying something.

"As sure as my ass is black," Shane assured him. "That mutha fucka Frost is violating."

"Then he gotta get dealt with," Angelo said.

"Man," Gator sighed, as he got out of the car. "Fuck this waiting shit."

"Gator, what the hell are you doing?" Angelo called after him.

"Man, I got this. Y'all niggaz wait like five minutes, then follow me inside." Without another word, Gator slipped inside the bar. Angelo looked at Fritz who looked at Shane. Each man held the same confused expression. None of them knew exactly what Gator was up to, but they were sure it was going to be colorful.

Bone sat with Ahmad inside of Pan-Pan's, watching the traffic. There was a time when their visits this far south would've been short and to the point. But times were changing. Their crew was getting larger, so they were becoming increasingly bold. Tommy didn't have eyes and ears everywhere. It was in these blind spots that Bone and his followers lurked, spreading their influence. They had infected a good number of Tommy's lesser soldiers and he had his head too far up his ass to notice.

Bone turned around and saw the huge form of Fat Mike appear in the doorway. He was led by a weasel-faced man wearing a pair of green polyester slacks that looked like they were a size too small. He damn near tackled a woman who was coming out, trying to make sure that he was the one to open the door for Mike.

Mike stepped into the spot and looked around as if he had smelled something rancid. He squeezed past the tiny line of people waiting for their orders and made his way to where Bone was sitting. Bone had noticed him come in, but he acted surprised when Mike's shadow loomed over him.

"Oh," Bone said. "I didn't see you come in. What up, Mike?" He extended his hand.

"How's it going, Bone?" Mike replied, taking the young man's hand. "Glad you decided to come and speak to me."

"Hey, you said you had something that might interest me," Bone said with a shrug, "so here I am."

"Sure, sure, kid. See, I got something that I think will work out for the both of us."

"Oh, yeah?"

"Sure do," Mike said as he plopped onto the two stools to Bone's right. "We've got a common interest," he whispered, "New

York and all the riches in it. There's a lot of dough on the streets, man."

"Yeah, I know it," Bone said coolly. "But I got my own thing going uptown. Fuck makes you think I give a shit what goes on in the rest of the City?"

"Because I know you ain't no shit-for-brains corner boy. You're a leader, much like myself. We see things on a grander spectrum than most people. That's how I figured you'd see the beauty of my deal."

"I can't promise you anything," Bone admitted. "But I'll hear you out, Mike."

"Fair enough. I'm sure it's no secret that there's tension between the Clarks and my crew. We've been having sort of a difference of opinion. Alas," Mike said, shrugging, "I think our business will soon be concluded."

"What's that got to do with me?" Bone asked, trying to hide the greed in his voice.

"I know we've only been doing business for a short time, but I know who you are, Bone—Poppa's fallen angel. That was a shit deal you got, man. Sure, you got a little light fingered, but that's only because they weren't giving you the proper respect. You should've been promoted along with the other lieutenants. It stinks to get passed over."

Mike paused to study the effects of his words on Bone. He could see frustration etched all over the man's face as he relived the humiliation in his mind. Mike knew he had him. Bone already had a grudge against Tommy. All it would take was a few well-placed words to push him in the right direction.

"Stinks like hell," Mike continued. "Guess there's not a lot of loyalty amongst thieves?"

"Okay," Bone said, frustrated. "You know your history, so what?"

"I'm getting to that. Bone, let's call a spade a spade, no offense. Things are changing on the streets. New rules call for new blood. Tommy and me did some pretty big things, but he's getting too big for himself. He doesn't understand business. If somebody puts you on top, you don't repay them by spitting in their face. His fifteen minutes of fame are over."

"What are you saying to me, Mike?" Bone asked, knowing full well what Mike meant.

"Bone," Mike said seriously, "I think you know what I mean. I'm offering you Poppa's operation. You'll be the head nigg— I mean the guy in charge. Not only that, but you'll have my full support. No strings."

Bone fought back the smile that was trying to spread across his lips. He was finally going to get a shot at greatness. With the Italians behind him, his crew would soon be able to rival any on the streets.

"Okay," Ahmad cut in unexpectedly, "the deal sounds sweet enough, but what's the catch? You claim to be able to help us take the streets, what do you get out of all this, Mike, and what price do you ask of us?"

Mike looked to Bone, to see if he should answer to his henchman. Bone nodded and Mike continued with his speech.

"Simple enough, gentlemen. I get to keep moving my work and we're both rid of a common pain in the ass. What could be sweeter than that?"

Bone waved Ahmad silent before he could say anything else. Bone saw a golden opportunity being laid at his feet. He would be able to repay Tommy for his slight and take over the empire. Killing Poppa would be hard, but not impossible. As he thought about it, he knew just who to call in for support. It would involve some risk and a few lives to be sacrificed. But it was a small price to pay for a chance at revenge.

"Okay," Bone continued, "say we accept your terms. Killing Poppa isn't gonna be easy. He's got a strong crew behind him and Tommy isn't gonna lay down for it."

"Now you're catching on," Mike responded wickedly. "Tommy is powerful, but only because Poppa made it that way. If we cut out the foundation, the house of Clark will fall."

"So you mean . . ."

"Indeed I do," Mike assured him. "Sit with me for a while and let's discuss our future."

Gator paused in the doorway, allowing his eyes to adjust to the dimly lit lounge. He stepped into the tiny place and immediately gagged from the stench of someone smoking a dipped cigarette. Gator knew a few cats who smoked sherm in Florida and Cali, but he didn't know that the habit had made its way to New York.

He held his breath as he moved through the light crowd to the bar area. Sitting at the end of the bar was a cat matching the description that Shane had given him. Frost was a little bastard who wore a lot of ten-carat jewels. Gator examined the jewelry from a distance and reasoned that it would be a waste of time to rob him.

Gator sat a few stools down from the little man and ordered a Corona. He sipped the beer slowly, keeping his eye on Frost. The little man seemed to be tipsy as he flirted with some girls who were way too young to be in a bar. He still wasn't sure that it was him until one of the girls called his name.

"That's right, baby," Frost slurred. "I put the 'g' in gangsta. Frost is that nigga."

The girls giggled and hung on Frost's every word. As long as he was buying drinks, they would laugh at him and boost his ego. Gator, on the other hand, was trying to figure if he should kill Frost inside the bar or try and get him outside. Gator's gold choppers ground together as he began to formulate a plan in his head.

"Did you say Frost?" Gator asked, loud enough for his target to hear him.

"Who the fuck is that?" Frost squinted.

"It's me," Gator said moving closer. "I know I ain't put on that much weight?"

"I don't know you, man."

"Frost, you really gonna act like you don't know ya boy?" Gator inched closer.

"I said I don't know you."

"It's Ty," Gator lied. "Remember? We used to work for Tommy Clark together."

Frost relaxed a little at the mention of a familiar name. He didn't really recognize the man with the cornrows, but he had worked with so many different people during his run with Tommy that it was hard to remember them all. Frost figured that Gator was just another dick-riding nigga that heard he was getting it and wanted to be down. He decided that he would humor him.

"Yeah, yeah." Frost sneered. "That was so long ago I almost forgot. What you up to, nigga?"

"Nothing much. Just got out of lockup."

"Shit, what you go down for?" Frost asked.

"Fucking drug charge," Gator lied. "Them niggaz had me down for a minute. Hard time, smell me? And I was fucked up."

"TC ain't hold you down?"

"Hell, nah," Gator barked. "Niggaz left me to rot."

"That's some cold shit," Frost frowned. "Coward-ass Clark niggaz."

"Yeah, but he did give me something when I touched down," Gator said as he got within spitting distance of Frost.

"What did he give you?" Frost asked, actually interested.

"A message." Gator smiled. Frost's eyes widened as he found himself looking at two rows of jagged gold teeth. "We know what you've been up to, Frost."

Frost smiled weakly at the big man. He could've shot himself for letting a stranger get that close up on him. He got caught slipping, but he wouldn't be undone that easily. "Oh, yeah?" He smiled. "Tell him that I said, 'Suck my dick!' " With a fake and a swing, a beer bottle shattered against Gator's head. When he staggered back clutching the gash in his head, Frost darted for the door.

Angelo was making his way to the bar entrance, followed by Fritz and Shane. Before he could reach for the door, Frost came running out. He brushed past a surprised Angelo and ran straight into Fritz's fist. Frost staggered backward and collapsed to the ground. Angelo bent down and yanked the little man up by his collar. Frost was dazed but well aware of what was about to happen to him. He would learn that his actions came with a hard price.

Gator came rushing out of the bar shortly after. He had a crazed look in his eyes as blood dripped from his head down the side of his face. He looked around until he found his target. With a snarl he drew his gun and approached Frost.

"Sneaky mutha fucka," Gator hissed. "Suck ya dick? Nah, why don't you suck on this!"

Before anyone could react, Gator leveled his .45 and dumped twice into Frost's face. Blood splattered on Angelo as part of Frost's jaw and skull came away. The body hit the ground twitching, but Gator wasn't finished. He stepped over the mutilated body and fired three more shots into Frost. The body had ceased its twitching.

Angelo nodded to his peoples and they made haste back to the car. Gator followed slowly behind the trio, touching his wound. He took one more look at Frost and shot him in the face before sprinting to catch the others.

A few hours after the Frost murder, Shai found himself in the Bronx, trying to find something to get into. After going through the motions with Tommy all day, Shai's nerves were shot. Things on the streets were beginning to heat up and lines were being drawn in the sand. Shai had a bad feeling about what was about to go down, but no one would listen to him. Poppa was too concerned with retirement, and Tommy was too busy treating him like a kid. Nobody seemed to be getting the bigger picture.

In an attempt to take his mind off things, Shai decided to hit the strip club. His entire day had consisted of hood shit. Guns and violence were the language of the streets. After all that Shai had seen and done throughout the last few days, he needed a change of scenery.

Swan was still MIA, so Shai found himself kicking it with his cousin Gator. When Poppa asked Shai to let Gator tag along, he naturally rebelled. He didn't feel like babysitting his country-ass cousin. He figured Gator would be loud and embarrassing, but he turned out to be real cool. Gator was country as hell, but he was gangsta with his. He didn't pester Shai about what to do and what not to do. Gator was more down-to-earth than anyone else Shai hung with—with the exception of Swan—plus he was down to bust on a nigga without question.

"Shit, I ain't seen you in years," Shai said, lighting the freshly rolled blunt. "What you been up to, cousin?"

"Shit," Gator said, in a Southern drawl, "I got in a little trouble back home. They had a nigga on the run, baby. Florida got too hot for the kid, so here I am in da Apple."

"Fuck you do, kill somebody?" Shai joked.

"Yeah," Gator said very seriously.

Shai shot Gator a look to see if he was playing, but there was no humor in his face. "Fuck happened to your head?" Shai asked, nodding at the bandage.

"Ah, this wasn't 'bout shit," Gator said, touching the wound. "Fuck-nigga hit me wit' a bottle earlier. He was loud talking 'bout Poppa, so we had to push his shit back."

"So, you're working for Poppa too?"

"I don't know what to call it." Gator shrugged. "I'm just trying to live. It's a lot of money floating around in New York. I just wanna get me some of it. Know what I'm saying, cuz?"

"Yeah, I can dig it."

"Say, cuz," Gator changed the subject, "where we riding to? We been coasting through this mutha fucka for about an hour and ain't got no destination."

"Be cool, man," Shai instructed, as he passed the blunt. He drove down a few more blocks, before finding the spot he was looking for.

It was a down-low spot not far from the Madison Avenue Bridge. The outside of the club wasn't much to look at, but the interior was nice. The foyer was an oval-shaped portal with a room off to the left for checking coats. The inside of the hall was a wide open space, with five tiny stages for the strippers to do their thing. The bar was a large horseshoe with a DJ booth suspended above it.

"This spot is all right," Gator said, looking around.

"Told you to be cool." Shai smirked. "My man Snoop told me about this place."

"Damn," Gator said, eyeing a light-skinned girl that was strutting her stuff. "Be sure to tell that nigga thank you."

Shai and Gator posted up by the bar and ordered some drinks. One after the other, girls came out and shook their moneymakers, while the men in the club tipped or gawked. Shai only half paid attention to the show. His mind was on the streets and what he could do to help ease the tension that Tommy was creating. A familiar form climbing onto the stage caught Shai's attention. He had to blink twice to make sure his eyes weren't deceiving him.

Honey stood wide-legged on the stage, wearing a leather halter and garter belt. Her blond hair was covered by a red wig, giving her an exotic look. Her arms and legs sported body paint in tribal designs. Shai looked on in shock as Honey began to go into her routine.

She was amazing to watch on stage. She moved with the grace of a gazelle, but her eye held the fire of a lioness. Honey worked the pole and the crowd as the patrons looked on like deer caught in headlights. Shai could feel his anger beginning to mount as the patrons tipped Honey and touched her at the same time. She wasn't Shai's girl, but he couldn't help the way he was feeling. It was as if they were violating her in some way and he didn't like it.

Honey got off the stage four minutes later, dripping with sweat. The light caught her damp skin, making her more beautiful than she already was. Shai watched furiously as a young cat whispered into her ear and Honey began leading him to the VIP section. He tried to remain calm, but the next thing he knew, his legs were carrying him in their direction.

"What up?" Shai called behind her.

"Shai?" Honey said, turning around, startled. "What are you doing here?"

"Taking in the sights," he said, glaring at the young cat icily. "I need to holla at you."

"Holla on ya own time," the young cat cut in. "She's busy right now."

"I don't think I was talking to you." By now Gator had eased up behind the kid. "Mind ya business, money."

"Fuck is you talking to, frail-ass nigga?"

"What!" Shai snarled.

At the same time the young cat moved, so did Gator. Holding his Corona bottle like a club, he swung around in an arc and smashed the young cat in the head. Glass and beer flew everywhere. The young cat wobbled and hit the floor. When the young cat's peoples moved to help, Gator spun and drew his pistol.

"Fuck is y'all niggaz trying to do?" Gator hissed. "Buck, nigga! I dare you!"

By now the other patrons of the bar had begun to scatter, no one wanting to catch a stray bullet. The bouncers moved in, but Gator had it for them too. When the first bouncer got close enough, Gator hit him with a chair. Seeing that the young men meant business, the other bouncers swarmed in, wielding bats and blackjacks. Gator stopped them all short, firing into the air. A miniature stampede broke out, giving Gator, Shai, and Honey an opportunity to escape.

Gator came out first, gun drawn and gold fangs bared. Shai followed, with Honey wrapped in his leather jacket. She protested a little, but allowed Shai to shove her into the backseat. The trio sped off into the night just as police were arriving on the scene.

For the next few minutes no one spoke. Gator sat in the passenger seat, gun in lap, staring out the window. Shai clutched the wheel, weaving in and out of the light traffic, looking in the rearview for signs of pursuit. Honey just sat in the back, still not believing what Shai had just pulled. Once Shai was sure that no one was pursuing them, he pulled over on a dark block. He put the car in park and hopped out.

"I need to talk to you," Shai said, looking at Honey. She just sat there, unmoving. "I said, I need to talk to you," he repeated. Still nothing. "Please."

For the first time since leaving the club, Honey looked up at Shai. His face was still twisted into a mask of anger, but his eyes told a different story. They were sincere and concerned. She wanted to be mad at Shai. She wanted to flip on him and demand that he put her in a cab, but when she looked into those soft brown eyes, she couldn't. Honey reluctantly got out of the car and allowed Shai to lead her around the corner.

"What's up with you?" he asked, trying to keep his voice even.

"What's up with me?" she shot back. "I should be asking what's up with you? That was some bullshit, Shai. You and your crazy-ass cousin coming up in my job wilding out."

"Your job?" he asked in a disgusted tone. "Ma, that ain't no place of employment. It's a flesh factory."

"Call it what you want to, but it pays my bills."

"Baby girl, that ain't no way to make a living. Showing all your goods to some thirsty-ass niggaz for a few singles. Come on, ma. That shit is degrading."

"Don't you come at me trying to pass judgment, Shai Clark," she said with emphasis. "What I do ain't no worse than what your family does. It's all in the name of a dollar."

"Don't bring my family into this, 'cause that ain't me."

"Well, this is me, Shai. I'm just trying to make it like everybody else. You think it's easy for a woman to raise a kid by herself? Look around you, Shai!" Honey swept her arms around. "New York ain't exactly the land of opportunity. Not everyone can be born into money. Some of us gotta get it how we get it."

"And you gotta get it by prostituting yourself?"

"Hold the fuck on," Honey said angrily. "First of fucking all, I ain't no goddamn prostitute. I dance, Shai. And that's it. I've made some messed up decisions in my life, but that's not what I'm about. I would love for a good man to come along and wanna take care of me and Star, but this is the real world. I gotta feed me and mine."

"You on some bullshit!"

"No, you on some bullshit, Shai. Matter of fact," she said, turning to leave, "you ain't my man, so I don't have to listen to this shit. I'm out!"

"Hold on," Shai said, grabbing her by the arm.

"Get off me!" she shouted, trying to pull away. Shai tightened his grip and pulled her closer. He and Honey were standing eye to eye. Anger was written all over her face, but Shai was turned on by it. She seemed so strong and defiant, a trait he wasn't used to in a woman. The closeness of her body and her breath grazing his cheek caused Shai to get an erection. Simultaneously, they both leaned in and kissed.

The two combatants kissed each other deeply and passionately. Soon Shai had loosened the grip on her arm and began exploring her body with his hands. Honey's skin felt like rose petals to his touch. As he explored her body, she explored his. Her hand slid down his muscular chest and abs to his throbbing penis. Honey was pleased by what she felt. She worked Shai's manhood out of his zipper and began to massage it, firmly. When he was fully erect, she pulled her thong to the side and allowed him to enter her.

Shai almost moaned out loud, feeling the heat that Honey's walls radiated. Vaginal fluid ran down his shaft and balls as Honey tightened herself around his penis. They started out moving slow and rhythmically, then stepped it up to simultaneous thrusts. Shai was trying to get as deep as he could and she gladly accepted him. They both let out animal-like groans as they reached their climax. When it was over, they stood there staring at each other silently.

CHAPTER 19

EARLY MONDAY MORNING Scotty walked into a restaurant located in downtown Manhattan. He gave the hostess his name and followed her down the aisles to his table. When he reached the table he saw the man he was sent to meet with. He was a squat-looking white man with salt-and-pepper hair. His wire-rimmed glasses hung slightly off the bridge of his huge nose. The man was Arnold Green, GM for the Knicks.

"Mr. Green," Scotty said, extending his hand. "Martin Scott."

"Good to meet you," said Green, shaking Scotty's hand. "Sit down, sit down."

"Thank you," said Scotty, accepting the offer. "Again, I would like to thank you for meeting me on such short notice."

"Not a problem." Green waved him off. "Any friend of Sol Lansky is a friend of mine. Now, I got the e-mail about the little problem you were having. One of your people is having some kind of trouble with my staff?"

"Actually, with you. The young man I'm coming to you about is James Tucker."

"That pervert? What about him?"

"I'm here to ask you to reconsider letting him go through the full tryouts for the team. I'm not asking you to let him on the team just because. By all means, let him earn a spot like everyone else. I'm just asking that he gets a fair shake."

"Fair shake, my ass. He's a fucking degenerate. I know his track record. I heard about the last poor girl that he got knocked up and then he tries to pull it on my own blood. Fuck him."

"Mr. Green," Scotty spoke softly. "I know that James has a checkered past, but I assure you that he is a good kid. I'm sure that if you would at least take this into consideration my employer, Thomas Clark, would be more than happy to return the favor."

"Thomas Clark?" Green asked, putting his fork down for the first time. "I should've known when I saw your black ass in that fifteen-hundred-dollar suit. I know about your employer. Poppa Clark is a drug dealer and a pimp. I'm not doing shit for Tucker."

"Mr. Green," Scotty said, fighting for control. "I think you should weigh your options."

"I'm not doing shit. You think you can come in here and muscle Arnold Green? Let me tell you something, boy. I know people. Connected people. If you and your tribe think you can come down here and bust my balls, then go ahead and try. I don't bend for fucking hoods. Get the fuck out of my face."

Scotty fought down the urge to lunge at the man and raised up from his seat. Green's bodyguard stared at him, but Scotty paid him no mind. He was more focused on the order he had to give. Poppa had told him to proceed at his own discretion and so he would. Green thought that he was a somebody, but Scotty intended to show him just how much of a fucking nobody he was.

. . .

Scotty left the restaurant and hopped into the back of the rented limo that was waiting for him. He gave the driver the nod and they pulled off into traffic. When they had gotten a few blocks, Priest melted from the shadows opposite where Scotty was sitting.

"Care to make a confession, my son?" Priest asked almost jokingly.

"The meeting didn't go well."

"A shame indeed. So what now?"

"Here," said Scotty, handing Priest a slip of paper. "This is the address. You know what to do?"

"Yes. I think that when I'm done, Mr. Green will see things our way." A broad smile crept across Priest's lips, causing Scotty's skin to crawl.

Poppa sat in his private booth at the back of the Caribbean restaurant, quietly eating his oxtails. As always, Butch sat a stone's throw away to Poppa's right. Angelo sat across from him, picking at his chicken and speaking to Poppa in a hushed tone. He was relaying the details of the hit on Frost.

"That boy has got issues," Angelo explained.

"Yeah," Poppa chuckled. "Gator does OD a bit, but he gets results. Did anybody make you guys?"

"Nah." Angelo shook his head. "We popped him outside, then got in the wind. Gator did that boy rotten."

"Serves the little bastard right," Poppa snapped. "Sneaky mutha fucka shouldn't have gone against the grain."

Poppa and Angelo talked a little more about business and other things. Shortly into their conversation, a shadow appeared over Poppa's table. Butch was already on his feet, stepping between Poppa and the uninvited guest. Poppa smiled and waved Butch down.

"You need to relax a little," Mike said to Butch. "How ya doing, Poppa?"

"I'm good, Mike. Have a seat," Poppa offered.

"Thanks," Mike said, cramming himself into the booth next to

Angelo. "I won't take up too much of ya time. I just wanted to talk to you about Tommy."

"Oh." Poppa raised an eyebrow. "What about him?"

"Well, I think that he might be a little confused about some things. See, he seems to think that youz guys don't wanna do business anymore. Now, I know this isn't the case, so it struck me as kinda odd when he came at me. Let's not even talk about the fact that he was disrespectful."

"Is that right?" Poppa said nonchalantly. "To be honest with you, I had heard something about the unrest as of late. You have one version and Tommy has another. I understand that my son can be a little bullheaded, but I'm afraid that there's little I can do about it. As you've probably heard, I'm retiring soon. My street affairs will be left in Tommy's hands. Any disputes that you might have over your narcotics relations will have to be taken to Tommy. Anything else, Gee-Gee and I can discuss as we always have."

"I don't think you understand." Mike said seriously. "Tommy is being unreasonable. If he continues like this, there could be a problem."

"I don't think you understand." Poppa matched his tone. "Any complaints you have, Tommy is the one to address. If he chose to stop dealing with you, then I'm sure he had a reason. Your people and mine have always dealt with each other *fairly* and I hope we will continue to do so. It displeases me to hear of you and Tommy's falling out. Truly, it does. These things happen in the game. I'm sorry, Mike, but I'm afraid I can't help you there."

"That's the way it's gonna be, Poppa?" Mike asked with ice in his voice.

"Tommy is lord of the streets," Poppa said, equally cold.

The two men eyed each other and their entourages did the same. Nicky fingered his pistol and Butch did the same. Angelo had already drawn his P89 and had it trained on Mike's ribs. The feel of death loomed ever present near the table.

"Okay," Mike said, getting up. "You're just as hardheaded as ya kid, but have it your way." Mike walked from the restaurant, leaving Poppa and his peoples in silence.

Bone strode into the Spanish restaurant feeling like he had just won the lotto. He knew it would only be a matter of time before an opportunity presented itself to exact revenge. Mike had laid a sweet deal out for him: total control of Poppa Clark's operations. Bone knew with the support of the Italians, taking down Poppa's crew would be that much easier. The tricky part would be taking Poppa out of the picture. This is what brought him to the Lower East Side in the first place.

The man that Bone came down to see was already there when he arrived. Frog was a short Mexican with a shaved head. Frog ran a crew of vicious young cats from the Lower, and was respected as an up-and-coming player in the game. He also owed Bone a debt for avenging the death of his older brother, Big Frog.

"What's up, homie?" Frog asked, giving Bone dap. "What brings you down this way?"

"Got a little business I want to talk to you about, fam'." Bone smiled. "Got a favor to ask. Something's come up and I think you can help me out with it."

"If I can, I will. What's up?"

"I need a nigga laid down," Bone started. "Before you answer, let me tell you what I offer in return. An entire housing project of your own in Harlem, in addition to expanding your own operations in lower Manhattan."

"Who?" Frog said greedily.

CHAPTER 20

SHAI, Angelo, and Swan sat inside of Popeyes on 125th with a small crew of soldiers, eating chicken and talking shit. Swan was feeling on top of the world about his new promotion and Shai was just as happy as if he had been made. No one deserved it more than Swan. He had been a loyal soldier and a ruthless field sergeant.

The young men wore smiles and dreamt of a bright future, while the soldiers wore grim death masks. By now the word had gotten out about Tommy severing ties with the Italians. It was a sensitive time in the streets and no one was sure what was going to happen.

"The natives look restless," Shai said, motioning toward the milling soldiers.

"Yeah," Swan said, sipping his soda. "Everyone wants to know what's going down. This could mean a war, son."

"You think so?" Shai asked.

"Looks like it," Angelo said flatly. "You know, you can't tell your brother shit. Now I know what Poppa means about him being hardheaded."

"Yeah," Shai agreed. "He be on some other shit sometimes, but that's just how Tommy is." He shrugged.

"I know and that's what scares me," Swan cut in. "The dagos ain't the only ones we gotta worry about. Without the Italians behind us, it's only gonna be a matter of time before the rest of these fool-ass niggaz start coming at us. There gonna be a lot of bloodshed, son. A whole lot."

Shai saw the look of concern on his friend's face. He was not a soldier himself, but he empathized with Swan. Swan had been hustling even before Poppa had put him on. The grind was all he had ever known. He thought that once he made lieutenant he could put down the gun and focus on getting money. That had all changed with the threat of war. Swan knew he would have to drop quite a few bodies, personally.

"It'll be all right," Shai said, trying to comfort his friend.

"Easy for you to say," Swan chuckled. "When this shit pops off, you'll be tucked safely in the mansion. We're the ones that have to be out here ducking gunfire. Every mutha fucka with a team is gonna be gunning for our spot once the Italians pull out."

"What about if y'all tried to unify the crews into one consolidated front?" Shai asked.

"Shit, that doesn't sound like a bad idea," Angelo said, scratching his chin. "But there's no way Tommy's gonna go for that. He wants all or nothing."

"Damn, why don't y'all go to Poppa with it?"

"Yeah, right." Angelo chuckled. "And look like turncoats or little bitches to Tommy? Don't think so. Besides, Poppa's backing his play. Tommy's the boss."

"This shit is crazy," Shai said, pacing. "I agree with my brother wanting to break from the Italians, but I don't agree with his methods. Everything has been cool for years, now we're going to war. Somebody's gotta do something."

"Shai," Swan said in a whisper. "We're lieutenants, but we ain't really Clarks. We got say-so over certain things, but Tommy is the boss. Period. If he declares war, no matter how selfish or stupid the reason, we gotta ride out."

"This is some bullshit. I'm gonna talk to Poppa."

"That's what we've been getting at all along," Angelo said seriously. "We know you ain't no solider, Shai, but you're Poppa's kid. If he sees you taking a more active roll in things, he's gotta hear you out."

"I can try and talk to him, but I really ain't for this shit," Shai protested.

"Shai, we ain't asking you to kill nobody," Swan assured him. "All we want you to do is try to bring some reasoning to the table. You've got clout that not even me and Angelo carry. The crew needs a more direct voice, son. You can act as a buffer between the soldiers and the bosses. Be the voice of reason to your hotheaded brother."

"You think Poppa and Tommy are gonna listen to me?"

"If we back you, they will," Angelo said confidently. "I'm just as loyal to this family as Swan, but I'm not real comfortable dying over some petty-ass beef between Tommy and Mike. And that's just what this shit is, *petty!*"

Before the trio could get any deeper into the conversation, Honey walked in, followed by Paula and Stacy. Shai's heart immediately began to pound, seeing her. His mind replayed their night of lustful sex and he could feel the erection coming on. He quickly regained his composure, not wanting to play himself in front of the troops.

"What's good, ma?" he asked, flashing his bad-boy smile and stroking her cheek.

"What's up, superman?" she joked.

"Listen . . . about that . . ."

"No need to say anything," she said, placing her finger over his lips. "I can't work that spot anymore, but it was worth it. Besides, I'll let you make it up to me."

"Oh, hell no," a voice called from behind Shai. He hoped his ears were playing tricks on him, but he knew they weren't. "I know this nigga ain't trying to play me," Jane continued. She was standing there with two of her friends, looking like a Triple Crown book cover. She was wearing a shirt that was too small to hide her slight potbelly and a knockoff Versace skirt. To cap it off, she had on a pair of suede boots that had to be roasting her feet. Jane always had a ghetto-ass mentality, but that day she looked the part.

Shai clenched his jaw at the sound of Jane's voice. There was no mistake in her tone that she was about to play herself. Jane was a tack head that Shai had made the mistake of getting involved with back in high school. Like most hood bitches, Shai found out that she was a headache and stopped dealing with her. This didn't stop her from harassing him whenever she got the chance. Jane just couldn't seem to get over the fact that Shai wasn't fucking with her like that. He was hardly in the mood for one of her flip sessions. He was trying to get at Honey and he didn't need Jane coming out of her face.

"Shai," Jane said, snaking, popping her gum. "How you gonna even do me like this? A bitch trying to be good to you, and you creeping with this ho?"

"Ho?" Honey said, looking Jane up and down. "No this bitch didn't."

"I got ya bitch right here," Jane said, pulling off her earrings.

"Oh, shit!" one soldier cried out.

"You gon let her clown you?" another soldier chimed in.

"Hold on, hold on," Shai said, stepping between them. "Jane, why don't you be easy?"

"Fuck you mean be 'easy'?" Jane snapped. "This bitch is all up on you and I'm supposed to be easy?"

"Shai," Honey said, annoyed. "Who is this little girl?"

"Honey, don't pay her no mind. She's just some tack head I made the mistake of getting involved with back in the day," he assured her.

"Tack head?" Jane snaked her neck again. "No the fuck you didn't. Shai, you need to stop stunting for your little jump-off, and act like you know."

"Bitch"—Paula stepped up, palming her razor—"you keep bumping your fucking gums and you gonna get what you're asking for."

"Jump if you want to, ho," Jane said, staring Paula down. "Shai, if you're finished talking to these lil' heifers, I need to holla at you."

"We ain't got nothing to talk about," Shai said, looping his arm around Honey's waist. "You see me wit' my shorty, so kick rocks."

Jane was lucky Shai stepped in when he did. Honey was about two seconds away from letting Paula scar her. She played her position though, leaning back into Shai's arms and staring Jane down. She could tell, by the look on the girl's face, that she was mad enough to try something. But mad didn't make her stupid.

"It's like that, Shai?" Jane sucked her teeth.

" 'Bye, Jane," he said, kissing Honey on the cheek.

Jane looked at the two of them as if she couldn't believe he'd chosen her. She started to cause a scene, but figured that it wouldn't change anything. Shai would get tired of the blonde and come in search of her bomb head. And when he did, she would be waiting with open arms.

As Jane was exiting the chicken spot, Swan taunted, "I still love you, Jane."

Angelo followed up with, "What you doing later? I got a whole dollar, and I'm dying to spend half with you."

The whole spot burst into a fit of laughter. Jane just put her head down and left. Once again, Shai had made her feel like shit. You'd think she'd be used to it by then.

Shai and Honey stood off from the crew, talking and enjoying each other's company. He whispered softly to her, while playing with her hair. They looked like two starstruck kids. Everyone looked on, surprised, 'cause it wasn't Shai's way to show affection publicly. This went on for about ten minutes, before Shai kissed Honey on the cheek and went to rejoin his awestruck crew.

"I've seen it all now." Angelo whistled.

"What's that supposed to mean?" Shai asked defensively.

"Nigga, you're in love!"

"Fuck outta here. I don't love them hoes," Shai joked.

"Well, you're feeling the shit out of that one," Swan cut in.

"Y'all niggaz don't know what you're talking about. Shorty is mad cool, but I wouldn't call it love."

"Whatever, young'n," Angelo pushed him playfully. "Just be careful with that one."

"What's that supposed to mean?" Shai questioned.

Swan shot Angelo a warning look. "I don't know nothing 'cept what people say. Nothing personal against her. I'd tell you the same thing about any chick."

"Yeah, okay," Shai said, not really believing him. In the hood, niggaz always had something negative to say. That's just how it went, but Angelo wasn't a typical hood nigga. He was one of the few cats that Poppa had on payroll that could be called a gentleman. Something was up and Shai would get to the bottom of it sooner or later.

Tommy sat in his father's office waiting for him to come in. He had told him that he needed to sit down about the situation with the Italians, but beyond that, he didn't go into detail. He knew that this was a very delicate situation and it had to be handled with care. He went over the script in his head again and waited for his father's arrival.

Poppa came into the office with a frustrated look on his face. Tommy tensed up. If his father was already in a bad mood, the news that Tommy was about to deliver would only make it worse. It was too late to turn back and the problem with Mike had to be addressed immediately.

"What's up, old man?" Tommy asked lightly.

"Rough day, son," Poppa responded. "Had to go see Scotty about that thing for James and that damn Mike."

"Mike?" Tommy asked, surprised.

"Yeah. He told me about the little falling out y'all had. When did you plan on telling me?"

"Poppa, I was just trying to get a handle on it before I brought it to you."

"Well, while you were trying to get a handle on it, those damn dagos could've tried to kill me and I wouldn't have even seen it coming."

"You're right, Poppa. Now what?"

"What're you asking me for?" Poppa asked sarcastically. "You're running the show now. I know why you did what you did, but you could've done it with more tact. Use your head."

"Sorry, Poppa."

"Don't be sorry, be careful. Now, Mike is in a bad way. You've wounded his pride and crippled his pockets. I'm not sure what he's gonna do, but I know he's gonna do something. Be prepared for it when it comes."

Tommy nodded as his father continued to speak. He knew the old man was mad, but he took it far better than he had expected him to. With that out of the way, getting ready to go at it with Mike was the order of business. The fat man could make things very uncomfortable for their crew, but they would hold their ground. The first move had been made, so Tommy had no choice but to play the game.

"The nerve of that little bitch," Paula said, looking at some Enyce jeans that were on sale at Harlem. "She came up in there looking like a goddamn streetwalker and had the nerve to be trying to stunt. She lucky I didn't blow her ass."

"She act like she was on something." Honey chuckled, looking at herself in the full-length mirror.

"She must've been, the way she was pressing ya man."

"What's that supposed to mean?" Honey asked, raising her eyebrows.

"Stop acting like you don't know," Paula said, thumbing through the sale rack. "I seen the way y'all was gazing into each other's eyes. Both of y'all looked like two lovesick puppies."

"You can't be serious?" Honey asked, selecting a pair of Baby Phat jeans with a matching shirt.

"Honey," Paula said, putting her hands on her hips, "this is me. I know you, so don't front. But I ain't mad at you though. The whole game plan was to get with that nigga and take him to the bank, right?"

Honey gave Paula a halfhearted nod. It was true enough when Honey originally got with Shai, it was all game. She would spend some time, maybe give him a little ass, then try and squeeze him. Somewhere along the line, the plan switched. The more she got to know Shai, the more she liked him. He could be a little arrogant at times, but she thought it was sexy. Besides that, his cock game was serious.

It was true, Honey was very materialistic. She liked for men to paper her and buy her gifts. This is what made her feel special. Shai, on the other hand, had made her feel more like a woman than anybody she had been dealing with prior, and he had hardly spent a dime on her. This wasn't part of the equation. Suddenly, she found herself at a fork in the road.

Shai and the others stood out in front of Popeyes, chatting about nothing in particular. The joke of the day had long since died down, leaving Shai with another lingering question. What did Angelo mean by "be careful"?

Before the issue could be pressed further, Tommy pulled up on the corner. He was dressed in a pair of jeans and Timbs. From the look on his face, Swan could tell that he was in a bad mood. The other soldiers didn't know what was bothering him, but Swan and Shai did.

"Swan, you about ready to go?" Tommy asked.

"Where y'all off to?" Shai asked.

"Got some business to handle," Tommy said shortly.

"Let me roll?"

"Ain't no place for kids, Shai. Swan will be back soon."

"Yo, fuck you, Tommy," Shai spat. "You always trying to play me. I ain't no kid."

"Shai, I'm trying to look out for your lil' ass."

"Well, don't do me no favors," Shai said, walking off.

"Dumb-ass kid," Tommy said, shaking his head. "Let's go, Swan."

"Maybe we should've let him come?" Swan asked.

"Now you're on your bullshit?" Tommy snapped. "Shai ain't built for this shit and that's the last time I'm gonna say it. Now, let's go."

Swan looked from Shai's retreating back to Tommy. He wanted to speak further on it, but Tommy was in a foul mood. The last thing he wanted to do was get into it with Tommy. Swan reluctantly followed his general.

"Did you hear the latest?" Max Wong asked, entering Billy's private study. "The streets are buzzing, brother."

"Max, what are you talking about?" Billy asked, looking up from his copy of the *Wall Street Journal.*

"Your boy, Tommy. Seems that Mike didn't like the idea of him leaving. The shit between them is about to get real ugly."

"Just as I said it would." Billy nodded. "With any luck, Tommy will have Mike in a box before the end of the year."

"He can't do it from prison," Max said seriously.

"What?" Billy sat up.

"I got word from cousin Hung at China Garden on Lenox Avenue. Says that Tommy had someone hit and the police have a witness fingering him as the one who ordered it."

"This is not good," Billy said, dropping his paper.

"Especially since you made a deal with him for all that heroin," Max reminded his brother. "What are we going to do?"

"I don't know if we can solve Tommy's problem," Billy said, picking up the phone, "but we can lend aid."

CHAPTER 21

ARNOLD GREEN STOOD IN front of his house looking down the street at the approaching school bus. His wife had promised to take the kids to their piano lesson, but she ended up having an errand to run. Arnold found himself forced to leave the office early to take his daughters to the lesson. It was an inconvenience for him to leave the office and come all the way home just to end up going back, but he would do anything for his girls.

The school bus pulled up and unloaded its cargo. Children exited the bus and went their respective ways. The bus driver closed its door and made to pull off. To Arnold's surprise, his daughters didn't exit the bus. Arnold found this very confusing, because he knew they had been picked up by the bus earlier that day.

Trying not to panic, Arnold called his wife to see if she had them. Hearing that he didn't, she panicked. After a futile attempt at calming her down, Arnold called the school. They informed him that someone had already picked up the children. Arnold immediately feared the worst.

Just as he was about to put in a call to the police, a black hearse pulled up in front of his house. The windows were tinted so Green couldn't see the driver. The door slowly opened and a man stepped out. He was of average height with a shaved head. A leather patch covered one eye and the other one was trained right on Green. As he stepped a little clearer into view, Arnold noticed that he was wearing a priest's collar.

"I take it you're Arnold Green?" Priest asked.

"Who are you?" Arnold asked.

"A man of the cloth, what else?" Priest said, as if Green had asked a stupid question. "I am a messenger of God and a deliverer of gifts. I have come bearing a gift for you."

"Listen, buddy," Arnold started. "I don't know who you think you are, but I don't have time for this shit. I'm fucking . . ."

Green's words froze in his throat, as Priest stepped away from the car, pulling a length of rosary behind him. The custom rosary stretched for about three feet and split at the end. The extensions were wrapped around the necks of Arnold Green's young daughters. Their hands were bound with duct tape, but Priest didn't need to gag their mouths; fear kept them silent.

"You bastard!" Arnold shouted. He made to lunge for Priest, but stopped short when he saw the silenced .22 that Priest had produced from his robe. He moved the gun back and forth between the two girls, taunting Arnold.

"I wouldn't do that," Priest said in an easy tone.

"What do you want?" Arnold asked, defeated.

"Only that you listen to reason, my son. The other day a man came to speak with you about doing a favor for my friend Tom. You were rude and dismissed him like he was beneath you."

"Is that what this is about?" Arnold asked, outraged. "You kidnapped my little girls because I booted that bum from tryouts?"

"Hardly," Priest said as he stroked the oldest girl's brown hair. Her eyes watered, but she dared not flinch. "This isn't about that piece of shit Tucker. I could care less if you let him join in your little games. This is about respect. Poppa Clark is a man that demands respect. You disrespected him by dismissing his representative. I am here to request that you rethink your rash decision."

"Anything," Green pleaded. "Just don't hurt my girls."

"Mr. Green," Priest said, tightening his grip on the leash. "What kind of man do you take me for? My Lord is merciful and so shall I be." He freed the girls and pushed them toward their father. "Poppa doesn't forget his friends. Nor does he forget his enemies." Priest glanced at the girls. "The choice is yours," Priest told him as he slid back into the hearse, "but I would reconsider if I were you. I trust we won't need to see each other again after today." He threw his head back and laughed as he pulled off.

Arnold Green hugged his daughters and tried to hold himself together. When Scotty had come to meet with him, he had mistaken him for a low-class lawyer working for a typical black gangster. After seeing how far they were willing to go to prove a point, Arnold Green, GM for the New York Knicks, began to realize that Thomas Clark and his crew were anything but typical black gangsters.

Fritz sat behind the wheel of the Taurus, chain-smoking. He had been following Bone since Angelo had called him, but still he came up with nothing. The kid's life was that of an average hustler. Come outside, set up shop, go to the weed spot, hit the block, and talk shit. Fritz was not enjoying his latest assignment.

He had a good mind to give the whole thing up and report in, when something very interesting happened. Bone was sitting inside a Chinese restaurant with his partner Ahmad. They had been sitting there for a while, but nothing noteworthy had happened. At least until their surprise guest came.

Fritz's jaw dropped when the guest got out of the cab. Even parked a few yards away, he knew the man's face. His blood boiled as the man went inside and greeted Bone with a smile and a hug. Fritz wanted to hop out and wet all three of the snakes, but those weren't his instructions. He decided to play this one by the book and pulled out his cell phone.

. . .

The meeting at Shakers had been a tense one. There weren't that many people there, just the family's most trusted comrades. The issue with the Italians had been the order of business. Random incidents had been occurring all over the City. "This one got shot over here." "So-and-so got bagged over there." If Tommy hadn't given specific orders to report any unusual activities, they might've gone unnoticed. In times of war, there were no such things as coincidences. The Italians had lifted their veil of support and the shit would be hitting the fan very soon. Things were unfolding a little faster than Tommy was prepared for, but he would never admit it.

CHAPTER 22

OVER THE NEXT WEEK or two, things were very tense on the streets. The heroin that the Wongs had supplied Tommy with was moving at an alarming rate. Tommy was making money, but he was still suffering losses. The conflict was building, but an all-out war hadn't popped off yet.

Just as Angelo had predicted, the other crews were starting to gain courage. Harlem was the heart of the Clark operations, so they didn't press the assault there, but the other boroughs were being infiltrated left and right. The Dominicans, Jamaicans, and whoever else had a stake in the streets wanted a piece of the Clark pie. Tommy's crew was holding them at bay as best they could, but it would only be a matter of time.

By now, everyone knew the Italians were no longer behind Tommy and were trying to capitalize on it. More soldiers were being lost than usual. If they weren't being randomly killed, they were being arrested on bullshit charges. The police that were still on the

Clark payroll had doubled their fees, knowing Tommy had no choice but to pay.

On a different note, Shai and Honey found themselves getting closer. The two could often be found in popular eateries or frequenting movies. Neither of them had expected to develop such strong feelings for each other, but it was happening. As unexpected as it might've been, they couldn't be mad at the twist.

Honey wasn't the only thing occupying Shai's time. He found himself spending more time with Swan and the other soldiers. He wasn't active in the conflict, but he would often act as counselor. Poppa and Tommy were oblivious to Shai's meddling, but Swan and the others were glad to have him. Shai had an edge, because he looked at things from a neutral standpoint. He would analyze certain situations and devise plans to counter them, plans that Swan and Angelo would gladly carry out.

One such problem was the dwindling support for the Clark family. The underworld citizens of New York City were being forced to choose sides in the conflict. They would have to ride with either Tommy or Bone. Quite a few of them had chosen to side with Bone, because he now had the support of the Italians. They still respected Tommy but hesitated to side with him because he was slowly becoming the underdog.

Shai saw this problem unfolding and quickly devised a plan to counter it. He began a recruitment campaign, spearheaded by Angelo and other loyal lieutenants. They began to go outside of the City proper to gain support. They sent word to the independent crews, who were loyal to neither side. They reached out to places like Newark, Mount Vernon, and Westchester County. The message was simple: "Support the Clarks and reap the benefits when the conflict was finished." Shai promised each crew leader a spot within the organization in exchange for their support. Just as Shai had anticipated, the promise of wealth and power was enough to draw more soldiers into the fold. It wasn't a massive turnout, but they managed to recruit over a dozen more soldiers and supporters. That meant a dozen more guns to be bust. The wayward crews saw it as a way to come up, but Shai saw it as a means of replenishing their ranks as well as spreading the already massive Clark territory. Fair exchange.

The moves that Shai was making gained him a great deal of respect as a tactician from the select few who knew of his involvement. It also helped to boost the morale of the ones who thought it was all Tommy's doing. Whichever the case, it restored hope to the Clark family. Tommy had no idea that Shai was secretly manipulating events through Swan, but Poppa wasn't so easily duped.

"Nigga, what?" Tommy asked, staring at Dave in disbelief.

"I ain't shitting you, T." Dave shook his head. "These mutha fuckas been stomping ass all through the hood. Word is somebody dropped a dime about you ordering the hit on Heath."

Tommy was sitting in the back of Shakers, surrounded by a few of his soldiers, his cousin Gator, and Angelo. As soon as he hit the streets, he began to hear the rumors about the police looking to question him about a murder. Tommy knew he was too smart to get caught with his hand in the cookie jar, so someone had to be running their mouth.

"How much do them pigs know?" Tommy asked.

"Hard to say." Dave shrugged. "You know how rumors get twisted around and shit. What I do know, is they don't put the love on a few of our peoples. Including my man, Bump."

"That's fucked up," Marshall said. "Bump is one of us, meaning he's untouchable. That was disrespectful. What we gonna do, Tommy?"

"We gonna get to the root of this shit," Tommy said angrily.

"All kind of weird shit has been happening lately," Dave mumbled.

"Fuck is that supposed to mean?" Tommy asked curiously. "You know something that you're not telling me?"

"Well," Dave spoke up, "we didn't think much of it at the time, but niggaz been creeping through our hood. You know, we thought they might've been just trying to shake us, but—"

"Get to the point, lil' nigga," Gator said, speaking for the first time.

Dave considered arguing with the newcomer, but one look at his sharpened gold teeth killed that idea. He sucked his teeth and continued addressing Tommy:

"Fucking Bone and his peoples."

"Dave, why the fuck are you just now telling me this shit?" Tommy demanded angrily.

"Tommy, so much has been going on lately, we really didn't sweat it." Dave shrugged. "Mutha fuckas have been trying to invade our other spots, but we thought they wouldn't have tried for Harlem. This is us, baby. We figured they were just stunting."

"Looks like they were doing more than stunting," Marshall said sarcastically.

"Fuck you," Dave shot back. "If y'all niggaz did a better job of holding the block down, maybe this shit wouldn't have happened."

"Y'all New York niggaz argue like some bitches," Gator chuckled. "Cousin T, fuck you wanna do? These niggaz need to die, let's blast 'em. Niggaz need to get snatched, let's grab 'em. Let's make something happen 'round this mutha fucka!"

"I agree wit' you on that, cuz." Tommy nodded. "Something needs to be done. Angelo, get Scotty on the jack and have that nigga meet me at the precinct."

"What you gonna do, T?" Angelo asked, pulling out his cell.

"Like I said, Tommy Clark don't hide from nobody, including no faggot-ass detectives!"

Gator filed out of Shakers with Tommy and the others. As he went to step into the truck, his cell went off. He knew that only three people had the number and two of them were with him. It could only be his uncle.

"What's up, Uncle T?" Gator spoke into the receiver.

"Chilling, nephew," Poppa responded. "Where are you?"

" 'Bout to roll with Tommy and Angelo."

"Nah, hop in a cab and shoot out this way. I need you to do something."

"Be right there." Gator hung up the phone and informed Angelo and Tommy that Poppa had called him back to the mansion. Gator said his good-byes and flagged down a cab. He told the driver where he was going and slid back in the seat. He couldn't imagine what Poppa wanted him to come all that way for, but when the boss sent for you, you didn't ask questions.

Shai stood in front of his bedroom mirror admiring himself. He was looking sharp in a pair of faded Akademik jeans and a powder blue button-up. On his feet were his trademark white-on-white Air Force 1s. He had a date with Honey that evening and he wanted to make sure that he looked like a winner, which he felt he always did.

A soft knock on the door drew Shai's attention from the mirror. Tommy wasn't home and Poppa's knock was far louder. It could only be his sister. "Come in, Hope," he shouted.

"What's good, Shai?" Hope asked, sticking her head in the door.

" 'Bout to head out," he responded. "What you want, girl?"

"I just wanted to see what you were up to. I've hardly seen you since you've been home."

"I know, chicken dinner," he said playfully. "I've just been busy. We can do something this week, shorty."

"Shai," Hope said, becoming serious, "can I ask you something?"

"Sure, sis. What's up?"

"People are saying things—"

"Hope," he cut her off, "I told you about listening to gossip. I haven't been creeping with anyone's daughter."

"No, Shai. That ain't what I meant. They're saying that you're a part of what's going on."

"Hope, what are you talking about?"

"Shai, I'm not a stupid kid anymore. You think I don't know what Tommy and Poppa do in the streets?"

"Hope, don't concern yourself with that kinda stuff. Tommy is gonna be all right, don't worry about it. And you know that ain't even my style. I'm a lover, not a thug."

"Shai, I just don't want anything to happen to you."

"I'll be okay," he said, stroking her cheek. "Your big brother ain't going nowhere."

Hope wanted to believe him, but she knew how powerful the call could be. She saw young men come and go in her father's army, so she knew what the business was. She knew that Tommy was too far gone to save, but there was still hope for Shai. All she wanted was a normal family life, but being a Clark made that damn near impossible.

Shai came bouncing down the stairs, singing a happy tune. In a short while he would be back in the City, looking like money with a fine young thing on his arm. Nothing could spoil his mood. All that changed when he saw Poppa standing at the foot of the stairs with an angry look on his face.

"Did you think I wouldn't find out?" Poppa barked angrily. Shai remained silent, looking at his sneakers. "So, you wanna be a gangsta, huh?"

"Poppa, I—"

"Shai, if you lie to me, I'll break you in half! I know what you've been up to. I know about your little behind-the-back schemes. I know about the soldiers you've been rallying." Shai just looked at his father, dumbfounded. "Don't look at me like that. Tommy's running the show, but these are still my streets. I have eyes everywhere."

"I'm sorry, Poppa," Shai said sincerely.

"What the hell were you thinking, Shai? These people are killers. Anything could've happened to you out there."

"Poppa, I couldn't sit by and watch your dream crumble. I had to do something," Shai said heatedly.

"So you figured you'd play general? Shai, if you keep creeping off doing things your way, how can we protect you?"

"I can take care of myself, Pop. If we work together, we can beat this thing."

"Shai," Poppa said, placing a firm hand on his shoulder, "this is not a game. This is a war! When they come, they'll come hard."

"You're right." Shai nodded. "They'll come. And when they do, they'll be hunting for Clark blood. This includes Hope and me."

Poppa stared at Shai. He was mad as hell, but Shai was right. For as long as the streets were in turmoil, no Clark would be safe. He knew it and so did Shai. No matter how hard he tried to keep Shai out of harm's way, he seemed to find it anyway, just like his brother. Tommy had already chosen his path, but he would be damned if he let Shai go down the same road.

"Look, Slim," Poppa sighed. "I've been playing this game for more years than you been on this earth. Don't try to tell me about the streets. I trusted you to behave and you did something stupid, Shai. I'm disappointed, son."

"So what now, you gonna confine me to the house?" Shai asked.

"Hardly. I know that ain't gonna work. All you would do is sneak out every time I turned my back. I'm not gonna take your freedom. But I am gonna put your ass on a short chain."

"What's that supposed to mean?" Shai asked, confused.

"You wanna act like a baby, then I'm gonna get you a babysitter. Gator is on his way here and you two will be joined at the hip."

"Come on, Pop. I got a date," Shai pleaded.

"Well, it'll be a double date now. I'm not even gonna debate with you about this, 'cause I got some business to handle in the City. Gator is gonna hold you down until we get this business straightened out."

Before Shai could protest further, the doorbell rang. Shai answered the door and was greeted by his cousin/watchdog. Gator greeted Shai with a fanged smile and winked his eye. All Shai could do was shrug, and motion for Gator to follow him down the driveway.

After seeing Gator and Shai off, Poppa returned to his office. He had a full day ahead of him getting everything together for the casino. He had already spoken to Phil and confirmed that his people could begin working within the week. The ownership papers for the hotel were being faxed to Scotty's office. Everything was going according to plan. It wouldn't be long before Poppa would be able to retire and reap the fruits of his years of labor.

Poppa's concentration was broken by the ringing of his office phone. He looked at the antique communication piece and shook his head. Between his office phone ringing and his cell buzzing, he felt like screaming. He was suddenly looking forward to retiring.

"Hello?" he snapped as he snatched up the receiver.

"Poppa," yelled an excited voice, "I made the team!"

"James?" Poppa asked.

"Yeah," James said. "They called me back a day or two ago to resume tryouts. About an hour ago, my phone rang and I found out that I made it."

"Congratulations, James," Poppa said. "You've been given another shot. Don't fuck it up."

"I won't," James said sincerely. "You know, if it wasn't for you, I wouldn't have this opportunity. Thanks."

"Hey, if you wanna thank me, give me the money back that I gave Priest to visit your little friend," Poppa joked.

"You got it, man, but I wanna do something for you."

"You don't have to do anything for me, James."

"Yes, I do," James insisted. "Let me take you to dinner tonight."

"James, I told you—"

"Come on," James cut him off. "We'll get some dinner and celebrate over drinks. Nothing fancy. I just wanna say thanks."

Poppa started to refuse again, but then he thought about it. It had been quite some time since he had gone out for anything other than business. He needed to stop acting like an old man and start learning to enjoy life. After his retirement, he would have a lot of free time on his hands. Might as well get used to having some type of fun.

"Okay," Poppa agreed. "Where, James?"

"We can meet at BBQ's on Seventy-second."

"Okay, I guess that'll work. What time should I be there?"

"Ah," James stammered, "how about a couple of hours?"

"That'll work. See you then." Poppa hung up with James, then picked up his hand radio to call his bodyguard. "Butch," he spoke into the box, "what's your location?"

"I'm making the rounds with Danny," Butch replied.

"Bring the car around in about twenty minutes. We're going into the City."

"Business or pleasure?"

Poppa smiled devilishly before answering, "Pleasure."

"You did good, boy," Freddy said, pressing his gun to James's temple. "Play your cards right and you might live through all this."

"Fuck you," James spat. "They're gonna kill your ass."

"I doubt that, thanks to you." Freddy smiled. "See, you just made my buddy Mike a rich man and sponsored me for membership. When we waste Poppa, I'm gonna be able to write my own ticket."

James thought about lunging for the gun, but decided that he'd never make it. Even if he was able to take Freddy down, the man behind him holding the shotgun was sure to cut him down. A lone tear ran down his cheek as he wondered for the hundredth time how he got caught up in this bullshit.

This is how it all came about: After the incident with Priest, Arnold Green tells his wife the whole story. She panics and suggests they call the police. Arnold knew they would be dead if they did that. It just so happened that Mrs. Green and Freddy's wife were members of the same PTA association. Smelling an opportunity,

Freddy gets with Mike and they come up with a plan. That's how James ended up getting his door kicked in and his ass snatched by the Italians. He was the perfect pigeon to get to Poppa.

"Don't worry about it, James," Freddy said, flipping open his cell phone. "If it'll make you feel any better, you'd have never made the team anyhow." Freddy burst out laughing and dialed Mike's number. "Mike," he said into the receiver, "it's me. Took care of that thing for you. Yeah, everything's ready. Yup, I called the detective. Tommy is either headed to jail or the morgue. Huh? Got that mutha fucka right here. James," Freddy said, covering the phone, "Mike says, 'Thanks for the help.'" Freddy had a good laugh and went back to the phone call.

James looked at Freddy and gritted his teeth. He knew that he had stepped into a world of shit, but there wasn't much he could do about it. If he had been thinking, he'd have just let Freddy shoot him as opposed to making that phone call. There was no turning back now. He felt that Freddy wouldn't kill him, but if they tried for Poppa and missed, he was going to wish he were dead.

CHAPTER 23

SOL SAT IN HIS den, sipping herbal tea and watching a video tape of the 1994 NBA finals. He had been so busy overseeing the operations of the casino, that he hadn't had much time to himself. He had planned on relaxing at home, doing nothing. Until the phone rang.

"Sol here," he sighed.

"Sol, how ya doing?" O'Connor asked on the other end.

"Billy, what's the word?"

"Not good," O'Connor said. "Seems we've got some trouble."

"What's wrong?" Sol asked, sitting up.

"Seems that Tommy might've gone too far. A friend of ours has a snitch that can link him to some dirt. *Serious* dirt."

"Geez, Billy. Tell me you're joking?" Sol asked.

"Wish I could. I just got the wire about five minutes ago. Somehow it got lost in the shuffle, so I got it late."

"Shit," Sol cursed. "Did you warn Tom?"

"I called his house and he was out for the evening," O'Connor said. "I tried his business phone, but didn't get any answer."

"Don't worry about it," Sol said, getting up from the chair. "I've got his private number in my Rolodex. Bill, see what you can do to find out who the CI is, I'll get word to Poppa."

"Listen, Sol," O'Connor said. "I know this probably isn't the right time to talk about it, but it needs to be addressed. I hear that Tommy isn't doing business with our friends anymore."

"I had heard something about that, but hadn't gotten the official word," Sol agreed. "It seems that your friends haven't been playing very fair."

"I dunno about all that, Sol. I sat down with Mike about this a while ago. It seems that Tommy is getting too big for himself. He's not even officially a boss yet and he's overdoing it."

"Tommy is rash," Sol said. "But not the tyrant some people might make him out to be. I really don't know who has the more valid point in the situation, Bill. It isn't my problem. I'm Poppa's business partner. I've got nothing to do with what goes on in the streets."

"Sure, Sol," Bill said. "If this thing blows up, it could get ugly. Mike is a capo."

"Capo or no, Tommy did what he thought was best for his operations. It's business."

"Yeah," Bill agreed. "But the Clarks made a lot of friends through the Cissarros. Gained a lot of weight. Kinda makes you wonder how people will take it if things don't go so well."

"I wouldn't worry about it, Bill," Sol assured him. "Tommy's a smart kid and meaner than any fucking dog I've ever seen. It was a risky decision, but he made it. Tommy's gotta live with his decision, no one else. Poppa's leaving all that bullshit to him and the young guys, so we can get the casino. The project is going smooth and by the end of the month, we'll be able to start advertising. Turns out our little plan is moving just as fast as we thought. Thanks to you putting in a call to the senator's assistant. Thanks."

"Anytime, Sol," Bill said. "I don't mind doing favors for my friends, as long as they don't blow up in my face."

"Bill, don't worry about that. Focus on getting into that office. Poppa and Tommy have got this under control."

"I hear ya, Sol, and I know Thomas is a personal friend, but you gotta look at it from different angles. Poppa is a classic character and a savvy businessman. I got a lot of respect for that guy, but I gotta question his judgment. Is it the wisest thing in the world to leave such a delicate operation to Tommy? Tommy might start a war with this cowboy shit. People start dropping in the street and Poppa's name is attached to it, where does that leave us?"

"I see where you're coming from, Billy, but Tom is a friend of ours."

"Sol," O'Connor sighed, "sometimes, even the best investments have unforseen drawbacks. The question is, are Poppa's drawbacks greater than his worth?"

"Bill," Sol said, "I understand you. Really, I do. But I don't think you understand. You and Poppa come from two different worlds. Things are done a little differently down there. I can respect your concerns, but Poppa is my friend and I won't back out on him. Thanks for the heads-up, Bill. I'll call you after I get hold of Poppa."

Sol hung up the phone and made his way over to his desk. He and Poppa had warned Tommy time and again about doing things the right way. Tommy was usually very careful, especially as far as murders were concerned, but he had slipped. Sol just hoped that it wouldn't be too late to fix this mess.

"Tommy," Scotty said. "Let me do all the talking."

"Go ahead with that shit." Tommy waved him off. "I'm a grown-ass man. These faggots don't put no fear here," he said, beating his chest.

Tommy slung a few choice curses at no one in particular and stormed up the stairs into the precinct. Scotty tried to stop him, but Tommy was stubborn as hell. He and Herc just looked at each other and followed Tommy inside, hoping he didn't make the situation worse.

"Can I help you?" the desk sergeant asked.

"Yeah, you can help me," Tommy said, raising his voice. "You can tell me why two of your dicks have been mentioning my name and murder in the same fucking breath?" Tommy continued before the sergeant could answer, "Let me tell your something, I ain't no fucking killer, I'm a businessman. All this bullshit y'all putting on the streets is wack and the shit needs to stop. Word to mine."

"Sir, who are you?" the sergeant finally got a chance to ask.

"Thomas Clark, Jr.," Detective Brown said, coming from the back room. Detective Alvarez was close behind him.

"Brown?" Tommy asked in disbelief. "Doo-Doo Brown, is that you? Man, I ain't seen you since you was in uniform, chasing them lil' project niggaz around. How's that coming?"

"Real fucking funny," Brown said, tightening his jaw. "Word is you and Poppa stomped on Prince's whole crew, not long after Santana went down. Had every capo and their families murdered. Real ugly."

"I don't know shit about that, dawg," Tommy lied. He knew just what Brown was talking about. Tommy and Herc had personally tracked Prince's remaining capos to their rabbit holes. They forced them all into one place and let them know that the Clark family meant business. First the capos were made to watch while a young butcher called Johnny Black hacked their families to pieces with machetes. Then Johnny decided that the men required a proper send-off. He turned on the kitchen stove and blew out the pilot so the gas would escape into the air. Johnny lit a candle in the bedroom where the men were tied and left. Minutes after he hit the streets, so did the capos' body parts.

"Man," Tommy continued, "I should've known that it was yo' dick-riding ass spitting that bullshit about me. You still mad, huh?"

Brown took a step toward Tommy, but his partner held him back. "Look," Alvarez said, addressing Tommy, "we just wanted to ask you a few questions about a—"

"Any questions you have for my client can be asked in private and only at my discretion," Scotty cut in. "Martin Scott, Attorney—"

"I know who you are." Brown looked at him in disgust. "Fucking worm," he mumbled under his breath.

"Gentlemen," Alvarez said, addressing all three of the men. "A man was murdered and we have reason to believe that Tommy was involved."

"Where's your proof?" Scotty asked.

"We have a witness, who—"

"Okay," Scotty cut him off, "so you have somebody that says Tommy did something, what else is new? Detectives, it's no secret to anyone in this building who my client is. His father is a respected businessman and pillar of the community. It's not uncommon for rumors to get way out of hand when they actually have no truth to them."

"That's bullshit and you know it," Brown snapped. "Heath, the numbers man, was murdered and Tommy gave the order. We're gonna nail his ass for it!"

"Big talk," Tommy laughed mockingly, "for a low-rank cocksucker. Nigga, you ain't shit," Tommy said venomously. "Would be an Uncle Tom mutha fucka like you to try to hate 'cause I'm eating. I ain't no fucking angel, but I sure as hell don't have nothing to do with no murders."

"That's enough, Tommy," Scotty said, placing his hand on Tommy's shoulder. "Detectives, if my client isn't being charged, we're leaving."

Alvarez looked over at his partner and could've sworn that he saw steam rising from his head. He was just as tight about the whole thing as Brown, but what could they do? Other than what Amine said, they really didn't have anything on Tommy. They had to let him go, but they didn't have to close the case on him.

"No," Alvarez said, folding his arms, "but we would like to ask him a few questions."

"What the fuck ever." Tommy threw his arms up. "Let's get this shit over with so I can get from 'round you silly-ass niggaz."

"Right this way," Alvarez said, motioning toward an office door. Tommy strode down the hall as if he didn't have a care in the world. Scotty followed behind them looking stressed. Herc sat near the desk sergeant, shaking his head. Tommy was his boy, but he was becoming a little extra with his attitude. He felt as if he was untouchable, and in a sense he was; as long as Herc had strength in his body, he would see to that.

Shai and Gator picked their dates up from the hair salon on 132nd and Lenox. Both of the ladies were looking good enough to eat. Paula had on a one-piece body suit and filled it out nicely. She had a horse ass and a little waist, causing Gator to eye her like a hungry dog. She returned his stare fearlessly.

Honey was on point as usual. She had on a skirt that was tight around the ass but loose toward the knee. Her black, button-down blouse curved with her body and held close to her breasts. Shai stared at her openly as he held the passenger door for her.

Gator and Paula hit it off right away. She took one look at him and was hit. He spit some wild-ass line at her with his Southern accent and she went for it. Gator was a kind of cat who was totally different to her. Shai and Honey didn't seem to mind. This left them some time to get better acquainted.

"Did you miss me?" he asked playfully.

"Shai, I just saw you the other day." She smiled.

"Shit, every moment away from Shai Clark is enough time to miss him."

"You are so stuck on yourself."

"Nah, but I'm stuck on you."

Honey couldn't help but blush at the statement. "Where are we going?" she asked, changing the subject.

"Damn, you're nosey," he joked. "You'll find out when we get there."

"Knowing you, it's probably some loud-ass club or social event," Honey teased him.

"Nah." He smiled. "Nothing like that. I got something different in mind."

"I don't give a fuck where we go, as long as we get there," Gator added from the backseat. "A nigga can catch cabin fever sitting in the back of this mutha fucka."

The whole car burst into laughter.

Lucius smiled liked the cat that swallowed the canary. Just as Bone had promised him, he was finally starting to see some paper. He was still hustling for Tommy, but soon he would make his separation from their squad. He was on top of the world, and nothing could knock him off his high horse. Had he known he was being watched, he might not have been so cocky.

CHAPTER 24

POPPA ARRIVED AT THE restaurant ready to have a good time. The pressures of all that had been going on were checked at the door. This night would be pleasure. Normally he would've had several of his security team with him, but he didn't feel like being crowded. He was just going to dinner with James, so he doubted that it would require an entourage. He had a soldier named Sam drive the car, while he kept Butch at his side.

Butch got out of the car and held the door for Poppa. There was no parking in front of the restaurant, so Poppa instructed Sam to come back when he called him. He figured if he was going to be a while, it didn't make any sense to have Sam riding around aimlessly. Butch didn't like the idea of being shorthanded, but Poppa was the boss.

As Butch led Poppa into the restaurant, a cold chill swept across his neck. Butch stopped short and looked around. There were a few people scattered throughout the place, but other than that Butch couldn't see anyone or anything that might've posed a threat. Still, he kept his hand close to his gun.

"What's wrong?" Poppa asked, noticing his man tense up.

"Nothing, I guess," Butch said, still looking around. "Just thinking how light this crowd is around this time."

"What's so unusual about that?" Poppa asked.

"It's happy hour," Butch said.

"Cut that shit out, Butch. You're gonna make me paranoid." Poppa waved him off and went to find James who was already seated.

"What's up, son?" Poppa asked, shaking James's hand.

"Glad you could make it." James smiled uneasily.

Butch caught a hint of something in the man's smile, but Poppa seemed comfortable around him, so he brushed it off as nerves.

"I see you've started without me," Poppa said, motioning toward the three empty liquor glasses on the table.

"Yeah," James smiled weakly. "Just a little celebrating."

"I know that's right," Poppa agreed. "I'm proud of you, kid."

"I couldn't have done it without you. No matter what, I'll always be grateful for all that you've done for me. I mean that, Poppa."

"Don't even worry about it, James. You can make it up to me by getting some season tickets."

Poppa ordered a bottle of champagne and the three men ordered their meals. Butch was on the job, so he didn't drink, but Poppa ended up getting a little tipsy. Butch had noticed a few odd things throughout the evening. James seemed to keep looking around nervously, as if he were waiting for something to happen. When the little Italian waiter brought their meals, James damn near jumped out of his skin. Butch wondered if Poppa's little athlete might have a coke problem.

Poppa and James talked about sports and life for the better part of two hours. He was more than pleased when Poppa instructed him to call Sam. Sam assured Butch that he was a few blocks away and would be there within minutes. Butch got up and went to stand by the entrance.

"James, thanks for the dinner." Poppa smiled.

"Hey, don't worry about it," James said nervously.

"Well, I need to be going now. You need a ride somewhere, James?"

"No," he blurted out. "I mean no thank you."

"James, are you high?" Poppa asked suspiciously.

"Nah, just a little buzzed," James lied.

"Some people ain't got no stomach for liquor," Poppa joked. "Come walk me to the car, James."

"I'll be right there," James said, backing up. "Gotta take a leak."

Poppa shrugged his shoulders and headed for the front door. James stood in the rear of the restaurant, where the bathroom was located. He leaned against the wooden door and began to cry. He knew he was going out like a crab, but what choice did he have? It was a choice between Poppa's life or his and Poppa lost.

The detectives grilled Tommy for over an hour. They asked him multiple questions about the murder and his personal life. Each question they asked him, Tommy either gave a smart-ass answer or Scotty wouldn't let him answer it. When asked where he was the day Heath was murdered, Tommy said he had been in a bar drinking, which he had been. There were dozens of witnesses that could verify that. When asked about his relationship with Amine and Legs, he claimed he had never heard of him. The detectives had nothing on Tommy.

"Listen," Scotty spoke up. "We've been over all of this a dozen times. If my client is not being charged, we're leaving."

The detectives didn't like it, but they had to let him go. They knew Tommy ordered the hit, but they couldn't prove it. The more frustrated they got, the wider Tommy's smile got. He was guilty as hell, but he knew that without evidence, they had nothing. Their only hope would be the testimony of their two witnesses.

"Okay, smart-ass," Brown said. "I guess you can go, for now."

"Nigga, like I told you," Tommy said, with a smile, "what murder?"

"Just get the fuck outta here, Clark," Alvarez cut in, trying to defuse the situation. "We'll be seeing you again."

"Fuck outta here," Tommy said, standing. "You chumps is outta your league. I'm a Clark, baby. That name means something 'round here. Y'all need to take yo' asses out and try to catch some of these real criminals. Like punk-ass police that beat up on kids."

The detectives and Tommy shared knowing glances.

"Whatever," Brown said. "Scott, you and your client, get the fuck outta here." Scotty and Tommy left the office, leaving the detectives feeling stupid.

"What do you make of all this shit?" Tommy asked, lighting a cigarette.

"Too early to tell," Scotty responded. "It doesn't seem like they have anything on you. At least for now."

"What the hell is that supposed to mean?"

"It means that they know something they're not telling you just yet. They wouldn't have gone through all this trouble if they didn't. Somebody is talking."

"I figured as much," Tommy said, as if Scotty were late in catching on.

"Any idea who?"

"I got a few. Angie," Tommy said, motioning for his lieutenant to join them. "What's your take on all this?"

"Well," Angelo began. "I'd say use the process of elimination. Who knew about the hit?"

"Me, you, Poppa, Amine, and Legs."

"Right," Angelo nodded. "Now, I know I ain't the rat and I'm willing to submit to whatever test you like to prove it. It couldn't have been you or Poppa. Who does that leave us?"

"Amine and Legs. Where are those two fucking knuckleheads?"

"Legs is still out of town with his girl," Scotty cut in. "He checks in once a week, as instructed. Nobody knows where Amine is."

"He hasn't been seen on the streets," Angelo said, "but I've been hearing a lot of crazy shit. The boy has got a big mouth. That's probably our leak."

"Scotty," Tommy snapped. "I want you to find out if the police have him in custody. If they do, find out where."

"If the police do have him, we aren't going to be able to get to him," Scotty informed him.

"You let me worry about that. Just find out."

Honey was thoroughly surprised when she saw where Shai had taken her. She had expected him to take her somewhere floss, but she was wrong. Shai had instead opted for something simple. The quartet would be enjoying an evening of bowling and drinks at Chelsea Piers.

"Shai, you never cease to amaze me," Honey said, as he led her into the dark bowling alley.

"You've never been bowling?" he asked.

"Well, no. And never quite like this. The balls glow in the dark," she said.

"That's why I like it down here," he confessed. "It's a different vibe."

Honey followed Shai through the alley, to the area where they were issued shoes and balls. Honey was thoroughly impressed by the place. The whole bowling alley was dark, with the exception of the neon balls and the multicolored splashes down the lanes. There was a bar on each level and a small food court on the main level. It felt more like a club than a bowling alley.

Honey sat there, sipping her cosmopolitan, and smiling. She hadn't had this much fun in ages. Normally, when she hung out with her girls or a guy, it would be at a club or in a restaurant. Shai had put her onto something totally different. Honey had looked at bowling as something mostly squares did, but she was having a good time.

"Shai," Honey said, leaning in close to him. "I want to thank you."

"For what?" he asked.

"For making me feel special. Even though you found out I strip, you still treat me like a lady."

"Why shouldn't I? I'm not interested in what you do for a living. I'm interested in *you* as a person. You're a special lady, Honey. Real special."

Honey couldn't help but smile. Shai had a rep as being a player, but he was actually a sweetheart. Most cats treated her like a whore or a showpiece, but Shai didn't. He made her feel like a woman. She had initially gotten with him to try to get into his pockets, but her feelings had changed. She really liked him. Paula always said that there were no happy endings in the hood, but this was one time she might've been wrong. Shai made Honey feel like she was the queen of the world. All she ever wanted from a man was respect and affection and Shai had shown her both. Honey decided to try something she had never done before and be honest with Shai.

"Shai," she began. "I really dig you."

"I dig you too, ma," he said with a smile.

"And because I dig you, I feel that it's only right that I be honest with you."

"Honey, please don't tell me you used to be a man," he joked.

"I'm serious, Shai," she said, looking him directly in the eyes. "Listen, when I first got with you, I didn't really know who you were. But as I began to put the pieces together, I realized you were the little brother that Tommy always talked about."

"What does Tommy have to do with this?"

"Shai . . . Tommy and I used to see each other."

"Ain't that about a bitch," Shai said, trying not to sound hurt. "You used to fuck with my brother, now you're working on me? Who's next, Poppa?"

"It wasn't like that, Shai."

"So what was it like? Damn, Honey. Why didn't you tell me this before?"

"Shai, I didn't know at first. Then when I found out who you were, I couldn't figure out how or if I was gonna tell you at all. Shai, we weren't supposed to fall for each other, but it happened. I'm sorry for not telling you, but I'm not sorry for falling for you."

"This shit is too much," Shai said, standing.

"Shai, wait," Honey pleaded, but Shai just kept walking.

Shai felt an abundance of things at that moment, but the most distinguishing emotion was hurt. As much as he hated to admit it, he had fallen headfirst for Honey. He had even thought that she might've been the one. She had issues, but who didn't? Shai liked the way it felt being with Honey. Her smell, her touch. All of these things made him want to explore her more. But she hadn't been honest with him. He understood her point of view, but his ego wouldn't let him accept it.

But Honey wasn't the only one to blame; Tommy had just as big a hand in it as she. He knew Shai was seeing Honey, but didn't bother to tell him about their past. Maybe it was a passing fling, or maybe it was more. It still didn't excuse Tommy for his deceit. Shai had to get up out of there and clear his head. He informed his party that he was ready to leave, and they followed him out.

Gator and Paula were having a ball, so Shai didn't want to ruin that because he was going through some bullshit. He agreed to continue the date, but had little to no conversation with Honey. The group decided to move the date to Times Square. They hit a few different spots and did some light window-shopping. They didn't have a particular destination, they were just four young people out having a good time. Until the bullshit started.

Honey and the group were coming out of another store, when she saw a familiar face. Her heart jumped into her throat at the sight of Ahmad's little brother, Rah. He was a notorious troublemaker and was sure to try and start some shit if he saw her. Honey tried to turn her head before he noticed her, but she was too late.

"Yo, what up, shorty?" Rah said, loud enough for the whole block to hear him. Honey ignored him. "Oh, you can't speak? I hear that, hot shit. You wit' ya lil' boyfriend," he said, motioning to Shai, "so you ain't got no rap for a nigga. Let's see what Bone has to say about this."

"Don't you niggaz ever learn?" Shai asked, coming to her rescue. "We've had this conversation already."

"Wasn't nobody talking to yo' punk ass," Rah said to Shai.

"Fuck is you talking to," Gator said, stepping up. "I'll lay you out, faggot."

"Chill," Shai said, holding his cousin back. "Why don't you take that shit uptown, shorty? This is grown folks' business."

"Yeah, pop that shit now, Shai *Clark*," Rah laughed. "After tonight, y'all niggaz ain't gonna be worth shit on the streets. The Clark reign is over."

"Fuck is you talking about?" Shai asked, stepping toward Rah.

"Don't worry about it, son. You'll find out," Rah said, backing up to where a police car was parked. He hadn't missed the fact that Gator was reaching under his shirt. "Tell the family I said hey." Rah burst out laughing and jogged across the street to where a car was waiting.

"You wanna chase that nigga?" Gator asked.

"Nah, fuck him. Fuck was he talking about though?" Shai asked curiously.

"Maybe it had something to do with the meeting ya brother and them had? They was talking about beef wit' the Italians and maybe other crews."

Just then it hit Shai. That's what the fuck Rah meant. Everyone knew that Mike had pulled out of the relationship with Tommy, but he still needed a dope outlet. It all made sense. Bone's sudden popularity, the other crews' newfound courage. Fat Mike had sided with Bone. The upstart had been flexing a bit more muscle, but he still didn't have what it took to come at Poppa or Tommy. That would change if he had the full strength and influence of the Italians behind him.

"What's wrong?" Honey asked, noticing the look on his face.

"Baby," Shai said, grabbing her by the hand and heading for the car, "we gotta go. I gotta get to my family."

"What's wrong, cuz?" Gator asked, grabbing Paula and following.

"There's gonna be a hit tonight. I don't know if they're gonna try for Poppa or Tommy, but I gotta warn them." Shai pulled out his phone and called Tommy. "T," he said frantically, "I thought they had tried for you already. Man, it's some bullshit going on 'round here."

"Slim," Tommy cut him off, "slow down. What are you talking about?"

"A hit," Shai damn near screamed. "Fucking Bone. The Italians and Bone are gonna try to kill you or Poppa."

"Shai, didn't I tell you to stay out of this? I'm gonna kick your lil' ass!"

"Tommy, could you stop being a dick for two seconds and listen? Mike is with Bone. They're gonna try and hit one of you, if not both, tonight!"

"Shai, how do you know?"

"Would you please not question me on this, there's no time for it. Where are you?"

"I'm on my way uptown."

"Head back to the house, Tommy," Shai said. "We gotta warn Poppa."

"I don't think he's home. He said something about coming into Manhattan today. I think he was going to BBQ's on Seventy-second."

"Tommy, find him. Find him now. I'm on my way, so I'll meet you there." Tommy tried to protest, but Shai had already hung up the phone.

Shai and the group hopped in the car and headed uptown. There was no time to drop the girls off, so they had to come along for the ride. Once again Shai found himself in the middle of some gangster shit. It was becoming quite routine with him. There was no telling where this next adventure was going to take him, but he hoped his people would come out on top in the end.

Scotty was as silent as the grave during the ride uptown. Even though Tommy didn't seem to think so, his legal situation was a serious one. If the police had a witness fingering him as the one who gave the hit on Heath, Tommy was fucked. With the jacked-up legal system, ordering a murder was just as bad as committing one. But Tommy didn't seem to see it that way. He thought the same rules that applied in the streets carried over to the judicial system. If he wasn't careful, he'd find out different.

Tommy's cell phone broke up the blunt session that he was having with himself in the backseat. "Hello," he said easily. Fritz confirmed his suspicions about Lucius switching sides. He asked if he should murder him where he stood, but Tommy instructed him to wait. He wanted to punish the traitor personally.

"What's good, T?" Herc asked.

"We've got another rodent problem," Tommy said flatly.

Before he could elaborate on it further, his phone rang again. Suddenly his face turned white as a ghost. "Slim, slow down. What are you talking about?"

Sam came out of the corner store and headed back to the car. He had stopped to grab a quick bite and a pack of cigarettes before picking up his employer. Since coming to work for Poppa, everything in his life had been sweet. He moved out of his tenement and into a nice apartment, plus he was getting money—all for driving a car. When he had first come to work for Poppa, two weeks prior, he had certain reservations about working for a kingpin. As it turned out, it was the sweetest job in the world.

Sam walked to the car, paying no attention to the little Mexican with the flower cart. As soon as Sam got the car door open, the Mexican made his move. He pulled a large knife from the cart and snuck up behind Sam. Sam's body stiffened as the blade went into his back over and over again.

The Mexican shoved Sam's body into the car and hopped behind the wheel. He stopped briefly at the corner to pick up another Mexican who was holding a duffel bag and they sped off.

Poppa had almost made it to the door when his phone rang again. Only a few people had that number, so he figured it must be important. "Hello," he said.

"Hey, Tom," Sol said. "Did I catch you at a bad time?"

"Nah," Poppa assured him. "I just finished having dinner with James. He ran to the restroom, but he should be back in a second if you wanna congratulate him. Our boy just made the team."

"That's great, Tom," Sol said. "But I got something a little more pressing to talk to you about. Have you heard anything about Tommy catching a beef?"

"A beef? What kinda beef?"

"A serious beef."

"Hell no," Poppa declared. "Where did you get this from?"

"Our pal, Billy boy."

"Goddamn that hardheaded-ass kid!" Poppa said, a little louder than he meant to. "How bad is it?"

"Seems they've got a witness. Don't know much else about it though. Bill's gonna see what he can find out."

"Thanks for the heads-up, Sol," Poppa said, walking out of the restaurant. "I'm gonna talk to Bill and see what he knows. But first, I'm gonna call that bonehead-ass kid of mine."

"Don't upset yourself about it, Tom." Sol tried to calm his friend. "Kids do dumb shit. I don't think it's as bad as it sounds. We don't even know the whole story yet. Worst-case scenario, he got a little sloppy and we fix it."

"Or worse, he got a little sloppy and his ass does time," Poppa corrected him. "Shit. I'll call you back in a few." Poppa hung up without waiting for an answer.

Tommy had really put his foot in it this time. To even have his name associated with a hit was dangerous. The police already hated the Clarks, now they had a reason. If they brought Tommy down on that murder, it would ruin Poppa's entire plan. Not only would he see his boy go to prison, but this would fuck up his retirement plan. If Tommy went to prison, who the hell was going to run the business? Poppa figured he would just have to put his retirement on hold. Retirement or not, he was still the boss of the family and Tommy had to be checked. Before he could dial the number, his phone rang again.

CHAPTER 25

"HELLO," Poppa said, in an irritated tone.

"Pop, it's me," Tommy said. "Where are you?"

"I should be the one asking questions," Poppa said.

"We just dropped Scotty and Angelo off, and we're headed downtown."

"What the hell is up with you and this beef with the cops?" Poppa questioned.

"Pop, we can talk about it later. Your crazy-ass son Shai seems to think that one of us is in some kind of danger."

"That boy smokes too much weed," Poppa joked.

"I know it, but he was pretty shaken up by it. Seems to think that the Italians are out to have us murdered."

"That's crazy, Tommy. Mike was upset because I backed your play, but he ain't nuts."

"Still, something has got Shai tweaking. You still in Manhattan?"

"Yeah, but I'm cool. I got some backup."

"How many guys you got with you?"

"Just me and Butch," Poppa said. "Sam went to get the car."

"Poppa, I want you to go back inside and wait for me. I'll be to you in about five minutes."

"Tommy, you're talking crazy. Ain't nobody out here but white folks. Besides, I see the ride," Poppa said, noticing his car. "I'm 'bout to . . . What the fuck?" were the last words Tommy heard before he heard the gunshots.

Shai mashed on the gas, as they zipped in and out of traffic. He was driving so recklessly that Paula had started crying. Shai didn't mean to scare her, but he needed to get to his father. Tommy was a gorilla, so anyone would be hesitant to come at him. That same rule might not apply to Poppa. Shai had a bad feeling about the whole thing.

Poppa's vehicle coasted to a stop in front of the resturant. Butch looked around before approaching the truck. He reached for the door handle to open it for Poppa when something occurred to him. Sam hadn't so much as rolled the window down when he came to pick them up. Usually the young man would roll the window down and try to say something witty. This time he just sat behind the tints. Something wasn't right. By the time Butch had realized what he had done wrong, the little Mexican had put his brains on the rear window of the truck.

Poppa looked on in shock as armed Latinos began to pour from the truck, waving guns. Poppa saw Butch on the ground twitching and knew he was up shit's creek. Between the men that hopped from the car and the ones that joined in the fray, there had to be at least ten of them. Poppa was out-gunned with nowhere to run. It was then that his survival instincts dusted themselves off.

Poppa grabbed a man that had been coming out of the restaurant and used him for a shield. A wave of bullets tore into the unfortunate man's legs and chest. Poppa would pray for the man later, but right then he had to get up outta there. Poppa pulled his revolver from his shoulder holster and let off two shots. One went wild and the other one hit a gunman. Poppa knew that he couldn't win this fight with five revolvers, let alone one. His best bet was to take out as many of the soldiers as he could and escape with James through the back.

Poppa pushed the corpse-shield into the gunmen, causing some of them to stumble. He raised his gun and let off three quick shots. Before they could recover, Poppa jumped through the front door of BBQ's. He crashed hard on the ground and rolled down the carpeted steps. Poppa got back to his feet just in time to see the Mexican soldiers rushing behind him.

The people and the staff were running back and forth, trying not to get shot. Poppa dashed through the crowds of people, knocking over tables and bodies, trying to slow the soldiers down. He looked over his shoulder to see that they were still pursuing him. Poppa's only hope of escape would be to make it to the kitchen and go out the back way.

One of the soldiers tripped Poppa up, causing him to stumble, but he never lost his balance. Poppa rolled over one of the tables and fired on the gunman. The gunman's face exploded as a bullet slammed into his face. Poppa went to fire on the other gunmen, but he was out of bullets. After flipping the table, Poppa dashed through the kitchen doors.

"This way," a waiter who was directing people through the fire door said. Poppa ran in the direction of the fire door, smelling freedom. He thanked the man and went to step through the door. That was when the man shot him in the back.

Poppa turned around and looked at him shock. Micco, who was Frog's right hand, stood there smiling, wearing a waiter's uniform. Poppa staggered down the side alley, trying to make it back to the front of the restaurant. Micco hit him once more in the back, but Poppa kept going. When Poppa had almost made it out of the alley, the gunmen caught up with him.

The first gunman to reach him hit Poppa in the back with a shotgun. The force of the blast sent him spilling out into the street.

People screamed and pointed, but no one dared help Poppa. The gunmen took turns unloading different weapons on Poppa's corpse. When he wasn't twitching anymore, Micco reached down and slit his throat.

The gathering of Mexicans didn't know what hit them when Herc hopped the curb and slammed the truck into them. Bodies flew all over and the ones who managed to avoid the truck scattered. Before the truck had even stopped, Tommy hopped out blasting. He fired from his twin nines not even bothering to seek cover. When he looked over and saw his father, it fueled his rage.

Herc took one in the chest as he exited the vehicle. That still didn't stop him from cutting loose with his sawed-off. A hail of buckshot splattered the Mexicans, causing them to back up. Herc spent the shotgun and started busting his .357s. They managed to back the Mexicans down, but they seemed to keep coming. One managed to get off a lucky shot and hit Herc in the neck. As his body slumped down against the truck, his last thoughts were that he had failed Tommy.

Tommy was in a blind rage. He snarled, sending spittle running down his lip and chin. He was squeezing the triggers of his hammers so hard that his knuckles threatened to rip through the skin. Through tear-flooded eyes, all he could see was his father lying dead and the Mexicans continuing to advance. Hearing the sirens in the distance, the Mexicans began to withdraw, but Tommy kept firing. Even when both guns were empty, he kept squeezing the triggers. When the police arrived on the scene, all they saw were dozens of dead bodies and Tommy holding two smoking pistols.

"Drop your weapon!" a uniformed officer shouted.

Hearing the officer's voice snapped Tommy out of his trance. He looked around the scene as if he were seeing it for the first time. His father lay dead among several other bodies. "Drop the weapons!" the officer repeated. Tommy looked at his hands and realized he was holding two pistols. When he went to raise his hands in surrender, the officers opened fire. They hit Tommy at least a dozen times before he finally crumbled to the ground.

When Shai arrived at the scene, the police had the whole area taped off. Bodies and spent shell casings were everywhere. The first person he saw was Scotty. He hopped out of the car to ask about his father, but the tears in Scotty's eyes told the tale. He followed his eyes and saw his father's dreads sticking out from beneath a white sheet.

Shai dropped to his knees and began crying his eyes out. He couldn't believe that his father was gone. He was numb as he knelt beside his father's body. Poppa was everything to him. Father, mother, mentor. His world and his hopes died with his father. The streets had claimed the greatest player.

Scotty tried to console Shai, but it didn't help. Shai felt like he was having a breakdown. Angelo and Gator were standing near the ambulance, where Tommy's unconscious body was being loaded. Shai ran over and pushed past the line of policemen.

"Tommy!" he shouted. "What happened? Tommy!"

"He can't hear you, Shai," Scotty said. "They hit him up pretty bad."

"Somebody tell me what the fuck happened?" Shai demanded.

"Don't really know." Angelo shrugged. "They dropped me and Scotty off and came to check Poppa. Next thing you knew, we got the call 'bout the shooting. By the time we got here, Herc and Poppa were dead, and they're not sure if Tommy's gonna make it."

"We gonna get these mutha fuckas," Gator sobbed. "Lay hands on my family. All these mutha fuckas is going to sleep. We gonna get 'em, Shai! You hear me?"

A rage began to build inside of Shai, a rage that he had never felt before. Murdering his father was the ultimate violation. His thoughts raced, but he couldn't focus on anything but the body at his feet. He couldn't think about Honey and school was the farthest thing from his mind. All he could think of was revenge.

"Yes, Gator. I do."

. . .

Bone and Ahmad arrived at the ass end of the carnage. They watched from a distance as Shai knelt over his father's body. Police and ambulances were everywhere. Angelo almost spotted them, so they decided to leave the scene.

"That shit looked ugly," Ahmad said. "Niggaz aired Poppa the fuck out. I can't believe it."

"Believe it," Bone said, lighting a cigarette. "Just goes to show that no one is untouchable. Not even old Poppa Clark."

"What do we do now, Bone?"

"The game is wide open, my nigga," Bone said, letting out a cloud of smoke.

CHAPTER 26

GATOR, Swan, Scotty, and Sol stood and watched as Shai took a baseball bat to his trophy collection. He had been crying his eyes out since his father's murder the night before. Poppa was all they had and someone had taken him from them. Blood would be spilled for this infraction.

"Mutha fuckas!" Shai roared. "Mutha fuckas!"

"Calm down, Shai," Sol pleaded. "You're going to give yourself a heart attack."

"Fuck that," Shai sobbed. "They took him and they're gonna pay."

"Shai," Scotty cut in. "We don't even know who did it. It could've been anybody."

"Yeah, we don't know who did the shooting, but I know who gave the order. Mike is the only one who would've backed a play like this. That mutha fucka is gonna get his head handed to him. I'm killing him personally."

"Shai, you can't go about it like that," Sol said. "What about school?"

"Fuck school!" Shai snapped. "These niggaz gotta die."

"Sol is right," Scotty cut in. "There's too much heat on us now. You gotta do this the right way. Don't fuck your life up because you're angry."

"We got soldiers for this, Shai," Swan spoke up. "I'm gonna put every nigga out on the streets to find out who killed Poppa. Mike will get his when the time comes."

"His time is fucking up," Shai responded. "That's what fucked Tommy up. He played too many games. I don't intend to play with these mutha fuckas."

"Shai, this ain't you." Scotty shook his head. "These people are gangsters. This ain't your war."

"I want in," Shai said. "You can't deny me this."

"Shai, I can't let you do this. Poppa wouldn't allow it."

"I want in," he repeated. "He was my father. I want the mutha fuckas who did this to pay for it. I want in."

"You think this is a fucking game?" Scotty said heatedly. "Poppa was just murdered, Shai. He was untouchable and they got him. War ain't no fucking joke. Stay in a child's place."

"I'm so sick of this kid shit," Shai barked. "I might not be a bad-ass killer like Tommy, but I can hold mine. My father was killed yesterday. Killed because of this senseless shit. If you think I'm gonna sit by and do nothing, you're crazy." Shai stormed out of the room.

"Shai," Swan called after him.

"Let him go," Scotty said. "We'll handle this until he can get it together."

Shai sat in his father's office, punishing a bottle of gin. Normally, he didn't drink but lately his life seemed anything but normal. As he looked around the office, he was reminded of his father. Shai tried to hold it, but the tears made their way down his face.

"Shai," Swan called from the doorway. "You a'ight?"

"I'm good." He wiped his eyes. "I'm good."

"Listen . . . I'm sorry about Poppa. We'll all miss him."

"This shit is fucked up." Shai banged his fist on the desk. "My father is gone and I'm supposed to just chill? Get the fuck outta here. I gotta do something, Swan."

"Shai," Swan leaned in, "I love your brother. He's my leader and my friend. But you're my heart. We've been down since shorties. I can't tell you what to do, but if you're determined to roll, I'm with you."

Shai gave his friend a brief smile. He was glad to know that Swan was with him. He was ready to do what he had to do to get revenge, but he knew nothing of war. Swan was seasoned.

"Thank you, my nigga," Shai sobbed. "We gotta hit the streets and find out what happened and who was involved. I ain't going out like this. When the time comes, I'm gonna lay my hammer game down."

"Now you're speaking my language," Gator said, strolling into the office. "Y'all niggaz in New York don't know nothing about killing. You think I'm gonna let my cuz run off into the streets without an expert at his side? Whatever y'all niggaz is up to, count me in."

The three young men stood there and looked at each other. They were all from different backgrounds, but they had a common bond: love for Poppa Clark. This bond would now become their purpose, to lay Poppa's killers in a hole beside his.

"Do you see this shit?" Gee-Gee ranted, waving a copy of the *Daily News*. "Do you see what you've caused?"

"I did what I had to do, Mr. G," Mike told him. "You said if I had a good reason, then I could move against Poppa. So I did."

"You fucking whale," Gee-Gee said, grabbing Mike by his tie. "These niggers are destroying the City. Don Cissarro is having a shit fit behind this thing."

"Don't worry about it," Mike said, trying not to appear as afraid as he really was. "The don will understand."

"Understand?" Gee-Gee laughed. "Mike, you acted on your own and killed the most notorious black gangster in Harlem. Heads will roll for this."

"Don't worry, Mr. G. I'm gonna take care of everything."

"Easier said than done." Gee-Gee chuckled. "You murdered their don. Even flying under the Cissarro banner, you think they're not gonna try you?"

"Fuck 'em," Mike said, smoothing his shirt. "Can't no niggaz compete with our thing."

"'Our thing' ain't got nothing to do with this." Gee-Gee shook his head. "You acted on your own, so this is your problem."

"I'll take care of it," Mike huffed.

"I sure hope so. You either make this right, or you've got a fucking problem. Are we clear?"

"Crystal."

"You heard what happened to Poppa?" Lucius asked.

"Who the hell hasn't?" Leon replied. "The whole hood is talking about it. Looks like the Clark empire is crumbling, huh?"

"Seems like it." Lucius rubbed his hands together. "Ain't you glad I got you in with Bone?"

"Yeah." Leon nodded, not really sure. "But what if we're making a mistake?"

"What mistake? Poppa is dead and Tommy is crippled, and about to be indicted. The Clark legacy is over."

CHAPTER 27

"TELL ME YOU'RE LYING," Ahmad said, slapping his hand against his forehead. "My little bother couldn't be that stupid."

"Yes he is," Tammy said, clicking her gum. "We was downtown the other day and he ran up on Shai. Shai was trying to dead it, but Rah just kept talking. That's when Shai left and Poppa got murdered."

"Thanks, Tammy," Ahmad said, handing her a hundred-dollar bill. "If you hear anything else, you bring it directly to me. Understand?"

"Yeah," she said, taking the money. "I'll keep you posted."

Ahmad made sure that Tammy had completely gone before throwing a tantrum. He smashed a lamp and kicked over his living room television in a rage. If the murder could be linked to them, they had a serious problem, all thanks to his dumb-ass brother. Bone's team was strong, but they would be slaughtered by the Clarks. This shit was getting ugly real fast. Bone wasn't going to take the news well.

Ahmad began to panic as he thought of his brother on the streets without him. There was no doubt that word of his brother's conversation with Shai had already gotten back to the Clarks. There were probably killers combing the streets at that very moment. He needed to get to his bother, but he had no idea where he was. This was why he always got on him about not carrying a cell phone.

Ahmad grabbed his jacket and his gun and headed for the door. Bone was traveling with soldiers, so he was protected, but the same couldn't have been said for Rah. Ahmad had to reach his brother.

Rah sat on the stoop with two other knuckleheads, shooting the breeze and looking at ladies. It was a fairly nice night, so there were plenty of them out. Rah passed the bottle off to his man Randy while he perused a big-butt female.

"Miss," he called after her. "Come on, don't even act like that." When she still didn't stop, Rah got nasty, "Fuck you then, bitch!"

Rah and his peoples fell down laughing. Rah poked his chest out and headed back to where his friends were sitting. He gave them dap and felt like the man for his public display of ignorance. He was feeling himself so much that he didn't even notice the shadows closing in on him. By the time anyone noticed, Gator was right on top of them.

"What's up, fellas?" He smiled. The three men sat there in shock as Gator pulled two nines and began hitting the stoop. They tried to run, but it was already too late. Bullets shook the young men and mingled blood with the urine and other soot on the stoop.

Rah took off running in the other direction. He figured himself lucky for not taking a bullet, but it was all part of the plan. He had made it about a half block when someone stepped out and clotheslined him. Rah nearly backflipped from the impact. He lay on the floor clutching his neck and gasping for breath. When Rah tried to get up, Swan placed a boot on his chest and a gun to his head.

"What up, pussy?" Swan smirked.

"Chill, yo," Rah pleaded. "What the fuck is going on?"

"Don't play wit' us, nigga," Gator said, kicking him in the head. "You know just what the fuck is going on. Get yo' ass up." He grabbed Rah by the shirt and lifted him to his feet.

"Don't kill me," Rah cried.

"We ain't gonna kill you, yet," Swan told him. "Somebody wants to see you."

"Who?"

No sooner than he asked the question, a stretched Lincoln pulled to a stop on the curb. Gator opened the back door and pushed Rah inside. He stumbled and fell at someone's feet. When he looked up to see who it was, he found himself staring at an angry Shai.

" 'Sup, nigga?" Shai asked.

"Shai, man," Rah said, crawling to his knees. "What's this all about?"

"I told you to stop playing," Gator said, easing in beside him, followed by Swan.

"I don't know why y'all snatched me," Rah confessed.

"I think you do," Shai said, giving the driver the nod to pull off. "You laid hands on my family, you fucking punk." Shai punched Rah in the nose. Blood splattered on Shai's dress shirt, but he didn't seem to care.

"I didn't have nothing to do with that," Rah cried.

"Oh, yeah?" Shai questioned. "You seemed to be pretty fucking involved the other day." Shai punched him again. "Who gave the order to kill my father?"

"I don't know," Rah lied.

"Swan." Shai raised an eyebrow. Swan took a box cutter from his pocket and slashed Rah across his forearm. "Last time," Shai warned him, totally ignoring his scream. "Who gave the order?"

"It was the Italians," Rah whimpered. "Promised us a piece of the pie if we took y'all down."

"Is that so?" Shai hit him again. "You gunned my father down in the streets"—a blow to the jaw—"that's a'ight though. You're going to serve as a warning to all these bitch-ass niggaz out here. Ain't nothing soft about the Clarks. Gator!"

"You ain't even gotta ask me twice." Gator grabbed Rah by the back of the head and forced his face into the back of the driver's seat. Rah tried to plead, but nothing could be heard over the sounds of Gator's hammer barking.

Ahmad had been combing the streets for his brother for hours, but there was no sign of him. He cut down 188th and Broadway, but slowed up when he saw all the police on the block. Some people had been killed before he got there. He feared the worst, but a girl he knew confirmed that none of them was Rah.

Ahmad turned around and went back the other way. He had searched everywhere, but couldn't get a lead on where his brother might be. Ahmad put one foot in the street, but jumped back when the Lincoln came speeding around the corner. The back door opened and someone pushed a body out. The corpse came to a rolling stop at Ahmad's feet. He looked down and almost fainted at the sight of what was left of his little brother.

Bone held the cell phone to his ear in disbelief. He just nodded dumbly while Ahmad raged on the other end. Bone told him where they would rendezvous and ended the call. He looked at his body-guards and sighed.

"Trouble?" Rudy asked. He was a thick man who sported a handlebar mustache.

"They hit Rah," Bone said sadly. Although Ahmad and Tracy's younger brother had been a pain in the ass, Bone never wished harm on him. He didn't know how he was going to tell his son's mother that her little brother had been murdered.

"So it begins," Justice said, rubbing his salt-and-pepper beard. He was the old head of their crew and more of the thinker. "The Clarks know we were in on the hit. Now what?"

"I tell you one thing," Bone said, heading for his car. "I ain't gonna make myself a target out here. Let's go get Ahmad and roll back to the spot." Just as Bone reached for his car keys, a black Hummer wheeled around the corner. Bone and his team watched in amazement as Fritz came up through the sunroof holding two Mac 11s.

"MUTHA FUCKAS!" Fritz screamed as he applied pressure to the triggers. The night sky lit up with muzzle flashes and explosions of lead. Fritz swept the Macs in a crisscrossed pattern, trying to lay everything on the block down.

Bone happened to be standing right next to his car. He dove to the ground, just barely escaping the storm that splattered the young man coming out of the bodega. The young man spun left to right, before finally backflipping. Fritz howled in frustration and emptied one of the Mac clips into Bone's car.

Justice drew his weapon and fired on Fritz. The bullet hit him in the arm, sending one of the Macs flying into the streets. In the very next motion, Fritz drew his Glock and started letting off. Justice took a bullet in the stomach and went down. Hearing the police sirens in the distance, the Hummer pulled off.

Bone's heart was beating at a hundred miles a minute. The boy from the bodega stared at him with dead eyes, while Justice squirmed and moaned and gurgled blood. Death surrounded him everywhere he turned. He knew that the situation had become serious. Bone could either lay low till it all blew over, or he could counter. He chose to counter.

"Turn this mutha fucka around," Fritz barked at Angelo. "That nigga is still breathing. Turn this bitch around, Angie."

"Nigga, be cool," Angelo snapped. "Police gonna be all up out this bitch in a hot minute. You bleeding all over this mutha fucka and a smoking gun is gonna look kinda funny. We'll get another crack at that mutha fucka. Watch and see, dawg."

CHAPTER 28

"**WHAT THE FUCK WERE** you thinking?" Scotty questioned the trio. "What gives you little mutha fuckas business to execute anybody?"

"The right of my father's murder," Shai barked. "I'm not gonna sit for this shit."

"Shai, this is not for you. People are going to die in this war. I don't want you to end up on the slab or in the pen. Why can't you just fall back?"

"Falling back is not an option," Shai said coolly. "The bottom line is this: My father was murdered and my brother will probably never walk again, if he happens to live through his injuries. Scotty, you've been a dear friend to my family for a great many years, but you're not a Clark. As of this moment, I am officially assuming control of my father's family. This includes bringing his killers to justice. Now, you can stay on and help us pull this off, or you can leave. The choice is yours, Martin."

Scotty couldn't believe what he was hearing. He looked to the other lieutenants for support, but found none. They all backed Shai.

He threw his hands up in mock surrender. He always knew there was a touch of Poppa lingering beneath Shai's surface, but now he was seeing it firsthand.

As Shai and Gator were heading out the front door, Sol was coming in. He had bags under his eyes from the last few trying days. He had been helping Scotty handle all of Poppa's business. From funeral arrangements, to his investments. Tommy might've been the head of the Clark family, but Sol had established himself as the pillar.

"Hey, Shai," Sol said, shaking his hand. "How you doing?"

"Just trying to put my father's affairs in order," he said. "As of this moment, I'm taking control of the family. I'll be running things until my father's killers are brought to justice."

"Do you think that's the reasonable thing to do?" Sol asked.

"Sol, reason flew out the window when the first shot was fired. These people don't understand reason, so I will speak to them in a language they do. Now, will you help me make things right, or try to give me a speech like Scotty did?"

"You know me"—Sol raised his hands in surrender—"whatever is best for the family. You have my support, Shai."

"Thank you, Sol. The next order of business is to gather all of my father's business associates together and deal with the casino. I want the project to continue as planned."

"I'm glad you feel that way." Sol gave him a half smile. "That's kinda what I wanted to talk to you about. Can you come back in the office for a second?"

Shai looked at Gator, who simply shrugged and kept going out the front door. Shai followed Sol down the hallway to Poppa's office. When he got there, Scotty was already seated with Phil and Antonio, going over some paperwork. Shai was suddenly very confused.

"Come on in, Shai." Sol waved to him. "We've got some things to discuss."

"What's going on?" Shai asked, taking a seat off to the right.

"Why don't you sit at the head of the table, Shai," Scotty suggested.

Shai was still a little confused, but he did as he was asked. Once Shai was in the proper seat, Scotty continued, "Shai, I know this is a tough time for you, but we need to discuss your father's business holdings."

"What's to talk about?" Shai asked. "I figure if Tommy lives, everything goes to him. I'm just the stand-in."

"Not so, Shai," Sol cut in. "Not long before your father was murdered, he had a meeting with Scotty and me. In this meeting, Thomas Clark named one Shai Clark as his successor."

"Get the fuck outta here," Shai said in disbelief. "Why would he have done a fool thing like that? I don't know shit about how to run a business."

"This is the way the old man wanted it, kid," Scotty explained. "Nobody knows why he did it like this, but he did. He was very clear on that point."

"This is too much," Shai said, slumping in the chair. "My father built his empire from the ground up. He knew the ins and outs of everything. I'd probably just fuck it up."

"Shai, you wouldn't be alone." Sol patted his hand. "Scotty and me will be with you all the way. You can do this, Shai. Your father wouldn't have entrusted this to you if he didn't feel he could. Congratulations."

Each of the men nodded and wished Shai well. He looked out over the gathered faces and wondered why. Once again, Poppa had pulled a rabbit out of his hat. He had divided his kingdom between his two sons, giving Shai domain over the heavens and Tommy the earth. This was an unexpected twist for Shai, but it changed things considerably.

The day of Poppa's funeral was a major event. People came from everywhere to salute the fallen king. They laid Poppa out in a pearl white casket with gold handles. People were sobbing and falling out, but Shai held his composure. It's not that he wasn't sad, but he knew that he had to show strength.

Honey sat at Shai's side, holding his hand. She hadn't known Poppa that well, but she felt it only right to pay her respects. She hadn't intended on sitting up front, but Shai insisted. Even though she hadn't been up front with Shai about the Tommy situation, he had managed to forgive her. He wouldn't admit it, but Shai was falling in love.

The main event of the whole thing was Mike's performance. He sobbed and acted as if he were really broken up by Poppa's death. Swan as well as a few of the others in attendance wanted to drop him on the spot. Sol and the presence of the law prevented that. Mike having the nerve to come to Poppa's funeral only made Shai want to kill him more.

"I'm sorry for your loss," Mike said to Shai.

"Are you?" Shai asked with a raised eyebrow.

"Poppa was like a brother to me, kid. Whoever did this will pay. Don't worry, Shai. I'm gonna handle everything."

"Thank you for your concern," Shai said, unmoved. "But I have everything under control. I have assumed control of my father's family. I can assure you this, Mike: Any and all parties involved will be punished." Shai made sure he was looking Mike in the eye when he said this.

"Sure, kid." Mike smiled. "If you need me though, you know how to find me."

"Indeed I do," Shai responded.

Mike was a little taken aback by the way Shai had come at him. The first time they met, Shai was a little cocky but respectful. The young man before him was quite different. He was cold and confident. It seemed that the youngest Clark boy might prove to be a problem after all.

Shai looked around at the long faces of the people surrounding him. "So much death," he whispered. Shai hadn't even been in New York for a fraction of a season and his whole world had been rocked. When he thought of the name Clark, it used to bring a smile to his face, now it only brought visions of death. He had seen men killed and he had given the order to murder, but he felt as if nothing had changed. He was only doing what he had to do.

Shai always knew his people did dirt, but he never understood it. Even as an adult, he didn't grasp the full scope of what his family was involved in. Over the last few weeks, it made perfect sense. His father played in a game far bigger than that of politics. This was a game that was played for souls.

A cold chill ran over him as he began to recount the things that had gone on while he had been home. Much blood had been spilled and more was to come. This wasn't the way Shai wanted it, but he knew it had to be. He used to think that his father shielded him because he wasn't strong enough for the game, but he was beginning to understand that this wasn't entirely true. Poppa had already sacrificed his soul so that his children wouldn't have to. Tommy had made his choice and Shai was getting worse by the year. Hope was the last ray of light in the Clark dynasty.

" 'Sup, lil' sis?" Shai asked, sitting on the folding chair next to hers. "You okay?"

"Hey," she sobbed into a handkerchief. "I'm cool, I guess. I just never . . ." Every time she tried to speak, she began crying. "Daddy is gone, Shai."

"It's gonna be okay." He hugged her. "Me and Tommy are gonna take care of you."

"Tommy?" she asked, looking at him with red-rimmed eyes. "Tommy is lost. Has been for a few years. Even if he does survive the shooting, he's gotta face the charges they're bringing against him. And even if he beats that, he's gonna be right back out there, doing his thing. I can't take this anymore, Shai. Y'all think I don't know, but I do. People talk."

"Don't listen to people, Hope," he told her. "Gossip is always a variation of the truth."

"You think I don't know about Poppa and Tommy? Shai, I can't even have a boyfriend because the guys are all afraid of getting killed or beat up by Tommy or one of his flunkies."

"Hope, it's not like it sounds. You know Poppa was a good man and so is Tommy."

"I know they were, Shai," Hope said, wiping her eyes. "But they did wicked things. I want to get away from here, Shai."

"Hope, where will you go? We're your family."

"Shai," she pleaded. "You don't understand. I have to get out of here. If I don't, I'll go crazy. Every day I wonder if someone is gonna jump out and try to snatch me. I can't live like this, Shai. Please. Maybe I could go stay with Mom for a while?"

"You can't be serious." Shai looked at her. "News flash, baby girl. Mom is a fucking junkie. She walked out on us before you could even breathe on your own. What the fuck would make you think she wants anything to do with us? That bitch didn't even come to the funeral. Listen, Hope"—he caressed her face—"soon, this shit is gonna be all over. I'm gonna get back into school and take you with me. We never have to come back here if you don't want, okay?"

"Shai, I'm not a kid anymore. Don't tease me."

"Sis, I'm dead serious. I gotta help get this shit worked out, then we're gone. I promise."

"Okay, Shai," she sobbed. "Okay."

Shai gave his sister a hug and sealed his promise with a kiss to the forehead. He meant every word of what he had told her. Poppa's murder had to be avenged, but Tommy could have the streets. When it was all said and done, all Shai wanted to do was play ball and run his father's company to the best of his abilities. When it was over, he and his sister would say good-bye to the rotten Apple and look to make a normal life for themselves.

Detectives Brown and Alvarez watched the exchange from a distance. They couldn't belive how well things turned out. Poppa was dead, they had Tommy on a murder, and the Clark family was crumbling. They had managed to kill two birds with one stone. The case was wrapping itself up, and they hardly had to do anything. Detective Brown was about to go over and say something to the last remaining Clark male, when Alvarez grabbed him by the arm.

"Let him mourn," Alvarez said sympathetically. "Let him mourn."

Shai stood alone, near where the procession had parked. He said his good-byes to his father, the man who had given him life and inspiration. Tommy and Poppa had taught him everything he knew. They were both his parents and advisers. He didn't agree with everything that they said, but they would never tell him anything wrong.

He shook off his foolish feelings and tried to focus on the business at hand. He was nineteen years old and in control of a quite sizable corporation. Running it would be no easy task, but in addition to that, his father's murder still had to be addressed. Everyone was against him playing a role in the erupting street war, but Shai was beyond the point of reasoning. Shai had the Clark name behind him and a few loyal soldiers. There wasn't much anyone could do to stop him.

Watching Rah die had been a strangely pleasant experience, but he was a small fish. Rah was one of Bone's peoples but still small. Shai needed the head. He thought of countless ways that he would make Bone suffer before he died, but he needed to get to him first. Bone wasn't as heavy a hitter as Tommy, but he still wouldn't be easy to touch. Especially after the hit Fritz had fucked up. Shai needed an angle.

"Slim," Swan called out, bringing Shai out of his plot. "You a'ight?"

"I'm cool," Shai said, shaking his head. "It's just that all this shit is a bit much, ya know?"

"Yeah, man. The streets will do it to you. More often than not, I wanna go crazy, but I hold it together. Fate has a bigger plan for me, just like it has for you. I know you got a lot of shit bouncing around in your head, son, but you gotta man-up. The streets are going crazy right now, 'cause there's no one to take charge. I know you going through something right now, but dead that shit. We got bigger problems. Crews are going against crews and those greasy-ass Italians are just standing by, waiting to pick over whatever's left. We need your head to be right, Shai. Ride or die, fam'?"

Swan's words were sharp, but very true. A war for control of Poppa's turf was popping off in their backyard and he was daydreaming. He needed to be a solider for his family and his people. Poppa raised his kids to be warriors.

"We ride, Swan," Shai assured him. "Taking this on is gonna take soldiers and money."

"Baby boy," Swan said, putting his arm around Shai's shoulder, "you just don't know how far your name goes. I got a plan to fix that bitch and them sucka-ass niggaz. Let me run it down to you."

The little Mexican hung from the basement wall by a filthy strap that was nailed into the brick. He felt like he was going to die at any moment and in truth, he was ready to. His captors had been torturing him for the last three hours. He cursed himself for smoking cigarettes, 'cause if his wind was up, he would've escaped.

They never even saw the black guys coming when they ran up. They were all wearing masks and carrying guns. The Mexican and his crew managed to kill one of the kidnappers, but they were holding superior firepower. The Mexican's crew took off, but when he tried to follow, he was captured. Now he hung from a wall awaiting his fate.

"Talk, mutha fucka," the first masked man said.

"I tell you all I know," the Mexican rasped. "They pay us to kill the nigger and promise more territory."

"You think he's lying?" the second masked man whispered.

"Doubt it," the first masked man said. "We've been whipping his ass for a minute and he hasn't told us much more than that. Besides, that's enough. I'm gonna get this info to Shai. I think he'll want to hear this."

"What about this nigga?" the second masked man asked.

"Kill him."

Alvarez came strolling out of the captain's office whistling a tune. He walked right past his partner, but never broke his stride. Brown looked at him, confused, and followed Alvarez from the station house. The Puerto Rican detective was nearly back at the car before his partner caught up to him.

"What's the deal?" Brown asked.

"Just got word from the DA's office," Alvarez said, sliding into the passenger seat.

"And?"

"And Amine is singing like a bird. Names, dates, the whole nine. Seems like Heath owed Tommy some money. When the guy doesn't pay up, *bang!* Tommy gets him clipped."

"Conspiracy?"

"That's what the warrant says."

"Shit, if Tommy does pull through we're gonna fry his ass."

The two detectives shared a merry chuckle and hopped into their car.

CHAPTER 29

LUCIUS, Leon, Gator, and Fritz sat at a booth inside Nikki's sipping straight Hennessy and reminiscing about Poppa. Fritz had wanted to jump on Lucius more than once, but Gator held him back. The traitors would get theirs, but it would be as Tommy had wanted it done. Public, but quiet.

"I can't believe he's gone," Lucius sobbed into the arm of his suit jacket. "He was like a father to me, yo. That nigga gave me my start."

"He was good to all of us," Fritz hissed. "Anybody that was down with this shit is gonna get laid out."

"Word up," Lucius agreed. "Niggaz gotta get it, yo. If you ask me, I think them Italians did it."

"We all got an opinion about the shit," Gator said, opening a beer bottle with his teeth. "One way or another, it's gonna come out."

Unlike Lucius, Leon didn't miss the looks that Fritz and Gator were shooting at them. The two men definitely knew something that they weren't telling. Leon didn't like it and wished for the hundredth time that he had brought a gun with him.

Gator looked around and noticed that some of the people from the funeral had begun to file into the little bar. There weren't that many, but there were enough to make their point. Gator gave Fritz the nod and let him know it was showtime. Fritz nodded back. And pulled his .45 from under the table.

"So what we gonna do now?" Gator asked.

"What you mean?" Lucius asked suspiciously.

"What the fuck you think I mean?" Gator leaned in. "Poppa is gone, Tommy is laid up. Shai is running the show now, but he ain't no street nigga. With the Italians out of the picture, things are gonna be rough as hell. I didn't come to New York to starve, dawg. If the well goes dry, I ain't got a pot to piss in."

"He ain't lying," Fritz cut in. "I tried to get at Angelo about it, but this nigga is all twisted over Poppa. I mean, I loved the old man too, but I got mouths to feed, yo."

Lucius sipped his drink and eyed the two men. He was trying to figure out what their angle was. He hadn't been dealing with Bone long enough for Tommy to find out, so they couldn't have been trying to pick him for info. Besides, that wasn't their thing. These two were killers. But they couldn't have come to hit him, because Nikki's was too crowded. Lucius decided to try his luck. With the two killers on his side, his crew would be much stronger.

"See," Lucius said, downing the last of his drink, "that's why y'all need to fuck with a nigga like me. See, I saw this shit coming. Seen it a long time ago, but no one listened to me."

"What you talking 'bout, yo?" Gator asked.

"I'm talking about getting with the winning team, son. I cut a deal with Bone and them to get a bigger piece of the pie."

"You crazy?" Fritz asked. "Tommy would kill us all."

"Not likely." Lucius waved him off. "Even if that nigga does wheel his ass out the hospital, the police gonna snatch him for the murder. That boy is a sinking ship, but we ain't gotta go down with him."

"So you're with them now?" Gator asked in anticipation. Leon looked to his partner hoping that he would catch on and shut up, but he didn't see it when he answered:

"Damn right."

Fritz cut loose with his .45, tearing Lucius's knee to shreds under the table. Lucius hopped up and fell to the ground. Leon tried to run, but Gator hit him in the back of the head with a beer bottle. Leon staggered and fell to the ground. Gator stepped over him, holding a nine and fired two shots into his face. Leon twitched once and died.

Fritz smiled as he watched people running back and forth, trying not to get hit up. He turned to finish Lucius off and found himself staring down the barrel of a small .22. Lucius hit Fritz once in the neck and once in the face. Fritz crashed into the table behind them, sending liquor flying through the air. Lucius tried to turn his gun on Gator, but was too late.

Gator stomped the heel of his Stacy Adams shoe into Lucius's face, smashing his nose. Gator put a knee in Lucius's chest and began to punch him in the face. When Lucius tried to raise his gun arm again, Gator grabbed it. He smiled wickedly and sank his gold teeth into his forearm.

Lucius howled in pain as Gator tore away skin and muscle. Blood dripped from his face as he leaned in close to Lucius. "Snake mutha fucka," he whispered. "This is for my uncle." Gator broke a beer bottle on the ground and jammed the broken edge into Lucius's face.

Shai sat in the backyard smoking a blunt and thinking about what he was going to do. There were dozens of guests milling around the property, but they all steered clear of him. Shai had left specific instructions that he was not to be disturbed unless it was by the guest he was waiting on. When Shai felt the presence over him, he didn't have to turn and see who it was.

"What up, Snoop?" Shai asked, blowing out a ring of smoke.

"Ain't nothing," Snoop said, sitting in the chair opposite Shai. "I got that info you wanted." He slid a manila envelope to Shai. "Seems there were quite a few hands involved in your father's murder."

"Talk to me," Shai said, thumbing through the files.

"Well, it was definitely Mike that gave the okay for the hit. Seems he went to some of the other crew and tried to get them to waste either Poppa or Tommy. Preferably Tommy, but Poppa filled the spot. I'll bet my ass that he struck a deal with Bone, but his people didn't do the job."

"They didn't?" Shai asked, surprised. "Then who the fuck did?"

"An unexpected player," Snoop said, pointing at a picture of a man with a shaved head. "Calls himself Little Frog. He runs a crew of Latinos from the Lower East Side."

"We don't even know them, why would they move on my father?"

"Same reason as everyone else." Snoop looked around. "Power. Your father is the man, Shai. He ran all of this shit and he did it fairly. Niggaz knew they were gonna starve if Tommy took over. He wasn't gonna let nobody eat but his people. They were scared of the future."

"This shit is not for me, yo," Shai said, clutching his head. "These mutha fuckas ain't got no respect for life. All over some fucking dope? This shit doesn't make any sense to me, Snoop."

"Fuck it, Shai." Snoop shrugged. "These are the scraps they left us. We're all just out here really trying to get by. Not everyone had the same success that Poppa had. That nigga had his marbles up."

"Yeah, and some niggaz had him laid down."

"Shai, you don't see what I'm getting at," Snoop said, becoming serious. "What your father did was illegal, but he put his heart into it and made it pop. It isn't what he did that made him such a respected man, but the passion with which he did it. Poppa never laid down for anything when it came to his trade."

"Just like I won't lay down for him dying," Shai declared.

"You sure you wanna go there with this?" Snoop asked.

"Real sure, fam'. I gotta see this gets done right."

"Then there's something else you might want to know." Snoop sighed. "A little know-nothing mutha fucka named Amine is the one who put the finger on Tommy in the Heath murder. He's giving the police enough evidence to fry your brother."

"Shit!" Shai cursed. "Where is he now?"

"The police got him."

"Damn, so we can't touch him?"

"I didn't say that, Shai." Snoop smiled. "I said the *police,* not the feds. These local mutha fuckas are stupid. He's on the Island, but he's in PC."

"Who do we have in there?" Shai asked anxiously.

"Nobody. When they brought that rat fuck in, they moved all of Tommy's people to booking or other detention centers. They do have a little sense."

"It might take some doing." Shai scratched his chin. "But I think I have a plan. A nigga owes my people a favor. I think I'm gonna reach out to him."

The men's conversation was broken up by a trio approaching from the direction of the house. The first was a tall man wearing a gray suit and a black overcoat. His hair hung down across his Asian face and touched his cheeks. The second was a squat man with brown skin and a shaved head. The third was a petite woman carrying a briefcase. The tall man stepped up first.

"Clark?" he asked politely.

"Who wants to know?" Shai asked, standing.

"Forgive the intrusion during your time of mourning. My name is Ichiro. I am looking for Tommy Clark."

"He ain't here. I'm Shai Clark, what can I do for you?"

"We have been sent here by Billy Wong to help you with your problem. I think you will find our skills to be quite an asset in these . . . dangerous times."

Shai looked at the trio to see if they were on the level; sure enough they were. If there's one thing he learned growing up in a house with Tommy, it was how to spot a killer. Snoop looked on, confused, while Shai just smiled.

. . .

Legs stepped off the bus at Port Authority and looked around. He hadn't been gone for a long time, but it seemed like it. He wanted to shoot uptown and see what was up with the crew, but he wasn't here for that. The caller on the phone had given him specific instructions and Legs intended to follow them to the letter. Too much hung in the balance.

Legs searched around until he found who he was looking for. A red-faced officer stood near the curb writing out a parking ticket. Legs looked at a sonogram picture of his unborn child and fought back a tear. He sucked it up and approached the cop. Without hesitation, he punched the officer in the face.

The officer staggered back and fell into the street. It took all of two seconds for more police to come and proceed to whip Legs's ass. They clubbed and kicked him, before cuffing him and throwing him roughly into the paddy wagon. He sat in the back of the wagon and wondered when, if ever, he would get to see his child. Legs had made a deal with the devil and it was time to pay.

Ahmad drove the Blazer through the streets of Harlem like a man possessed. He shoveled cocaine into his nose as if it were going to run away. Bone had urged him to calm down, but he wasn't trying to hear it. The Clarks had taken from him and now he would take from them. The cocaine that flooded his system told him to drop any member of the Clark family on sight.

"Slow this mutha fucka down," Rocky protested from the backseat. "You gonna get us pulled over with this heat in the car."

"Stop crying," Ahmad snorted. "That bitch called me damn near a half hour ago and said that lil' nigga Swan just walked into Poppy's restaurant. We gotta get there before he leaves."

"Ahmad," Steve said, "maybe we should think about this. I'm all for killing this kid, but doing it on Spanish Poppy's turf?"

"Fuck that," Ahmad said, taking another snort. "He dies wherever I see him."

Ahmad bent the corner of 149th Street so hard that he almost flipped the truck. He really wanted to get at Shai or Tommy, but Swan would do just as good. He had taken over as Shai's second in command. When he got to Broadway, the first thing he saw was Swan and another man coming out of the restaurant. His whole body tensed with anticipation. Had it not been for Rocky placing a firm hand on Ahmad's shoulder, he might've tried to hop out on him. They calmly pulled to a stop in front of where Swan's ride was parked and began to file out.

"Something doesn't feel right," Brown complained. "With all the shit that's been going on over the last few days, it should be jumping."

"Don't look a gift horse in the mouth," Alvarez told him. "Maybe everyone is still mourning."

"Not fucking likely. These bastards have been trying to kill each other since Poppa died, then it all just stops? I don't buy it, partner. Something's gonna go down, I'd just like to know what."

As in response to Brown's question, a transmission came over the police scanner: "ALL UNITS, ALL UNITS. WE HAVE RE-PORTS OF GUNFIRE ON WEST 148TH STREET."

"Unit one-one-four en route," Brown said into the receiver. "Punch it, J!"

The Buick lurched into traffic in the direction of the gunfire. They didn't know for sure if Tommy's family was involved, but it was a pretty good guess. Brown leaned back in the passenger seat and thought how much easier his job would've been if they got there too late and Tommy's crew were all dead.

Swan had just finished the negotiations with Spanish Poppy and his crew. Shai had instructed him to go uptown and holla at the kid about resuming the relations that Tommy had chosen to sever. They agreed to resume supplying the Clarks with cocaine, as long as they had exclusive rights. This meant that they couldn't buy coke from anyone except Poppy. This suited Shai just fine. In return, they agreed not to up the prices and to lend support to the Clarks in their cause of punishing Poppa's killer. Spanish Poppy had a lot of love for the old man and didn't like the fact that he had been murdered so close to retirement.

Swan was feeling pretty good about the turnout. He was aware that Shai had a lot on him, making the transition from a schoolboy to a gangsta and he wanted to make it as easy as possible. He knew in his heart that Shai wasn't made for the life, but he insisted on seeing his father's affairs put in order. Swan had no choice but to ride it out with him, even if it meant his life.

Dave was saying something to Swan, when he stopped short. He turned to see what had drawn Dave's attention and peeped several men creeping. Swan's instincts told him that something wasn't right. When he recognized Ahmad, he knew what time it was. By the time Dave shouted a warning, Swan was already in motion.

Swan dove behind a car, drawing his Ruger. Seconds later, bullets struck the spot where he had been standing. The gunmen were thrown off by Swan's quick reflexes, but they quickly recovered. Ahmad stepped up blasting away with his nine. He hit damn near everything but Swan.

Rocky was a better shot. He moved forward with his Desert Eagle and gave Dave three. Dave got hit once in the arm and twice in the chest. He staggered from the impact, but his vest had withstood the shots. Or so he thought. Dave touched his chest and his fingers came away bloody. Rocky smiled, knowing the armor-piercing shells were well worth what he paid for them.

Dave felt the burning in his chest spreading to his arms. His mind raced in every direction, keeping him from reacting. His whole young life flashed before his eyes as he slid down the side of the car. With his last bit of strength, Dave let off a burst from his Mac 10. Rocky took at least five to his face and torso, killing him painfully. Dave's last thought was, At least I got to take one of them with me. He was dead at the age of eighteen.

Seeing his man dead sent Ahmad into a rage. He fired shot after shot, turning the car into Swiss cheese. Swan tried to move, but the gunmen had him penned. He tired to look around the bumper of the car and a bullet grazed his shoulder. He was up shit's creek.

Hearing the shots, Spanish Poppy's men came out of the restaurant blasting. Swan used their diversion and came up from behind the car. He squeezed off two shots. Ahmad took one to the chest and went down. The remaining shooter turned his attention back to Swan. Swan dropped back behind the car just as a flurry of bullets struck the car and a man coming out of the store.

There were bullets flying everywhere and Swan was stuck in the middle. He heard police sirens in the distance and knew he had to do something. Lying flat on his stomach, Swan could see the shooter's legs on the other side of the car. He aimed his pistol and took out the shooter's ankles. When he hit the floor, Swan put two in his side for good measure.

The shooting had stopped, and Swan was unharmed with the exception of a gash on his shoulder. Spanish Poppy's men had started disappearing into their foxholes. Swan knew he had to leave, but he wasn't done yet. He approached Ahmad, who was still gasping for air on the ground.

Ahmad wanted to curse Swan, or maybe even try and continue the fight, but he couldn't. The bullet had entered through his chest, and ripped up his lung on the way out his back. All he could do was gurgle blood as Swan stepped over him and fired three shots into his anger-twisted face.

CHAPTER 30

DURING THE NEXT FEW DAYS, it rained blood in the streets of Harlem. After Ahmad's death, Bone had gotten low, but that didn't stop him from playing a part in the feud. The Clarks went at Bone's. Frog and his men used the chaos to try and gain a hold in Harlem. They killed Tommy's people as well as Bone's.

The Clark family had begun to show signs of wear. Not only were the Clarks at war with other crews, but they were at odds with each other. With Poppa being dead and Tommy going to jail, the Clark throne was vacant and everyone wanted to claim it. Everything was falling apart and Shai was left alone to hold it together.

Shai sat behind his father's desk staring vacantly at the wall. Gator sat to his right, while Swan was on his left. Scotty sat directly opposite Shai, and Angelo sat quietly to the side with his hands folded. He hadn't been himself since his partner was murdered. Angelo now had a personal stake in the war.

Shai's life seemed to be going downhill at an alarming rate. His father had been murdered and Tommy was currently occupying the infirmary at the Federal Detention Center on Pearl Street. The police had hit Tommy up something terrible, but he lived through it. He would never walk again, but he would stand trial for Heath's murder.

"Shai, we gotta do something," Swan pleaded. "It's chaos out there, man. Everyone is wilding out, trying to slide into a place of power that rightfully belongs to you."

"I have eyes," Shai said, casting a glance at Swan, then back to the wall. "You don't think this is fucking with me too? This shit has gotten out of hand. My father is dead and they're gonna try and fry my brother for this Heath shit. We've lost over a dozen soldiers, maybe more, since this thing popped off. How many more will have to die before we say enough?"

"We need to ride on all these niggaz," Gator said, picking at his bandage. "We got the guns and the muscles, let's stomp these mutha fuckas and be done with it."

"Ain't that simple, fam'," Shai said, standing up and moving around the table. "We've got the guns and the soldiers, but we don't have the organization. We're at war amongst each other and other crews. Our forces are spread too thin because everyone has an agenda."

"At this rate, we're gonna get mashed out," Angelo added.

"Shai," Scotty cut in, "this is just why your father never wanted you involved with this part of the business. These niggaz ain't playing out there. The stakes are far higher than the rewards. This is why he didn't want you to play. Poppa had a bigger plan for you, but this is the way fate decided to deal the cards."

"My nigga"—Swan placed a hand on Shai's shoulder—"what I'm about to tell you ain't pretty, but it's real. These niggaz is bugging, 'cause they ain't got no direction. They need someone to step in and lead them. Shai, when this is done, nobody's gonna be mad at you for walking away."

"As much as we all hate to admit it, Shai has to put this back right." Angelo sighed. "As long as I get to kill me a few mutha fuckas, I don't care."

"There's just so much going on, man," Shai huffed. "All this killing and shit, what are we doing? I don't know shit about running something like this and if I don't move right, I'm gonna fuck it up. I ask the most high time and again, why me?"

"Why not you?" Sol said, strolling in casually. "Shai, even though it's a wicked business, it was your father's legacy. Poppa made it safe for kids to play and old folks like us to come and go safely. Don't let these fucking animals undo that."

Shai nodded in understanding. It *was* his father's legacy. Poppa hustled, but he made sure the hoods he hustled in were kept correct. The way things were going wasn't right. The sheep wandered unattended by their wounded shepherd. The reckless murdering that had been going on the last few days was not how his father would've wanted it.

"Swan," Shai whispered, "speak to our people. We'll settle this thing once and for all. Quietly, if possible. If not, we fight."

"That's what I'm talking about." Swan smiled. "Whatever you need from me, dawg."

"All I need from you is strength and wisdom, old friend." Shai patted him on the back. "Scotty"—he turned to the lawyer—"I need you to arrange a visit with Tommy for me."

"That can be arranged." Scotty nodded. "He's still in the ICU, but you're his brother. They shouldn't have a problem letting you see him."

"Make it so," Shai said.

When Shai left his father's office, he had a lot on his mind. There were armed soldiers posted all throughout the house, as well as the surrounding grounds. Everyone wore a grim mask. The odds against the Clarks were formidable, but not insurmountable. He knew that ending the war and putting things in order wasn't going to be an easy task, but it was his duty to do so. As he rounded the hall corner he bumped into a teary-eyed Hope.

"What's good, sis?" Shai asked, wondering what had happened to her.

"You're with them now?" she whispered.

"Who?"

"You know, Shai. I heard you guys talking."

"Be easy." He patted her cheek. "Nothing has changed. I got you, sis. Things are crazy now. Tommy's in no condition to do much about it, so I'm just helping the guys hold it together. Once things die down, this shit is getting handed over to someone more qualified. I ain't no gangsta, Hope."

"You don't even see it," she sobbed. "They're gonna change you, Shai. You're gonna end up like them."

"No, I won't," he protested. "This was Poppa and Tommy's life, not mine."

"My friends don't even wanna hang with me anymore. They say that you're the new king and it's too dangerous to be around me."

"Baby girl, don't believe everything you hear. Listen, as soon as this shit is over with, we're out. Wherever you wanna go. I was even thinking about going to Europe for a while. Maybe the summer?"

"Shai"—she wiped her eyes—"promise me you won't become one of them."

"You got that." He smiled. "Now go get dressed. We're going to see Tommy tonight."

Hope's mood seemed to brighten a bit. Shai sighed and continued walking through the house. The next few steps would have to be executed precisely. Shai was gambling for the lives of all his people and their families. He glanced out the window and saw that storm clouds were forming in the distance.

"Fitting," he whispered. There was a storm brewing indeed. Shai just had to make sure he and his were the only ones holding umbrellas.

Micco and his daughter's mother, Rosa, were just coming out of the theater on 44th and Broadway. They had been to see a play and had an expensive dinner in downtown Manhattan. Since they had started making more money with Bone and the Italians, Micco had made it a point to treat himself to the finer things in life.

He headed east on a lightly populated block, touching and kissing Rosa. Micco found a dark corner and ushered her into the shadows. He licked and played with her breast tenderly, as he thought how good life was. Rosa's eyes rolled back in ecstasy as her man grazed her spots. When she opened them, she saw they were not alone. Two Asians dressed in dark suits stood there looking at them. Micco, feeling Rosa's body stiffen, looked over his shoulder to see what was going on.

Kinnada Ichiro pirouetted toward the couple and produced a small dagger from a fold in her business skirt. With a swipe of her petite arm, she lopped off one of Micco's ears. Rosa tried to scream and Kinnada plunged the blade into her mouth and out the back of her head.

"Rosa!" Micco screamed, pulling out his Glock. He tried to aim it at Kinnada and Gabriel Ichiro made his move. He pulled out a hook-like object that was attached to a chain. He whipped the weapon hook first and it latched on to Micco's arm. With a yank he pulled it from the young Mexican's body. Kinnada removed her blade from Rosa's throat and used it to saw off Micco's head.

CHAPTER 31

LEGS WALKED DOWN THE prison corridor in step with eleven other men. Inmates lingering in the hall or near their cells tried to shoot intimidating looks at the newcomers. Everyone knew that these men were bound for PC—protective custody. This was where they sent the men who were courageous enough to do the crime, but didn't have the stomach to be housed with the other inmates.

When they had first brought Legs over, he immediately started a fight with another inmate. He told the guards that he was in fear for his life because of it. They immediately shipped him from general population to PC.

Amine laid on his bunk reading a magazine. He had done a lot of reading just to pass the time and keep himself from going crazy. The feds were supposed to have him moved until the trial, but he was still stewing on the Island. He glanced up from his magazine and thought that he had seen a ghost. "Legs?" he whispered.

"Amine?" Legs smiled, approaching the cell door. "Fuck is you doing in here?"

"I was gonna ask you the same thing, man. I thought you got low."

"I did, till a mutha fucka turned me in," Legs said angrily. "These niggaz was gonna fry me for that Heath shit, so I did what I had to do. Ya know?"

"You cut a deal?" Amine asked.

"I had to, yo. I know you think I'm a sucker," Legs fronted. "But I got a seed on the way. I need to be there for him or her."

"I can dig it." Amine nodded. "Between us, I cut one too. I didn't wanna do it, 'cause that ain't gangsta, but it was me or him."

"So you're the one that got Tommy knocked?" Legs asked, trying to hide his rage.

"They got him?" Amine asked. "Damn, I feel a little better now. Not that I wanted them to knock T, but I got a life too."

"Move along," a beefy guard barked.

"Yo." Legs leaned in. "I'ma get wit' you later, fam'."

"A'ight," Amine said, giving him dap. "It's good to be with you again, partner. I just wish it was under different circumstances."

"Me too." Legs turned away, so Amine wouldn't see the tear running down his face. "Me too."

Honey sat on the stoop of her building watching the tiny raindrops hit the ground. Her white shirt was damn near transparent and the rain killed her perm, but she wasn't even tripping over it. Her relationship with Shai had become strained. His father's death had fucked him up more than most people realized. He didn't care about school, basketball, or anything else. All he ever thought about was revenge. They used to do things together, now she had to make an appointment just to see him. The change in Shai had begun to frighten her. No longer was he the cocky young man that she had fallen in love with. Shai was becoming something else altogether.

"Girl," Paula said, coming down the stairs, holding an umbrella. "You don't feel this rain?"

"I'm cool." Honey waved her off.

"Honey, what's been up with you?"

"I'm worried about Shai."

"That crazy mutha fucka? Shit, he's just like his brother. He done had damn near every nigga in the hood killed. That boy ain't hardly playing with these mutha fuckas."

"Be quiet, Paula," Honey said, defensively. "Those are just rumors."

"Rumors, my ass," Paula declared. "Poppa is dead and Tommy's ass is a cripple, who you think is putting all these niggaz to sleep? Santa Claus?"

Honey wanted to deny it, but she knew Paula was right. Shai had stepped to the plate and taken over his father's empire. She had tried to console him, but he wouldn't have it. Shai was determined to settle the score. All she could do was stand by him and try not to let her bullshit land her on a hit list.

"Paula, I just don't want nothing bad to happen to Shai," Honey sobbed.

"Oh, shit." Paula stepped back. "Honey, if I didn't know any better, I'd say yo' ass was in love?" Honey remained silent. "Girl, you love him, don't you?"

"Yeah," Honey said, sobbing. "I love him, P. I love him and I don't want to lose him."

"Oh, baby," Paula said, hugging her friend. "It's okay, baby. Have you told him how you feel?"

"How can I? I slept with his brother and kept it from him. He says he forgives me, but I don't buy that. You know how them Clark men are."

"Honey, Shai isn't your typical Clark. He's doing some things that are out of his character now, but it ain't him, Honey. They forced his hand. Go to him, Honey. Let him know how you feel before it's too late."

Before Honey could respond, they heard a car engine approaching. A black town car pulled up to the curb where they were sitting. Angelo stepped out, wearing a gray business suit and holding a nine at his side. He scanned the block, before going around to the other side and opening up the back door. Shai sat in the back of the car, puffing a blunt and looking lazily at Honey. When he waved her over, she came without hesitation.

"What's up?" Shai asked coolly.

"Hi," she whispered.

"How you been, ma?"

"I'm okay, I guess." Honey stood there, fidgeting nervously.

"So, you gonna just stand there getting soaked, or you gonna get in?"

Honey looked back at Paula, who was motioning for her to get in the car. She cast a glance at Shai, whose face held a half smile and slid in the back next to him. Angelo's hawk-like eyes made one more sweep of the block before he climbed in himself. The engine roared and they were off.

There was an uncomfortable silence in the car. Angelo sat up front, stone-faced, staring at nothing at all. She could remember times when he would have been locked into a witty conversation, or making jokes with one of the other soldiers, but not that day. Things were different, and it seemed that the trying times had killed even Angelo's jovial spirit. Shai just stared out the window while Honey waited for him to say something.

"So, what's good, baby girl?" he asked, still not looking at her.

"Not much," she said, in a submissive tone.

"Honey, I'm sorry about the way things have been between us. I ain't trying to throw shade, shit has just been real hectic. Poppa left a lot of unfinished business that I gotta put in order. I'm trying to do everything on my own and still help Tommy fight this case."

"Shai," she spoke up. "About that Tommy thing . . . baby."

"Honey"—he cast his brown eyes on her—"I can't let what went on between you and my brother sidetrack me. You should've told me, but it happened before my time. I care about you, Honey. That might make me one of the dumbest niggaz to drop out of a womb, but I can't help it."

"I care about you too, baby," she said, taking his hand in hers.

"I know you do, baby. I know. I can't say that I'm pleased by the way you chose to carry yourself, or my brother for that matter, but what's done is done. I know you're sorry and you never meant to hurt me, but the question is, will you make this right?"

"Of course," she said, anxious to get back into Shai's good graces. "All I want is a chance with you, Shai. Whatever you want me to do, baby. Just name it."

"Glad you feel that way," he said, with his smile taking on a wicked twist. "I need you to do something for me."

Tommy lay in the hospital bed, trying to figure out where he did wrong. He had always been so careful with his shit. He calculated and planned for the day when his father stepped down and handed the business over to him. All of it went out in a hail of smoke. Even though his mind was still sharp, his body was broken and no good to anyone. Tommy was paralyzed from the neck down.

His bout with self-pity was nearly as short as his reign. The door to his room opened up and Detective Alvarez spilled in, followed by his partner. Tommy wished that he could get up and choke the sarcastic bastards, but he couldn't do shit but frown.

"What up, T?" Brown said, sitting on the edge of his bed. "You don't look happy to see us."

"Fuck you," Tommy croaked.

"It speaks." Brown smiled. "I didn't think you could answer us with all of these tubes running in and out of you." Brown took the oxygen tube that ran into Tommy's nose and squeezed it. Tommy gagged a few times before Brown released it. "Bad-ass drug lord, breathing through a tube and shitting in a Pampers. How does it feel, shit head?"

"Enough, partner," Alvarez cut in. "Tommy, you're in a bad way. The game is over for you. Your father's army is crumbling and you're going to jail for a very long time. Why don't you help us help you?"

Tommy laughed weakly. "You crazy? My father didn't raise no rats. Do what the fuck you want."

"Think you're smart, huh?" Brown said, grabbing Tommy by the face. "You know, it wouldn't be hard to do you in here and make it look like an accident."

"If you don't get your hands off my brother, I'll kill you!" barked a voice from their rear.

Shai stood in the doorway with rage flashing in his eyes. He was flanked by Scotty and Hope. Brown started to reach for his pistol, but Scotty stopped him short with a defiant glare. Even though the young man was the Clarks' lawyer, he was once one of their soldiers. Scotty still had quite a bit of street left in him.

"Let's not go there with this," Scotty said, keeping his voice even. "I think you both know that we don't have much to lose at this stage of the game. Please, leave my client alone with his family."

Brown thought about trying Scotty, but Alvarez laid a hand on his shoulder. He gave his partner the nod and led him out of the hospital room. As he passed Shai, he gave him a cold stare. "I look forward to putting a hole in your little ass too," Brown remarked to Shai.

"Talk is cheap, mutha fucka," Shai said defiantly.

Shai waited for the detectives to leave before he approached his brother's bedside. When he looked at Tommy, he couldn't even be mad at him anymore. The police had tore his brother up. Most of his body was covered in bloodstained bandages and he had tubes running in and out of damn near every hole in his body.

"Tommy." Shai nodded.

" 'Sup," Tommy said, not wanting to make eye contact. "How you been?"

"Better," Shai said, sitting on the bed. "But things are starting to look up for us."

"I hear you're the man now," Tommy groaned.

"In a manner of speaking," Shai answered, still wearing an emotionless face. "I've assumed control of the soldiers, and Sol informed me that all of Poppa's legal holdings have been turned over to me."

"That's heavy burden to carry, Slim."

"I'll manage."

"Things are pretty bad on the streets, huh?" Tommy asked.

"Manageable at best. At least we've rooted out most of the snakes. No offense, T."

"Fuck you, Shai," Tommy chuckled. "I guess I deserved that."

"Quite the contrary," Shai said, stoking his brother's forehead. "I've learned a lesson in all this: trust no one. But as I said, all is forgiven. Honey will actually be very instrumental in helping us dead all this shit."

"What the hell are you cooking up, Shai?"

"Let me worry about that. You just get better."

"Little brother's all grown up, huh?"

"It happens to the best of us, Tommy."

"What about school?"

"I'm still going back. I'm just holding down the fort till you get better. That's all."

"Shai," Tommy sobbed. "Look at me. I don't think I'll be getting much better. I'm no good like this."

"Tommy, don't talk crazy."

"It's not crazy, it's real. I'm fucked up, Shai. I rolled the dice and they fucked me. I can't do shit like this. To make matters worse, that fucking snitch Amine is gonna put me away."

"I wouldn't worry about him," Shai said, patting Tommy's hand. "You've taken care of me all my life. It's time to return the favor."

"Shai," Tommy cried freely. "You don't owe me shit. Just take Hope and get the hell away from all this."

"Can't do that." Shai shook his head. "It's like you said, my name is Clark. Be only a matter of time before someone comes for me. I gotta make this right."

"Shai—"

"There's no more to be said," he cut him off. "This is the way it has to be. Win, lose, or draw, this shit ends."

Tommy looked into his brother's eyes and saw the same blackness that greeted him every morning. The balance of power had shifted and crashed down on his little brother's shoulders. He wanted to hug Shai and tell him how sorry he was for failing him, but he couldn't. All Tommy could do was lay there and weep.

CHAPTER 32

FOR THE LAST FEW WEEKS, James Tucker had been running. He moved from one place to another, each time narrowly escaping death. He had crossed a man who had been good to him. All he ever did was disappoint Poppa, but the man had always allowed him back to make it right. There was no making this right. It was because of him that Poppa Clark was dead.

Poppa's men had all the bus, train stations, and airports covered, so there would be no escape any of those ways. The one route they hadn't thought of was the water. James had rented a boat for a supposed fishing trip, but he was really going to blow town with it. He would sail somewhere, anywhere, and make his escape.

James boarded the twenty-foot boat and tossed his bags on the deck. It was broad daylight, so there were plenty of people about. James figured that even if Poppa's people did catch up to him, they wouldn't touch him here. Just to be on the safe side, James held his nine close.

After untying the boat, James began the task of sailing out. Piloting the boat wasn't the same as driving a car, but he'd figure it out eventually. As the boat began to make its way out to sea, James breathed a sigh of relief. He felt bad about what he did to Poppa, but there would be time to beat himself up over it when he was safely away from New York.

The boat had made it a good ways when the engine stalled. James tried to restart the motor, but it wouldn't kick over. James left the control panel and made his way to the back of the ship to see if something was caught in the rudder. When he leaned over the side, a cord flipped up and wrapped around his neck. James was jerked over the edge of the boat and into the water.

"Greetings, sinner." Priest smiled, hanging from the rear of the boat. "We missed you at the funeral."

"Help!" James screamed. He tried to tread water with one hand and unwrap the rosary with the other.

Priest pulled himself into a sitting position on the back of the boat, tugging James closer. "My son, my son. I loved Poppa Clark as if he were of my flesh. Your cowardice is the reason that he is no longer with us. Are you ready to repent?"

"I'm sorry." James struggled, trying to put some distance between himself and the blades. "They made me do it. I swear on my mother."

"Doesn't much matter now," Priest said, fumbling with the engine. "I am only a guide to the great beyond. It is up to the most high to judge you."

The blades came to life and began to churn the water. One of the blades nearly missed James's face as he thrashed about. He knew that crossing Poppa would catch up with him. When James opened his mouth to scream, the rudder's blades tore into his face and gums. Priest sat and watched as the blades slashed James's face to bits. Once the man was dead, Priest took the helm of the boat. He would coast around for a while, until the sharks were done with the man's body.

. . .

Honey sat in the motel room, looking out the window. It had been raining nonstop for the past few days. Bone had sent some of his people to bring Honey to him. She sent Star to her sister's and reluctantly accepted his summons. For the past few days, they had been held up in the hotel room, snorting coke and sitting around. Honey felt like she was going to go crazy in the room, but she put her feelings to the side for the greater good.

"What the hell is wrong with you?" Bone asked, scooping coke into his nose. "You've been looking out that damn window for over an hour."

"I feel like I'm going crazy in here, Bone," she admitted.

"Girl, you know I can't be out on the streets. It's too much shit going on out there. Don't worry, when it dies down, everything will be cool." Bone slapped Honey on the ass and went into the bathroom.

Honey thought that he would never leave. He had been a pain in her ass for days. Honey snuck over to her purse and pulled out her cell phone. "It's me," she whispered. "Get a pen and write down this address."

Shai paced back and forth, looking over the sea of faces. Those who remained loyal to the Clarks were assembled and awaited their leader's instructions. Shai had called a war council to finally put an end to the drama that had plagued the City. Swan stood at his side in the position of field general, while Angelo served as his adviser.

The troops had begun to lose hope. They were losing men and money. There was more than enough product to sling, but the constant fighting made the streets hot. You had to keep one eye open for police and assassins. Just when they were ready to give up, Shai had come down from the mountain.

"My niggaz," Shai began. "I thank you all for coming. I know these haven't been the easiest few weeks out here. The little war that we've been sucked into was something that none of us wanted. A lot of people have turned their backs on us, but it's all good. The Clarks have always stood independently. I'm not my father or my brother, but I am a Clark and therefore it falls to me to make this right."

"We're with you, Shai!" someone shouted from the crowd.

"Fuck the dagos!" another man shouted.

"Easy, easy," Shai urged them. "With Italians at our back door and every fucking crew in New York at our front, the odds don't appear to be in our favor. I do things a little different than my brother. We will not stage a head-on charge and only get the satisfaction of clipping a few choice snakes. We will make a calculated strike and eradicate all of our enemies."

"I'm down for whatever," Born spoke up. "If you got a plan, I'm sure as hell listening."

"A'ight, y'all, listen up."

Gee-Gee sat and listened as the young black man spoke. He couldn't believe what he was hearing, but somehow he didn't feel like it was a lie. Fat Mike had been causing all kinds of trouble. He was a good earner, but a little too ambitious for the old man's taste. Something would have to be done about him sooner or later.

Once again, Legs and Amine had become the inseparable pair. They ate their meals and moved through the prison together. Amine felt comfortable again, having his partner with him. He felt bad for Legs, but at least he had someone else to do time with. He was totally at ease.

Legs, on the other hand, was stressed out. He had known Amine for years. Through thick and thin, they had been peoples. But Amine violated the code. He snitched and had to answer for it. It wasn't really a choice for Legs. When Swan had contacted him, he was very clear: Legs had brought Amine in, so he was his responsibility. He was also very clear when he told Legs that if Amine testified, his child would never be born.

"Damn, I hate this shit," Amine said, looking at his tray. "What I wouldn't give for some real food. How 'bout you, Legs?"

"Huh?" Legs asked, distracted. "Yeah, man."

"What's been up with you, kid? You ain't been yourself."

"This place is getting to me, I guess."

"Don't worry about it. Soon the feds are gonna move us. I hear they can set us up in a real nice spot." Amine continued to rant about what he and Legs were gonna do with their lives when it was all over. He never even saw Legs pull the shank from his waistband.

Legs looked around to make sure no one was looking, then he moved on Amine. He jammed the pick-like blade into the back of Amine's neck. Amine dropped his tray and gagged. He tried to turn around, but Legs held him in place with the blade. He couldn't bare to look into his friend's eyes. When Amine wouldn't go down, Legs broke the blade off. Amine clutched at his neck, but couldn't get ahold of the lethal object. His legs flailed about as the life drained from his body.

Legs just knelt there and cried over his friend. He hated himself for what he had to do, but at least Shai would take care of his girl and his baby. He knew the youngest Clark would keep his word. Legs stepped over Amine's body and returned to his cell.

The white Benz wagon pulled around to the back of the motel parking lot. Gator hopped out of the car, followed by Angelo, and two other gunslingers. At Angelo's side was an M16 machine gun. Gator carried a sawed-off pump, while the gunslingers had various handguns.

Gator carefully checked his surroundings. They were in a rural town in New Jersey, so all he had to do was look around to see which cars didn't belong. He immediately spotted an Expedition and a Lexus, sitting on 20s. Those cars definitely did not belong. Gator signaled his people and they began to fan out around the parking lot.

The gunslingers were to cover the parking lot, while Angelo and

Gator approached the room from opposite sides. There was no way to tell how many cats Bone had with him, but they were sure he wasn't alone. Angelo peeked inside the room and saw Honey lying across the bed with Bone. There was also a third shadow cast against the wall, but it was coming from the door. Angelo held up three fingers and Gator nodded.

Gator took two steps back and slammed his boot into the motel door. The flimsy wood gave on the first try. Bone spun around in shock, but Honey knew what time it was. She jumped off the bed and ran into the bathroom. Once inside she locked the door and got into the empty tub.

The man who had been hiding tried to draw his gun, but the door had his arm pinned. Gator flipped the shotgun backward, with the barrel against the door. He pulled the trigger and sent a hail of buckshot into the man's groin. Without missing a beat, he snatched the door forward and placed the shotgun to the side of the man's head. The gun bucked again, splattering the man's brains on the wall.

At the sounds of gunfire, the door of the room next to Bone's swung open. The first man to step out caught the full blast of Angelo's M16. The second gunner hopped over his fallen comrade and fired on Angelo. He dodged the bullet and let the M16 go from the hip. He laid the gunner right next to his man.

It seemed like enemies were coming from everywhere. The gunslingers did their part, laying down anyone trying to creep on Gator and Angelo. Gator stepped over the man lying in the doorway and went for the prize. Bone tried to draw, but Gator whacked him across the jaw with the shotgun. Bone cried out like a girl and fell to the ground. Gator was about to finish him, but Angelo stopped him.

"He's mine," Angelo said, trading the M16 for a small .38. "It's 'cause of yo' snake ass my partner is dead." He shot Bone in the arm. "A life for a life."

"Come on, man!" Bone shouted. "Y'all got it, if you want me gone, I'm gone. Just don't kill me."

"Yeah." Angelo chuckled. "We do want you gone. The game is

over and the Clarks are still in power, son." Angelo put one in Bone's head.

To everyone's surprise, a man jumped out of the closet blasting away with two nines. Gator took two slugs to the back and hit the wall. The slugs felt like little fire pellets in his back. His left arm hung numbly at his side, but he was still standing.

The man turned his guns on Angelo, who was already diving for cover. The bullets slammed into the wall and the television, but never touched him. The man momentarily forgot about Angelo, who was only holding a .38, and turned to Gator. The few seconds that the man had taken to fire on Angelo had given Gator enough time to balance the shotgun against his hip and fire.

The buckshot hit the man in his chest and sent him flying into the wall, causing his pistol to fire. The slug hit Gator just above his heart and dropped him. Angelo put two more into the man with the .38 and crawled toward Gator.

"You hit bad?" he asked, trying to examine Gator's wounds.

"Get the fuck off me." Gator waved him off. "What does it look like?" Gator cocked his head and heard the sirens getting closer. "We're fucked."

"Nah," Angelo said, lifting him to his feet. "We're getting the fuck outta here."

Honey had just poked her head from the bathroom door to see if the coast was clear. She almost threw up at the sight of all the dead bodies. "Oh, my God," she whispered.

"Girl," Gator snapped. "You better quit praying and come the fuck on."

Honey gathered her wits and followed the men outside. The gunslingers had already made it back to the truck when they heard the sirens. They weren't stupid enough to leave the lieutenant and the killer though. They parked the truck a few yards up and waited on their people.

"Shit," Gator said, almost making himself and Angelo fall. "I ain't gonna make it, dawg. Gimmie the sixteen and get the fuck

outta here." He looked over his shoulder and saw the first Jersey
state patrol car jump the curb. "Hurry up, man."

"Gator, I ain't gonna leave you."

"You ain't got no choice," Gator informed him, as he put the
sawed-off to Anglo's ribs. "This ain't no time to argue. Tell cuz I
went out in style."

Angelo looked at Gator in amazement. At that moment, he had
more respect for the country boy than anybody else in the game. He
nodded to his comrade and handed him the machine gun. He started
to say something, but Gator's glare gave him pause. Angelo hugged
Gator, then ran off with Honey in tow.

The troopers were swarming into the lot, on foot and by patrol
car. There were easily a dozen of them to Gator's M16. They surrounded him and ordered that he drop his weapon. Gator looked at
the white faces and drawn pistols and gave that infamous smile.

"Okay, mutha fuckas," Gator said, hoisting the machine gun.
"Let's dance!"

CHAPTER 33

FROG PACED THE FLOOR of the project apartment, chain-smoking and taking shots of tequila. Getting involved in Bone's little scheme hadn't played out the way he had expected. He had lost his most trusted friend and a good deal of the homeboys. To make matters worse, the Italians didn't keep up their end of the bargain. Shit was not going well for Frog, and being cooped up in the house wasn't helping.

"What's good, man?" Victor said, waking into the room holding an AK.

"This shit is driving me crazy, bro," Frog ranted. "These fucking niggers got me boxed in."

"Fucking A, man. Tommy was bad enough, but that fucking Shai is a real bastard. Always so fucking cold. That kid has got issues."

"We're gonna have issues if we don't get this shit tightened up," Frog told him. "We gotta be ready if these monkeys come for us."

"We're ready, bro." Victor smiled. "We've got the whole project locked up tight. Our men are posted everywhere. They won't be stupid enough to come in here for you."

No sooner than the words had left Victor's mouth, they heard the first gunshots.

Swan plowed the black Hummer right through the project's fence. The truck spun out and crashed into the front of the building. The other four SUVs followed his lead and rolled into the projects. Men began to hop out of the various vehicles, carrying all sorts of firepower. The people who had been outside ran for any type of cover. The housing project had been in the grip of the Mexicans, but that night they would be liberated.

"Lay all these mutha fuckas down!" Swan said, standing on top of the Hummer, waving an AR-15. "No civilians, but every mutha fucka claiming Frog, dies!" The men moved to carry out Swan's orders. They had been on the defensive long enough, it was time for them to lay down their claim to the hood. Shai had given them new life.

Swan ran toward the building where Frog was supposed to be hiding, followed by six killers. They got halfway to the building, when a wave of Latinos came rushing out. The Latinos were gunning down everything in their path. Swan ducked behind a bench and let the AR spit. He laid down quite a few of the enemies, but they kept coming.

"These mutha fuckas is coming out in packs," Born said, kneeling beside Swan. "I hope we got enough guns."

"Fuck that," Swan said, wiping his forehead. "That nigga Frog doesn't leave here alive. If I gotta tear this mutha fucka down brick by brick, his ass is dead."

Swan popped from behind the bench and sprayed the front of the building. When he had an opening, he pulled a concussion grenade and charged the front door. Swan chucked the projectile through the front door and took cover. The grenade shook the lobby and cleared the way for Swan.

"With me!" he shouted, charging into the building. Latino soldiers were sprawled out all over the lobby. They were unconscious and bleeding from the ears. Swan left two men in the lobby to finish off the wounded. He sent two more up one stairwell and the last two followed him up the other.

"What the fuck is going on down there, homes?" Frog asked.

"Sounds like World War Three," Victor said, running to the window. "There's fucking niggers everywhere."

"We gotta get out of here, man," Frog said, checking his pistol. "Get the money from the back and let's go."

Victor ran to the back room and began snatching money from shoe boxes stacked in the closet. He dumped money and drugs into the duffel bag and headed toward the door. Victor froze as a cold chill ran down his neck. He turned around and found himself face to face with Jin Ichiro. Victor tried to reach for his gun, but the brown-skinned Ichiro was too quick. He grabbed Victor's arm and snapped it in his mammoth paw. When Victor tried to scream, Jin clamped a hand over his mouth and snapped his neck.

Frog began to wonder what was taking Victor so long, so he headed toward the back to check on him. Halfway down the hall, Jin appeared from the bedroom. He moved with blinding speed, but Frog was quicker. He put three in the big man and slumped him. Forgetting about the money, Frog ran for his life.

"I don't buy this shit, Mike," Nicky protested. "All of a sudden, this jig wants a sit-down. Something is up."

"Nicky, don't be so fucking paranoid," Mike said, biting into his slice of pizza. "This kid is scared to death. He ain't from the streets and don't know shit about running his father's business. He needs us to get the wolves off his back."

"Shai's been doing a pretty good job of that on his own," Nicky pointed out. "He's been getting people clipped left and right."

"That ain't him, Nick. That's his people acting off instinct. This little prep school brat is in up to his ass and he knows it."

Shai came strolling into the pizza parlor, flanked by Angelo and two soldiers. Two more men, armed with automatic weapons, waited outside with Mike's people. This was to be a meeting of bosses about the state of the streets.

"Thanks for agreeing to see me," Shai said politely.

"Hey, who am I to refuse a friend?" Mike smiled. "Sit down, fellas." Mike waited until the men were seated before he continued speaking, "Let me start off by saying I'm sorry for what happened to your brother. There was no love lost between us, but I wouldn't wish that shit on anyone."

"Let's cut the bullshit," Shai said, surprising everyone. "You and I both know that you're not sorry for what happened. In fact, I have it on good authority that you played a large role in the recent events."

"You hold on a fucking second," Mike spoke up. "You come in here under a flag of goodwill and accuse me of murder? You got big balls, kid."

"Indeed I do," Shai said, adjusting his suit jacket. "Let's be clear on this, Mike. I'm not Tommy. I'm not so blinded by the lust for power that I don't see what's going on. You made a lot of money selling heroin to my brother. When he wanted to pull out, you caught feelings. I know you harbored ill feelings towards my family and I know you gave Bone the authority to kill my father. What I want to know is why?"

Mike was impressed by Shai's deductive reasoning skills. It seemed the youngster had figured out the whole scheme. Mike thought that he had covered his tracks, but Shai had showed him differently. Had to give him credit for that. Mike reasoned that he had Shai at his mercy, so there was no need to hide it anymore.

"It wasn't personal, Shai," Mike said with a grin. "Me and Poppa made a shitload of money together. He knew how to play ball. Tommy . . . he had to be a hard-ass about it. We've both been making money off the drugs, but Tommy felt he didn't need me anymore. I had to show him different. Tommy forced my hand. You understand, don't you?"

"Indeed," Shai said, returning the smile. "Mike, I'm not going to sit here and pretend that I like you, or I accept what you've done to my family. You're a coward and a fucking snake. That still doesn't change the fact that my family has to eat. I've come here today to lay things to rest and resume our relations."

"I'm supposed to believe that?" Mike asked suspiciously. "You come in here talking about making peace, but as soon as my back is turned, you'll try to put a knife in it. Why shouldn't I just have Nicky blow your brains out and be done with it?"

"Because I'm more use to you alive than dead," Shai said, not moved at all by the threat. "Bone has proven himself to be a fool. You tried to insert him into power and he's just made a mess of things. His people can't handle an operation of this size, and my people won't follow either of you. That's why you need me. You have my word that I will not try to take revenge against you for the murder of my father. Besides, business is business. Is it not?"

"Sure as hell is," Mike said, giving Shai a "got you by the balls" smile. "Spoken like a true businessman." Mike rubbed his hands together. "Okay, Shai. You call off the dogs and everything goes back to normal. These are acceptable terms, Shai. You rein in your people and I'll do the rest."

Mike couldn't believe his luck. Just like he told Nicky, Shai was coming to make nice. The kid wasn't cut out for war and he had come to kiss Mike's ass. Things would be sweeter under this Clark than the two before him.

"I do have a question, though," Shai said. "The Mafia rule is Deal and die. You managed to orchestrate a drug war to further your own gains, but never raised Mr. G's eyebrows?"

"That's old-world bullshit, kid. These old bastards don't understand the money in drugs. I've made a pretty penny right under their noses. The best part is, I don't have to kick anything back, 'cause they don't know I'm doing it." Mike damn near fell over laughing, while Nicky looked at him in disgust.

"Damn," Shai said. "You're smarter than most people give you credit for."

"What can I say." Mike beamed. "Don't worry about a thing though, Shai. We're gonna do some nice business together."

"I look forward to it," Shai said, standing. "Good night."

The ascension of the stairs was by no means easy. It seemed as if Latinos were popping out of every crack and crevice. Swan had lost one of his men, but they were still two deep. There was no way to know what waited for them on the top floor, but they had come too far to turn back. It had to end.

The two shooters who had taken the other stairwell made it to the top first. When they burst out on the twentieth floor, Frog was on his way down the hall. They were momentarily startled, which was all the time Frog needed. He fired his weapon, taking out both gunmen.

"Down," Swan whispered after hearing the gunshots. He only heard a few shots, but there was still no way to tell how many people were up there. He eased his head through the stairwell door and saw Frog running back and forth like a caged rat. When he tried to step out, Frog took a shot at him.

Swan gritted his teeth and took cover. There was no way that he could come at Frog directly, he needed an angle. He motioned for his comrade to take up his position, while he went around to the other side. They had come too close to let Frog get away.

After the meeting with Mike, Shai and his team filed out of the pizza parlor. No one said a word as they walked the block and a half to the waiting cars. The first car was a white limo owned by Mr. G and the other was the truck carrying Shai's people. Mr. G sat next to Snoop in the back of the limo, still wearing the headphones.

"Thanks, Snoop," Shai said, tossing him the tiny microphone that he had stashed in his shirt collar. "Have you heard enough, Mr. G?"

"Quite enough," he said, removing the headphones. "Shai, I'm man enough to admit when I've made a mistake. I can't tell you how sorry I am about all this shit that's gone on the last few weeks."

"What's done is done." Shai shrugged. "I just hope we can put an end to this war now."

"Consider it finished." Gee-Gee nodded. "I hope we can continue to do business, aside from the drugs, that is."

"Anything is possible, sir. I have to put my family in order before I can do anything."

"Well, you know how to reach me, kid."

"Indeed I do, sir." Shai nodded. "And Mike?"

"Oh, don't worry," he said, patting Louie Bonanno on one of his massive shoulders. "He'll get what's coming to him."

Swan crept silently around to the opposite stairwell. He could hear Frog exchanging shots with the gunman on the other side from his vantage point. He eased the door open as silently as possible and homed in on Frog. He popped him once in the leg, sending Frog crashing to the ground. Frog reached for his gun, but Swan mashed his boot on Frog's hand.

" 'Sup, nigga?" Swan said, placing the machine gun to Frog's forehead. "I believe we've got a few things to discuss."

Mike was working on pizza pie number two when Mr. G walked in, followed by Louie Bonanno and another soldier. Mike's eyes opened as wide as saucers when the underboss walked in. Nicky thought about going for his gun, but Louie had already drawn his weapon.

"Mr. G." Mike smiled. "What's this all about?"

"Just some old-world bullshit," Mr. G said, waving his killers forward. "You knew the rules, Mike, yet you ignored them."

Mike tried to plead, but it was useless. Louie and the other soldier cut loose with their weapons and gunned Mike and Nicky down. Bullets tore into both flesh and glass as the windows shattered. Gee-Gee tossed a wad of bills to the petrified owner and made his exit.

"Get the fuck off me," Frog shouted, as he struggled against Swan's grip.

"Shut the fuck up." Swan smacked him. "You ain't in no position to give orders. Didn't you know Poppa was a made man?"

"Fuck Poppa and fuck you!" Frog shouted, as Swan and the other shooter dragged him across the rooftop gravel.

Swan pulled Frog to the edge of the roof and looked out over the City. "You see this? This was Poppa Clark's city. That man was the closest thing I had to family and you bean-eating mutha fuckas took him. That's a'ight though, 'cause he can settle up with you himself."

Swan grabbed Frog by the neck and tossed him off the roof. Frog's screams could be heard for blocks as he plummeted twenty stories. When he hit the ground, the very concrete split from the impact of his skull.

Detectives Alvarez and Brown stood in the aftermath of the gun battle. Both blacks and browns lay sprawled in the streets. Benches were riddled with bullets and trees had been uprooted. The Lower East Side housing project looked like what it was: a war zone.

"I don't fucking believe this," Brown fumed. "All this work down the fucking toilet."

"Take it easy," Alvarez said, lighting his Newport.

"J, ain't nothing easy about this. There's at least twenty mutha fuckas laid out over here and our star witness's codefendant jams a knife in the back of his skull. Our whole case is shot to shit, partner."

"Does look bad, huh?" Alvarez smirked, blowing out a ring of smoke. "We were busy worrying about nailing Tommy and Shai turned out to be the worst of the bunch. Slick little bastard."

"The worst part is, we can't charge him. We know he was be-hind this shit, but he never once got his hands dirty. With his back-ground, there's no way in hell we could convince a jury that he orchestrated the slaughter of two drug crews and put one over on the Italians. That little fucker is probably gonna ride off into the sunset, laughing at us."

"I doubt it," Alvarez said, replacing the sheet over Frog's corpse. "Poppa is dead and gone. Even though Tommy's probably gonna walk on this charge, that'll be the only walking he's ever gonna do again. You think little old Shai is just gonna walk away from the game like that? Don't think so, partner. She's got him now. I don't think this is the last we've heard from our little ball star."

BOSS OF BOSSES

THE VERY NEXT DAY, Poppa Clark's estate was buzzing with people. The war was over and there was much to be discussed. The Clarks had won, but Shai didn't feel like a winner. During his stay in New York he had ordered the execution of quite a few people. It had been a mess, but it was finally over.

Now came the task of rebuilding. There were still people who had to be dealt with, and relationships solidified. Shai's first order of business would be his father's casino. Shai would see that the construction of the place was completed. Poppa had come too close not to see his dream through. It would be the perfect way to honor his memory.

Honey appeared in Shai's bedroom that morning. They had gone over quite a bit, but there was still much to discuss. She had done some shady shit in her dealings with Shai, but she hoped that the request that he had made of her helped balance the scales.

"Come here, ma." Shai motioned for her. Honey entered the room and sat on the bed next to him. "You did real good. I know it was hard, but I appreciate you looking out like that."

"I told you, all I want is a chance," Honey restated.

"And a chance you've earned." Shai caressed her face. "Things are different now. I need to know that the people around me are trustworthy."

"Baby, I will be."

"I'm glad to hear it." He nodded. "Melissa, I need you to know something before we go any further. I'm digging you. Because I'm digging you, I'm allowing you into my world, but it is indeed a cold one."

"I know, Shai," she whispered. "I'm with you, baby."

"For as long as you are loyal to me, I will take care of you. The moment you betray me, you will die. Can you deal with that?"

Honey felt fear grip her about the throat. She couldn't believe that Shai had just come at her like that. She couldn't say that she blamed him though. Trust was something that you had to earn. Honey still had a long road ahead of her, but she was willing to take that journey. For once she had someone that was good to her and she didn't want to fuck that up.

Right after Shai had gotten dressed, Angelo came to get him from his room. He smiled at his friend and allowed himself to be led down the hall. Quite a few people had come to see Shai. He was the man that had restored order to the streets. While he might not have felt it, Shai was a hero. Shai was just about to enter the office and greet his guest, when Hope stopped him in the hall.

"What's up, sis?" he asked.

"I'm okay," she responded. "You?"

"Maintaining."

"Now that it's over, we can leave, right?" she asked.

"Hope," he said, turning his eyes away. "I know what I told you, but I just can't leave Poppa's business undone. I just need to—"

"You promised," she hissed. "You promised me that you wouldn't be like them."

"Hope," he sighed. "I'm sorry. I hope one day you'll understand."

Shai continued into the office where a host of guests were waiting for him. Hope stood in the hallway crying her eyes out. She might not have lost Shai in body, as she had her father and brother, but she had lost him in spirit.

Poppa's office held quite a few important people. All of the lieutenants were in attendance; Mr. G had sent two of his people and even the Wong brothers were there. Shai nodded to the guests that he passed on his way to the head of the table. He stared at Poppa's chair for a long while, without moving. The very thing that Poppa had kept him from wound up being his destiny.

Swan set it off. He stood directly in front of Shai and slowly began clapping. Mo Black came next, picking up on the youngster's lead. Soon everyone in the room was clapping in unison. A lone tear ran down Shai's cheek as he sat in his father's chair. One by one, the guests came forward to kiss his cheek and pay homage to the new king. Shai's fall from grace was a long one that had landed him smack-dab in the fire. The prince of angels was now the lord of the underworld.